- IN THE GIANT'S SHADOW BOOK TWO -

THE
OCEAN
BEYOND

PETE A O'DONNELL

ISBN: 978-1-7349090-1-2

Ill-Advised Stories
PO Box 6072 Warwick, RI 02887
www.illadvisedstories.com

Dedication

To my daughters, Anna and Riley, my
        cartoon buddies and the best part
        of my life.
    may your life be full of wonderful stories
        and adventures.

Also By

The Curse of Purgatory Cove

The Stars Beyond the Mesa
In the Giants Shadow Book 1

And for younger readers:

The Adventures of Sparkie and Spazoid
Portal's World

Chapter 1

Dawn arrived at Nalanda Station and with it left the fear of ghosts haunting the narrow stone corridors, set aside for monks. Through the rock it was impossible to tell the time of day but Kavaris Dell, first of his order could feel the cycle of this place in his bones. They ached as he hurried to a stairwell that was a little too tall and steep for human legs. He took the first step, then the next, lifting his robe out of the way.

He grumbled and glanced at a thin wire stapled to the stone ceiling. Every couple of feet was a dimly glowing bulb. Kavaris Dell knew why more weren't present and the reason they kept them so low. He'd been the one who ordered it, keeping the voltage undetectable and unattractive. Still, it would've been nice to be able to see better. Those lights were placed by human hands and the wire was nearly a hundred years old, but the walls were far more ancient.

How old? Kavaris Dell didn't know. Thousands of years, maybe millions? It didn't really matter; this place belonged to the Order now and to those they served.

He came to the top of the stairs breathless and entered the lighthouse. "What is it?" he asked, not surprised to find Andavarri reclined, half hanging from the wall. It didn't matter to her that this area was only for the monks and that the monks could only be human. She saw his annoyance and waved her tail contently, a surge of color passing over her dark purple skin.

The Long-Wolf tended to go places she didn't belong and know things she had no right to. Kavaris Dell ignored her infractions, considering her too valuable to punish. Above them, massive windows of curved glass came together in a dome, looking out on the tangerine-colored clouds of Altor, the gas giant.

Below that dome, in the center of the room, was a raised dais with machines as ancient as the walls, with the look of brass and black onyx. They glowed and hummed in a way Kavaris Dell had never seen before. In the time he'd been here, some had never come to life at all. Studying the machines too closely was frowned upon. It was one thing to theorize their purpose but attempting to learn how they worked was forbidden.

"Is someone going to answer me?" he demanded. The monks in front of the machines were younger men who'd taken the vow to serve. They turned toward their elder.

"It's one of the voids, master. It's surfaced," a monk answered, pointing to a spot on the planet that pulsed with energy like a beacon in the clouds. The phenomenon was large enough to swallow a world.

A prickle of fear touched Kavaris Dell as he stared at it. The voids were always there, moving beneath the clouds, but rarely did they show themselves.

Each race living on the moons that circled the gas giant Altor knew to be afraid of the voids. It didn't matter which world they called home, the Ice-Carvers, the Long-Wolves, the Drakes, the

Grannusians and the humans, all had an instinctive dread when the voids surfaced, when those openings to nowhere made themselves seen.

"How long have these machines been active?" Kavaris asked, as he climbed a short flight of steps to the dais. He was trying not to look up at the planet and the bizarre spot as he approached the monks.

"Only a few minutes," the same monk answered.

"You're recording, of course?" Kavaris Dell asked, nodding to equipment that'd been moved into the room, human technology. A table was covered in small computers and monitors, cameras and displays for the sensors.

"Yes, of course," the monk answered, "but there's something else." He brought Kavaris Dell's attention to a screen that showed the view from an exterior camera pointed toward the gas giant and the void space. Kavaris Dell felt uncomfortable looking at it. The study of the voids had been outlawed as well. The monk touched the screen, magnifying the view, focusing in on one spot. Something was in front of the void, floating in the space above Altor. It was shining, reflecting the distant light of the sun, twinkling like a tiny diamond. "Dear lords," Kavaris Dell whispered in a trembling voice.

"The automatic monitors caught it. I've just gone over the recording. It came out of the void," Andavarri said from behind him. Kavaris turned and looked back at her. Her purple flesh was dark and her eyes unreadable, waiting to see what the old man would say. Andavarri had a face like a shaved wolf. She always looked like she was sneering with a bored sort of disapproval, but that look was gone now. She was as conflicted as the monks.

"Can the Golems recover it?" Kavaris Dell asked.

"Yes, if you want them to? If you think it wise," she said.

It took him a moment to answer. He looked back at the display, wondering if he was making the right choice. "Send them," he said. Andavarri nodded before turning and moving down from the raised platform. Her long sinuous body didn't make a sound as she left the room.

Kavaris Dell watched her go, then ran his hand back over his bald head, looking up at the spot. With the fear still in his voice, he said, "May the Æesir forgive me." But he knew the Æesir didn't forgive, they only punished.

∞

Andavarri had little time. She slipped down the stairs on both her hands and feet, then hurried through a corridor, coming out of the monk's private areas onto a balcony overlooking one of the grand halls. She glanced over the edge at the combat field. Broad columns lined the massive chamber running to the far end where incredibly tall windows let in light from the twin suns reflected off the gas giant's surface. Two teams of humans were on the combat field below, preparing to go through one of their foolish training exercises. Most of the other humans at the school were gathered, ready to watch the barely organized brawl that they called a combat simulation.

Andavarri ducked behind a column and reached in her pouch, taking out a small crystal. Not many knew how the Long-Wolves controlled the living flames of their Fire Golems. While she was certain the military scientists of different human dynasties had figured it out, she felt no urge to advertise. She held the stone to a nodule at the base of her skull. A small fold of skin hid a similar stone that'd been surgically placed. The connection was made, and she saw through the eyes of the Fire Golems.

Outside, in the vacuum of space four statues of rough volcanic rock stood immobile, waiting on a platform overlooking Altor. They could be formed to look like anything, but here at the Station the monks preferred the Golems appear human, or as close as possible.

Andavarri held an image of the diamond in her mind and commanded the Golems to go forth. She could feel them lift from their bodies. It was unpleasant as she sensed their perspectives change from one focus to all directions as they flew away from the statues that housed them, becoming their true form, living flame. She held the connection for only a moment more. Long enough to look back at Nalanda, floating on a rocky satellite, too small to be called a moon, but larger than the other particles that made up Altor's rings.

Only the straight lines of the station's walls distinguished it from the rock it was carved into, rising like a castle with towers and turrets and parapets. She saw the seven grand halls and their massive windows. The station was laid out in a starburst, rising from the rock. Those windows had held back the vacuum of space longer than any of the races around Altor had existed. It was a place left behind by a mysterious race that was long since gone. Only the ghosts remained.

Andavarri didn't need to give the Golems any more instructions. They were the perfect servants, strong, adaptable and most importantly sentient, capable of assessing a situation and making decisions. All it took was for her to tell them she wanted the diamond object and they'd do whatever it took to bring it back. With little concern for their own safety and faster than any shuttle, they'd dive into Altor's gravity well, skirt the edge of the void space, and retrieve it like a dog with a stick.

Andavarri had other concerns now, mainly what to do with this information. It was too late to conceal it. Something new was coming and everyone would find out eventually. She glanced over the balcony at the humans getting ready for mock war. They were always playing games, those young nobles, those violent creatures. Games of deceit and war. They love their blood sports. 'There were so many houses that they were hard to keep track of, but there were only a few that mattered.' Andavarri thought of the diamond and knew this was beyond them.

She nodded as she decided to tell the stewards of the other races. She'd make it a gift to them and hope the favor was returned. She wouldn't leave it to the monks to decide who should know. Without hesitation she dove over the balcony. Her wide toes and finger pads stuck to the rock as she started down the wall, heading toward the classrooms and Regin, the Ice Carver.

Chapter 2

Streaking down to the gas giant Altor, the Fire Golems went to the edge of the wormhole and closed around the diamond vessel. Something else was there, a Drake, one of those massive creatures from Uppsala. They carried him back to Nalanda, to the landing platform where their stone bodies waited.

Inside the ship five young people huddled together, refugees from Earth. They watched the flames enter the statues and saw them come to life and carry the vessel into the hanger bay.

Through the vessel's walls they felt the floor rumble as the massive stone doors closed behind them. Then they watched as an odd collection of beings closed in on the diamond vessel. Kavaris Dell, Andavarri and Regin the Ice-Carver entered, but there was one more on his way. His heavy footsteps shook the floor.

Inside the vessel, Chris couldn't shake the feeling he was waking from a dream as he sensed the massive being approach. He didn't know how long they'd been in passage, but only a couple days before climbing in this diamond vessel he and his brother Alex had arrived at a research institute in the desert of Northern Arizona where his mother, an astrophysicist, went to work. Things had gone terribly wrong there. He was still struggling to accept the notion that the Earth might be gone forever.

"What is that? What's happening?" Katy asked. It was tight in the Diamond vessel and uncomfortable.

"I don't know," Alex said.

"There are aliens outside and it sounds like something big is about to join them," Amita offered while pushing at Ben who was climbing toward the latch. He wasn't careful about where he put his feet, which was mostly on Chris. The latch was made of a hardened material that looked odd on the smooth crystal wall, as if it'd been added after. Before anyone could stop him, Ben opened the hatch and was sliding down the side of the ship to the floor.

Being much more careful not to step on anyone, Chris followed him. He was halfway out the hatch when he stopped, looking at the creature that stood in the doorway, blocking nearly the whole entrance. It was over ten feet tall with armor plating and pointed snarled barbs. Stooping down, it held a staff the size of a small tree with a lantern hanging from it. He was a Drake but much larger than Tearmai, the one that'd traversed the wormhole.

"Would you look at the size of that guy?" Ben called, ignoring the look of surprise on the faces of the other creatures there. The massive Drake took a step forward and Ben put his hands up. "We come in peace."

The lantern flashed, pulsing with energy as the Drake leaned forward and stared past its beak-like snout. With a grumpy sort of menace, its voice rumbled out, "This is strange . . . very strange."

Chris felt the light from the lantern touch him like a physical force. 'Strange,' the creature had said. Chris couldn't think of a better word. He glanced at Ben. Everything that'd happened since he started hanging out with the scientist's son could be defined that way, especially the last few hours, Chris thought. Not that time had much meaning anymore. They'd fallen through a wormhole, tossed through by a smaller Drake named Tearmai, in a vessel made of mirrors. Then they arrived here, a place straight out of the sci-fi novels Chris loved so much.

The creatures were talking to each other, these beings who'd come to greet them, but he understood very little of what they were saying. He clung to the diamond ship, their escape vessel from what may have been Earth's destruction. There was another pulse of light that brought Chris's attention back to the lantern. The Drake stepped forward.

Chris could feel his heart pounding. Something was digging around in his head. A foreign touch reached out to his thoughts, working in his brain from the outside. Another pulse, it hurt a little. He looked at the lantern and saw a creature encased inside it. He knew what it was. A Lightening Bug, like Brash. He'd seen his mother, less than a relative hour before, carried off by a creature that he and his friends had tried to save. It had said it was there to help them. It wanted to shut down the wormhole, but when that was no longer an option, it'd kidnapped his mom and carried her off into the void.

Another flash. "Stop that!" Chris yelled, covering his eyes. He peered out from below his hand at the strange creatures that'd come to meet them. There was some sort of purple lizard with a face like a shaved wolf, a six-armed simian creature with white fur and then there were the living statues, like volcanic rock, still burning with internal heat, glowing red from their core.

The oddest one was the old man. He was bizarre for how normal he looked, dressed like a priest in a red robe with a white beard ready to celebrate Christmas mass.

Chris saw Andavarri, the purple creature, go to the old man and say, "They've come through the void-space in outlaw technology. We'd be better off getting rid of them, blasting them out into space before the Æesir come to punish us." Andavarri stared at the two boys as she spoke. She sneered in disappointment at the sight of more humans. Then her eyes widened as they fell on Tearmai who'd been laid on the floor.

He'd been a student here. She looked around at the others, Fafnir the ancient Drake, Regin the Ice-Carver, their faces were unreadable.

Chris heard Andavarri and was too shocked to think about how odd it was that he now could understand her. Her words sounded foreign at first, but slowly started to make sense like a barely remembered language returning to him.

The old man, Kavaris Dell shook his head. "We're safe for now," he assured Andavarri, but his face was painted with concern.

Chris looked at Tearmai, the smaller Drake lying on the floor. He appeared dead. 'How could he not be after what he'd been through?' The Drake had tried to help them close the wormhole but he'd been too late, instead he'd sent them here. They'd come through together, but he hadn't been protected by the vessel.

He'd been exposed to the currents of the void, that bizarre twisting of time and gravity.

There was another flash from the lantern, from the Lightening Bug encased in it. The pain came again lancing into Chris's head. "Where's my mother!" he yelled, feeling dizzy. He stared at the Lightening Bug and noticed for the first time that its body was shrunken-in and broken. It didn't move. Outside of the energy pulses, it showed no sign of life, frozen in the brass and amber of the large Drake's lamp.

"Where is she?!" Chris demanded, the dizziness overwhelming as he struggled to stay in place. He noticed that his words sounded different. He was forming unfamiliar sounds, shouting them.

Thump, thump! The Drake's massive footsteps echoed through the room as it came closer. "Calm yourself," Fafnir said slowly. The deep voice rumbled through Chris like the vibrations of a truck on a bumpy road. He met the creature's eyes, which were deep set, shining blue as it added in its carefully paced speech. "The pulses are reorganizing the pathways in your brain, making it so you can understand us. It can be an odd feeling."

Chris looked at the Lightening Bug in the lantern, barely able to imagine what that meant. These creatures were able to control people in their sleep, and now it was rewiring his brain. He wanted to tell it to stop, but before he could find the words his attention was taken by Ben. The reckless boy had gone up to one of the statues. Unafraid he waved his hand frantically in front of the Fire Golem's one glowing eye. "You guys can understand me now?" he asked.

The statue was over two meters tall, towering over Ben, but he didn't hesitate to lean in and tap on the piece of volcanic rock that made up its chest. "This is so wild. What are you?"

Fafnir let out an annoyed sigh and said, "They won't answer. They are quiet beings."

Andavarri snorted. "'Beings?' Not quite. They're barely alive. You'd be better off talking to a wall."

Ben smiled and nodded, then waved his hand in front of the Fire Golem's eye again, "Hi." The statue tilted its head down. "Thanks for saving us."

Andavarri crossed her arms, leaning back on her long tail, staring at Ben. "I think there's something wrong with that one."

The small simian creature said, "Try not to judge them too harshly." The Ice Carver stepped forward, turning his bright eyes toward Chris. "Excuse my Long-Wolf friend, Andavarri is— an acquired taste. I am Regin. Please, tell us who you people are?" he asked.

Chris looked at the furry creature. He opened his mouth and the words came out in a foreign language. "Um, Sure—" he started, but then someone pushed past him from below. Amita climbed up on top of the ship, quickly took in the room, then slid down its mirrored side, touching the ground. Unafraid of the living statues, she stepped past the Fire Golems and went to Tearmai's side. The small Indian girl gently touched the Drake's arm. The creature had saved her from a terrible fall back on Earth and from freezing in a pool of icy water. She'd only known him for a little while, but in that time, he'd been a friend. Amita didn't have many of those.

Chris started again trying to answer Regin, "We a—" but then looked down to see someone grabbing his leg.

His bruised and battered brother, Alex was below him. "What's going on?" Alex asked. His brown skin was pale from blood loss and injuries.

"Sorry, Um. . . Regin," Chris said over his shoulder to the small furry alien. He wasn't sure how to explain anything he was seeing to his brother. He opened his mouth, but then decided to offer his hand instead.

"You'll have to come up," he said as Alex took it.

It was a struggle for him to climb with his injuries but with Chris helping he was able to get on top of the ship. Although Alex had been able to see everything from the inside as the walls of the diamond ship were transparent, it still took him a moment to accept what was in front of him. It looked like they were inside the walls of some ancient temple. Just yesterday he'd been complaining about having to spend the summer in Arizona. Now he was here, looking at strange creatures and somehow understanding them.

"How many of them are there?" Andavarri asked, staring at Alex.

The brothers ignored the question, turning back to the hatch. Katy, Ben's sister, was still below with her eyes covered in gauze. Her encounter on Earth with Brash and another creature had left her blind.

"Katy, reach up. I think we might be safe here," Chris said to her.

Alex strained to help his brother. Both took a shoulder and worked together to lift Katy out. Being careful of the burns on her arms, they got her to the top of the ship. "Let me get down, then I'll help you guys," Chris said.

The Fire Golems stepped forward as Chris turned to slide off. He glanced back as one of them reached out its rocky arms, offering to help. Chris saw the one glowing-red eye and waved it off. "Yeah, I think I'm good," he said, climbing down himself.

Above he could hear his brother talking to Katy. "It's alright, Chris is right below you," he was saying, helping her to the edge of the ship. Chris could see Alex wincing in pain, but his older brother didn't let the discomfort show in his voice. He remained calm and reassuring as he helped Katy down.

Chris took her around the waist. "Almost there," he said, listening to Amita behind him.

She had her head on the Drake's chest. "He's alive! I can hear it, he's still breathing. How's that even possible?" Amita looked up and around at the strange creatures that surrounded them. Tearmai had been in the hard vacuum of space. Even for a creature as tough as a Drake, it seemed impossible to survive such an ordeal.

Amita waited for one of the creatures to say something. She looked to Fafnir, the large Drake. He moved forward. His voice full of concern as he demanded, "Step back!"

Chris watched Amita stay where she was, next to her friend who needed help. Her hand went from his chest to the side of his face, that's when Tearmai's eyes flew open. They searched around in panic as Fafnir called again, "Step back!" but he was too late and he was moving too slow to be able to save her. Tearmai's arm shot up into the air, ready to come down and crush Amita.

Chapter 3

The small Drake should've been dead, but Tearmai's armored chest swelled as his lungs filled with air. Amita felt a thrill, though she was concerned about the look in his eyes. They were darting around in a crazy panic. He turned toward her, raising one of his massive arms, then his clawed fist came slamming down with a blow that was meant to kill.

Fafnir watched in horror, moving too slow to stop it. "The Madness," he warned, seeing the look in the younger Drake's eyes. Somewhere in his distant memory he recalled the effects of the void. Centuries ago, before the gods, explorers would touch the edge of the void spaces only to come back changed and dangerous. Tearmai had done more. He'd fallen through it.

Amita opened her mouth to scream but the air was pulled from her lungs as she was suddenly dragged away. She looked down and found a furry clawed arm around her waist. Regin the Ice-Carver had heaved her to safety. He was smaller than Amita, but incredibly strong with long wiry arms. His wide, simian eyes looked at her. "Thanks," she said after seeing the spot where she'd been. The floor was broken, smashed into pieces.

Tearmai was getting to his feet. His arms were wider and longer than his legs making it possible to swing back on his fists, moving like a pendulum. Crouching down he prepared to lunge. He stared around the room like a cornered animal. His kind eyes were the first thing Amita had noticed about him on Earth, but any gentleness was gone, replaced with confusion and anger. His gaze fell on Ben.

Amita watched Ben back up, saying, "Hey buddy, it's me," moving towards the diamond vessel. Chris stepped out from behind him, pulling Katy out of the way. He half-dragged half-pushed her to the old monk, before hurrying back for Alex.

"Tearmai, it's me." Ben held his hands out in front of him. "Remember, we went on a road trip together?"

The Drake let out a sound that wasn't quite a growl, more like a moan of pain. He charged. His legs flung forward, then his arms swung ahead, galloping, closing the distance to Ben.

A Fire-Golem tried to stop him, stepping into his path. It was pulverized for its effort. Stone exploded across the room in a cloud of volcanic dust. The force of the Drake smashing into the rock released the hot living plasma inside which floated up into the air.

Tearmai wasn't slowed at all, bashing ahead till he crashed into the diamond vessel. Alex tried to hold on as the ship was tossed across the floor. He was flung from the top, hitting the ground with a grunt of pain. The rest of the Fire Golems closed in, but they weren't going after Tearmai. They went to the diamond ship and placed their hands against it, steadying it.

Ben and Chris ducked, narrowly avoiding being crushed. Chris pulled Ben to his feet. "Run, Ben!" he yelled, looking back at Tearmai. The Drake had gotten to his feet as well. Turning, his gaze fell on Ben again.

"What'd I do?" Ben asked, trying to scramble away. The Drake stalked forward, making snarling noises, ready to pounce. Ben closed his eyes with no chance of escape. Suddenly he felt like he was standing in front of a fireplace. He opened his eyes to see the flame from the Golem drop down over the Drake.

Tearmai had already been confused and enraged, but as the flame closed over him, he began to flail in panic. His powerful clawed arms tried to pull at the fire, but with nothing solid to touch, his claws tore into his own armored hide as he opened his mouth to scream. No sound escaped and he fell to the ground, gasping for air. After a long moment, the Drake stopped struggling and went still. The flame lifted up and away, floating above the unconscious body.

Ben looked at Chris. "Seriously, what did I do?"

Amita stepped forward a little. She nearly went to Tearmai again, but Regin held her back. "Be still child," he said softly.

Looking at him, Amita noticed for the first time that the fur on his face was combed into a little beard tied in a point, and that he wore a leather jerkin covering his core but allowing his legs, his four arms and his three tails to move freely. He looked like a defective stuffed animal. Like some toy factory worker had lost count of how many appendages one of those dangling monkeys was supposed to have.

Chris ignored Ben's question, got up and went to the ship. His brother was on the ground. "Alex, are you alright?"

Alex nodded as he struggled to get to his feet, unable to say anything while wincing in pain. Behind him Kavaris Dell stood over Katy, who'd fallen when Chris moved her out of the way. "Let me help you, my dear," the old man said. As she got to her shaky legs the monk touched the gauze over her eyes. "What's happened to you?"

"She was hurt. Are you alright Katy?" Ben asked, standing just beneath the flame.

Katy nodded. "I think so."

Fafnir, the large Drake, stepped forward to look down at Tearmai. He held his lantern out and the Lightening Bug glowed softly inside. "It's the madness from the void. I remember it. But it's been so long. In the days when there were still explorers."

Kavaris Dell glanced at Fafnir, the monk's face pinched a little, unhappy to hear this. He waved with his hand and two Golems stepped forward going to Tearmai and lifting him.

Standing in the pile of stone left from the destroyed statue, Ben looked up at the flame, "Hey, thanks for saving me by the way. Sorry your, um, body got all smashed up." The flame didn't make any gesture to show it heard him.

"It's foolish to thank a Fire Golem," Andavarri said, shaking her head disapprovingly. Ben grumbled something under his breath that even if Andvarri had heard, she may not have understood. No one can really explain exactly what an ass-hat is.

Across the room Alex managed to stand up with Chris holding him under the shoulder. His brother's stomach, wrapped with gauze, was starting to bleed. "Do you guys have doctors here? My brother needs help!" Chris called, feeling Alex become heavier as he started to slump over. All eyes, human and alien, turned toward his panicked voice.

The old man in the priest robe came to him. "I am the Kavaris, Kavaris Dell, first of my order. We are trained in medicine."

"And he's the master of this place," Andavarri added, making it sound like an insult.

"This place has no master but for the Æesir," Kavaris Dell said as he leaned down to pull up Alex's shirt. He touched the blood. It was as red as the robe he wore. "You've been badly wounded. This is from combat, isn't it?"

"We were attacked," Chris said, watching the blood drip down from his brother's stomach, staining the old man's hand. "Something called a Hunter came through the wormhole."

Kavaris Dell glanced at Chris in surprise, then turned back to the others.

"A Hunter, you're sure?" Fafnir asked.

"That's what Tearmai called it," Amita said. "It was there for Brash, but a lot of other people got hurt too."

Kavaris Dell still stared at Fafnir and Regin as if expecting answers. "Brash was there with Tearmai?" he asked.

"Yes, you know him? Did they come from here?" Chris responded. "Do you know what the Hunter was?"

The Kavaris didn't answer. He stood up and wiped his hand on his robe, leaving it wet near the edges. "Let's get your brother to the healing chambers, then we'll worry about your questions. We've many for you as well." He started back toward the door, expecting them to follow.

Regin motioned with one of his furry arms to the statues. "Allow the Fire Golem to carry him." The stone beings turned from the diamond ship and moved toward them in a line. They had been standing in a circle around the vessel, unmoving as their red eyes reflected off its surface.

Alex was pale, but looked up as the statues approached, and shook his head. "I'll be alright," he said, leaning heavily on his brother as they started forward. "I can make it." Amita carefully took Katy's gauze wrapped hands, falling in step behind the Golems that picked up Tearmai. It took two of them to carry him. One holding his feet and the other with its arms under his back.

Alex and Chris followed slowly to the door. As they passed beneath the large Drake, Alex looked up at the lantern. "Ask him where our mother is," he muttered into Chris's ear.

"I kind of already did," Chris said back.

"Ask him again," Alex insisted.

Chris looked up at the massive Drake. He motioned with his head toward the lantern, struggling to look past his brother. "Brash was a creature like that. He kidnapped our mother and went through the wormhole with her. Did she come here?"

Kavaris Dell was already out in the hall. He turned back and said sharply, "No—" then more quietly he added. "You're the only ones to ever come through the void . . . That I know of anyway. In fact, we don't understand how this is even possible." He pointed to the diamond. "This thing is strange to me."

Kavaris's eyes fell on the Long-Wolf Andavarri. Her long reptilian hand was on the side of the ship and her tail pointed in concern. The ship's reflective hull rippled like water under her fingers. When she turned to see Kavaris Dell staring at her, she quickly took her hand away. The Kavaris shook his head with a frown, then started back out into the hall. Regin had already gone ahead, looking one way, then the other, making certain it was empty.

"I will stay here," Fafnir said, stepping toward the ship. His voice came out in the slow, heavy and measured beats of his species. "Forbidden or not, we need to know how these children came to us. How Tearmai found this." He stared pointedly at Andavarri as if expecting an answer.

The Kavaris looked back at the massive creature. He frowned, then nodded. "Fine, but when you are done, it will have to be locked away or destroyed," he said pointing at the ship.

"Of course." The Drake motioned to Tearmai. "Keep me appraised."

The Kavaris looked at the unconscious form before nodding yes. He started down the hall, while the other fell in behind him.

Chapter 4

Walking a little in front of her, Amita held Katy's hand and could feel her shivering. It was chilly in the hallway, but Katy's trembling wasn't just from the cold.

"Are you alright?" Amita asked.

Katy kept moving and held tight. "Just don't let go," she said with her head down, wandering in the darkness behind the gauze.

Not knowing what to say, Amita softly touched Katy's shoulder. She could hear the boys behind her. Alex was breathing hard and so was Chris with the effort of helping his older brother. Ben had come over to check on his sister. The stimulation, combined with exhaustion, made Ben more excitable than usual. He was buzzing about, flitting from each group in their party. She wondered how long it'd been since he'd taken his ADHD meds.

She looked at the wide corridor with a high ceiling, made from the same stone as the landing bay. Dim bulbs hung from a few strings of wire lit the way but did nothing to banish the strange shadows that danced across the walls, cast by the Fire Golems with their flames seeping out. Light radiated from cracks in their stony bodies, leaking and filling the air with an eerie glow. Amita noticed how a few doorways they passed looked different from the others, as if they'd been added after, made from a hardened plastic.

Hoping to warm Katy, Amita moved closer to the living statues to feel their heat. She wanted a better view of the tunnel. She noticed every detail including the lifeless form of Tearmai.

"What is this place?" she asked Kavaris Dell, who was beside them.

The old man glanced down at her, then back at Katy. He smiled gently and said, "It's called Nalanda. It's a sanctuary, a monastery and a mystery, a place where we try to teach and reach understanding. It falls short of being a school, though I've tried in my time here." His voice had a practiced wisdom.

"That's great," Amita said, "but what is it actually? I'm assuming you guys didn't build it. I can see where you've retrofitted things for human habitation. And what are people even doing here? Are you from Earth?"

After an awkward moment of silence he answered, "No, we didn't build it and I don't know what this Earth is." Then he moved ahead of her. They passed a few other men in red cloaks like Kavaris Dell's. They bowed their heads as the group approached, unwilling to make eye contact.

"Earth is a planet. It's our planet, and if you didn't build this place then who did? Also, if you're not from Earth, where did you come from?" Amita called out as she leaned into the floor a little. "And another thing, how does the gravity feel so normal here? On an asteroid this size, we should all feel lighter."

Kavaris Dell had been moving ahead, trying to get further from her. He stopped and glared over his shoulder. "There may be time for some of your questions later. But for now please be quiet."

Noise came from further down the corridor. Some sort of action, heavy thuds and smacking with an occasional grunt or yell. "What's that?" Ben asked moving ahead of the group. Somehow, despite the fact that he couldn't possibly know where he was going, he'd slipped to the front.

"Those are war games," Andavarri spat out. "The sound of you humans playing."

"It's training," Kavaris Dell added. "By the laws of the Æesir, noble human children are sent here to learn. That of course includes combat training. It's only to be expected by their families, and we have one of the best instructors around, Edith, a warrior I handpicked myself. She's also the head of security."

"Funny that you didn't contact your mercenary about our arrivals." Andavarri nodded toward the group.

"This isn't a security matter. In fact, I wanted to keep it as quiet as possible," Kavaris Dell said before turning back to the group. "Unfortunately, the healing chambers are close to the great hall where our students train."

"It only makes sense to keep emergency medicine nearby," Regin offered.

"And since we'll be going so close to the combat field, I would ask that we try to move silently. I've no wish to call attention," Kavaris Dell said just as Chris looked up from under the weight of his brother.

"Um, Alex," Chris whispered.

His brother's complexion was ashen as he asked, "What's up?"

"I don't see Ben." In the distance painfully bright lights poured into the dark hall from a large space where combat was taking place. Chris tried to peer past it, but he didn't see Ben anywhere. Somehow, he'd managed to pull ahead of the others. Chris hurried his pace a little, but it was hard with his brother leaning so heavily on him. Alex, to his credit, did his best to help.

"We should be less concerned with secrecy and more concerned with where these children came from," Andavarri said as they reached the end of the corridor and out onto a raised walkway. A broad set of stairs led down into the grand hall. Ben was already halfway down them by the time the others caught up.

In the center of the room, on a platform raised above the floor, was a massive metal cage that stood three stories tall and was half the length of a football field. Obstacles were scattered throughout from ceiling to floor. Hunks of rock and sheets of metal hovered, making a confusing three-dimensional maze. The bars of the cage were thick. A person could've passed through them if not for the fact that they were glowing dangerously, lit by bands of energy.

Students dressed in fitted jumpsuits of dark grey crowded near the cage, staying only a few feet back from the raised platform. Many of them looked younger than Amita. For the most part, the crowd remained quiet. Low whispering filled the air as they watched intently, without cheering. Tension filled the room that had nothing to do with the combat. Older students crowded the balconies around the hall, staring down at the battle.

Inside the cage, at one end, some of the metal sheets had been stacked together making a crude fort with thick walls. Several defenders stood near it, and inside was a small device, a red marker the size of a football, pulsing with light. The defenders and the other team were dressed in the same grey jumpsuits, but black segmented pads had been added to cover their most sensitive parts. They wore helmets with their faces exposed. The ones defending the wall had shoulder pads painted red. The ones attacking wore green.

Each one carried a small staff, angry devices that sparked with electricity at their ends. Their faces were bloodied from the roughest combat. Five from the green team made a push toward the wall, while seven from the red stayed in tight, blocking their way.

The combatants varied in age and size. Some were girls and some were boys, but a few on the red team could have been adults. Four of them were giant, towering over the others, broad and thickly muscled like NFL players. Chris couldn't help noticing that even though their faces were human, some of those larger players had skin shaded the color of Andavarri, a deep purple.

The five from the green team came in fast. With their smaller size and agility, they attempted to use the obstacles to gain an advantage. The floating rocks moved a little, wiggling in their orbits as the team hurried through the debris field, charging the fort. One small girl scaled a rock, then jumped from the hovering stone. Yelling a war cry, she held her staff down and pounced on one of the largest opponents.

Her target, the biggest brute on the red team, appeared to be the leader as he was shouting orders at the others and pointing out where the attacks were coming from. His size and purple skin was so odd that it took Chris a moment to notice that his staff wasn't in his hand, instead he had it slung over his shoulder. The brute looked up just in time to see the girl as her weapon came down on his broad shoulder, making contact. He twisted a little as electricity flashed on his armor, then swatted the staff away, following one hand with the other and smashing the girl in the abdomen. She went skidding across the floor from the force of the blow.

After looking up and seeing she wasn't safe, she tried to scurry away on her hands and knees. The brute stormed toward her giving a savage kick, knocking her legs out from under her and sending her rolling across the floor. The brute didn't let up, lifting his leg higher this time with the intention of stomping down and smashing her into the ground. Chris could feel his brother tense up. He knew Alex wanted to rush over and help the girl, but there was nothing they could do.

That's when a stern voice called out. "Vyktor, enough!" It growled from outside the cage. All eyes turned toward a woman dressed in black, standing above the crowd. The armor she wore didn't look like it was meant for any sort of game. It was as scarred as her close shaven head, with pieces of tactical hardware clinging to her muscular frame. She stood with her hands behind her back. The brute inside the cage paused, his foot still in the air.

"That's Edith," Kavaris Dell whispered to the group, nodding at the woman in black as he tried to hurry them along. They'd slowed, distracted by the combat, except for the Fire Golem, who'd kept going, carrying Tearmai toward a broad set of doors. Kavaris Dell didn't seem to notice that Ben, who stood watching intently, was only a few steps from the bottom of the staircase.

Edith looked at the brute and spoke in a tone that sounded like each syllable was encased in ice. "If you're going to finish her, then finish her. Stop messing around."

With a glance at Edith and a growing frown, Vyktor took his staff down from his back, held it with both hands and drove it between the girl's armored plates, almost like he was trying to shove it through her. She screamed as electricity sparked and twisted across her body. Her scream stopped, but Vyktor still held the staff on her, making her body flop for a moment more. When he pulled it away, the girl wasn't moving.

"What the hell's going on?" Katy whispered.

"You don't want to know," Amita answered in disgust.

After seeing their teammate go down, some of the greens tried charging Vyktor, but the brute swept his staff in front of him. The rest of the reds surged forward and the greens were forced to dive for the obstacles. The fighting was intense. Sparks flew as staffs were jabbed ahead, flashing off the metal plates, rocks, and the armor of the combatants. The green team fought hard while backing away, retreating. The red team followed with Vyktor leading the charge.

"We need to be going," Kavaris Dell said in a low tone, waving them on. He was grateful no one had looked their way. He held to the fleeting chance of keeping their arrival secret from the nobles, but it still escaped his attention that Ben wasn't with them. The teen had gone down the stairs to watch the combat, and was quiet for now, enthralled by what he was seeing.

Vyktor's rage was impressive as he stormed ahead, bashing his opponents, but he didn't notice another combatant moving high over his head where the obstacles nearly touched the ceiling of the cage. Looking to be Alex's age, this green team member was jumping and using the floating pieces as cover as he moved toward the red team's base. He glanced down occasionally, to see how his group was doing. When he saw them back into the obstacle field with the red team following, he started moving faster, making larger jumps to pick up time. He dove like an acrobat toward their base and landed on the wall, then grabbed the red flashing marker, tucking it under his arm.

The distance between the fort and the first obstacle was a far stretch, but the young man went for it anyway, running along the top of the wall and leaping as if he were unafraid of falling. He grabbed a hunk of rock that floated three meters above the floor with a single arm and hung for a moment trying to swing his legs up to find footholds. His toes touched, giving him just enough leverage to hold on. He jammed the marker under his chin so he could use his other hand to climb up. The whispering of the crowd faded, as they watched this green combatant work his way to the top of the rock. When he finally managed to pull himself up, the whole room breathed out a sigh of relief.

He stood, trying to find a path back toward the other side of the combat field. His teammates weren't doing well and the only way to end the game was to get the marker back to their base. The crowd watched in silence, not making a single sound. Except for one person.

At the bottom of the stairs, looking up in awe, Ben said aloud, "Man, you guys should be charging for this!" Ben's voice tended to be loud, but in the massive room it sounded like he'd spoken through a megaphone.

Kavaris Dell glared while Ben's face became as red as his hair. Everyone turned to look at him, from the combatants to the students around the cage, to Edith. Her eyes were darkly hooded, but they seemed to light up with something unnatural as she turned her gaze on him.

Ben brought his hands up. "Um, sorry. I-ah, didn't mean to interrupt." He backed up the stairs slowly.

Amita let go of Katy's hand for a moment and rushed down to grab Ben. "Would you get up here!" she growled through gritted teeth, dragging him behind her.

Above the cage, the student with the red marker was looking too. He'd crouched down, trying to keep his balance. Like everyone else he was curious. Here were five strangers, wearing clothing like he'd never seen, being led by Kavaris Dell and most of the stewards of the indigenous races.

On the ground, Vyktor glanced toward Ben. He wasn't the curious type. If anything, he was more upset that the combat had been interrupted. He turned back to the nearest green team member, one of those quick little mice that he so desperately wanted to crush and as he looked around, he happened to glance up. Maybe he heard a noise, or maybe he noticed how some of the students outside the cage weren't watching the fight on the floor. Either way, his eyes drifted up and he saw the leader of the green team, Cormack, clinging to a rock.

Vyktor snarled, thinking what a coward to hide above the combat floor. Then he saw the marker in Cormack's hand. His mouth dropped open and he roared in rage.

Cormack looked down. "Oh damn," he cursed as he watched Vyktor coming toward him.

Vyktor grabbed one of the floating obstacles and pulled it toward himself. Usually they didn't move, but with his incredible strength he was able to drag it down before climbing on and riding it up. Jumping on another and another, he went higher while calling to his team, "He's there! Ignore the rest!"

All of the red team started after Cormack who was already on the move, jumping from obstacle to obstacle, nearly slipping more than once. The red team wasn't as fast, but they were closing in from every direction, moving with panic and rage. Vyktor was the nearest. More than once Cormack leapt free as the brute reached for his legs.

Ben was still trying to watch as Amita pushed him along. She shoved him ahead of her, hurrying to get out of sight of the crowd while Chris and Alex purposely blocked his view. Katy held tight to Amita as the small Indian girl led her toward a set of double doors and barely broke stride kicking Ben in the back side to encourage him.

"Hey—" Ben started to say, but he stopped, looking ahead at Kavaris Dell, who stood in the broad doorway to the healing chamber. He did not look happy.

Chapter 5

When Alex passed through the doors of the healing chamber, he wanted to look back just as badly as Ben. To see if the leader of the green team would make it across the combat field, but he kept his eyes forward, focusing on the ramp in front of him. Turning in a tight circle at a steep pitch, it brought them to an upper level. He let the pain in his gut keep him focused. Each breath was agony as his feet shuffled forward, sliding across the stone floor with Chris helping.

His younger brother stayed quiet, glancing back every few minutes to check on Amita and Katy. Chris is alive and for now we're safe, keep that in front of you, Alex told himself. We'll figure everything else out as it comes our way. His eyes wandered down to Regin. He watched the creature's strange gait with its extra arms. Alex found himself staring, not sure if he was actually awake or if this was some sort of fever dream brought on by his injuries.

At the top of the ramp the lights were brighter and the white stone walls formed like a honeycomb, curving and turning from the entrance to create smaller rooms. Alex could hear machines turning on. He stared past the opening where the ramp ended and could see a window that looked out on the combat cage. The balconies that the older students watched from were at their same level. Despite the drama being played out in the cage, Alex felt his eyes drawn elsewhere. Sensing someone staring at him, he searched the balconies till his eyes met another's. A girl about his age was looking at him from across the room. She was distractingly beautiful.

With a small gesture Andavarri sent the Fire Golems with Tearmai off into one of the side rooms. Kavaris Dell followed, glancing in. The Golems came out and closed a heavy door behind them, leaving Tearmai inside as a lock cycled shut.

"What's going to happen to him?" Amita asked.

"We'll do what we can," Kavaris Dell said, turning to her. "But for now, he needs to be kept secure. We don't want him attacking anyone else. Drakes are powerful creatures, but they're usually docile." He touched Alex's shoulder and motioned to a table. "Please, over there."

Chris helped Alex across the room and onto the cold, solid exam bed. Alex's eyes were still on the window and the cage. He could see Cormack jumping from obstacle to obstacle. The red team was stretching out their batons, trying to touch him with the charged ends. Paying little attention, Alex was still looking at the girl in the balcony. She wasn't dressed in a jump suit. None of the students in the balconies were. Their clothing was more elaborate and expensive looking.

The girl didn't break eye contact with him. He noticed that her shoulders were bare, her dark hair was held by a jewel-encrusted band, and her dress sparkled in the lights. It was hard to look away. She smiled knowingly, then returned her attention to the match.

Kavaris Dell helped Alex take off his shirt. "Who is that?" Alex asked, pointing with his head toward her.

Kavaris Dell washed the blood from the shirt off his hands and glanced up to see who Alex meant, but by the time he did, Andavarri had answered. "That is Princess Maeven Tamerlane, the emperor's daughter," she said.

"You have an emperor?" Amita asked in disbelief.

"He gave himself the title," Regin explained. "Though, in truth, he controls enough resources and has enough loyalty from the other lords that he may very well have earned it."

'A princess, there isn't much chance that she actually saw me,' Alex thought, looking at the girl. At least fifty meters separated the window from her balcony. Not to mention he was halfway across the healing chamber with a piece of glass between them. Still, as he stared at her, he somehow knew that she could sense him. He saw her smile a little, the corner of her lip lifting, and felt that he needed to look away. He leaned forward and looked down, trying to see the match.

∞

Out in the cage Cormack jumped down from the obstacles toward the open space between the floating debris field and the green team's base. Moving fast, Cormack rolled when he hit the ground. The red team wasn't far behind him, but some of the greens, the two largest members, were covering the base. They nodded as Cormack charged past them, hunkering down and setting themselves in the way of the other team.

Four of the reds came in fast, but the green defenders stood strong. They took shocks from the batons, using their bodies as barricades while Cormack ran ahead at a full sprint. He didn't look back as he dove behind their base.

He slammed the red marker on a pedestal and a buzzer sounded through the hall, ending the match, but as Cormack leaned back to catch his breath, he saw that the red team was still advancing. Their leader Vyktor had come down from the obstacle field, while the two green team members who'd guarded the base were trying to get to theirs.

Screaming in rage, Vyktor dropped in front of them, kicked one in the chest, then smashed his fist into the face of the other. He didn't stop, continuing to kick them while they were on the ground.

"Hey it's over," someone said. One of Vyktor's own team, who was half his size, stepped forward to try and stop him. The boy reached out grabbing Vyktor's shoulder.

Vyktor shoved him so hard that he slammed into the bars four meters away. As the brute was going back to the downed greens, Cormack came charging at him.

He threw his entire body at Vyktor with his leg out in a flying kick. It was like hitting a brick wall. He bounced off and fell to the ground where he had only a heartbeat to back away from Vyktor's foot, which came stomping forward.

Vyktor didn't notice that the field around the cage had shut off or that Edith, the woman in black, had come in.

"Enough!" Edith yelled, grabbing Vyktor's wrist and twisting it back while throwing her shoulder into him. Edith was strong, but Vyktor was still half a head taller and twice as wide.

Vyktor tried pulling away, but the instructor wasn't letting go. She jammed her knee behind his leg and brought him to the ground, still holding his wrist. "Enough!" she shouted again, bringing the knee to his shoulder blade, using leverage to force Vyktor to the floor. A little more pressure and Vyktor's arm would break. He punched the ground with his other fist as the struggle ebbed slowly out of him.

∞

In the healing chambers Alex sat up to watch, but Kavaris Dell pushed him back onto the table. "That's enough of that for now."

As soon as Alex's shoulder touched the bed, a lip rose along the sides, covering the edges. Kavaris Dell pulled away the blood-soaked bandages to reveal the deep wound across Alex's abdomen. Alex winced a little, feeling the stitches being tugged roughly by the old man while the dried blood cracked. Kavaris Dell wasn't gentle, as he took a hose and sprayed the cut. The liquid stung with antiseptic.

Kavaris Dell opened a cabinet and took out a jar of viscous gel. He watched a display while pouring it over Alex's stomach, spreading it with his fingers. The gel began to glow with tiny blue creatures swimming in and out of the cut.

42

"What is that?" Alex asked in alarm, sitting up and looking at the tiny creatures.

The monk pushed him back again. "They are Dioepea, microorganisms. They're going to start stitching your wound, but the bruising on your organs and the shattered ribs may take a bit longer to heal. Your cells will regenerate rapidly. . . It might be uncomfortable."

The feeling in Alex's stomach started as a strange tingling, but quickly turned into something closer to an electric shock. Trying to get used to the sensation, he grabbed the edge of the table and closed his eyes, then opened them again and stared at the window, trying to focus. He looked for the girl on the balcony but she was gone. Instead, he tried to remember what she looked like.

∞

Across the room Katy could only listen. Everything was darkness. She could sense the faint pressure of the bandages on her arms and she remembered the spot where Amita had held her. Katy wouldn't say it aloud, but she really wished Amita hadn't let go. She'd heard the youngest of their group over by Tearmai's door. 'Tearmai? He saved me and I don't even know what he looks like.' Her eyesight had been gone before he came for them. She'd felt him guide her to the diamond vessel and lift her up, but she'd never actually seen him.

Someone stepped in front of her. She felt hands touch her face, felt the gauze being cut and lifted. How strange that I'm not pulling away. Katy had no idea who was in front of her, who was touching her, but she welcomed the contact. It was more than the nothing she'd been walking around in for the past few hours.

"What happened to you?" a voice asked. It was soft and a little raspy with age. "How did you lose your sight?"

Katy took a moment to answer, and when she did, her voice sounded foreign to her. "When the Hunter came for me, there was a light. It was so sharp. It was . . . powerful and it hurt. I think it was Brash. He came back when the Hunter was going to kill me, but Brash—I could feel it. He was brighter than anything— I felt him shove me. After that I couldn't see anymore."

"There was an explosion too," Chris added coming over. Kavaris Dell was being gentler with Katy than he had been with his brother. Holding a device up to her eyes he pulled her lids open with his fingers.

"'Brash?' You're sure that was his name?" Kavaris Dell asked.

"He was the one who took our mother," Chris offered.

The old monk looked back at Regin, who said in response, "His name is so fitting."

The old man stared at the little alien for a long moment, waiting for him to volunteer more. In a very human gesture, Regin shrugged, holding all four of his furry hands in the air.

"Go fetch Chooth for me. This is beyond my skills," Kavaris Dell ordered before turning back to the display.

"Of course, the one we really need is Eir."

"And who knows when she'll return from Grannus?" Regin agreed, heading toward the ramp. He was about to leave when a large group came stumbling up. The seven members of green team, many of them trying to help each other along, were groaning as they limped into the room.

Cormack was in the middle, his face painted with concern, carrying the girl who'd jumped down on Vyktor. She was small, but he was still struggling, trying to keep her steady while her head hung back in semi-consciousness. "We were victorious," Cormack said grimly to the room.

Kavaris Dell left Katy's side and went to them. He held up his arms in a vain attempt to block their view of the healing chamber. His red robe acted like a poor curtain. "This way, this way." He hurried the team out of view of Alex and the others, guiding the greens into another room.

Regin watched for a moment, waiting for them to clear the ramp while Andavarri sidled up next to him. "I'll help you find Chooth," she offered.

Alex called after them, "Hey, we want to know about Brash."

Regin stopped and sighed before answering, "Brash was here like Tearmai. He was one of the stewards, like us." He pointed toward Andvarri and himself. "He was the only one that could do it because he was the last of his race. But he was young and, well—"

"Brash," Andavarri added.

"Yes, exactly." Regin continued. "The rest of the Lightening Bugs vanished or were wiped out by humans on Uppsala. Brash disappeared weeks ago, along with Tearmai. We had no idea where they went, till now. Somehow, they found their way to you. Now please, let me go get your friend some help."

Alex nodded, then Regin and Andavarri left. He looked around the room at the others. They were alone for the first time since coming out of the ship. Ben was by the window, Amita was checking out some of the machines and Chris was by Katy. With the gauze gone he could see how pale her eyes were, how the blue had been washed away or covered by milky scars. The flesh around her eyes was red and burnt, and her forearms were still wrapped in bandages. Alex could tell his brother wanted to reach out and touch her arm. He wanted to tell Chris to go ahead, to reassure her.

"So, does anyone have a clue where we are?" Katy asked, causing Chris to jump back, startled.

"Your dad was opening a wormhole. We're on the other side of it," Amita said.

"So, these people are all aliens, even the people people, like the ones without fur and claws and you know, purple skin?" Ben asked.

Amita shrugged while Chris and Alex looked at each other, neither sure how to answer.

"Wait! There's someone here with purple skin?" Katy sounded confused.

"There were a few out there fighting. And the other one was less a person and more of a wolf-lizard thing." Chris offered.

"With a bad attitude," Ben added. "You don't think that has to do with their color, do you? What's purple on a mood ring?"

They heard the doors open at the bottom of the ramp and heavy footsteps coming up. Edith walked into the room. Her eyes were dark as she looked over the healing chamber. Her gaze fell on Ben. "Where is Kavaris Dell?" she asked in a voice that made Ben shiver.

He pointed to the other room as Kavaris Dell returned. "Don't worry. Your students will be fine, despite the brutality of your exercises," he said, pulling the sleeves of his robe down.

"That's not why I'm here," Edith answered. She leaned forward to Kavaris Dell, whispering.

He listened, then stepped back, turning pale at what he heard. "But they haven't done anything? No sign of attack?" he asked, leaning a little on Edith's armored shoulder.

She shook her head, no.

Kavaris Dell turned back to the room, to the five refugees. "I'm sorry, but there's something I must attend to immediately." Edith started to leave with the monk directly behind her.

"Wait, what's going on?" Chris asked.

Kavaris Dell looked back over his shoulder. "I'm afraid your arrival may have attracted some attention," he said in a distracted tone as he disappeared down the ramp with Edith.

Ben watched her go, then told the others, "That Edith lady should probably be purple too."

Chapter 6

As soon as the monk's red robed figure disappeared down the stairs, Amita started walking away.

"Hey, where are you going?" Chris demanded behind her.

"We need more information and we're not going get it hanging out here," she said.

Alex sat up and took a deep breath. "You need to stay," he said through gritted teeth.

Ben came over to him. "Yeah, if it's information you want, we can check out these machines." Ben pointed to a display on the table, which showed Alex's body outlined. The wounded areas were painted in swollen red. "There's got to be a way to get more out of this thing." He started touching buttons.

When a shrill and steady alarm beeped, Alex reached over and grabbed Ben's arm. "Knock it off," he growled turning his attention back to Amita, "Look, I get it, we need to understand what's going on, but this place could be dangerous. We need to stay together. You think I don't want to know what happened to my mom, or hell, what's happening to Earth right now? None of that matters though if we wind up dead. Our first priority needs to be survival."

"We need to do a lot more than survive," Amita said, shaking her head as she wandered around the corner. She heard Alex call behind her, but her attention was on the next room where she saw the green team being treated, their armor in piles, littering the floor.

Standing between the medical beds where most of his team sat, Cormack looked up. His face was painted with concern, but when he saw Amita he smiled and nodded. Amita smiled back at the handsome young man and waved shyly. He was leaner than Alex with dirty blond hair that had been left a little long. His eyes hinted at an Asian heritage and his skin was the light olive of someone who'd grown up under a hot sun but hadn't been home in a while. Amita noticed many of the team members had similar traits. Everything about them screamed islander, wearing jewelry made of shells and white pointed teeth from sea predators.

Cormack had started walking toward her when she heard the doors open again. She glanced down the ramp to see Regin returning with company. Next to the furry alien was the strangest creature Amita had seen yet.

She stared in fascination, barely noticing Chooth's face, which resembled a moray eel. The creature's body had the vague form of a human being with two arms and two legs coming off a central trunk, but what made up the rest of his body was far from human. Chooth was a composite, made of a number of smaller creatures, slugs and fish and shelled crustaceans all working together. He was covered in eyes and antennas with little claws interspersed throughout. They clung to a framework of glass bottles and tubes pumping liquid to his arms and legs.

He wore a loose robe of simple brown cloth that did a poor job of covering his strangeness. Someone else may have been horrified, but Amita was intrigued. "Wow," she said as she followed the creature and Regin back into the room with Alex and the others.

The new arrival nodded to Amita, then looked over the group as Regin said, "May I introduce Chooth. He is a student here, but he's been trained as a healer."

Ben and Chris stood with their mouths open, while Alex wondered if he was hallucinating.

"He's going to take a look at—" Regin glanced at Katy, then back at the others. "I'm sorry, I failed to get your names."

It took Ben a moment to close his mouth and form an answer. "She's Katy, she's my sister. I'm, ah Ben." He finished introducing the others, pointing around the room while constantly turning back to stare at Chooth.

Regin smiled. "Excellent, now that we are acquainted, Chooth here is going to take a look at your sister's eyes."

Katy could sense someone standing nearby. She reached out, touching Chris's shoulder. "Is he one of the purple ones?" she whispered.

Chris was staring at Chooth, "Um . . . no, he's not purple."

∞

Kavaris Dell followed Edith through the stone corridors leading back to the lighthouse. He tried to remain composed by staring at the woman's dark armor as it blended in with the walls. Edith had a calming effect. Her voice hadn't revealed any concern when she gave him the news. She wasn't the kind to let fear show, but she moved with haste, knowing that to test the patience of their visitors was to welcome destruction.

The warrior stopped at the staircase, the same one that Kavaris Dell had climbed earlier that morning. "I'll wait here for you," she said. She'd been to the lighthouse before as head of security, but she knew the rules. It was a place for the monks, for those who'd taken the vow to serve.

Kavaris nodded to Edith, glad that at least one of his instructors was willing to obey him. He looked up at the tall steps, lifting his robe and starting up them. 'How long ago was it,' he wondered, that he took his sacred vows, 'seventy years, maybe eighty, could he really be that old?'

He remembered well the day he'd been blessed. How could he forget it after watching his township decimated, burnt to the ground, destroyed for their wickedness? He'd been twelve, the lone survivor, left to be a witness. 'How many more years did he have left? How much longer would he serve the Æsir? It could end today for him,' he thought.

Back in the lighthouse, his eyes went to the glass dome ceiling and to the clouds of Altor. The void space hovered on the surface, pulsing with energy. Fewer monks were here than before. Standing with their heads bowed, they were reverent, as they should be, but he wondered how many of them were secretly shaking with fear.

As he passed one monk, the young man looked up and said, "They've done nothing. They only wait."

"How many?" Kavaris asked.

"Three," he answered. As Kavaris Dell moved away, the monk said behind him, "Blessed be your encounter."

Kavaris glanced at the dais in the center of the room where the machines were still active. Strange lights played across their surfaces. Kavaris wondered what they were for, but then he lowered his head as well, knowing that to investigate them further would be unwise. He walked toward a doorway on the other side of the room.

The portal dilated as he approached. It was a bronze iris that spread apart, opening on the inner half of an airlock. Kavaris Dell tried not to be startled, but his heart beat faster as he looked in. Someone was standing on the inside. A slight glow came from the figure who was mostly swallowed in shadow as darkness like a cloud danced around him as if he were partially made from a nightmare. The being moved into the lighthouse. His very real steps echoed on the stone. Kavaris looked up, feeling awe and unbridled fear. The Æesir were here.

He was looking at his god, the destroyer the monks worshiped. He was taller than Kavaris Dell by half a meter, covered in armor that was grey and ancient. His jaw was shaped like the bottom of a human skull and his eyes were unseen behind his helmet. Horns were on his head and spikes on his shoulders. In his hand was a broad axe that glowed with power. He was made for man to be afraid of, the very sight of him uncovered weakness.

Kavaris Dell fell to his knees, his eyes going to the floor. "Why have you come to bless us, lord?"

He saw the axe blade touch the floor, glowing red with heat. The floor began to warm. "I'm not here to bless you. You know our blessings only come with fire." He bent down a little, reaching his hand out to Kavaris Dell's chin. His gauntlet was inlaid with human bone. He took the old man's face and lifted it toward him. The touch was incredibly cold. "I've come because I'm curious. Tell me, what has come through the void?"

∞

Refusing to lie back, Katy sat with her feet up and her hands around her knees. Glass walls had risen a meter and a half all around her, enclosing her in what looked like a fish tank on top of the table. A valve opened and water started pouring in. Katy was still dressed as it filled. "I don't know about this." Even though she couldn't see, she was turning her head frantic and afraid. Her hands found the top of the tank. "Couldn't I just put my face in a bowl or something? Do I have to be all the way under?" The bandages that'd been on her arms were gone, exposing the angry electrical burns. Her skin had thickened, but the edges were raw. She tried not to move them, afraid of tearing the ridges of the burns open.

Regin climbed up onto the display. Using his extra arms and legs to support himself he reached down and kindly touched Katy's shoulder. "It's going to be alright. This is the best way for Chooth to examine you. The Grannusians are the finest healers circling Altor. They can perform miracles, but they need to be in their natural state."

Chooth had taken off his robe. He was standing next to the tank. "Please don't be afraid," he said while Ben and Amita bent over examining his odd body. Amita was trying to understand how the system of water bottles worked to keep Chooth's body parts moist, while Ben was counting the number of eyes he saw. Each little shrimp-creature had its own set while the worms appeared to be blind. They still wiggled as if they could sense him standing too close.

"You two certainly are curious," Chooth said.

"Sorry." Ben stood up, a little embarrassed but Amita continued her examination ready to reach out and touch Chooth when someone entered the room.

"You can't really blame them. You are the handsomest Grannusian I've ever seen," Cormack said as he came around the corner and leaned against the wall.

Chooth looked at him. "I see your morning exercises went as well as usual. Your mother will be happy that you didn't mess up that pretty face."

"And we won," Cormack said. "If that counts for anything."

"Is everyone okay?" Chooth asked.

Cormack nodded. "The Tairnish team was brutal, but our people are still breathing."

"Are many in need of my services?"

"The machines are working on them, but if you wouldn't mind taking a look after. . ." He pointed to Katy. "When you're done here."

Katy's head was turned toward the new arrival. She leaned toward Regin. "Who is that?" she asked.

Amita gave a distracted answer. "He's another human, the one from the steel cage match, the good looking one." Her attention was still on Chooth.

Cormack's face turned red as he waved awkwardly to the group. "Yeah, hi, I'm Cormack."

Chris and Ben glared at Amita, who just shrugged. "Are you aware of everything they're sensing?" she asked, reaching out to touch a shrimp-creature. It pulled away from her, digging deeper into Chooth's body.

"Mostly, each part of me has its own nervous system that can operate independently, but most of the parts have to be together, or at least in close proximity, in order for me to be me, for my personality and intellect to function. Otherwise, I'm not myself. I become . . . diminished."

Regin touched a button on the table-tank and it started to lower, sinking till it was level with the floor. The water sloshed around Katy who was grabbing the sides while Regin took down an air hose, handed it to her and helped guide it toward her mouth. "It's time to lie back, my dear," he said.

"It's going to be alright," Chris assured her, although looking at the tank and at Chooth he wasn't so sure. She put her head in the water. Air bubbles floated to the surface when she breathed.

"Okay," Chooth said, looking back at the group. "Try to stay calm, this may seem odd." In a wave each part of his body jumped forward. His legs bent down, but by the time they were in the air they'd already come apart, spreading into his component pieces. The largest was his head, which was like an eel with a puckered tail for a spinal cord. So many parts dropped into the tank with large splashes that the water churned with the chaos of all the little creatures landing. The frame of hoses and water bottles that had been his body slumped to the floor in a pile.

Through the ripples Chris saw Katy start to panic, nearly spitting the air hose out. Her hands surfaced then she suddenly relaxed. Her hands floated down to her side, as the panic faded and she became unnaturally calm. Small creatures swam and climbed over her like a swarm, but it didn't seem to bother her. Chris looked at Regin. "What was that? Is she alright?"

"Chooth can release a mild sedative in the water. Your friend absorbed it through her skin. It'll make it easier to help her."

Time passed while they all watched. For twenty minutes the water churned and bubbled. When it finally calmed, Katy sat up, then slowly let her body float while leaning back on her elbows. Some of Chooth's parts supported her from below. The breathing tube fell lazily from her mouth as she opened her eyes. Her irises still had that milky white color, but her dark red burns had softened and faded back to a more normal shade.

Chooth's head came up near her face. "I'm sorry, the damage to your eyes is like nothing I've seen before. I've begun healing your burns, but your sight . . . it's beyond my ability." He turned to Regin. "We need Eir. She may have seen something like this."

"Who is Eir and where are they?" Chris asked.

Katy interrupted before anyone could answer, singing to herself. "Oh where, oh where is Eir?"

"Maybe dial back the sedative," Cormack offered.

"It'll wear off in a moment." Chooth's parts started coming closer together in the tank, forming a solid mass.

"That's too bad," Katy said. She was already sounding clearer.

Chooth reached over the side to grab his water frame from the floor while saying, "To answer your question though, Eir is our master healer, the steward of our species here on Nalanda Station. She's one of the oldest of my people, but she's gone back to Grannus, to mine and Cormack's home world."

"Prince Cormack's people live there now, anyway," Regin interjected, wanting to be clear.

"We've lived there for quite a while," Cormack shot back, looking at Regin, waiting for him to argue. When the Ice-Carver remained quiet, Cormack continued. "If it's Eir we need, then we should try to find her. I've got state business, so I'm returning to Grannus on the next supply shuttle. You're all more than welcome to join me. There have been troubles that I need to look into. That's why Eir returned in the first place, but she's been out of communication."

"What kind of troubles?" Alex asked.

"The waters that the Grannusians call home is poisoned," Regin answered. "There's been mass pollution in their food chain. Chooth witnessed it while he was home visiting. He returned to Nalanda Station to warn us and tell Eir. The master healer went home to investigate, but weeks have passed with little word. The humans say they know nothing."

"Because we don't," Cormack shot back.

After climbing out of the tank, Chooth stood next to Cormack and touched his arm. "It's alright, my friend. I can't believe your mother or any of your people would sink that low."

Cormack nodded as his lips twisted. His face was still tight with concern as he turned back to the group and forced a smile. "Anyway, the shuttle leaves in twenty hours and the offer stands. If Eir is who we need for your friend, then I say come with me and we'll find her. I would love to welcome you to my world. It's a brighter place than this." He motioned to the drab walls around them.

Alex and Chris looked at each other, not sure how to respond. Ben summed up their thoughts. "But we just got here," he said.

Chapter 7

Hours had passed and the grand hall was empty. When three red robed monks entered the healing chamber, they offered little explanation. They briefly checked Alex and Katy's wounds, then said, "Follow us, your chambers are ready."

Alex struggled to his feet, while Ben rushed up next to Chris, who was helping Katy out of the tank. Ben seemed calmer now after sleeping for a bit. They led Katy to the ramp where she reached out to the wall.

"Are you alright?" Ben asked. Katy nodded, but she didn't say anything. Water dripped from her, soaking the floor.

Amita came last. She waited while the medical machines cycled down, then took one last look at the room Tearmai was in. The door had been locked the entire day. She put her ear against it and heard a scratching sound followed by a low moan inside. Amita touched the door for a moment longer, then hurried to catch up with the others.

Chris looked around when they reached the darkened hall. Up high, in the massive black space, the cage and the balconies were shadows making him feel small and cowed. At the far end, he could see a window and the edge of the gas giant. It was shadowy now, a gray murky form, blocking the stars. They were on the dark side of the planet. Night had fallen on Nalanda Station.

Katy shivered. "Can we get her something to wear?" Ben asked, trying to warm her by rubbing her arms. Till then the only sound had been their footsteps and the chattering of Katy's teeth.

One monk looked back and said in a hurried voice, "You can all change in your chambers." He motioned ahead, never breaking stride, moving through the darkness.

"I'll be okay, Ben. Just show me the way," Katy said.

They entered a passage, following low lights on the ceiling. Not a single person was in the narrow corridor where currents of cool air seemed to breathe about them. It was better than being out in the open space of the hall, where a feeling of being watched came from the very walls.

As they turned a corner, they came to four lifeless and dark figures. The Fire Golems stood guard over the passage. Amita looked at them and remembered the way they had lifted Tearmai as if he weighed nothing.

The Drake hadn't left her thoughts, not the entire time they were in the healing chambers and not now. Regin and Chooth had checked on Tearmai earlier, spending a fair amount of time with him in that locked room, but they said little about it when they came out. She had tried to follow them in, but Regin said, "I have no wish to endanger you."

When Kavaris Dell finally returned to the healing chamber, Amita had shot up. She opened her mouth to speak, but he held up his hand for silence and said, "Even though you aren't 'nobles,' you'll stay here at the school. You'll be treated like any other student, but you'll be housed apart, in the monk's quarters."

They didn't understand what any of that meant, and Kavaris Dell didn't seem open to answering questions. Appearing shaken and distracted, he turned to Cormack, who had still been present. "If you're not injured, then you're still expected to attend classes. The healing chambers are for those in need, for those who didn't fare as well as you." Kavaris Dell sneered, nodding toward the room with Cormack's teammates.

Cormack didn't like being spoken to that way, but he said nothing as he left. Kavaris Dell glanced at the door where they'd placed Tearmai. "Now please tell me exactly where it is you've come from."

Chris told the whole story from beginning to end, about the facility in the desert, about the Hunter, the Lightening Bug, and about the Drake. Then he told him about the wormhole they went through, that was slowly swallowing the Earth. Kavaris Dell asked a few questions, but for the most part he only listened. He ignored Ben and Amita's interruptions, holding his finger up and telling Chris to continue every time someone tried to break in. Even Alex wasn't able to get information from the old man.

When Chris was done, bringing his story to a close with the diamond vessel, Kavaris Dell nodded and turned to leave.

"Wait, hang on a second." Alex called from his bed. "What happened to our mother? How do we get her back? And how are we here?"

"I'm afraid I can't help you with those things. Investigating the wormholes, as you called them, or the void spaces is forbidden. I have no idea how

Brash came to your world or what he may've done with your mother. But you're here now. This is a place of learning and that's what you'll be doing, but you'll be learning what we teach. You're under my protection. I suggest the first thing you do is familiarize yourself with the rules. Everyone must follow them, even you. Our consequences here may be more severe than you're used to." He turned and unlocked the door where Tearmai was and went in.

When he came back out, he was with Regin. The Ice-Carver turned to the group, shaking his head before following Kavaris Dell to the exit. Kavaris Dell stopped at the ramp and told them over his shoulder, "Try to rest, you'll begin your education tomorrow." Then he left.

Ben waited till the monk was out of earshot before he said, "Well, that sucks," summing up everyone's thoughts.

"They're not going to help us find out what happened?" Chris asked, feeling exhausted.

"No, they're not," Amita growled. "These twits aren't here to learn anything. The things they teach are probably just enough to keep them in power. We went through a wormhole right into an idiocracy. It's a damn dystopian nightmare." She pointed in the direction the old monk had gone.

"Settle down," Alex ordered. "We're alive and that's better than the alternative. Our first priority is staying that way."

Amita couldn't stop herself though, talking at a frantic pace as she laid out the facts the way she saw them. "It's mad as a bag of ferrets. We've got no information and no way of getting any. Our world is being consumed as we speak, and we've fallen into the power of some religious cult who, despite the fact that we're pretty far from Earth, are to all appearances human. And that wormhole, just from what I saw, looks stable. I didn't even think that was possible, but what do I know? They're only theoretical after all, except there's a real one, right out there anchored in the upper atmosphere of a gas giant, but I'm not allowed to study it. On top of that, we're going to have to go to some sort of Hogwarts in space where they'll teach us a pile of horse flop and feed us just enough garbage to keep us in line."

Ben asked, above Amita's rant. "Hey Katy, is there any more sedative in that water?" Floating just below the surface, Katy didn't respond. She hadn't said much after Chooth climbed from the tank.

Chris went over and touched Amita's arm. "I know its nuts, but there's not much we can do about it right now. We're all tired, Amita. When was the last time you slept?'

"I'm not big on sleep." She threw his arm off and went to sit against the wall.

Chris stared at her for a moment, then settled down onto the floor next to her. It wasn't till hours later that the monks came. Alex passed a good amount of that time sleeping, while the glowing organisms stitched him up. A scar was left behind on his abdomen when he awoke, but not much else. It still hurt to breathe and if he moved too fast, he'd feel the edges of his broken ribs and the bruising beneath his skin.

Katy stayed in the tank, floating away the hours, letting the bath of chemicals and nutrients work on her burns. By the time she climbed out, the dark torn edges of the wounds were gone. The burnt skin sloughed off, leaving behind pale, new looking flesh, but her eyes were unchanged. They stayed white, staring at nothing.

Ben had joined Chris and Amita on the floor. The two boys eventually slumped and wiggled down till they were flat on the ground, where they fell asleep almost on top of each other. Amita stayed sitting next to them, leaning against the wall. Her eyes may've closed, but she wasn't sure if she slept. Her mind worked over everything she'd seen, every detail that had been spoken. She was afraid.

A few hours later Chooth came out of Tearmai's room. Amita was the only one who looked up. Chooth was moving slowly, his body slumping. Each creature, every part of him was exhausted. The snails and slugs barely clung to his frame. He checked on Alex and Katy, who were both drowsy from the meds and the process of healing.

"How is he?" Amita asked, pointing to Tearmai's door.

"He's sedated and he'll have to stay that way for a while. Being in hard vacuum, even for a little while, did damage to his internal organs. He needs to heal before I can hope to address his other issue, the madness from the void," Chooth said and started walking away.

Amita looked at Chris and Ben. Chris was ignoring the fact that Ben was using his shoulder as a pillow. "We're all scared, but you need to get some rest," Chris said softly to Amita, but she didn't listen. The five were alone till the monks came for them and took them out into Nalanda.

After passing the Fire Golems they traveled further in the low light, past a row of doors made of a fiberglass material that didn't fit with the rest of the hall, like they'd been added after. It wasn't the first time Amita noticed that not everything at the station matched. Changes had been made for the human inhabitants. Amita had known right away that someone else had built Nalanda long before humanity had started living here. She could see it in the way the halls curved and turned, the way the windows and balconies suggested bizarre shapes.

She of course wanted to ask the monks about it, but they didn't seem willing to answer questions. As they moved at a worried pace through the halls, Amita could see that they were uncomfortable with being out at night. When they opened the door, Amita glanced back and saw that Ben had dropped his sister's hand to stop and stare at the Fire Golems.

"Come on," she called to him.

The quarters they were assigned followed the same honeycomb pattern as the healing chambers, just on a smaller scale with curved walls leading to entrance ways. Curtains hung between the rooms and mattresses had been laid on the ground. The bathroom was a basin and a hole in the floor. "That's not a very impressive space toilet," Ben said, looking down at the dark tunnel that seemed to go on forever.

In the center of the common room was a large cabinet that looked like it'd been converted from a shipping container, repurposed by adding shelves. One of the monks opened it to reveal clothing inside, jump suits like the students wore in the grand hall and simpler clothes, loose fitting pants and shirts. A monk handed out the bundles. "The pants and shirts are for class. The one-piece suits are for combat training, though I imagine it'll be a while before you're expected to participate in that. We'll retrieve you in the morning for breakfast. Sleep well, you'll be safe in here for the night," he said patting the door reassuringly before turning to leave.

Chris looked at the bathroom, then turned to the bedrooms. One was for the girls with two mattresses and the other was for the boys with three.

Ben had gone to the door after the monk closed it, "'combat training?' Is he serious? And safe from what? What's this door supposed to keep out?" he asked, turning back to the room and looking at the others.

Chris shrugged. He was holding Katy's hand and noticed she was still wet and shivering. "Do you think you could help her?" he asked Amita.

"Sure," Amita said.

But Katy held onto him, "Are we going to talk about Cormack's offer?" she asked.

Chris stepped away. "We'll talk about it tomorrow." His footsteps were heavy as he pulled the curtain out of the way to the boy's room. Alex followed behind him.

Both were exhausted.

Ben watched them lay down while he was still at the door. "Seriously, guys, aren't you worried about what the monk said, about what's out there?" No one answered.

Chapter 8

Nalanda Station was a place of territories with common spaces, such as the grand halls and classrooms, and private areas set aside for the monks and for the different races. Long Wolves, Drakes, Grannus and the Ice-Carvers, both large and small belonged in the Extraracial territory. And the nobles were given dormitories separated by royal houses.

Through diplomacy these sections were set aside as sovereign ground for the different dynasties and their loyal partisans. Soldiers guarded their doors and servants worked inside their walls. Often lesser houses served the greater. Through conquest, marriage, mediation and conspiracy, those that claimed royal birth frequently found themselves beholden to more powerful houses. This was the place Tara's family held, bound to serve the Tamerlane's.

For nine years Tara had been handmaiden to Princess Maeven Tamerlane, daughter of the emperor. She was pale and blond, the daughter of a duke from the icy north of Uppsala where the trees of the arbor moon once grew the tallest. Her's was an old family, and a proud one, but they weren't powerful enough to stand against the Tamerlanes. The trees no longer stood in the North. The land was dotted with craters, left over from when the Tamerlanes seized control of the entire world, when they claimed Uppsala for themselves, bringing each house in line, crushing them under orbital bombardment.

Those craters would fill with icy water, making perfectly round ponds that dotted the landscape like mirrors. Tara had looked out on those ponds when she was young, thinking they were beautiful. Looking back, she knew what they truly were. A reminder that her life would never be her own. Her father would always serve, just as she would.

After the match she followed Maeven to her quarters. The princess had said nothing after the Tairnish defeat, simply turning and leaving. Tara was expected to follow, like a loyal pet. She tried not to resent Maeven for it. They were friends after all. And what better friend to have than a powerful one. Still, when Maeven was in a dark mood, it was hard not to be afraid.

They'd been together since Tara's seventh birthday, when she'd been more of a playmate than a servant.

Growing up, Maeven had shared all her secrets with Tara, even the terrible ones. It'd been by choice then. Tara still knew more than she should, but now it wasn't because Maeven told her.

Genetic engineering was a forbidden science, but it hadn't always been and some cultivated traits still showed up in people like Tara. They weren't spoken of, and they certainly weren't studied, but being able to sense the thoughts of your enemies had once been the goal of that genetic tampering. Whether those scientists had succeeded long ago in creating a telepath, no one knew, but in Tara's bloodline, some people were born with abilities. They were vague and fell short of something measurable. Still, the Tamerlanes found it useful to always have a member of Tara's family nearby during negotiations, and they found it necessary to always keep Tara's family subservient.

Here at Nalanda Station, among the other houses, with politics ever present, Tara knew her friendship came second to Maeven's responsibilities. Maeven was the emperor's hand and had to remain strong.

"Something must be done," Maeven said. They were in her private quarters, a series of rooms in the Tamerlane domicile set apart from all the other nobles. It was larger than any other private quarters on the station. The common honeycomb pattern had been demolished and decorated with wood from Uppsala. The finest panels of white milk-wood covered the stone, making the room bright and cheerful. The ceiling had been excavated as well and made smooth with clay and hung with elaborate crystal lighting.

"Done about what?" Tara asked.

Maeven looked at her as if the answer should've been obvious. "About Cormack, of course, and Vyktor as well. Today's combat exercise showed me quite clearly. Cormack is too damn clever, too good. And Vyktor, when he's older, he's to be one of my chief war councilors. Can you imagine that lout commanding the entire Tairnish army? He's a fool, a raging idiot. They're both problems."

Maeven had kicked off her shoes in the center of the room. They were tall wooden heels inlaid with jewels. Tara hurried to pick them up and place them in a cabinet with several more. "Vyktor's young, untested," Tara offered. "With time—"

"What time? Imagine . . ." Maeven was standing in front of her mirror, looking at her dress, which was lovely of course, but she sneered at it as she began to shrug it off. "Help me with this," she ordered. "We don't give time, not to our enemies, or to those that can hurt us. Stupid is stupid. Look at Cormack, look at the moves he makes. He's loved by his own people and liked by the teachers and other races. Not that that matters, but he's also the favorite of most of the other houses, even some that are supposed to be loyal to the Tamerlanes. And he didn't take any time to gain these things. It's just who he is. He's a damn ray of sunshine. Meanwhile, he cuts me down every chance he gets. He talks about me and spreads the rumors of witchcraft. Think of the damage those rumors could do. I am telling you; something must be done."

Tara helped Maeven out of the dress, then went to the closet to retrieve her uniform. It was a simple outfit. A white shirt and dark pants, the same as everyone else's, but of course Maeven's was made from better material and cut precisely to complement her body. The princess stayed in front of the mirror, starring at herself naked. Trainers and a healthy diet along with good genetics, some of it engineered in the days when that was still allowed, made her a perfect physical specimen. Still, she sneered at herself.

She turned to Tara. "Something must be done and soon." She took the uniform from her and pulled the shirt on while Tara took an elaborate piece of metal shaped like a badge from a wooden case. On it was a spear crossed with a sword. A tree was beneath them, the coat of arms for the house Tamerlane. Tara wore a similar badge with a snowflake and a tree. Maeven's wasn't pinned though. Her badge was hung by a piece of silk that she wore around her neck. After Tara draped it over her, Maeven added, "Then there's the other matter. These new arrivals. I'm sure Cormack has already found out all about them. My father must be informed, but I'll want more information before I contact him."

"Perhaps I can help you with that," someone said from the door. Tara jumped a little at the voice. She had no sense for alien minds and neither of the girls had heard the door open. Maeven still faced the mirror, not bothered at all, even by the fact that she was half naked.

She calmly pulled her pants on before turning toward the voice, having recognized Andavarri. She would've been disappointed if the Long-Wolf hadn't come to see her. After all, the Tamerlanes ruled Andavarri's world too, or at least had the loyalty of the humans who did. "So, tell me," Maeven said, "who are these new people?"

Andavarri bowed deeply before telling the princess.

∞

Ben lay with his eyes open. He was listening to Chris and Alex, who were both breathing heavily, deep asleep. He didn't get it. Didn't know how they could pass out like that. Not with the massive enchilada of crap that had happened. They were somewhere in space, far from everything they knew. The whole Earth was on the other side of a wormhole, probably getting chewed up right now. His school, and everyone in it, were likely being flushed into outer space. True, most of them were un-mitigating turds, but he still couldn't sleep thinking about them.

Ben stared at the stony surface of the ceiling. It made him think about the Fire Golems. He thought of the one that'd saved him, how it'd sacrificed its body for him. That was awesome, but then the Golem came back as living flame, taking the Drake out. Ben remembered how the heat had felt on his face. He was certain it was alive, no matter what that alien said. He looked at Chris, wanting to ask him about it.

'Chris is sleeping, I shouldn't wake him,' Ben thought, giving himself a mental pat on the shoulder for not bothering his friend. Instead, he got to his feet and headed for the door. He wasn't sure why. This was normal for Ben, moving and acting, then wondering about his motivation later. All he knew was that a Fire Golem was outside the door and he wanted to talk to it.

"Where are you going?" Amita whispered. She was sitting at the end of her mattress.

"I want to talk to one of them," Ben answered.

"The Fire Golems?"

"Yeah, those guys."

"I'm not sure they talk," Amita said, getting to her feet.

Ben's shoulders fell as he stepped back. He hadn't thought of that.

"But they are right outside, so we could find out," Amita said.

He smiled, then opened the door and Amita slipped out behind him. He carefully closed it, trying to keep it from latching so they could get back in.

The Fire Golems stood in the shadows, tall, dark and rigid, two on either side of the hall showing no signs of life. Ben walked toward one, looking up. "Do you think the fire part is inside them right now?" he whispered to Amita.

"I don't know," she said. "They wouldn't be very good guards without it."

Ben reached up, tapping one on the chest, not noticing Amita wandering further down the hall. "Hi," he said, waving his hand, then staring, waiting for something to happen. He glanced over his shoulder to Amita. "I don't know. I think these ones might just be rock." When she didn't answer, he turned to look for her. "Hey, where are you going?"

"Exploring," Amita said. She was almost out of sight, around the corner. "I'm tired of not getting answers, I'm going to go get some for myself. You coming?"

Ben looked around the darkened hall and thought again about what the monk had said that they should be 'safe' in their quarters for the night. He wondered again what he meant, but when he opened his mouth he muttered, "fine," and went chasing after her.

Ben didn't look back at the Fire Golems, otherwise he would've seen a lone eye in the center of each of their faces begin to glow. Then their heads turned to watch Amita and Ben disappear into the dark.

Chapter 9

"How's that sense of direction working?" Amita asked, looking back at Ben. "Do you think you could find your way to the room?"

"Yeah, definitely," he said. "We've only taken a few turns. It feels like more because the tunnels are curved. Why, do you want to head back yet?" It wasn't the first time he'd asked, or the first time Amita ignored him. They'd been out for a while, exploring the darkened passageways.

They left the Golems behind, going further into the monk's private territory and passing doors much like their own. At one point, Amita turned off, taking a smaller passageway cut into the wall. It was so narrow they had to move single file.

Tight and dark, it wouldn't have been Ben's pick, but Amita swore she saw light ahead. They came out into a wider corridor, more like the ones near the hanger bays where the diamond vessel was. They weren't anywhere near it, but Amita noticed how the walls looked similar, machined with a smooth finish. The cross tunnel, the dark narrow one, felt like it'd been part of a mine with rough walls carved from the asteroid that Nalanda sat on. The hall that led to their room was somewhere between the two. 'Age and time,' Amita thought, 'this place had been built over generations, with different stages of construction and no central plan.'

Softly glowing lamps lined the walls of this larger passage as it ran straight, fading into the distance. Ben looked one way, then the other. They were somewhere in the middle of the passage, and he didn't see many exits. When he remembered the hanger bay entrance, the way it blended in with the wall, he wondered if he'd even recognize a door without seeing it open.

"Well?" He held his hands out flat motioning in either direction, asking Amita which way.

"You're the one who always knows where he's going," Amita said. Her voice began at a normal volume, but she dropped it almost to a whisper when she heard it echo back. "Which way do you think?"

"I'd go that way. Back to our room," Ben pointed behind them.

"When did you become such a chicken?" Amita asked.

"First off, not a chicken. I just don't want to die. And I started becoming more concerned with said dying not too long after showing up in a creepy alien space station that feels more like the setting for a Frankenstein movie."

Amita shook her head. "We need information and I'm tired of people telling me we'll talk about it later."

"Yeah, fine, but I don't see anything informative here. Just walls and more walls."

"Let's try this way." Amita started off, picking a direction at random. Between the lights were small openings like the one they came from. They were hidden in the shadows and hard to see. "Are you going to be able to remember which of these we came through?"

"Yep," Ben said. "I've been counting." Looking ahead he noticed another one of the openings in the wall. It appeared slightly different, but he couldn't tell how.

Amita came to a sudden stop. She held her breath as she turned away listening for something behind them, looking over her shoulder at the empty passage. There were no corners where anything could hide.

"What is it?" Ben asked.

"Shush," Amita demanded as she waited to hear it again, wondering, did the sound come from one of the openings. Her eyes went over each one, attempting to see in the shadows past the lights. She tried to remember where the black spaces had been, between which lamps. A few of the lights concentrated in one spot had gone dark, making a black void further down the passage. It was a good distance away, but it hadn't been there before.

"Ben, look at that." She pointed while keeping her voice low.

"What . . ?" He asked, even though he saw it right away. The spot of darkness was impossible to miss as it grew, filling the hall.

"That's where we came from," Ben said. "The tunnel we came through was back there." He pointed. "You didn't hit a light switch or anything, did you?"

"Have you seen any light switches?" Amita demanded.

"No, but—" Ben stopped, then pointed again. "Did you see that? Another one went out." Without being fully aware of it, he grabbed Amita's arm and started backing away from the darkness. His pulse quickened as a tingling started down his spine. They could both hear something coming from the dark spot. They couldn't quite call it footsteps, more like a shuffling, like metal sliding on rock. The sound was so faint, but it was coming closer, moving with the darkness as more lights faded.

Never taking his eyes off the lights, Ben walked backwards, making his way to the passage he'd noticed ahead. He dragged Amita with him, feeling the hair on her arm stand up. Ben's breathing sounded too loud to him but the more he tried to silence it the louder it got. They reached the opening and he understood why it was different. It led to stairs that went up and away.

"Come on," he said, starting to climb.

"Wait," Amita said. "I can see something." She peered into the approaching blackness, making out a shape. Something was taking form and it seemed familiar. "What is that?" Amita asked, her curiosity greater than her fear.

A shape started to form that Amita recognized. She held her breath again, but this time it was involuntary, catching in her chest as her whole body froze. She knew right then that they'd made a terrible mistake coming out here because she understood what she was looking at. Her hand went to her mouth, attempting to stop her scream.

The last time she saw this thing, it had been bent over the bodies of her parents. It was a Hunter, like the one on Earth, the one that had nearly sliced Alex in half and tried to kill Katy. Amita would never forget the monstrous shape and it was still fresh in her mind. To her, it had only been the night before when the wormhole breached its containment. Amita had been face to face with the creature while her parents lay in the street, unmoving.

The monster, proceeding through the shadows in hall, was the same height and width as the one on Earth. Its knees had that same weird angle and it carried those same swept-back blades on its arms, making that shuffling sound as they dragged across the ground.

'Katy destroyed it,' Amita thought, 'it couldn't follow us here.' She kept telling herself that as she backed away, placing a foot on the first step, trying to be as quiet as possible. She wouldn't take her eyes away from the monster.

As the lights faded around it, it was hard to see, but this Hunter was different. The one on Earth had been made from a deformed human body. This creature didn't look like it was made from a deformed anything. Its head was completely alien with an array of dark eyes, a thick cranial ridge above them, its jaw split apart with bug-like mandibles and a thick tongue lulling out.

Something else about it was different. The creature on Earth had been dark. This thing looked greyish and smoky, almost insubstantial. When it came near the lamps on the wall, the light passed through it, like the creature wasn't completely solid.

Wandering through the darkness, zigzagging back and forth across the hall, it seemed to be attracted to the lamps. When it came close to a light, it would reach out with its long fingers, keeping its blade swept back out of the way. The light would dim and go out when the creature touched it. Its shoulders would slump, then it would turn and go on to the next one.

Amita felt Ben's hand pulling on her, but she didn't think the creature had noticed them. Curiosity was winning out over fear again as she watched.

Ben pulled harder. "Come on!" He was already a few steps up.

"Knock it off," Amita snapped, twisting away from his grip.

She turned back to the hall. The creature was no longer moving. It'd stopped dead center in the corridor and its head rolled around as if searching for something. It had heard her.

It turned, looked straight at Amita with black eyes that glinted, reflecting the hall lights. Then it started forward.

"Go, go!" Amita ordered, waving her hands as she hurried onto the stairs.

Ben didn't hesitate. He dashed off while Amita tried to keep her steps quieter. When she thought she was far enough she broke into a sprint. Neither of them looked back as they climbed the stairs that turned in a tight circle, going higher and higher.

The steps were tall, forcing both Ben and Amita to use their hands. Amita could hear Ben plodding ahead of her and tried to look up. "Ben," she called but he was too far away, out of sight, around the corner.

The sound of his panicked breathing was far too loud for Ben to hear anything over. He climbed and climbed till with a final push he suddenly found himself on a solid floor with no more steps in front of him. After tumbling forward, he glanced back to see Amita bounding up the steps behind him. She stopped just short of crashing and tripping.

Ben lay on his belly with his whole body lifting and falling as he struggled to breathe. "Is it-—? Is it-—?" He couldn't get out the rest of his question.

Amita smacked his leg. "Get out of the way," she said trying to get in the room while struggling to catch her breath too. She stood with her hands on her knees, looking around. Her eyes fastened on the massive glass dome above them and on the dark surface of the gas giant beyond it. Then her gaze went to the room with its gold wiring inlaid walls and raised platform in the center covered in strange machinery.

"Whoa," Amita said, not waiting for Ben to get up as she climbed over him. She went around the platform till she found a short flight of steps. Some of the machines she recognized, display screens and cameras, control boards and hard drives. All of it, even what she assumed was human tech, looked different from anything she'd seen on Earth, but she knew with time she'd be able to figure them out.

The artifacts that belonged here at Nalanda, the onyx machines with gold inlay glowed in the strangest ways with lights sparkling and fading beneath their surfaces. Amita had a feeling their purpose would deny explanation. Of course, she was willing to try. She went to one block of black stone shaped as a hexagon with a raised corner and watched the lights dance across its surface. Then she touched it, bringing a hand down in the middle and sliding a finger along the gold wiring. She could feel the machine pulsing through her flesh, feel it wanting to work. Silently, Amita told it to go ahead. To her surprise, it listened.

Meanwhile, Ben was staring up at the planet behind the huge glass dome. In the distance he could see the horizon of the gas giant and the glow from the twin stars slowly coming around the world. The rock that Nalanda Station was made from circled closer and closer to the bright side of the gas giant as daylight crept over the planet's curve, awaking some primal instinct making both Ben and Amita feel better.

Suddenly, glowing tangerine light formed into a solid display in front of the windows, blocking the view of the outside. "Hey, what did you do?" he asked.

Ignoring him, Amita stared at the display, bringing it into focus. She concentrated and dialed back the gain, till they were looking at the entire planetary system. "This is where we are. I asked it to show us," she said.

"Asked what?" Ben demanded, but Amita ignored him.

The whole room was filled by the display. In the center was the gas giant with its rings, and circling it were five large worlds, though they seemed small in comparison with the giant.

Ben got right in front of her. "Amita, I don't know what you're doing, but I'm supposed to be the impulsive one." He tried to grab her hand and pull it away from the machine, but Amita chopped down hard on his wrist.

"Ouch!" Ben yelled, holding his hand. "Come on, I know this is cool, but that ghost thing could still be out there looking for us."

Amita was focused on bringing the display in closer, like a camera moving past the planets, dropping down till it was just above the rings. She saw Nalanda Station from the outside, then the camera turned and looked back out toward the stars. Amita was trying to connect the dots, trying to understand exactly where they were in relation to Earth, but she sensed Ben coming closer and knew he was about to become more insistent.

She looked at him. "That thing couldn't hurt you, Ben. Didn't you see how the lights were shining through it? It was no more real than this display, like a three-dimensional image of the thing from Earth. You could've put your hand right through it," she assured him.

A voice that wasn't Ben's answered her. "I wouldn't count on that." It seemed to slither in from thin air. Ben and Amita both turned to the stairs where Andavarri stood back on her hind legs with her arms crossed, staring at them. A Fire-Golem stood behind her, glowing subtly. "If you did indeed see one of our ghosts, then you're very lucky to still be around. Young ones, like you, are their favorite to take."

Amita kept her voice steady as she asked, "What was it?"

Andavarri started toward them. "A ghost, like your friend said." She pointed to Ben.

"No way. You're trying to scare us." Ben waved his hand dismissing the idea.

Andavarri came around the platform. "No, I'm not. This place is much older than any of the races that now call it home, and the ghosts have always been here. They only come out when we pass through darkness." She pointed past the display toward the murky world outside. "Try thinking about it." Andavarri asked, motioning to the machine Amita was touching.

The display changed again, showing the rings with Nalanda Station lit a little brighter to mark it while it circled the world. Andavarri slipped between the two of them reaching her long fingers out to come down next to Amita's on the stone. The display turned faster. "One rotation is twenty hours," she said. "We are in darkness for a little less than half of that. During that time, I assure you, you'd be much safer in your chambers. You see, at night we occasionally have students go missing. We never see them again."

Ben backed away, not caring to have the alien so close. He didn't like the way she moved, so much like a snake, or the way she smelled, slightly of sulfur.

Andavarri smiled a little at his discomfort, showing her long teeth. "It's rare, but sometimes a student is foolish enough to seek the ghosts out. They become curious and want to know what they are." She turned and looked down at Amita. "I suppose we'll never know what they learn."

Amita didn't move away. She held her hand on the display. "It looked like the thing that came through the wormhole. Brash and Tearmai called it a Hunter."

Andavarri nodded, "Yes, they are related." She stared at Amita for a moment more before she added, "The Hunters are machines, weapons really. They can claim a body, take it over and repurpose it. They were found on the dead world." The display changed again, focusing on one of the moons circling the gas giant. It was a black, burnt looking place, but its surface was covered with obvious signs of past habitation, straight lines marked places where buildings and machines had once been. "Humans tried using them in their wars, but they were outlawed by the Æesir. Any that were found were taken and destroyed. We've no idea who made them."

"'The dead world,' that doesn't sound ominous at all," Ben said, looking at the display.

"It should," Andavarri said darkly. "You see, here at the station the ghosts are mostly harmless. They grab a student every now and then, but what does that matter? On the dead world they are far more lethal. Anyone foolish enough to land there never makes it back."

"Then how did the humans get the Hunters off?" Ben asked.

Andavarri looked at him, narrowing her eyes, "That's a good question and if you find the answer, please let me know. That technology would be quite valuable."

"If it wasn't outlawed," Amita pointed out.

Andavarri held her hands out, agreeing. Then she said, "For now, no one is supposed to be in the lighthouse except the monks. You will find their punishments quite severe. I believe it's time you two returned to your room." She waved a hand toward the stairs.

"Definitely," Ben said and grabbed Amita's arm, pulling her away from the machine. The display blinked out of existence.

The Fire Golem stood just to the side of the first step. Amita walked past, but Ben stopped. "You didn't rat us out, did you?" he asked the stony creature.

The Fire-Golem looked down. It didn't say anything. Andavarri, who was following behind them, answered for it. "Of course it did. They alert me of everything. That's their purpose."

Amita turned back. "Why you? I thought the monks run this place."

Andavarri laughed a little before answering, "It's true. The monks may be in charge, but the Golems know who their masters are. My species created them. We breathed life into rock. Now go." She pointed toward the stairs again.

Amita glanced back at the room. Even if it weren't allowed, even if it were dangerous, she knew she'd be back here. She knew this was where she'd find answers.

Chapter 10

Not long after Ben and Amita returned to their room, someone knocked at the door. Ben rolled over, refusing to wake up, while Amita had never slept. Her eyes had been on the ceiling the whole night, but it was Chris who pulled himself out of bed and stumbled sleepily toward the sound. Alex called behind him, "Who is it?"

As he opened the door, Chris rubbed his eyes, then looked down at Regin. His tails were waving happily. Chris stared at the furry alien, who nodded and said, "Greetings, my young friend. Kavaris Dell has given me permission to retrieve you and your companions, to take you to the dining hall for breakfast." Chris looked at the room, then at the alien again. Everything that happened to them came flooding back.

"Um, okay. . . Do you want to come in?" he asked after a long pause. He stepped aside and watched Regin enter. The small simian creature used his center arms and back legs to walk while his tails followed like a bridal train.

They made a line at the sink as the group tried to pull themselves from bed. Ben made a mess splashing water over his face and neck, then went to help Katy, getting her a fresh set of clothes and tying her hair back in an unruly ponytail.

"I'll do it, Ben," Katy said taking his hands. "Just see if you can find me a brush or something."

He went to the sink and found some grooming equipment the monks had left. "How are you doing?" he asked, handing her a simple comb.

"I'm fine," Katy said, but her voice was distant.

Ben stared at her, waiting to see if she'd say more. "Should I get Amita to help you get dressed?"

"No, just pull the curtain," Katy said turning away.

When they were finally all out in the passageway, Regin took Katy's hand. "This way, my dear," he said. "I think I should prepare you. The dining hall can be an active place. You've been kept isolated so far, free and safe."

"Safe from what?" Alex asked.

"Plots and plans, the standard fare of human nobles," Regin explained. He saw that they didn't understand. "What a wonderful world you must come from that you don't have to worry about such things."

Voices echoed through the passageways. Regin spoke louder to be heard. "This school was established nearly a hundred years ago by the Kavaris monks to educate the different human dynasties according to the rules of the Æsir. You see, humanity had been constantly at war. They'd developed dangerous technologies, weapons that could wipe out entire worlds. The monks hoped that by bringing people together, they could prevent darker times. The other races came as well so they could learn and sometimes teach." They turned a corner and came into a grand hall, full of long tables filled with hundreds of students.

In the center was an open kitchen with stove tops. Shelves of plates and produce were piled high near serving stations set up in a long line. Humans in drab brown uniforms and Drakes, none of which were bigger than Tearmai, in aprons served the nobles from silver trays. The servants moved around the room clearing empty tables and picking up trash.

All the other races were eating. One table was filled with Long-Wolves sitting on benches so their tails could hang back out of the way. Their purple skin was subtly different from Andavarri's. They were a lighter shade and appeared smaller. Fire Golems were serving them or standing guard nearby.

Not far from the Long-Wolves, Vyktor sat alone, grumpily shoveling his food. His blockish head, broad shoulders and oddly shaded purple skin made him stand out. A few other large humans sat at his table, but they'd huddled at one end, giving him space.

Ice-Carvers, like Regin, took up half of another table. They were constantly turning their heads, looking around, anxiously watching everything. A few of the Grannusians sat at the same table with their robes pulled tight around them, hiding their strange bodies.

Drakes who weren't serving sat on the far side of the room at a table with creatures that Chris hadn't seen before. They reminded him of the Ice-Carvers, having six appendages like Regin and tails that flowed behind them in the same way, but they were taller and bulkier, as large as the Drakes. Their faces were different too. Where Regin had taken care to pull his fur back from his face, neatening it, these creatures made no attempt at grooming. They looked altogether more savage, with deep set eyes and broad mouths full of sharp teeth. The meat they were eating was raw and bloody. Sharing their table, the Drakes stayed far away, huddling at one end, eating vegetables.

Chris saw Regin raise his head a little and look over at these fierce creatures tearing into red clumps of flesh and bone. Regin shivered, turning away as if trying to control a nervous twitch.

Cormack sat nearby with some of his teammates from yesterday. He waved happily and got up when he saw the group enter. He was coming toward them when Chris heard Regin say, "It'll be okay."

"No, I can't!" Katy snapped. Chris turned and saw her pull back from the little alien. Her face was colored with fear. She tore her arm free and stepped back. Her head swung left and right in panic, desperate to get out of the noisy room. She bumped into Alex and tripped over Amita's foot, starting to fall as her pale eyes searched blindly for help. Chris reached out for her, but Cormack jumped in first, taking her arm and holding her up before she hit the ground. Katy wrapped her arms around his waist and clung to him like a lifeline.

"It's going to be okay. It's all right. Just focus on my voice, you're safe. We met yesterday in the healing chambers," Cormack's voice was soft and calm in her ears.

The panic ebbed away as Katy focused on him, listening. "I remember. . . I'll be alright." She got to her feet repeating it.

Chris and Ben stepped closer to Katy. "We're all here with you," Chris said. "Just stick with us, okay?" He had to look over Cormack who was still holding

Katy's arms, steadying her. Cormack started guiding her to his table.

"It appears you're in good hands," Regin said, excusing himself. "I'll be back after you eat to set you up with your classes." He scurried away, going toward the other Ice-Carvers. Chris watched him, wishing the little guy hadn't run off so fast. He followed the others to Cormack's table, feeling unsure about everything, but especially about this overly helpful new guy.

Several students got up, bowed respectfully and moved out of the way, giving Cormack and the group their seats. Cormack helped Katy to a spot, then motioned for the others to sit.

"What's up with that?" Ben sat and nodded toward the students who gave up their spots. "Are you big man in the prison yard or something?"

Cormack tilted his head, not sure what Ben meant. "Um, no I'm heir to the throne of Sidhe, the next chief of my clan."

"Oh, right . . . And what does that mean?" Ben asked.

Cormack looked at the room, wondering how to explain it. "If you look around, you'll see that some of us are sitting apart or at the head of tables." He waited for Ben to nod. "These are the future leaders of the human race, lords, chiefs, kings." He pointed to Vyktor. "Supreme leader of the Bogatyr collective."

"That's a long one," Ben interjected.

Cormack nodded, then pointed to Maeven, "She'll be empress if she keeps the title." Alex glanced over, knowing she was the girl from the balcony. He'd had a hard time not staring at her since he came in the dining room. She hadn't looked back, but he sensed that she was watching him.

"Either way," Cormack continued, "We're the ones who are supposed to be in charge someday. On Grannus, my clan is one of many, but we're the one the others look to for leadership."

"Oh," said Ben, "so you're kind of a big deal then?"

"I guess." Cormack stood, waved to one of the servants in brown, holding six fingers up indicating their number.

When he sat back down, Katy asked bluntly. "Does the offer still stand about bringing us to your world and finding your healer?" She couldn't tell, but everyone from Earth was staring at her.

Chris was the first to speak. "I thought we were going to talk about that first?"

"We are talking about it, right now," Katy said.

Cormack cleared his throat. "Of course, if you wish to come with me, you're more than welcome." He took a small black device, a little thicker than a DVD case, out of his pocket. When he touched it, a clock appeared. "Chooth and I will be on the supply transport, the Enbarr, in sixteen hours, just before dawn tomorrow, but you're going to have to decide today so I can tell the captain. They get sensitive if you change the payload too close to departure, it throws off their calculations," he said as a couple servants brought over plates of eggs and bread.

"So, can you just leave the school whenever you want?" Amita asked.

"Well, I can take a short recess for matters of state. Finding Eir is important," he said.

"No, what I mean is can you physically leave anytime? Like are there always shuttles?" Reaching across the table, Amita picked up the black pad and examined it. It was heavy and inelegant with bulky buttons on the side. She tried touching them to see what would happen. "You see where we're from we don't have much in the way of space travel. Our world was pretty much on its own."

Cormack nodded, finally understanding, "It's true then, you guys really did come through the void space, from somewhere else?"

Amita nodded as Cormack continued, "Um, the supply transports go out to the different planets on a regular basis, but they have to wait till the orbits are right. Nalanda Station is the closest place to Altor, so they have to climb orbits to get to any of the worlds. It can take a few rotations to build enough momentum. Even then it's tricky getting the shuttles in and out of the gravity well. I don't understand all the mechanics of it. I'm no engineer, but I've been taught a few things in combat theory." He took the device from Amita's hand, touched a sequence that opened a display screen, then handed it back.

"Hey, that looks like an I-pad, you know if cavemen designed it," Ben said, eyeing the screen. "Let me see." He tried taking it, but Amita turned away, keeping it out of his reach.

"We call them monitors. Everyone is issued one when they arrive at the school. Most of our educational material is on it."

"So, you still have to worry about gravity wells, inertia and orbital mechanics?" Amita asked, trying to clarify.

"Whoa, big words," Ben said, still reaching for the monitor. Alex finally grabbed his hands and pushed them down onto the table.

Cormack nodded yes, and Amita continued. "Then how do they control the gravity on this station? The rock it's on isn't spinning, is it?"

Cormack looked around a little, checking to see if anyone was listening, then leaned down toward her. "This place is special. It's old. There are things here, machines that make the gravity. Even when the transports approach, it's the station itself that brings them in using some sort of field technology. Otherwise, even with a Fire-Golem's help, we wouldn't be able to get through the debris field in the ring. The monks use the machines, but no one's allowed to study them. They don't even like us talking about them."

"Does the station have some sort of artificial intelligence?" Amita asked.

"What's that?" Cormack tilted his head.

"Thinking machines. They operate independent of humans," Amita explained.

Cormack started, "No, that sort of thing—"

"Is outlawed by the Æsir," Amita interrupted. "I'm starting to sense a pattern." She bent down and started eating, her eyes wandering, looking around the room. Alex and Chris started eating as well, but they were both watching her and wondering what she was thinking.

"Um, so are we going? I mean we're going, right?" Katy sounded a little desperate when an immediate answer didn't follow. Amita's eyes met Chris's. He could tell she was about to say something she didn't want.

∞

Across the room, Tara was bringing Maeven a tray of food. It was light fare, eggs and fruit, prepared special for her by her own chef, who stood apart behind the stoves in the center of the room.

Tara had tasted each thing on the plate, making sure it was all fresh, but also making certain it was safe. When she placed the tray in front of the princess, Maeven looked up at her. Then Maeven's eyes drifted over to Cormack, who was sitting with the strangers.
She didn't look happy.

She slipped something from her sleeve and handed it to Tara, who looked at the small vial. It held a clear liquid. Maeven nodded and Tara knew what she was supposed to do. She headed across the room.

Chapter 11

Vyktor looked at his people, the other Tairnishmen, and scowled. They were careful to keep their eyes diverted and to stay quiet while they ate. A few were of his bloodline, the Bogatyr, with skin the same pale purple and bodies engineered to survive the harsh environment of Tairnish. Even though that kind of bioengineering was illegal now, many of the traits remained such as the size and the aggression.

He looked down at the tiny fork in his hand and the food in front of him, a pile of eggs and some sort of fried meat. He wasn't enjoying it, not like he usually did. Even his water tasted awful. Since his failure in the cage, nothing felt good. It wasn't just the loss. It was the fact that he'd been shamed in front of the whole school. 'Edith had made him look like an idiot.' The thoughts circled in his mind.

True, he'd lost his temper, and going after the other side when the match was over was bad sportsmanship, but to a Tairnishman war wasn't a sport. You never let an enemy leave the field capable of attacking you again. Even their victories should be losses.

He glanced over at Maeven just as Tara was leaving her. He knew the princess had been watching. She was always watching and he knew she wasn't happy with him. The treaty between their families was an old one. The Bogatyr collective had always respected power and no one was more powerful than the Emperor Tamerlane. Even if their philosophy about government was different, they were allies. He stared at Maeven, but she wouldn't bring her eyes up to meet his. Then he sensed someone moving. The person sat down across from him.

'What fool is bothering me,' he wondered but held his tongue when he saw Tara.

"She's not happy," she said.

Vyktor had a sharp answer for her but stayed quiet. Tara stared at him till his shoulders dropped and he muttered, "I know."

She watched his broad face fall. 'He's younger than he looks.' Tara put the thought aside as she continued with some guilt, "My mistress doesn't care for failure. If someday you are to be her war chief, commander of the Tairnish navy, the tip of the spear, then you'll have to be better." She sensed his misery coming off him in waves. He was like a wounded animal.

Vyktor nodded. "I don't have to be told that."

"You don't?" she asked pointedly. "Look at Cormack," Vyktor turned his head. "Someday you may have to defeat him in a real war," she said while taking the vial from her sleeve. Her hand moved quickly when his head was turned. In a single gesture she poured the contents into his mug. She stared at him, feeling sorry for him.

Vyktor slammed his fist down as he looked back at her. "When it happens, it won't be some stupid game."

"Oh, I see, his scheming will only serve him in games. Is that it?" Tara demanded.

"He's a coward," Vyktor said, taking up his drink. "He wouldn't be able to stand in front of me in real combat." He finished the mug in an angry gulp and slammed it down.

Tara watched him for a moment, looked at his eyes, waiting for his pupils to widen. The drug worked fast. He felt it, she could tell even without her abilities. "It really was clever the way Cormack sent his people into a fight they couldn't win, sneaking up behind your defenses," she said. All he needed now was the catalyst. "A child like you would never think of such a strategy."

He looked at her as his blood boiled. The drug raged through his system, dimming his thoughts and fueling his anger. She turned toward Cormack. "He's better than you. He's smarter and he's quicker too. You're nothing, you giant lout. Tell me, how will you ever measure up with someone like Cormack around? You should've finished him yesterday. Instead, you let Edith pull you off and embarrass you. Who will ever respect you now?" She turned back, watching for a moment as his anger became uncontrollable, hoping it wouldn't turn on her.

Vyktor's rage consumed him. He looked for Edith, the combat instructor, in her black armor. She was all the way on the other side of the room, too far away to help. He looked at Cormack, knowing Tara was right. The princeling needed to be dealt with, but he knew that to attack someone here, in public, would bring shame on his house, that he'd lose his place in his family, and that he'd face dire consequences from the monks, or worse he'd lose his right to lead. He didn't care though, reason was gone. His mind was foggy with hatred. Vyktor got to his feet and started toward Cormack. He stopped only for a moment when Tara grabbed his arm.

He looked down at her. She motioned to his knife on the table. "You don't want him to be clever again," she said.

∞

Across the room, Amita was doing her best to ignore Katy's question. She turned to Cormack. "So, what you're saying is that the technology at this station is more advanced than what you have on your world?"

"Well, I mean the Grannusians, Chooth's people, have developed some amazing things with their biotech, things humanity wouldn't ever have imagined, but most of it is archaic now. They don't build like that anymore."

"Nothing like what's here, though? No way of studying the void spaces, right?" Amita asked.

Cormack looked around before answering in a low voice. "You're not allowed to study them, and the machines here— the monks are the only ones allowed to have anything to do with them," he said.

Amita held up one hand, waving for him to continue and answer her question. Finally, he said, "No, of course there is nothing on Grannus that compares to here. We have ships and space stations, but they're not like this place."

Amita nodded and took a deep breath before looking around at the others and saying, "There are problems we need to solve." She pointed to Katy's eyes. "But let's be honest, just yesterday we came through a wormhole that Earth was being absorbed into. Our families are back there, along with the rest of the human race."

"Our mom is on this side," Alex said.

Chris pointed to Cormack. "And, I'm not claiming to be an expert, but I'm pretty certain he's human."

Amita stared at Cormack as if considering a problem. She shook her head and continued talking to the group. "Okay, yeah, but still, if we have any hope of understanding what happened to us or of getting back. I think it's here." She turned to Cormack. "I'm sure your water world is lovely but—" Amita stopped midsentence, gazing up in shock as the human mountain Vyktor came rushing down on top of Cormack.

Vyktor slammed into the prince, throwing him across the room and smashing his chair to pieces. The massive human stood for a moment, sweating and staring wildly at his victim, sucking air deep into his nostrils as his chest heaved up and down, then started toward Cormack again.

Alex saw the knife held down by the brute's side first. Vyktor squeezed the small blade, knelt over Cormack and brought it high over his head.

Alex jumped from his chair to throw his whole body at Vyktor's back. Grabbing the Tairnishman's wrist, he twisted both his arms around it while dropping his shoulder into the brute's spine, wrenching his hand back.

Vyktor growled and pulled forward, throwing Alex through the air and into a table. Somehow Alex stayed on his feet, but he couldn't get out of the way of Vyktor's fist. It slammed into his chest and shoulder. Then the knife came. Vyktor drove it into Alex just above the hip. The blade slipped in and slipped out.

Vyktor turned from him, going toward Cormack again. The dazed prince was still on the floor, attempting to get up, fumbling around. Alex looked down at himself, knowing he'd been stabbed. The pain was instantly intense and sickening.

Alex saw blood dripping from the blade and watched for a moment taking a deep, agonizing breath. 'This is stupid,' he thought taking a step forward. Instinct and training got him to move. He wasn't willing to back off, not for this guy.

Chris came around the table, but Alex waved him back, pointing for him to stay where he was, not wanting his brother to go up against the psycho with the knife. Alex ignored the pain in his side and grabbed a chair. Swinging it over his head, he brought it down across Vyktor's back. The brute turned in surprise.

The chair held together. Alex swung it again, driving it forward, pushing the legs into Vyktor's chest. The brute stood like an unmoving wall with his shoulders back and his arms wide, smiling at Alex as he was about to smack the chair away.

Alex saw an opening. He smashed the chair down onto Vyktor's foot and stepped up on it giving himself a little extra height. He sprung forward and drove his fist into Vyktor's throat. Vyktor grunted and choked, while Alex brought his other hand down on the giant human's wrist, chopping the nerve on his forearm.

When the blade fell from his hand, Alex didn't hesitate. He grabbed it from the ground and brought it up to slash across Vyktor's abdomen, then brought it down again, slamming it into Vyktor's knee cap.

Vyktor screamed in pain as Alex backed away and picked up the chair again. He swung it like a baseball bat, dropping Vyktor to the ground. Alex finally moved out of his reach. He watched the big kid try to pull the blade out of his knee, but it was buried deep.

Everyone was staring, including Chris, who looked horrified. He came around the table as Alex glanced toward Maeven, who was watching closely. When their eyes met, she nodded to him. Alex touched his side and felt his brother's hand reaching for his shirt. He was saying something, but Alex had trouble understanding him above the noise that had erupted in the room.

Monks gathered around, and the woman in black armor came over as well. Alex looked at Vyktor. He was still trying to get to Cormack, who'd gotten off the ground. Vyktor was crawling toward the prince, still desperate to end him as he held his knee and left a smear of blood across the floor.

Edith walked over and looked down at Vyktor with disdain. When she viciously kicked him in the head, he finally stopped moving.

Alex's whole body became heavier as he lifted his hand and looked at his blood. It was more than he expected. "You gotta be kidding me," he said before everything went dark and he dropped down on top of his brother.

Chapter 12

Amita's face was lit by a faint glow. Sitting on Chris's bed, she had been staring at the monitor for hours. Ben was on his own bed, watching her. Occasionally, she'd shake her head in amazement at something she read or throw her hands up in frustration. Ben scrolled through his own monitor, disappointed by the choices. All the games felt like homework and when he finally found some movies, they were all super boring. The quality sucked and they were stodgy, like that Downton Abbey show his aunt liked.

The whole day had been a drag. The most exciting part had been the fight at breakfast. He couldn't believe the way Alex tore that big guy apart. Ben thought about all the times he'd annoyed Alex, promising himself that he'd avoid doing that from now on. Afterwards, they'd all gone to the healing chambers where Alex had been laid out again. Edith, the combat instructor, had helped Chris carry him.

Alex woke up a little on the way, but never fully, and not while Ben and Amita were with him. Chooth had come in to examine him. Apparently, the knife clipped his liver and that was bad. He was rushed into surgery, into the tank again with a tube shoved down his throat. Chooth kept him sedated through the procedure.

The Grannusian stuck his eel head out of the tank and told Chris that he was going to keep his brother sedated to heal. "Since he can't avoid trouble while he's awake," he said.

"But he's going to be alright?" Chris asked.

Chooth nodded. "With rest."

Regin had come to the healing chambers with an offer to give them a tour of the station. Chris said he wanted to stay with his brother, "But you guys should go, try and get your bearings around this place." He was looking at Alex. "Just try and stay out of trouble, okay?"

"I won't leave their side," Regin promised.

"There's really no point in me going either," Katy said. "It's not like I'm going to see anything anyway." Cormack was standing next to her and put his hand on her shoulder, consoling her. Ben watched this and noticed the way Chris's face tightened.

Ben felt bad for Chris. One thing his sister had never been short on was the attention of guys. Katy never sought it out, not that Ben had seen, but guys tended to fall for her. They'd start by pretending to be her friend, but they always had that puppy dog look, just like Chris. Some of those guys became possessive, calling Katy a tease or telling lies about her when she didn't return their feelings.

None of them ever really bothered to get to know her. They didn't know what an amazing artist she was, or that she'd ride her bike for miles to get to the beach at dawn before the crowds. They just saw a pretty girl.

Ben took one last look at his sister, realizing for the first time that she might not ever draw again or stare out at the ocean. "You coming?" Amita called when she was halfway down the ramp, interrupting his thoughts. Ben hurried to catch up and they left with Regin to take the tour. The place was so big that it was hard to remember everything they saw and a lot of it started to look the same. They checked out classrooms and landing bays, grand halls and offices, the gymnasiums, the entrances to the alien sectors and the entrances to private areas of the nobles' houses, which were all guarded. Ben was certain they never crossed into the area they'd been in the night before, when they saw the ghost. Regin was avoiding the lighthouse, although they did go into an astronomical lab with an observation platform and a few telescopes.

They'd stopped for lunch and for dinner, staying close to Regin the whole time. He gave them monitors and had them sit in on a few classes. Math, biology, astronomy, all pretty boring stuff to Ben, but he did his best to pay attention. Then Regin brought them back to their room. It was empty. "Wow, I can't believe they're still hanging out in the med ward," Ben said.

Amita nodded and said "yes," in a clipped voice, as she dove into the monitor. She hadn't really looked up since then. Ben asked her some questions but had only gotten one-word answers. He wasn't sure why she was hanging out on the boy's side of the room, but he didn't mind the company. Even a distracted Amita was better than being alone.

Ben had no idea how much time passed before the door opened and Chris came in. He looked tired. "How's Alex?" he asked.

"Still unconscious, but he's out of the tank. Chooth laid off the sedatives for a bit so I could talk to him. I guess he thought it'd make me feel better, but Alex was still pretty out of it. That empress girl stopped by, though, right when he woke up. She had her handler or whatever she is with her, that other girl Tara." Each of Chris's steps were heavy with exhaustion.

"Really? How'd she seem?" Ben asked.

Amita moved over and Chris sat down to start taking his shoes off. "I don't know, imperial I guess," he said. "The Tara girl seemed okay, but the princess didn't really talk much, not to me anyway. It's kind of funny how she managed to show up right when Alex was awake." He considered it for a minute, then shrugged. "Chooth got weird around her. He seemed nervous. . . Anyway, she went right past me to Alex and whispered something to him. I don't know what.

"When she turned around, it seemed like the first time she noticed me. She asked me if my brother was a warrior on our world. I told her he planned on being a soldier like our dad. Then she nodded like she thought that was a good idea and left. Tara had to say goodbye for her. I guess that's how royals do it." Chris shrugged again, then looked at the others. "Weird, right?"

"Yeah, man, but what isn't weird here?" Ben responded.

Amita had the monitor down on her lap. "Did you guys find anything interesting?" Chris asked, pointing toward it.

Amita nodded and picked up the device. "Interesting? Yes. Useful? I'm not really sure."

"You think any of this stuff is interesting?" Ben asked.

"It paints a picture," Amita said. "You have to read between the lines but—" She didn't finish her thought as Chris interrupted her.

"Hey, where's your sister?" he asked Ben, noticing for the first time that Katy was missing. Chris turned back to Amita and said meekly, "Um, sorry. I just thought if we're going to go over this, she might want to be in on it."

Ben and Amita looked at each other. Then Ben said, "We thought she was still with you."

"No, she left with Chooth. He was supposed to bring her back here. That was a few hours ago, just before they started shutting off the lights."

"Oh," Ben said. He wasn't scared yet, but a thought entered his head that he didn't like. "Did you guys talk about anything? Like leaving here?"

"Not really, I mean with Alex all banged up I figured it was a dead subject. I guess she tried bringing it up. But . . ." Chris thought back. "I may have shut her down. You know I was still really worried about Alex. You don't think she'd—?"

Ben got up. "She has before."

"What?" Amita asked. Her attention had drifted back to the monitor.

"Ran away," Ben said. "She tried running away before, back in the desert."

"Yeah, but that was on Earth and from her dad. Here, we're talking about another planet. Running from us. To another planet. Or I should say, to another moon," Amita said as if she couldn't believe anyone would do something so foolish.

Ben shrugged. "I don't know if you noticed, but doing stupid stuff is kind of a family trait. Dad, wormhole. Me, pretty much everything."

"We've got to go find her. When did that Cormack guy say his shuttle was leaving?" Chris asked.

Amita glanced down at her monitor, which had a small clock in the corner. "Soon, I think."

Chris went to the door with Amita close behind. He looked back at Ben who was searching around the room, opening a closet and lifting the bed, trying to find something. Finally, he gave up and picked up his monitor, held it at the corner and gave it a practice swing. "What are you doing?" Chris asked.

Ben swung it again like a weapon. "You know, just making sure I'm ready in case we run into trouble."

"You don't think Cormack is going to fight us, do you?"

"He's afraid of ghosts," Amita said, then held up her monitor with a map on the screen. "It works better this way, Ben." She went past Chris, out into the hall and the two boys fell in behind her.

Leaving the monks' area, they passed the Fire Golems. "They didn't try to stop us," Chris said, staring back at the statues.

Amita was looking down at her monitor. She nodded when Ben said over his shoulder, "Yeah, but don't think that means they won't rat you out."

"What do you mean?" Chris asked. "And what's all this talk about ghosts?" He'd noticed how Ben approached every corner carefully, peeking around it before he'd continue on. At first, he thought Ben was just being overly cautious, but as they went on, he had to wonder. Admittedly, the place creeped him out too. The stone walls made the station feel like a medieval castle and with all the lights turned down, it was the perfect setting for a horror movie.

"We went out last night and we saw something," Amita said.

"What?" Chris asked as they came into a grand hall. The lights along the side left the center of the room in darkness. They stayed close to the wall and Ben never took his eyes off the long, shadowy center of the room where their footsteps echoed in the silence.

"We went exploring," Amita said. "And while we were out, we saw something. Andavarri said it was a ghost."

"Yeah, but you saw it and said it looked like that Hunter-thing from Earth," Ben pointed out.

Chris clutched Amita's arm. "I think you need to tell me everything."

"There's not that much to tell, and anyway it'll have to wait." She pointed toward a set of double doors framed by two human guards. "That's the entrance to the Sidhe clan's private chambers, Cormack's family."

"I got this," Ben said. He strutted toward the guards with his shoulders back on pace to walk right between them and through the door.

One of the guards grabbed his shirt while the other pointed a polearm, glowing with power, at his chest.

"Where do you think you're going?"

"It's cool guys. I'm friends with Cormack," Ben said. The guard brought the polearm closer. "Back off man. We're here for my sister." Ben slapped the weapon away, but it came right back up, this time sparking with electricity.

Chris pulled Ben back. "Slow down," he said, holding up his hand. Both guards had weapons pointed at them now. "Look, my brother saved Cormack's life at breakfast. How do you think he's going to like it if you zap us?"

One of the guards growled, "The prince isn't here. He's gone to the transport bay, and if your sister is that blind girl, then she's with him. They moved the Enbarr's schedule up."

Ben and Chris's eyes met, then Chris said to Amita, "Find us a way there."

∞

Everything was a surprise to Katy. That's how she felt anyway. Every corner, every step was a mystery. As she walked forward, her mind was constantly spinning, asking questions like what is this and what am I touching. She felt like all she needed to do was open her eyes and the answer should be right in front of her. But, of course, her eyes were already open. They'd been open the whole time.

She could no longer blame her lack of sight on the gauze that'd been wrapped around her head. The pressure of it across her face, she missed it a little.

That's the thing about a Band-Aid, when you cover a cut with one, it's with the belief that someday you'll be healed. When it's gone and the damage remains, the hope leaves as well.

The others will be mad at me, but how could they understand? The worst part was last night when she slept, she'd had a dream. She was back in California watching the sunset. It felt like it lasted forever, then the lights from the boardwalk came on. The store fronts and restaurants glowed softly and she could see the whitecaps rolling in, but when she opened her eyes in the morning, she saw nothing, only darkness. What was she supposed to do, wait to sleep, wait to dream? And what if the dreams didn't come?

No, she needed her eyes. She'd have given anything to have them back. Cormack's hands guided her forward. It was odd holding onto a stranger for so long. He'd been guiding her through the halls coming from his family chambers. Now she sensed they were in a large space with machine noises, hissing and ticking, and their footsteps sounded like they were on a metal shelf. It echoed beneath them.

She heard a voice that was familiar. It was Chooth. Katy tried to focus on that, still holding tight to Cormack, "There's some steps here," he said. They'd already come down one long flight. Now, they were going up a shorter one, more echoing metal. "And there's a lip you'll have to step over." She reached out with her hand to feel the edge of a curved entrance, then lifted her leg up and over, certain that she looked ridiculous.

The sounds were less in here. They were in a smaller space that seemed like it was blocking the sound of machinery from outside. She flinched when she heard something start to move. "That's the airlock," Cormack said.

Another sound echoed in the distance, someone yelling, "Wait, Katy. Wait!" She heard her brother's voice. Raised voices and the sound of an altercation came from outside. Something slammed to the floor.

"What the hell are you doing?" someone asked. She recognized Chris's voice. She wasn't sure how to answer him, and by the time she opened her mouth, her voice was drowned out by the sound of the airlock closing with a heavy and permanent thump.

Chapter 13

Ben's face was pressed into the metal plating on the floor, and his arm was twisted back. He wasn't going to struggle anymore. "Okay, okay," Ben said. "I wanted to find my sister, that's all. She went in that door." He jerked his head toward the short flight of steps that Chris had just barreled up. Ben had been a step behind when they grabbed him.

The guys holding him wore the brown uniform of the station's servants, but out of the corner of his eye he could see the red robe of a Kavaris monk approaching. "Let him go," the monk ordered. Ben got to his knees, dusting himself off, looking up at the massive room. It was long, narrow, and incredibly tall with catwalks running on either side. Cranes and chain falls hung from the ceiling while machines similar to forklifts and metal stairs going up and down to different doorways crowded the floor. Pallets and crates were piled on the various levels, while more workers in brown uniforms moved through, checking the supplies.

In front of the airlock one of the servants was struggling to get to his feet after being barreled over by Chris a moment before. Ben turned to the monk, "My sister went in there. She's taking off with that Cormack kid."

The monk looked at the door, then down at his monitor. "She was accounted for in the departure papers. She must've had permission from the Kavaris."

"Permission? She's taking off for another planet," Ben said.

"Moon. Technically she's heading for a moon," Amita pointed out helpfully. She hadn't been grabbed or tackled. In fact, until that moment, the monk hadn't noticed her.

"Whatever," Ben said, before turning back to the monk. "You can't just let her go. You've got to open those doors. She can't run off to another . . . um, moon, or whatever. We just got here."

Windows made of thick, reinforced glass lined the wall. The monk motioned to one. "It's too late."

Ben went over next to the window, straining to pull himself up and see what was outside. Flashing lights ran along the length of another wall. He had to stare for a few moments before he realized that the wall was moving, pulling away from him. Slowly, he saw edges and curves as the shape of the thing became clearer. It looked like a huge brick with engines strapped to it. Small jets fired in sequence from all sides as the shuttle maneuvered away, dropping toward the gas giant.

"You gotta get her back. You've got to get both of them back," Ben said, still staring.

"Impossible," the monk answered. "We're already moving faster than the transport. They're dropping below the ring, closer to the planet to maneuver safely. It'd be incredibly dangerous for them to try catching up to us now."

Ben was still watching. The ship had gone from something massive to something small. It was like watching a coin dropped into a deep fountain, floating away.

"This is awful." He ran his hand over his head and turned back to Amita.

"She'll be alright," Amita said touching his arm. "Chris is with her."

"I know," Ben said. "But now we've got to tell Alex."

∞

Moments before the shuttle released Chris grabbed Katy's arm. He got to his feet as the airlock closed behind him. Turning, he banged on it "Come on, open up!" He glared back at Cormack.

"I'm sorry, my friend. Once it's sealed, it's already too late. In fact, we're running behind." Cormack glanced at a red light on the ceiling over an opening. "We need to be moving." He was holding Katy's other hand as he stepped over another threshold. Katy shook Chris's arm off and followed the prince.

"You're just going to leave your brother here?" Chris asked behind her. Katy pretended like she couldn't hear him and continued on, walking past Cormack, who'd stopped inside the door.

"Katy!?" Chris demanded.

"You wouldn't understand. This is a nightmare," she shot back at him.

"Yeah for all of us! That's why we have to stick together."

Chooth stepped over the threshold and looked at the red light, which started flashing. He said, "They're about to seal this door, Chris. If you don't come with us, you're going to be stuck in hard vacuum. Please?" He waved for him to follow. A buzzer sounded and the outer door began to move. For a moment Chris was tempted to stand his ground, not believing they'd actually close him out. Cormack looked up at the light as the buzzer sounded and the door continued to move. Chris saw the look on the prince's face. It was enough to convince him.

"A damn spaceship," Chris cursed as he jumped, crashing into Cormack. They both hit the ground. "I've always wanted to fly in a spaceship," Chris grumbled as he started to get up.

"Good," Cormack said laughing a little. "I really thought you were going to stay there." He helped Chris, then reached for Katy's hand again to lead her further in.

Chris looked back at the closed door. "Look, this is nice and all but we can't go with you. My brother's back there."

Chooth touched his shoulder, "It's too late. This transport is going. Come on, we need to get you strapped in before the shift."

Following him down a long walkway, Chris felt lighter the further he went. Eventually his feet left the ground. He pushed off from the floor and felt his stomach sink as Chooth reached out grabbing a hand hold on the wall. He took Chris's hand and placed it on one of the rungs.

By the time they entered the next room, Chris could no longer remember which way was up. The only chairs were attached to what should've been a wall. Cormack was hovering over Katy, helping her into one of the seats. He hooked her into a five-point harness and reassured her, touching her hand. Some of the other passengers Chris recognized from the breakfast table. They were Cormack's people and they were happy to see their prince. They smiled, nodding to him and held up their fists putting their fingers out in a flat plane at an angle to their palms. Cormack returned the gesture, going around and happily patting friends on their shoulders before getting into his own seat. Chris looked around at the smiling faces that hinted at Asian ancestry and thought that 'this is what it'd look like if Hawaii had a space program.'

Chooth helped Chris to an empty chair, then took the one next to him. As Chris pulled the straps up, struggling to connect them, Chooth explained, "We're not sure how Nalanda Station creates artificial gravity. As you can see its effects don't reach far past the station's interior." He motioned to the straps. "The worst part is when we maneuver away. We'll drop toward the planet, out of its rings, then we'll start climbing toward our moon Grannus." Chooth strapped himself in while the little eyes of the creatures that made up his arm turned away, tightening toward his center. In fact, Chooth seemed smaller, as if his whole body were trying to squeeze together. "Once we set a course and start accelerating, we'll be able to get up and move around," he said.

"Are you nervous?" Chris asked, trying to read the alien's body language.

It took Chooth a moment to answer. "Not about the journey . . . I'm more worried about when we get there. On my last trip home my people were being poisoned. I came back to Nalanda to tell our master healer Eir, hoping she'd be able to help. She left, going back to our home, and now she's missing." He held up his hands. "There was a tenuous peace between humans and my people. If the humans are doing this . . ." He glanced over at Cormack. "It means that peace is over."

Chris wasn't sure what to say. He'd been so worried about his own problems that he hadn't thought much about where they were going. He just didn't know enough. "I'm sorry," Chris said.

"It'll be okay. The currents will carry it away as it does all things," Chooth said.

Chris looked around. "So, how long are we going to be on this ship?"

Something was starting to happen. They could hear thrusters firing through the hull. "A few days," Chooth answered, pulling his head in tight.

"Awesome," Chris said, sounding a little strained. The thrusters were pushing them on course. He held his straps feeling the g-forces change, coming from different directions.

"If you need it, there's a baggy in the pocket of your chair," Chooth said, pointing.

"You have space barf bags?" Chris asked.

"Of course, nothing but the best," Chooth answered.

At first Chris ignored the suggestion, but after a moment he picked up the bag and held onto it just in case.

Chapter 14

Ben struggled to wake up. He sat, wondering why the lights were on. A monk stood just outside the door. "We must retrieve your friend before the trial. Come with me," the monk said as he stepped back out of the room.

"Wait, what?" Ben asked while rubbing his eyes. He didn't feel like he'd slept at all, having passed much of the night worrying about his sister. Somehow, it'd seemed more tolerable being here with her. She was the one anchor of normal in this strange world. He glanced over at Amita, who appeared just as confused as he was with dark circles under her eyes. They both felt better sleeping close together and Chris wasn't using his bed anyway, so Amita had crashed on the boy's side. She'd been reading last night when Ben finally fell asleep.

It was impossible to guess the time of day, but Ben had a feeling it wasn't long after they'd been escorted from the loading docks by a monk and a few Fire Golems. Ben had wanted to go to Alex then, so he could get his punishment over with, but the monks had insisted on sending them back to their room. The time had been halfway through the night cycle when the shuttle left, and the monk told them that moving through the halls at night wasn't a wise idea.

Ben wasn't sure if he'd met this monk before. They all started looking the same after a while. The only one that was different was Kavaris Dell and that was only because he was so old.

"Wait, whose trial are we going to?" Ben called. The monk either didn't hear or was choosing to ignore him.

Ben turned to Amita. "It's not us, is it?"

"I don't know any more than you," Amita snapped.

They got to their feet and followed the monk out the door, wearing their clothes from yesterday, but both were so tired that they didn't care.

"Excuse me." Ben was touching the top of his head, knowing his curly red hair would defy even the artificial kind of gravity. "But this trial isn't for us, is it?"

"Have you been accused of a crime?" the monk asked.

Ben looked back at Amita, who was pulling a scarf over her head. "Um, no," he answered.

"Then you should be fine." The monk kept walking.

They came to the healing chamber and went up the ramp where they were surprised to see Alex wasn't alone. Two girls were with him. One turned and nodded, while the other scowled at the interruption. In the middle of saying something, Maeven quickly hid her impatient sneer. She looked Ben up and down, then forced a smile. Even faking, it was something to see on a face that'd been bred to royalty. She wore the same simple uniforms as everyone else, but somehow, she did it with more style. Her dark hair was pulled back, and she had bright green eyes that were large and mesmerizing, above a perfectly symmetrical face with full lips which seemed to be in a constant state of pouting.

"Whoa, you're the princess, right?" Ben asked as he came to an immediate stop. Walking behind him, Amita stumbled up the ramp and into his back while Ben attempted an awkward bow.

Amita pushed him out of the way as Tara said, "This is Princess Maeven Tamerlane, first heir to the throne of Uppsala and the colonial empire, keeper of the sacred grove."

Ben caught himself before falling over. "That's a mouthful. Is your name that long too?"

Tara smiled more honestly. Her long blond hair was pulled back as well. She was pretty but looked thin and pale next to Maeven. "Just call me Tara," she offered.

Ben ran his hand back through his red curls, wishing he'd taken time to tame it. "Nice to meet—" he started to say, but he was cut off.

"And I'm fine with Maeven, as long as I'm here, away from my father's empire. Nalanda Station is a place where everyone must learn a little humility." The princess spoke quickly. "It's my understanding that the monks have decided to house you in one of their chambers. I came to offer you the hospitality of the Tamerlane royal quarters. My family has one of the finest wings at this old station and we have more than enough space to put you and your friends up," she said to Alex.

"Um . . ." Alex started to say. "I, a . . ."

Before he could finish stumbling through an answer, Maeven added at the same clipped pace,

"You were impressive yesterday. I've never seen someone attack a Tairnishmen in such a way."

Alex's face reddened. "I don't like bullies," he said. "And I'm pretty sure that big guy planned on killing that kid."

"Yes, it was shameful to attack someone in such a way. I don't know what Vyktor could have been thinking. The Bogatyr are a different breed. They are great warriors, but they are not great thinkers and Vyktor is very young and rash," Maeven pointed out. The monk broke in. "That's why I've come for you." He'd been waiting to speak, not wishing to interrupt Maeven. He went to a cabinet, took out some clothing, and placed it on the bed next to Alex, then looked at the readouts. Turning to another cabinet, he pulled out a chair with wheels on it. "It's a bit far to the tribunal room."

"Tribunal?" Alex asked.

"Yes, Vyktor attacked a noble in front of the entire student body," Maeven explained. "Such things cannot be tolerated. I'm sure justice will be swift."
Alex struggled to sit up. "So why do we have to go."

"Everyone has to," the monk said as he helped him pull on a shirt.
Alex looked around the room. "Where's Chris and Katy then?"

Ben stared at Amita, hoping she'd say it, but Amita stayed quiet, staring at the floor. "Yeah, about that . . ." Ben started.

∞

"I can't believe her. I just can't believe it!" Alex slammed his fist down on the chair. They were out in the hall moving toward the tribunal room. Several students were going in the same direction, glancing back at them questioningly.

The monk pushed Alex's chair into what appeared to be a dead-end cut into the rock. Other students had crammed into the corner. Above them was a dark empty space and on the walls were large metal rails. The floor began to move, dropping down to a lower level.

Ben stepped away from the wall, avoiding the moving stone. He leaned toward Tara. "You know on our world, elevators have walls; they're great big metal boxes. It keeps everyone's hands and feet from getting torn off." Tara smirked a little at how nervous he was.

"There's got to be some way of getting them back here," Alex demanded.

"They say there isn't, and I believe them," Amita answered.

"I assure you, there isn't," the monk agreed. "It'll be at least three weeks before the transport returns, but I wouldn't be overly concerned. They're traveling with young Lord Cormack. I'm sure they'll be safe."

"Quite safe," Maeven agreed, though her tone suggested something else.

They followed the crowd into a large auditorium with bleachers built against the wall curved into a horseshoe. A wide platform sat in the center with a podium. Kavaris Dell waited with the monks of his order. Over two dozen, surrounded him.

The monk pushing Alex's chair found a spot for them on one of the lower levels, then left to join the others on the platform.

Regin was sitting next to Amita with a few IceCarvers on his other side. The large Drake Fafnir stood beside the stands, leaning on his cane with a number of smaller Drakes nearby. Their passive eyes would drift up to him from time to time as if asking why they were there.

Andavarri was in the next row up with the other Long-Wolves. They sat above the Ice-Carvers, leaning forward in anticipation, their long claws practically on their neighbors' heads. The Ice-Carvers looked back at them nervously. They watched the entire room with an air of anxiety. Regin was the only one of his race that appeared completely calm.

Maeven excused herself, pointing up toward a large group of students. "I must join my house and its allies," she said, smiling at Alex and touching him lightly on the shoulder.

Tara followed, with Ben waving and calling behind her, "Later . . . I mean, I'll see you. You know, like later." Leaning back and trying to look relaxed, he realized too late that there was no back for him to lean against. If Amita hadn't grabbed him, he would have fallen over. Tara looked at him strangely, following Maeven up the stairs.

Amita laughed. "Nice one. Girls love a guy that'll go arse over tits for them." She reached up and touched his puffy hair. "At least you're wearing a helmet."

Ben pulled away, asking, "Did it really look that bad?"

Amita lifted a single eyebrow to answer him, while Alex said, "Yep."

Ben turned and saw Regin smiling too. He was pretty sure the little alien had just snickered.

Ben put his face in his hands and watched between his fingers as the entire student body filled the stands. They were excited, all talking at once, but the crowd went silent when a door on the opposite side of the room opened. Four Fire Golems entered with Vyktor in the middle of them. Heavy shackles held his hands together and his legs were chained as well. His eyes stayed on the ground watching his feet shuffle. Edith, the woman in black, came in behind him. She still wore her armor and carried a nasty looking weapon that could've been a lance or a gun, or a bit of both. The entire crowd watched while she remained close to the prisoner.

Vyktor was escorted to a spotlight focusing on the center of the floor. He kept his eyes on the ground until

Kavaris Dell began to speak. "Vyktor of the Tairnishmen, Fifth of Bogatyr collective, you are accused of attacking and attempting to harm another student, a member of a royal house, beyond the borders of the combat hall and outside the confines of an approved martial training exercise."

Slowly Vyktor looked up at Kavaris Dell. His face was hard and defiant, glaring at the old man, as if all he wanted to do was break his chains and attack.

Comfortable in his seat of power, Kavaris Dell wasn't afraid as he said, "The victim of this attack is not here to witness for himself. Urgent matters called him back to his world, so it will fall to another. Is there any who wish to speak and tell us what this young man did?" The monk's eyes fell on Alex.

Alex moved a little in his chair. He could feel the attention of the entire room falling on him. Regin leaned over and whispered in his ear, "If you wish to be a witness, you must stand, state your name and house, then say what you saw."

Looking at Vyktor in the center of the room, Alex leaned back toward Regin and asked, "What's going to happen to him?" Vyktor stared and their eyes locked. Despite his size Alex guessed Vyktor was no older than Chris, maybe younger. He looked at Edith, who was also watching him, and knew right then that if he said anything it wouldn't be good for this kid.

Before Regin could answer, Vyktor had turned away, shaking his head with disdain. He faced Kavaris Dell and said, "You'll need no witness, I freely confess to what I did. I was angry after my defeat in the morning combat training and I wanted revenge. It was my intention to murder Cormack of Grannus, house of the Sidhe."

"You admit this, knowing full well the penalty for such a crime?" Kavaris Dell asked.

"Yes," Vyktor said.

"Will you ask for mercy or say anything in your defense?" Kavaris Dell asked coldly.

Vyktor shook his head. "I've nothing to say. I've brought shame on the Tairnishmen by being foolish. I will only say this to my brothers, be more cautious than me. Watch for the plots and tricks of our enemies and our allies." He looked directly at Maeven.

"Does anyone wish to plead for the accused?" Kavaris Dell addressed the crowd. Vyktor held Maeven's gaze. She smiled. Slowly his face began to boil with rage.

Tairnishmen sat near her, a few rows above. Vyktor looked at the large humans, sensing them preparing to revolt. His people got to their feet, ready to slam down on the floor like an angry wave. He had cousins present, family who would die in his place if he asked them. They'd certainly kill as well. As Edith's lance dropped from her shoulder to her hands in a ready position, Vyktor found one of his younger brothers and shook his head, saying no.

He waited till his people sat down, then turned back to Kavaris Dell. "I've violated your law and your law is from the Æesir, those that bring order, those that are without mercy. I will not shame my people any further by pleading for my life."

Kavaris Dell appraised the crowd, waiting for anyone to speak. His eyes lingered the longest on Maeven, but when she said nothing, he let out a heavy sigh. "Very well. If no one will plead for you, then we shall commence with justice." He nodded to one of the monks, who went to a thick glass door next to the stage. The glass was encased in heavy metal panels with controls next to it. When the monk pressed a button, lights went on inside, shining down on an empty room.

He pressed another button and the doors rumbled apart, banging deeply when they finally stopped. With Edith holding her lance at his back, Vyktor walked forward.

"Wait, what's going to happen to him?" Alex asked Regin.

"He will be punished." Regin's voice was hushed.

Vyktor walked through the glass doors, then the monk pushed the button again. The doors slid shut with an even louder thud, and Vyktor stood in the small chamber, glaring back through the glass at the crowd.

His eyes were on Maeven.

Kavaris Dell said to the whole assembly, "The rules of Nalanda Station, handed down by the Kavaris order, are law. Any violation of those rules will be dealt with most severely." He nodded to the monk at the controls, who touched another button. Behind Vyktor the walls began to move, splitting apart to reveal the tangerine clouds of the gas giant Altor. No sound came from the chamber as the air escaped.

Amita, Ben and Alex watched in horror as Vyktor stood his ground. His cheeks were full with one final breath and his feet were planted firmly as the air around him rushed out. The purple color of his skin turned darker as he took one step back, then another.

"Your families sent you here, not so you could continue the wars from your homes, but to learn. Unfortunately, sometimes, those lessons must come through pain." Kavaris Dell stared at the crowd.

Every person in the room was watching Vyktor struggle to stay on his feet. Eventually he fell to his knees, then opened his mouth. His shackled hands went to his chest as he felt the pain of attempting to breathe in vacuum. The outer airlock door was fully open now. The wind from the air escaping had died down. He fell onto his elbows, then his body slumped to the ground. He didn't move again.

"Remember this," Kavaris Dell shouted while pointing. "Do not make me repeat this lesson." He stepped away from the lectern, then off the platform and the other monks fell into a line behind him.

One monk, the one that had worked the door controls, walked up to the lectern. "You may all now return to your classes," he said as a dismissal.

Immediately the room was full of voices as the students stood and started working their way to the bottom of the stands and out the door. Alex, Ben and Amita remained seated in a state of shock. Alex looked for Regin, but the furry alien and the other Ice-Carvers were the first out the door. Fafnir and the other Drakes had left as well. Only Andavarri remained behind. She sat watching the three. When the crowd thinned out and only a few students remained, she leaned down to Amita and said, "You may want to remember this lesson when you wander into areas you don't belong in."

Amita watched her go, then turned back to Alex and Ben, waiting for one of them to speak but none of them could think of anything to say.

Chapter 15

Fafnir left the tribunal chamber with the other Drakes close behind him. The human students moved much faster around them, hurrying to their classes. The quick little people were talking. Some even managed to laugh. None would miss Vyktor. They all knew he was going to come to a bad end.

He had been a brute, lacking refinement or any social skill. He only fit in with his own people, the Tairnishmen, and even they didn't seem to care for him much. It wasn't his viciousness that made him so unpleasant. More than a few students were sadistic and crass in their time here, but still managed to be well liked. The stories of Emperor Tamerlane, for instance, began with his years at Nalanda. He first started on his path to conquest at the school, but he had been sophisticated. He won people as friends and only harmed his enemies when necessary, or when his power was greater.

'Vyktor's greatest crime had been his awkwardness, his refusal to ever be more than a blunt instrument.' Fafnir thought about that phrase, 'Blunt instrument,' as he looked at his students. 'That's what the humans saw when they looked at Drakes, with their hulking size, powerful arms and slow thoughts. But Drakes were so much more.' Fafnir was over four hundred years in age, the oldest of his species and in that time he'd seen much.

He'd been there when the Æesir came. At the time he'd been a slave to a royal house. As the monks, the servants of the Æesir, spread the fire of their faith across the moons of Altor, Fafnir had ridden the wave, leading his own charge, seeking freedom for his people.

Drakes still labored in slavery today, but so many more were free, and they owed that freedom to Fafnir and a few others like him whose minds had quickened with time.

They owed much to the monks as well. True they were zealots, mad in their own way, but they believed all sentient creatures were equal to some extent. Everything that breathed was equal in its servitude to the Æsir, even the human royals. The Æsir didn't differentiate. Of course, that didn't sit well with the royals, but given a choice between bending the knee and burning, most were wise enough to swallow their pride.

'Everyone follows someone,' Fafnir thought as he stared at the Lightening Bug in his staff. Her name had been Ora. How he missed her, missed when she had been his direction. That's why it took so long for a Drake's thoughts to quicken. They'd been in symbiosis with the Lightening Bugs, the dream walkers, but when the humans destroyed them, the dream had ended.

Some power still resided in Ora's broken body, but it wasn't the same. The monks had their Æsir, but the Drakes had these beings, who touched and breathed the light of stars, sensing the edges of space and time. He wasn't surprised to learn Brash had gone into the void space. Lightening Bugs had no reason to fear it. When the crowd of human students thinned out, Fafnir stopped and pointed back toward the main body of the school. "Go to your classes, my young brothers," he said to the other Drakes. His students would follow him all day if he didn't dismiss them. "Remember what you saw here. Remember the cruelty of it. The rule of the Kavaris monks is harsh but know that it is necessary. Humans cannot understand without pain. They will not follow without fear. It is their way, learn it, but remember it is not ours."

The young Drakes nodded and left, moving quickly with their arms swinging like pendulums. A Drake was never late for class. It was a rule to be on time and Drakes always followed the rules. 'All except Tearmai,' thought Fafnir. He had done much that was suspect, but then again, he always had Brash with him. For Lightening Bugs, rules were pliable. Fafnir smiled a little and looked again at his old friend held in stasis in his lantern. Ora had once led him as only a Lightening Bug could lead a Drake. She'd been the one who put the thought of freedom in his head. He missed her deeply.

He continued toward the landing bays where the diamond ship waited. The hallways had emptied and the only sound was his heavy steps. He came to the large doors of the stone hanger, which were already open. Reflected in the ship's glass sides, he could see his friend Regin waiting with his hand resting on the vessel. "Their brutality is unending," Regin said.

"I've seen worse," Fafnir answered.

A moment of silence passed as Regin considered that. He may have been the elder statesmen of the Ice-

Carvers, but he'd never have as many years as the old Drake. No one really knew how long the massive creatures could live, but so far Fafnir had gone the longest. Ice-Carvers usually died violently continuing their species, and when they didn't, their sixties were the best for which they could hope. Regin was pushing that.

Regin let his hand glide over the side of the vessel.

"Have you learned anything from it?" he asked. Fafnir breathed out heavily. "It's ancient, much like Nalanda Station. I believe it was created for the purpose of going through the voids. I don't know where Tearmai and Brash found it, but it is reminiscent of something. Do you see it?"

Regin stood back, looking. Then he noticed how Fafnir was glancing to the hall where two Fire Golems stood guard.

"The control crystals?" Regin whispered. Andavarri would never speak of them, but Fafnir had been around long enough. He'd been a slave on Tairnish for a time, so he knew how the Long Wolves controlled the fire creatures. The diamond vessel looked like one of those crystals, not only in shape but in material as well, more like a thing that had been grown than built.

"Did they find it here? Would Andavarri know?" Regin asked.

Fafnir shook his head. "No, I don't think so. If the monks found it first, they would've destroyed it and if she had known, she would've leveraged the information."

"And I assure you that I would've known," someone said coming in the room. Regin and Fafnir turned to see Andavarri slinking in quietly. Neither of them knew how much she heard.

Fafnir held up his lantern, displaying the damaged body of the Lightening Bug. "Still, it may have been here. My friend Ora could see many things that others couldn't. Her senses were tuned to energies that the monks wouldn't consider looking for. Things forbidden by the Æesir. Perhaps Brash was able to find it while you or the monks weren't. Unless, of course, it came from somewhere else."

Andavarri ignored Fafnir's suggestive tone. "Ah, yes. The vaulted Lightening Bugs and their abilities. So wonderful. Too bad the humans exterminated them," Andavarri scoffed.

Fafnir looked back toward the ship. "Even if we can't know where this came from, we have to ask what Brash and Tearmai hoped to accomplish with it."

A glance passed between Regin and Andavarri. Immediately, Regin turned his eyes away. "Is there any hope for Tearmai?" he asked.

"Maybe when our healer returns from Grannus," Fafnir said. "Though in the old stories, when they spoke about the madness of the void, the only thing that helped were Lightening Bugs. I doubt Tearmai will be able to tell us anything without Brash."

"The humans said Brash came through the void ahead of them." Andavarri pointed out. "They were adamant that he entered only a few hours before them, but the sensors picked up nothing. So where did he go?" she asked.

"That's the question, isn't it," Regin said.

Fafnir held his cane tightly. His deep-set eyes passed from Regin to Andavarri. He was certain they weren't telling him something, but in his long life he'd known few that could keep a secret forever. He agreed. "That is the question."

∞

The transport Enbarr circled Altor in just over thirty hours, accelerating, moving out and away from the rings, pointing toward Grannus. Chris only knew this because he asked. He felt tired and heavier while the Enbarr used its thrusters and the velocity it'd gained from Nalanda Station to circle Altor building speed. "Space travel can be straining," Chooth had assured him, "but you'll get used to it."

The captain of the ship had come down to check on his passengers a few hours after they left. He counted heads and when he found he had an extra one, his eyes darkened. He looked at Chris, considering whether or not to throw him out an airlock. "Traveling between moons isn't like paddling a skiff. Our mass has to be precise." The captain glared at Cormack, who tried to explain why Chris was on his ship.

"My friend is a unique case. I'm certain my mother will be grateful that you've given them safe passage. She'll probably reward you for bringing both of them to her."

The captain's face changed as he considered this. He nodded, then moved over to Chris and Katy, taking them to a wall lined with small alcoves with beds in them. Sliding back the plastic doors, he said, "These will be your berths for the journey. Try and treat them well." The captain didn't seem to notice Katy was blind. "I'll be in the control room if you need anything, but your galley is stocked and you can help yourself to the consoles." He pointed to a small kitchen area with a few cabinets and a table. Shelves ran over a long desk with boxes and display screens stowed on them. Everything aboard looked well-worn as if the ship had been in service for years. Chris had no idea how big the crew of the Enbarr was. The only one he ever saw was the captain.

After a day and a half passed, much of which Chris and Katy slept through, Chooth came over to them. "We're sending a signal to Nalanda Station if you'd like to speak to your friends. They've picked up the contact and are bringing them to the comms room now." Lying on his back, Chris had been trying to read one of the monitors, trying to understand anything about this world they'd entered, but his eyes kept wandering to the ceiling with his head pounding. His body wasn't used to the acceleration of space travel. He hoped it wouldn't be this way for the entire trip.

He climbed off his bunk and tapped on the plastic partition that served as Katy's door. They hadn't said much to each other. Neither was feeling well and every time they talked it turned into an argument. Chris had accused her of being selfish, of abandoning her brother, which hadn't gone over great with Katy. "And who the hell are you?" she'd demanded. They'd gone round and round till Cormack separated them. Katy hadn't spoken to him since.

Chris reached out his hand and helped her over to the consoles that were lined up on a desk with small dividers to give each user privacy. Chooth typed in a few commands and a video feed came up. "We'll only be in range of Nalanda for a brief time," he said.

"Right here?" Chris heard Alex ask someone off screen as he sat down.

Chris watched his brother's face grimace as he moved. Then Amita and Ben filed in behind him. Chris wasn't sure what to say, so Alex started, "Are you all right?"

"Yeah," Chris answered. "I'm sorry though. I should've stayed with you. I wasn't trying to leave—"

"It's fine. You were trying to do the right thing." Alex's eyes fell briefly on Katy, he didn't say anything. Katy couldn't see the look, but she sensed the pause in conversation.

"I don't expect you to understand. Any of you," she said.

"Come on Katy," Ben said. "You had to have known this was a bad idea. This place is crazy. We've got to be able to count on each other."

"We got to be smarter than this," Chris grumbled.

"You know what, I don't need this." Katy stormed off with her hands out in front of her to keep from walking into things.

Chris turned back to the screen, "Yeah, so, that's where I'm at."

"She'll get over it," Ben said. "I tick her off all the time and she eventually forgives me."

"She doesn't need to forgive me," Chris said. "She's the one who got me stuck on this ship, heading for another planet. Man, I can't believe that sentence came out of my mouth."

"Yeah, my sister can be kind of impulsive," Ben said.

Alex and Amita shared the same look, staring back at Ben. "What?" he asked.

Amita turned back to the screen. "They're moons by the way, not planets," she pointed out.

Ben rolled his eyes while Chris answered, "Yeah, I know." He took a breath, then asked more calmly, "So how are you guys? How are things back there?"

Alex shook his head. "They killed that big kid, the one that attacked your friend, Cormack."

Chris ignored the 'friend' comment. "Wait, what?"

"There was a trial yesterday morning. The entire school was there," Amita said. "The guy admitted that he was trying to kill Cormack so Kavaris Dell had him put in an airlock. Then they opened it."

Chris's mouth hung open.

"These people don't play around," Alex said. "We all need to be careful. We're in a different world. Everyone here seems to be plotting and planning. You need to be like Dad, Chris. Try to keep your head, no matter how bad it gets."

Chris nodded. He knew exactly what his brother meant. Their father had been a Navy SEAL who had always told them that any situation is survivable if you can stay calm, if you can stand back and look at it. Your actions have to be decisive, but your assessment needs to be fluid, their father had said. Chris looked back at Cormack thinking how surly he'd been toward the good-looking prince. 'That probably wasn't the smart play,' he thought.

"This place is insane," Amita added.

Alex turned back to her. "It'll be alright, kid."

She shook her head. "I don't mean the execution or the politics. Those things are just brutal. What I mean is the way this whole system is set up. There are three different habitable moons circling a gas giant. Each has life on it, intelligent life. Do you know the odds of that?"

"It's impossible to know—" Chris said.

"No," Amita interrupted him, "It's just impossible. The odds are astronomical. Then you throw in the fact that humans are here at all. Explain that?"

"I can't," Chris said.

"Neither can I and I've been studying their records. It's all balls-up."

"'Balls-up, that's awesome,'" Ben snickered then he saw the look on the other's faces. "Um, sorry, not the time."

Amita ignored him and continued. "The only explanation is that these people were brought here." The signal started to become fuzzy.

"By who?" Chris asked as it flickered and went out. Left staring at a blank screen, he turned and looked back at Cormack, thinking about his brother's words.

He had to be careful. Right now, this young prince might be his only ally. Then again, they wouldn't even be on this ship if he hadn't talked Katy into it. Now his brother was back on the station, injured and having to look after Ben and Amita. 'What does Cormack even want with her?'

Cormack stood next to Katy. 'It's not what he wants, but who he wants,' Chris thought. Jealously flared, then he looked down at Katy, who was bent over. Chris wasn't sure, but it looked like she might have been crying. He immediately felt bad, knowing he was being awful. He got up and went over to her.

Cormack saw him coming and stood in his way. "I think she needs a minute," he said putting his hand on Chris's chest. Chris's face turned hot.

Be smart. He repeated his brother's words in his head, right before looking down at the prince's hand and reacting poorly. Chris wasn't his brother, but he'd wrestled. He had some training, and he'd gotten in enough scuffles with Alex to learn a few things. Wrenching the hand away, Chris grabbed Cormack's wrist, twisting it behind his back and bringing the prince to the floor. Even Chris was surprised by how fast he'd been. He looked down at Cormack and had enough time to think, 'Aw, crap,' right before everyone else in the room tackled him.

Chapter 16

When the transmission ended from Chris, Alex didn't feel any better. His brother was on his way to another world and he was here, still beat and tired.

He leaned back and breathed out, struggling to adapt, then looked at Ben and Amita. He'd have to watch them. They were his responsibility now. In his head he tried to line up his goals. Safety was first and information was second. He wanted to know what happened to the Earth, where they were and what happened to their mother, but if they didn't survive this place, they wouldn't get the chance to know anything.

"Amita, do you think you could get me one of those monitors?" he asked.

She pointed toward a red robed figure by the door. "I'll ask the monk. You're going to need one for class anyway. Not that the information in there is very useful."

"What do you mean?" Alex asked.

"It's all rising and falling dynasties. Human history repeating a pattern over and over again. The science we need, stuff that would give us proper information about how we got here, has been declared illegal— It's mad!" she yelled. Then she looked around and lowered her voice. "Sorry," she said before stepping away.

Alex watched her. He barely knew Amita, but something told him she'd be tough to keep safe. She'd been out more than him, but she still didn't seem to get how dangerous this place was. He thought about the execution. 'They didn't give second chances.'

Ben and Amita had gone to class after watching Vyktor die. They'd been there today too, up until lunch when they'd been pulled out and brought to the communications room. For Alex, this was the first time he'd been away from the healing chambers since the fight.

"They'll be okay. Chris is a smart guy," Ben said, patting Alex on the shoulder.

Alex glanced back at him, still not sure what to think of Ben. The fact that his eyebrows hadn't grown back didn't help. After a moment Alex said, "Yeah, I know, he takes after our mom. That doesn't mean I'm not worried about him though."

"Don't take this the wrong way, but I'm glad he's there. That Katy's not alone," Ben said.

Alex nodded. He was about to say something else, but then a monk came over and handed him a monitor. He had to place his hand on the screen so that it'd be keyed to him.

Amita and Ben were sent back to their classes, while Alex made his way to the dining hall with the monitor in front of him. The first thing he pulled up was information on Grannus. He wanted to know everything he could about the world his brother was going to. The opening entry stated that Grannus was ruled by Queen Daoine Sidhe. The family resemblance to Cormack was striking. 'God, Chris, don't do anything stupid,' Alex thought.

Looking down at the screen, Alex entered the room. Then he glanced and noticed how almost every table was empty, and how the cooks and servants in the middle were putting everything away and cleaning.

"You're a little late for lunch," someone said behind him. He turned to face Princess Maeven. Her eyes were shining as she smiled at him. "They keep things on a tight schedule around here. You've got to eat when they want, go to class when they want, and train when they want."

"Then why are you still here?"

"I don't like being told what to do." She bit into a piece of fruit and nodded toward Tara, who was waiting. "Luckily, I've got someone to keep me on track."

Alex glanced at the leftover food being packed away. The princess took his arm, "Come on," she said, taking him over to the serving counter. She didn't ask as she grabbed a plate. A few of the servants looked annoyed, but they didn't say anything, instead they turned their eyes to the ground. She handed the plate to Alex. He held it with one hand while Maeven hooked his other arm in hers and gently guided him toward the food. Her closeness was exciting to him.

"It's nice to see you up and moving," Maeven said. She had checked on him last night. They'd talked for a while before she returned to her quarters.

"Hopefully, I can avoid being stabbed for a few days," Alex answered.

Maeven leaned around him and loaded the plate with meat and something that looked like potatoes. "Anyone would think twice about attacking you after seeing you in action." Then she pointed to a table.

"I don't know where the monks expect you to sit, since you don't have a house, but you'll always be welcome to join me at my table. In fact, the offer still stands for you and your friends to lodge in the Tamerlane chambers. We've more than enough room and you can eat whenever you want."

"Thanks, I'll think about it," Alex said. He was certain the monks didn't want them hanging around with one specific house. They wanted to keep him and the others isolated. He felt her pulling at his arm, leading him out of the dining hall. "Where are we going?"

Maeven released his arm and took the plate, holding it out so he could pick at some of the food while they walked. "Class, of course. Like I said the monks are very particular about their schedule."

"They don't much care for food being taken from here either," Tara added as she fell in step behind Maeven. She tried reaching for the plate, but Maeven pulled it away.

"It's okay, I can carry it for him." She continued to hold the plate out to Alex. "You better start eating. They may take this when we get there." Picking something up that looked like pork, she held it out in front of him. "Go ahead."

Tara stared in shock. She'd never seen Maeven like this, feeding someone and caring for them. She thought back, remembering a pet the princess once had when she was young. A puppy that her father had given her. Tara tried to remember what happened to the animal when the princess became bored with it. She couldn't recall. It would've been hopeless as a hunting dog after the way it'd been loved. Maeven's father had no patience for useless things.

Tara observed Alex as he looked down at the offered food. His face, which was always somewhere between sullen and grim, broke into something she'd never seen on him before, a smile.

They reached an auditorium like the one where the execution had been held, minus an airlock. The room was full of students, humans and aliens. Kavaris Dell stood behind a podium watching Maeven enter. They were the last ones to arrive.

Amita and Ben were sitting near the front, and Ben waved to them, sliding over on the bench to open a seat. Maeven looked at the opening, then glanced up at the crowd of students. The Tairnishmen were sitting away from the emperor's other supporters, staring with blatant rage at her. It didn't matter to Maeven. Royal houses that served her father always left an opening for her.

Alex started toward Ben and Amita. "Please take a seat, so we can begin," Kavaris Dell said from the podium.

Maeven smiled sweetly at the old man and followed Alex. Ben scooted over making enough room for her, crowding Amita into an Ice-Carver. Amita elbowed him in the ribs while pushing back.

"Hey, gimme' a break," Ben grumbled while holding his ground. He wiped the seat off with his hand. "Come on, I kept it warm for you." He motioned to Tara, smiling even while Amita was shoving at him.

"Alright," Tara said, sitting down. The whole group was so tight that it was impossible to be comfortable.

"You mind moving down a bit?" Ben called to the Ice-Carvers at the end. The aliens turned their big eyes, staring at him strangely. In fact, the entire room was looking at him and the rest of the group. "Come on guys, just a little space," he called, while ignoring the frown he was getting from Kavaris Dell.

The Ice-Carvers moved reluctantly. Then Ben called again, "Thanks guys. You're awesome." Finally, he turned and faced the front of the room.

"Are you quite settled?" Kavaris Dell asked.

"Yeah, we're good," Ben answered looking to his group. He didn't notice the way Alex was covering his face or the way Tara was shaking her head.

"Excellent," Kavaris Dell said. His cheeks were nearly as red as his robe. He let out a long breath, glancing down at the podium before starting. "For those of you unfamiliar with it, I think you'll find this enlightening. It is, of course, my favorite subject, the 'Modern Age' and the coming of the Æsir." The lights lowered and an image was projected on the screen behind him.

"For nearly a thousand years humanity struggled and fought amongst itself." A slide show began behind the monk. Images of ships floating in space, exploding or half destroyed were followed by fields wiped clean by orbital bombardment. It changed to video clips of strange, pulsing energy weapons that tore apart the fabric of reality. "We pursued knowledge that was un-healthy for the survival of all

147

the races in this system." More images came up of creatures that appeared half-human, mutants who had their genes altered.

"But when the Æsir came, it was with righteous fire. They cut across our worlds, teaching, and setting our people on a course for survival. They showed us the way to Nalanda, to this place, so that we could learn from each other and no longer delve into those things we should not know." The image on the screen was of something coming up from Altor, a creature with horns, riding a rocket trail under a small pedestal. It was only a silhouette but what it was carrying was clear. This monstrous, armored creature was holding a glowing axe.

There were two more behind him, smaller and further away. Kavaris Dell pointed to the image. "These are our saviors; they came to set us on a righteous course.

"This image was taken over a hundred years ago from Prometheus Station, a military research facility, home to the assassins who'd learnt to walk through walls. It was taken moments before the station and the fleet protecting it were destroyed." The image changed to more ships floating in space, but now they were in pieces, making a field of devastation. He pointed again. "These men thought they knew what power was. They were wrong. Ground based observatories reported that the battle lasted all of five minutes. That's how long it took for the Æsir to purge this evil."

Kavaris Dell looked across the room to stare at each student, making certain they understood what he was saying. His eyes fell on Amita, who had her hand up.

He ignored her and continued. "Now as a monk of the Kavaris order, I've stood in the presence of the Æsir—" He was distracted again by Amita, who was now jabbing the air with her arm trying to get his attention. "I've been honored to speak with them, to be guided . . . by. . . What!?" he finally asked, no longer able to ignore her after she stood and started waving.

"So, you're saying your 'saviors' won't let you pursue certain avenues of study? Like the wormhole we came through."

"That's correct. We're not allowed to study the void spaces that move under the clouds of Altor. Knowledge of them led to the development of some of our deadliest weapons," he answered.

"There's more than one?" Amita asked.

Kavaris Dell had already turned his eyes back to his notes. He shook his head in frustration and spit out the question. "More than one what?"

"Void spaces, what we call wormholes. You said, 'void spaces,' plural, meaning you think there's more than one." Amita had stepped forward a little.

"It doesn't matter how many there are. Their study is forbidden."

"That's simply mad," Amita blurted out. "You seriously allow some sort of outer space boogeymen to keep you in a state of stalled research?" She glanced back at the others but ignored the way Alex and Ben were trying to get her to sit down.

"You've no understanding of the situation. The Æsir are our saviors," Kavaris Dell repeated.

"Are they? You don't even know who they are, do you?" Her hands were on her hips as she nodded at the screen. "Why am I asking, anyway? I bet their first rule is that you're not allowed to study them, right?"

"I've heard enough of this blasphemy! We've no time for your silliness. Go now before you say anything else imprudent and damn yourself." Kavaris Dell shoved his arm toward the door with his red robe flailing.

"'There is no sin, except stupidity,' Oscar Wilde. You gits are living it," Amita said. Then she glanced back over her shoulder at the room. Every eye was turned toward her, watching in silence. She held up her hands, "Okay, I get it. I'll just go."

Two monks had come to the door. "Bring her back to her quarters and keep her there," Kavaris Dell called after them as they escorted her out.

Ben watched Amita go, then turned and leaned over to Alex. "Did Amita forget that this guy put a kid to death yesterday?" He nodded to Kavaris Dell.

Alex looked at Ben and knew they needed protection. He knew if he didn't contain Amita and Ben, they weren't going to last here.

Chapter 17

Days passed while the Enbarr moved closer and closer to Grannus. The passenger compartment had no windows but there were video screens. One showed their approach to a deep blue world shining in the reflected sunlight from Altor and growing larger for half of each rotation. During the other half of the orbit, the Enbarr and Grannus were in the shadow of the gas giant.

Chris passed the time reading. His head no longer hurt and his bruises were healed. A few days out and the shuttle was no longer pushing to reach escape velocity from the gas giant, going in a wide elliptical orbit towards the blue world. Chooth floated in zero-g, describing their velocity as being slow in comparison to some ships, especially warships. "There isn't any getting up and moving around on those, not when they're on a mission. You could spend days strapped into an acceleration couch," he said, telling Chris about the fleets that patrolled between the different moons.

It was Chooth who'd helped Chris off the floor after Cormack's people tackled him. Some had kicked him while he was down and stomped on his back. Cormack tried to stop them. He held his shoulder, the one Chris had twisted and yelled for them to stop, but his people were too angry. They had swarmed over Chris. Apparently attacking their future king was a big no-no.

Chris had been embarrassed, not for being taken down, but for flaring up and going after Cormack in the first place. He knew he had a temper. He'd let it go on Alex a few times when he and his brother fought, but he'd never lost it with a person he hardly knew. He didn't like Cormack. The guy was too perfect.

Chris had apologized to the prince. Cormack had been gracious and accepting, taking his hand, but that didn't make things feel any less strained. Everyone on the ship watched Chris, waiting for him to do something else stupid. Chris tried to be smarter. Every time he looked at Cormack, he forced a smile and tried to be friendly. Sometimes, he felt like he was acting too friendly. Feigned fondness was awkward as hell.

At least Katy started talking to him again, which was good. Their bunks were on the same wall and as mad as they were at each other, the situation they were both in, being castaways from an Earth that might be gone forever, made it impossible for them not to talk.

It was easier when Chooth came to them. He was a caring voice to Katy and despite his oddness he was a friendly face to Chris. He'd spend hours next to their bunks asking them about themselves and the world they came from. Chooth was a great listener and storyteller, and he was curious.

Chris could not avoid hearing Katy confess to the Grannusian that it had been fear that made her accept Cormack's offer. She said, "What if my sight never comes back? What if this is how I'm forced to live? Walking around in the dark, I'm helpless and I hate it."

"You're not helpless, Katy," Chooth said. "Life is adaption and you will adapt to this."

"It's too much," Katy said. "I'm worried it's going to break me the way my mom broke."

Chris tried not to listen. What Katy was saying sounded so incredibly personal. Katy told Chooth how her mom had had a mental break down, that she'd been placed in a hospital after she tried to kill herself. Katy explained, "When she finally got out, she was normal for a little awhile. But it didn't last. She left a note, but I've never read it."

Chris wanted to say something, but he couldn't find the words. He was too shocked. After hearing that, he had to admit that he and Katy didn't know each other that well. Chris thought about his own mother, trying to imagine what had happened to her. He'd seen her enveloped in that light from Brash. Could she have passed through the void safely? He didn't know. She could be out here on one of these worlds right now. The next time he and Chooth spoke, he brought it up.

Chooth had looked over the humans on the ship then in a whispered voice he explained, "the science of how the void spaces work was outlawed by the Æesir. But they weren't as thorough in the purge of my people's knowledge." He looked again, making certain no was listening. "It was believed by many that the Lightening Bugs could enter the void safely and return."

"What happened to them? The Lightening Bugs?" Chris asked.

Chooth explained that humans had come to each moon of Altor as refugees. That they'd survived some cataclysm. Its exact nature was lost to time. On each world humans had started out peaceful enough. Then time and pressure led to them wanting to expand. "It happened on Uppsala, the Lightening Bug's world. As humans became more powerful, they became scared of the abilities the Lightening Bugs had, their dream walking."

"But you don't know where those humans came from?" Chris asked.

"No, I don't," Chooth said. "The oldest colony that I know of was on Tairnish, but that was a millennium ago. Contact between races wasn't as common back then. Even my people have risen and fallen many times."

As Chris became more comfortable with the alien, he started to sense that Chooth was just as nervous as he was. The closer they came to Grannus, the more he saw it. Their first few days on the ship, Chooth had been warm and friendly, but as time passed it seemed more of a forced effort by the Grannusian. Chooth was distracted. Occasionally he heard him talking to himself when he stayed in his own bunk, which looked more like a fish tank.

Two days before they were due to get off the ship, Chooth called Chris over to the viewing screen. "I'd like to show you something." A blue world had grown to fill the entire screen. The endless shades of aqua and indigo blended into the deep greens in a massive ocean that covered the moon's entire surface.

"This is what I wanted you to see, it's our destination," Chooth said pointing toward something circling over the horizon of Grannus, a white, flat disk with a stalk like a mushroom. Compared to the planet it was small, but compared to the ships that docked on it, it was massive. "This is my people's greatest creation. It has served for thousands of years as our bridge to the stars. We call it the solar blossom."

"How big is it?" Chris asked.

"Roughly ten kilometers across," Chooth answered.

Several structures dotted its surface, many of which looked man-made, but the disk itself was organic, like a giant bleached bone with shades of pink. Paler scars dotted the surface, spots that looked like healed wounds.

"Below it is the really amazing part." Chooth pointed to a line that was so thin it was almost impossible to see. "That is the tether. It reaches down to our world, anchoring the disk to our equator. Over the centuries it has survived countless hardships, war, weather, the radiation of our twin suns, but still it stands."

"It's a space elevator?" Chris asked. He was familiar with the concept from his years of reading scifi novels. None of them had suggested something like this, something that had been grown and that may very well still be alive. He looked at Chooth, at his body made from all its strange parts and realized how in awe he should've been of the Grannus. He'd been so worried about where they were, that he'd failed to see the amazing things around him.

They had been decelerating for days, now it would be a while longer before they took orbit around Grannus. The final maneuvering required them to be strapped in as the Enbarr dropped into the moon's gravity well and decelerated. Grannus wasn't as large as Earth, but it was close, about three quarters the size.

They never actually touched down on the solar blossom, but rather were attached by cables to one of the towers that'd been built on its surface. Maneuvering took hours and by the time it was done, without thrust, the simulated gravity was gone. Chris removed his straps, stood up and found himself floating toward the ceiling. That's when his leg was pulled back to the floor.

He glanced over to see Chooth holding him. "Careful. Floating is fun but cracking your skull isn't," Chooth said.

Chris nodded. "Thanks." As he looked across the room at the hatch, he watched the others move, crowding toward the exit. He remembered something his dad had said when they went diving on vacation. 'A hand for you and a hand for the boat,' his father had told him before opening the throttle. 'Being weightless was a lot like that,' Chris thought, as he used the chair backs to pull himself along. Everyone else gathered their personal possessions, but Chris had none. Even the clothing on his back was given to him. Cormack was at the front helping Katy, taking both her hands and guiding her toward the door.

The hatch opened. Outside the ship was a long gangway extended for docking. It was a corridor reaching up from the human bases on the surface of the solar blossom.

Armored soldiers waited on the other side of the airlock. Their bodies were covered in segmented pads much like Edith's back on Nalanda, but their gear was light grey, matching the walls of the corridor. The face plates on their helmets were pulled back just enough to see their eyes. With their weapons slung over their shoulders, they moved in, using small jetpacks, letting out short bursts of compressed gas. They helped Cormack, who was the first to the airlock, guiding him and Katy to a ladder that ran the length of the gangway with small lights softly glowing from its rails. Cormack placed Katy's hands in one of the soldier's, then the two started to descend. "Be careful with her," the prince ordered.

"Yes, my lord," the soldier said, moving away. The guard ignored the ladder guiding Katy down toward the solar blossom, using small bursts from his pack, getting far ahead of everyone else who had to make their way using the ladder.

Watching Katy go, Chris was worried. He didn't like having her that far away from him. He exited the transport, and started pulling himself along, getting further from the ship with Chooth not far behind. He scooted around the others ahead of him, coming off the rungs and using the outer rail. "Relax Chris! We're all going to the same place," Chooth called behind him.

Cormack turned around at the sound of Chooth's voice. He watched Chris struggle toward him, getting death stares from the people he passed in the corridor. Then the prince glanced at Katy and her guard, who were almost at the end of the gangway where an open airlock waited. Cormack rolled his eyes and started back toward Chris.

Everyone moved aside for the prince, letting him back through. When he reached Chris's side he said, "Chooth is right, Katy will be fine." He reached out, taking Chris's wrist and crouched down a little putting one foot on a rung as he said, "Here, let go."

Chris did as he was told, then Cormack pushed off from the rung. They shot down the gangway. "Come on, Chooth, keep up," Cormack called playfully to the Grannusian. Chooth shook his eel-like head, then kicked off as well, diving into freefall.

A little embarrassed at having his arm held, Chris couldn't stifle the thrill of being weightless and moving fast in an enclosed space. He smiled.

"Alright, try to turn your feet down. Like this." Using the muscles in his core, Cormack swung his legs under him toward the approaching airlock. Chris tried to do it too, but it was harder than it looked. The end of the gangway was coming up quick. Ahead of them, inside the airlock was a corner and a solid looking wall that they were quickly approaching.

"Come on, Chris," Cormack said. He reached over and pulled at his shoulders, helping him spin. Chris got one foot down, then the other. His landing wasn't graceful, but it was better than face planting.

They entered a wider hallway, passing through a docking station. It was one of the human towers that stood on the surface of the solar blossom. It had looked small from the ship, but inside it felt very much like an airport terminal with more space to spread out and more rails and ladders to help passengers along.

The group came to another airlock. When it cycled open it revealed the strangest place Chris had seen yet, the inside of the solar blossom. The walls were white and rounded, reminding him a bit of the slot canyon back on earth, looking like frozen ripples on a pond. When he touched them, he found that they were soft and warm, pulsing a little. As they descended the colors changed, bizarre light emanated from the walls themselves. The air was moist and thick. Occasionally they passed through a floating bubble of liquid suspended in droplets. They moved through the tunnels, still weightless, using banded stirrups of a fleshy substance that seemed to beat in their hands. Blue and purple lights blazed through the walls while the stirrups glowed a deep green. Signs along the way were printed for humans, but it seemed like almost everyone knew where to go as the tunnel became tighter. Occasionally, Chris had the sense that he was being watched, that tiny eyes hidden in the crevices of the walls were on him. He glimpsed them moving at the corner of his vision and felt like the entire structure was alive and pulsing.

After the tunnels they entered a large cavity. In the center of it was a metal cart with chairs, a box made for humans, with a roll cage firmly affixed to the bottom wall. Everyone in the party picked a seat and settled in. The armored guards helped Katy into one and backed out of the room, leaving the cavity.

"How are you doing?" Chris asked as he took the seat next to her.

"I'm okay," Katy said. "How about you?"

Chris looked around at the strange space, feeling like he was inside a massive creature's belly. "I'm good, I think. This is really, really weird," he said, laughing a little, "But kind of awesome too." Once everyone was strapped in, the walls of the cavity began to pulse and contract. Chris watched as they quickly closed in, dropping like cling-wrap over the cart. It made an organic burp, tightly crunching the sides. They were left sitting in darkness.

"What was that?" Katy asked.

"Um, I don't know," Chris said, reaching out to touch the material.

"It's the descender securing us," Chooth said. A pulse came from the wall, then another, and soon they came so quick that it was impossible to tell where one began and one ended. The cart moved, falling toward the planet. Chris held tight to the chair in front of him. They were being pushed through a forever long throat, moving at increasing speed. The force of gravity pulled at him as they accelerated. It was terrifying. Chris reached over for Katy's hand. He tried looking at her but it was too dark. It'll all be over soon, he told himself. They dropped and dropped endlessly. His eyes close as time passed.

Chris wasn't sure, but he may have drifted off to sleep. When he awoke in bright sunlight, he had the strangest feeling that he'd been drugged. He glanced back at Chooth, who was sitting out of reach, then he looked around at the other people. Everyone seemed to be opening their eyes for the first time after a long nap.

"It's an easier journey that way," Chooth said, knowing what Chris was thinking.

"You knocked us out?" he asked.

"He didn't. The solar blossom did," Cormack said. "I just wish it did it a little sooner." He wiped his hand over his eyes, then unbuckled himself.

The cart was surrounded by organic material that looked like a bean pod burst open. Above, the suns were incredibly bright in a clear blue sky, though from this distance it was impossible to tell there were two stars. A shadow lay across the land extending out into the ocean and going on forever. Chris glanced up, trying to shade his eyes. He saw the tether and the orifice at its bottom from which they'd been ejected. Several of the openings circled the tower like a row of mouths, releasing more pods. They were in an organic track that gave way to a set of rails, stopping them at a padded barricade.

The tether itself was thicker than any skyscraper he'd seen and so much taller. It reached up into the atmosphere till it disappeared. In the sky above, the edge of the solar blossom was a ghostly form, nearly invisible in the sunlight. It was impossible to think that they'd just come from it. Chris was still woozy as he tried to get up.

The area around the tether was empty, but not far away down a steep hill was a city encircling them, with clay shingled roofs and white walls that glistened in the sun. Beyond it was an aqua blue ocean dotted with small green islands bursting with plant life. They looked like broccoli caps floating on the water, held in straight lines by thin bridges. Little of the white rocklike surface they sat on showed through.

"It's so beautiful," Chris said as he stood, looking out. He'd never been to Greece, but he'd seen pictures of a place called Santorini. That's what this city reminded him of in the way the buildings rolled with the cliffs and hills, while overlooking the ocean. They were crowded tightly together with balconies and domes, while roads paved with shells twisted between them.

"It's something, isn't it," Cormack agreed. "This is where I grew up. It's called Anchor Home."

The two of them helped Katy to her feet and guided her out of the cart. "We could take a skimmer. But I think I'd rather walk. If that's okay with you guys?" Cormack said.

"I guess. Where are we going?" Chris asked.

"My home, of course." Cormack pointed to the tallest building in the city, which dwarfed all the other domes and roofs, rising twice as high, with towers and minarets tipped in gold. The palace stood apart from the city on a massive stone dock that extended out into the ocean. It was surrounded by a thick wall with guards patrolling it and technology poking up that could only be weapons emplacements. Cormack held Katy by the elbow as they started off. Many of the others from the cart followed him.

Chooth stepped past Chris, then looked back when he realized Chris wasn't following. "Come on. Exercise will help the effects of the tether wear off."

His lips curled back in a fishy grin. "And you might want to close your mouth. The insects you people attract can be aggressive."

Chris shook his head and started following, still staring at the palace in the distance. He couldn't believe he'd been ready to take a swing at Cormack. 'I'm going to be doing a lot more fake smiling,' he thought, as he glanced down at the prince.

Chapter 18

Cormack walked through the town, waving to people and saying hello when they came up to him. By the time they were a half kilometer down a lane, he'd gathered an impressive crowd. He always had a few handlers nearby, the guys who'd come down the tether with him, but none of them were armed. They tried to stay close as more people funneled out into the street.

Women with young children gathered around and men who ran shops were patting him on the shoulder. Cormack picked up the kids and talked to the adults as if they were long lost friends. Chris felt like he was part of a parade, but they were the only attraction. Looking ahead, even more people were gathering.

Katy was next to Cormack through the whole thing. He'd only drop her arm when he was giving one of the citizens a hug or a handshake, then he'd take her arm again, leading her along. Chris tried to stay near, but it was hard with so many crowding in. Over an hour passed and they weren't getting anywhere fast.

Chris glanced down at the palace and saw something approaching at speed. The skimmer was flying four meters above the street, causing people to duck, avoiding the downdrafts from its four turbines as it roared over them. It looked like a landing craft from World War II, the ones that stormed the beaches of Normandy with armored sides and soldiers filling it. Only it was fancier with flags and banners streaming behind it and, of course, it was flying.

The crowd moved out of the way as the vessel hovered just above the ground. "Looks like my ride is here," Cormack said to the people. A front ramp dropped and men in blue and grey armor marched out, carrying rifles that were different from Earth weapons, but looked like they might work along similar principles. They wore helmets that covered their faces as they formed two lines with flag carriers at the front.

One man removed his helmet and took a knee in front of Cormack. "My prince, the queen requests your presence."

"Of course," Cormack said. "That's where I was heading anyway." He started toward the skimmer, still holding Katy's arm. He turned back to Chris and Chooth. "Come on guys. Looks like our stroll is over." The soldiers filed back into the skimmer, crowding Chris to the side. It lifted off, heading back the way it had come. The floor shifted and moved under him as the machine climbed with its noisy turbines, accelerating. Chris leaned against the rail for support and looked down as they flew over the wall around the palace. Massive gun emplacements, many of which were pointed out toward the water, were manned by small platoons of armored soldiers. Ships beyond the wall floated in the sea, including other skimmers. Apparently, they were made to operate on water as well.

When they reached the palace, servants waited in formal uniforms with high collars and carefully pressed shorts. Cormack greeted a few personally, then asked one to guide Chris and Katy to the guest quarters. "I've got to meet with my mother," he explained. "I'll tell her all about you guys. She's probably going to want to make your acquaintance later." He was quiet for a moment, thinking. Then he almost reached to put his hand on Chris's shoulder, but he hesitated and said in a low cautious tone, "Try to be careful around her, okay? She can be a little intense and she is a queen."

Chris nodded, feeling nervous for the first time since they arrived.

Cormack turned to a servant. "If you'd be kind enough to find them something appropriate to wear." Then he smiled and hurried off, leaving them with the servant.

"Follow me," the servant said over his shoulder while walking away. Chris took Katy's hand and placed it on his arm to guide her through the large archways and across the tile floors. He glanced back to see if Chooth was following, but the Grannusian wasn't there. Without saying a word and without anyone directing him, he'd disappeared.

They were brought to a suite with two bedrooms, a balcony, and a massive common room. The servant laid out clothing for them, then showed Chris how the shower worked and took his leave. It was the first time Chris and Katy had been alone together since arriving through the void. "Do you, ah, want to use the shower first?" Chris asked.

"What's it look like?" Katy asked him.

"The shower?"

Katy laughed a little. "No, the planet. I have no idea what it looks like. It feels warm and I can smell the sea."

Chris took her arm and led her to the balcony. He looked out at an incredible view of the water breaking against the rocky cliffs. "It's beautiful," Chris said. "A real paradise."

"I wish. . ." she started to say, but then she stopped.

"I know, Katy."

She shook her head. "You probably don't know this about me, but I used to be an artist. I mean, I liked to draw anyway. I always kept a sketchbook with me. It was how I relaxed, like my own kind of meditation." She went quiet for a minute, then asked, "Are you still mad at me?"

Chris thought about it. They'd come so far and lost so much. The idea that the Earth could be gone seemed too big. It was easier to worry about his brother and Amita and even Ben but he couldn't say he was angry anymore. Katy's face was pointed toward the water. Some of her hair had broken loose from her ponytail and it was swirling in the sea breeze. 'She really is incredibly pretty,' Chris thought, feeling silly that it was the only thing that came to his head. "No, I'm not mad. Not anymore. . . I'm just concerned. We need to be careful, Katy. We don't know these people. We need to watch out for each other."

Katy put her hand out, reaching for him. When he took it, she said, "I'm sorry I dragged you here, but if there's any hope. . ." She pointed to her eyes. "I suppose I can't ask you to understand."

"It's ok," Chris said trying to focus on anything but the feel of her hand.

"It's selfish, but I'm glad you came with me. I don't want to be alone here,"

"I'm happy you're not alone too," Chris said. After that they were silent for a while. Chris led her back in and showed her where the bathroom was. He picked her outfit off the bed. It was a dress, kind of thin and short.

As he thought of everyone he saw in the streets, he wasn't surprised as they'd all worn a similar style clothing. Their outfits didn't need to be warm and they would want something that dried fast, since everyone's work probably had to do with the ocean. Of course, Katy's dress was much nicer than anything he'd seen outside the palace walls, made with a shiny, silky material. He handed it to her, holding it by the thin straps. "Here you go, I think it goes this way," he said.

Katy took it. "Shouldn't there be more to it?"

"Yeah, I thought so too," Chris said stepping back, closing the door behind her. He went to his own room, where he picked up the outfit he'd been given. It was embarrassingly small as well, basically a swimsuit with a formal sash and no real shirt to speak of. Chris lifted his shirt and looked at his belly, wishing at least once he'd gone on one of those early morning jogs with his brother.

An hour later the servant returned. Katy had filled a bath and taken her time in it, while Chris had been much quicker with the shower. "The queen is ready to meet you now," the servant said.

"I'll bring them down," Cormack offered as he came around the corner. He looked Chris and Katy up and down, checking out the traditional Grannus clothing. "You guys look great." Chris watched Cormack's eyes linger on Katy. It was an appreciative glance, but it wasn't as lusty as he'd expect from a high school-aged kid. Chris still put himself between them, holding out his arm for Katy to take. Katy couldn't see him of course, but Chris still felt an urge to suck in his gut.

They followed the young prince through the halls, coming to a grand set of stairs carved from the same white marble as the rest of the palace. Chris brought Katy to the rail, then started down slowly. He was trying to watch where she was walking, but it became difficult to pay attention when he saw the throne room that was in front of him.

The far wall was below the ocean's surface, which was held back by a massive wall of crystal. It glittered blue as the sun shone through, causing strange reflections to dance across the floor. The massive skull of a prehistoric looking animal dominated the room, resting on a raised platform and facing the ocean with its mouth propped open. Jagged white teeth, long and spear-like, still clung to the jaw and inside sat the queen on a silver throne.

Suntanned nobles, dressed much like Chris and Katy, milled about before the throne. Their formal wear stood out in sharp contrast to the soldiers who stood at every corner and entrance. They wore more of that advanced looking armor with the helmets and faceplates. They were hulking next to the nobles, bristling with firepower and tactical gear. Chris sensed they were all looking at him.

They reached the bottom of the stairs. Cormack guided them to the front of the throne where he kneeled before his mother. "These are the people I told you about, Chris and Katy. They came through the void space from another world. The monks at Nalanda Station didn't seem to know what to do with them, not until after they were visited by— well, you know who."

All the nobles in the room stiffened. Cormack didn't have to say the name of the Æesir.

Chris kneeled, tugging Katy's arm to let her know that's what they were doing.

Cormack's mother, Queen Daoine Sidhe watched, then leaned forward, staring at Chris and Katy as if they were some sort of curiosity or specimen. Her face was stern but attractive, worn less by age and more from governing. Her hair had turned white, but her olive skin showed very few wrinkles. Chris guessed that she was a little older than his own mom, maybe early fifties. Sitting next to her was a younger man. He was inside the sea creature's mouth as well, but in a chair that was much less ornate than the throne the queen sat on. He was in his thirties and handsome, though there was something Chris didn't like about him. He seemed to exude arrogance.

"So, you're the one who assaulted Prince Cormack Sidhe, heir to the throne of Grannus?" the younger man asked.

'I guess we weren't done with that,' Chris looked around the room as the thought flitted into his mind.

Those guards suddenly seemed far more intimidating.

"Um—" Chris started to say.

"Duke Sebastian, our altercation was small and unimportant." Cormack broke in before turning to his mother. "Those who reported it to you were only concerned for my safety after what happened on Nalanda." He motioned to Katy. "Chris was trying to reach his friend. I over-stepped, trying to stop him."

"You are gracious as always, my son, in forgiving him," the queen said.

Cormack enjoyed the praise, nodding as he added,

"His brother did save my life."

The queen nodded, but then she pointed out, "Still, there is no excuse for laying hands on the royal person." Two guards started across the room.

Cormack glanced at them nervously. "Please, Mother," he begged. "He was beaten for it and it was me that laid hands on him first." The soldiers took Chris roughly by both arms while Katy was pushed aside.

Chris didn't try to fight as he was brought to his feet. He could feel how strong the men were. The armor they wore was enhancing their strength. This whole journey was so unreal, like a dream, that it was hard to get upset. Some part of him had expected it to turn bad. He knew from the moment he heard about the execution that something like this could happen. Shivering, he pictured an axe falling across his neck and wondered why that image entered his mind. 'They'll probably try to drown me or feed me to a shark or something. It'd be keeping with the room's theme,' he thought before shaking his head as he tried not to laugh, surprised by how silly it all seemed. Then someone else entered the room.

With a splash the ocean spilled onto the floor as a muffled voice called out, "Your laws hardly apply to him. He is not a commoner, he's not even from our world, not from any of the worlds circling Altor." It came from the crystal wall where a portal had opened. A pocket of water extended in. As it fell away, Chris turned to see Chooth, who was leaving puddles behind him as his different parts came together. He was no longer wearing his cloak or the frame of bottles that kept his skin moist. "If need be, I will claim him and give him the protection of the Grannus."

"And what could that possibly mean?" Duke Sebastian asked.

"Test me and you'll find out, consort," Chooth said harshly. It was obvious he didn't care for this man. He turned to the queen and in a less belligerent voice added, "Though these travelers don't have a house, they were afforded all the rights of the noble-born by the monks. If the servants of the Æsir treat them as nobles, what would it say about you if you punished them as commoners?"

The queen turned her head thinking, then nodded and looked at Chris. "Very well. If Cormack has forgiven you, then this matter can be put to rest."

The two guards released Chris. He watched them walk away and pondered what would've happened if Chooth hadn't come in. So, they can't treat me as a commoner. That's good, but the kid they executed back at the station had been a noble too.

"Thanks," he said to Chooth, while getting to his feet.

The Grannusian nodded and turned toward the queen. "Has there been any word from Eir?" he asked.

"No, not since you left. We've had little communications from your people since it started. Since the poisoning," she said in a neutral voice, giving little away. Chris watched her face. It was impossible to tell how she felt.

"I think they've communicated quite clearly," Duke Sebastian said turning his attention from the queen and staring at Chooth. "There have been attacks at the volcanism projects. Your people have sent giant sea creatures against us, the Cirien-Croin. We've lost workers by the hundreds all along the rim. It's brought our work to a standstill."

"Cirien-Croin? You've seen one?" Chooth eyes widened as he asked.

"We've seen the devastation it left behind. Some recordings survived, mainly just the sound of men screaming." The duke pointed his finger at Chooth. "Your people blame us for the poisoning and now they've released this horror on the shallows."

Chooth's eyes narrowed. It was the closest Chris had ever seen him to angry. "Despite what you think, the Grannusian don't control every creature in the sea.
There are things that even we are afraid of, including that monster from the deepest part of the oceans. If

your drilling brought a Cirien-Croin to the rim, then it's you that's to blame. We would never inflict such a thing on anyone. They are merciless killers better left to the deep."

Cormack broke in. "Besides, the Grannusians are not violent. They never have been. They've gone hundreds of years without ever attacking humans."

"Never directly anyway," Sebastian said. "But with their abilities they don't have to be direct. And they weren't happy about the volcanism projects. They can't understand that we're not fish, we need land to live on. Growing islands is our only solution."

Chooth shook his head disagreeing, but he was unwilling to engage in an old argument. He turned to the queen, "I've come home to find answers and to find Eir. I must find her!" He nearly shouted. His voice was a primal growl that shocked the room while his whole body twitched. Outside the window, something large and dark swam by. Chooth took a moment, slowing himself. "Too much time has passed. This world needs its healer."

The queen nodded, but before she could say anything Cormack interjected, "We have to help him. We owe it to the Grannusians. And I wish to go with him, to help my friend. Please, Mother? We must know what's happening," he pleaded. "The Grannusians have been our allies. This poisoning, it's not just an attack on them, but on us. We need them."

"We've already sent expeditions," the queen said. Her eyes held Chooth's gaze. "Your cities were empty.

Your farms as well. We can find no sign of your people. Perhaps they're in hiding."

Chooth stared at the floor. "I can't give up hope."

"Were there bodies?" Chris asked, breaking into the silence that'd fallen over the room.

Everyone's eyes were on him. He wasn't sure why he'd opened his mouth, but he continued anyway. "If Chooth's people died of poisoning, then there should be bodies in their cities, right? If there were no bodies, that means they went somewhere else."

Cormack nodded. "Mother, as I said, we need to investigate. Allow me to go with Chooth and help him. I gave my word to this girl," he motioned to Katy, "That I would find her the healer. Please don't make me go back on it."

The queen looked at Katy, then smiled at her son, "You are so much like your father," she said. "I give you my permission, but I ask that you be careful and return to me quickly."

"You know Chooth won't allow any harm to come to me," Cormack said stepping next to the Grannusian.

"I will do my best," Chooth answered.

"Very well. I will have a submarine prepared for you." She turned to Chris and Katy. "And you two, do you intend to go with them as well?"

Chris looked at Katy. She'd turned to him expectantly. "If there's any chance this healer can help my friend, then we have to," he said, glancing out at the blue and endless ocean. His eyes were looking beyond the crystal wall. The light of the sun passed through it, but eventually, in the distance it

175

faded and there was only darkness. Chris wondered what a Cirien-Croin was and what other creatures might be waiting out in the deep.

Chapter 19

After class, the one where Amita was booted for arguing with Kavaris Dell, Alex turned to Ben as everyone was leaving and said, "We need friends. We need to be able to protect ourselves and we need resources if we're going to figure out what happened to us, to my mother and to everything else. I think we need to take Maeven's offer."

Ben was a little surprised, mainly because this was the most Alex had ever said to him. He nodded and asked, "Great, what offer?"

Alex explained it to him.

"So, we're going to be living with Tara and Maeven?" Ben asked. He was looking at the door where Tara had followed her princess to their next class. Alex shook his head. "We're not playing house. There are other nobles there too, members of her family and their allies. It's a big area with a bunch of rooms, kind of like an embassy for her government. We'd be protected there."

"And Tara lives there?" Ben asked again.

"Yeah," Alex answered shaking his head and throwing his hands up.

"I'm in then. We've just got to tell Amita." Ben stared at his tablet, looking at the schedule for the day. "We should get moving. We've got another class and I think you're going to like it."

"Oh yeah, what is it?" Alex asked.

"Battle theory," Ben said in a deep voice, then stared at Alex, tilting his head when he didn't see a reaction. "Man, I thought I'd get a smile out of you,

177

but all you did was frown harder. Are frowns like smiles for you?"

"Come on." Alex got up, heading out to the next class. It was a smaller room, tighter and more intimate than the auditorium where Kavaris Dell had held his class. Maeven wasn't there and neither was Tara. The boys took a seat as the instructor came in. It was Edith, still wearing her armor.

She stood in front of the classroom and all conversation stopped while she surveyed the students, her eyes sparkling with something that wasn't human. "Tell me class, in a battle what is the most important thing to have."

One student raised his hand. "Superior force," he answered.

Edith nodded, "True, being superior in fire power or numbers is a good thing, but history is full of battles
where a lesser opponent won the day."

Someone else said, "Better positioning."

"Explain?" Edith demanded.

"Control of the battlefield, having high ground or commanding the sky," the student answered.

"That is important. Always consider where you're fighting. Try and influence the field as best you can, but sometimes that's not an option. When you need to take an enemy's position, you don't always get to choose where that position is."

She turned her gaze to Ben and Alex. "What about our new arrivals." She looked right at Alex. "What do you think is the most important thing to have in battle?"

Alex thought about it for a second. He'd never learned military strategy in high school, but he liked history and when you had a father like his, you picked things up. "You need to have a clear objective," Alex answered. "You can plan all you want, have as big a force as you can imagine, but if you don't have a goal, it's all wasted."

Edith's scarred face showed something between a sneer and smile. "Very good, very good. So often noble families go to war over some insult or some point of pride. Those dynasties fall under the weight of their own stupidity, pride is never a purpose for war. You must have something you want, some goal. Controlling trade, claiming resources, increasing influence. Those are the larger objectives of war, but even on a small scale, even in single, hand-to-hand combat you must have a purpose. It could be murder, could be preventing murder. It could be defense or it could be a desire to show the world what you're capable of. Isn't that right, Alex?"

"Um, no - I mean yes - that could be a reason, but if you're asking if that was my reason for getting involved the other day . . ." Alex paused, moving uncomfortably in his seat.

Edith held him in her gaze. "Was it?"

Edith had a tone in her voice that Alex recognized. She spoke the way his dad had, always challenging him with the extreme focus of a soldier. He looked back at her respectfully, trying not to show fear. "It wasn't."

Ben glanced behind him. The entire class was watching, including many Tairnish students. Their wide, purplish faces were tight with rage as they stared at Alex.

"Why not," Edith asked.

Alex touched the wound at his side, feeling where the knife had passed through him. "I'm not a showoff and even if I were, letting everyone know what I'm capable of, that I'm tough or something, can only invite more testing. It's better if your opponents underestimate you. It's better if they don't consider you a threat at all. The best way to win a battle is to avoid it in the first place," Alex said.

"Ha." Edith let out a sharp, short laugh. "I disagree. Your answer is well thought out, but wrong." Her eyes ran back over the class again. "There is no avoiding war- Ever! If you live and breathe, you fight. Remember that. There is no safety. You defend or attack, or you're the sheep hiding behind the protection of others, at peace till the day you're slaughtered."

Ben looked at Alex expecting a reaction, maybe an argument, but Alex was quiet. He listened attentively through the entire class. When it was over, he got up to go while Edith nodded to him respectfully.

Ben and Alex split up just after the evening meal. Alex went looking for Maeven, while Ben went to the room to grab their things. Of course, they didn't really have 'things,' just the clothing they came through the wormhole with. His pile from Earth had been dirty and tossed in a corner. The monks never explained how laundry service worked on the station.

He brought Chris and Katy's stuff with him too. It was all rolled in a ball with a hoody tied around it that he slung over his shoulder. Ben stopped in the poorly lit exit from the monk's territory, looking up at a Fire Golem standing guard. It appeared to be nothing more than a darkened statue. "I just thought I'd let you know we're moving. Alex made up his mind and he thinks we'll be safer with Princess Maeven."

Ben gave the statue a tap on its chest. "So, um. . . I'm sure I'll see you guys around." He knew Andavarri was probably listening, but that's not who he was speaking to.

He didn't like Andavarri and she claimed that she controlled the Fire Golems, but Ben didn't believe her, not completely. Somehow, he knew she was lying. He just didn't know exactly how or why. There was more to these guys than the alien claimed. Ben could feel it.

He thought about those first few moments in the landing bay, when he'd seen the flames bring the statues to life, when one of them had sacrificed its body to save him. He could sense the intelligence from it. The flames were alive, he was sure. The Fire Golems, for his money, were the most amazing part of Nalanda Station and despite what Andavarri said, he had trouble believing anyone could create life, not like this.

He let his hand rest on its chest, feeling something warm inside. Slowly it became hotter and hotter as the center eye began to glow. "Woah, um sorry, I didn't mean to wake you up, or bother you or whatever." Ben pulled his hand back.

The statue tilted its head to the side, looking at Ben. A gesture that seemed to indicate that it didn't mind being bothered.

"I don't know if you heard me before, but like I said we're moving. I don't know if you guys hang around Maeven's quarters- you know the princess girl, but that's where we're going to be." The eye continued to stare at him.

"You know you're only telling Andavarri," a voice said from behind him. He turned to see Edith. Her eyes glowed softly while her armor faded into the shadows. She came toward Ben. "Everything they see, she sees," she said and motioned to the Fire Golem.

Ben looked at the red eye. "Did her people really create them?"

"That's what they claim, but who knows." Edith shrugged before continuing, "I came looking for your friend Alex. I'd like to speak with him."

"He's off looking for Amita. I was too," Ben said, though he'd almost forgotten that he was supposed to. "She got kicked out of class earlier and we haven't seen her since."

"Alex watches out for you two, I take it?" Edith suggested.

For some reason, this annoyed Ben. "He's been too banged up to look out for anyone. If anything, we've been watching out for him."

"I see. So, where is he right now if you've been watching him?" She smiled.

Ben was a little surprised by her warmth, "That's really not fair," he said.

She held up her hands, "I'm sorry. I'll leave you alone with your, ah, friend. I'm sure Andavarri will enjoy anything you have to say to it." Edith nodded to the Fire Golem.

Ben looked back at the Fire Golem after she left. "I don't blame you for having to be a spy. I know there's more to you than what she makes you do. You guys didn't save me because of her."

He looked down the hall where Edith had gone. "She thinks Alex is our protector - I don't know. Maybe he is. Maybe that's a good thing. . . I wish Chris were still around, and Katy too. I wish they hadn't left." He shrugged, took one last look at the Golem and started walking away.

He was too far away to hear the low, harsh noise, like rocks crunching against each other that came from the Fire Golem. A word came out. The creature touched its chest and said, "Protector." Then it went back to rest.

Chapter 20

The monks had taken Amita back to her quarters after kicking her out of class. Apparently, they weren't willing to guard a student's room. When Amita peeked out her door, she found an empty hall with only the Fire Golem left behind. She'd tip-toed past them, then left the monks' area. Reading her map, she looked for areas that were unlabeled. This led her deep into the station, where people seldom went, to dark places. The whole time, as she explored, she was expecting to hear the Long-Wolf's arrogant voice sneaking up behind her. At a point, as she delved deeper, she may have even welcomed it.

The station was still on the daylight side of the gas giant, so as much as she wanted to go back to the lighthouse, she knew it was going to be too crowded. 'Those monks who were supposed to be watching her were probably busy guarding the machines, making certain everyone remained ignorant. If the tech did anything interesting, they'd be just in time to destroy any useful knowledge,' Amita thought.

She felt jealous of Ben and his unusual sense of direction as she wandered down another hallway that looked like all the others. Her monitor displayed the floor plan of Nalanda Station, but even with a map it was easy to get lost in a place this big, especially when you were trying to avoid people and when no one had bothered to put up a sign.

Amita glanced at the map. She thought she was coming back up. Initially, she'd gone down, far into the station, taking less-traveled corridors that plunged into the rock. She worried she'd get lost below and never find her way back. The hallways in those deep places weren't used for the school. They were rough looking after being empty for ages. The map showed most, but other passages that hadn't been recorded, dark openings in walls and forgotten crevasses.

There were stairs going down and shifting gravity fields. She'd hoped there'd be some secret knowledge down in the depths, but the further she went, the more she got the feeling that nothing alive had been that deep in Nalanda for an awfully long time.

The lights strung along the walls stopped at a point, but she went a little further, using the glow from her monitor to shine in the dark. Amita didn't frighten easy, but sensing the black vastness of those tunnels, her nerve and her resolve faded. Just before turning around, she laughed a little saying, "There's probably nothing down here anyway." Then she listened to the strange echo of her voice coming back.

She followed the map, trying to find her way to the corridors that ran closest to the outside of the station, closest to the stars, but she was only able to guess where she was. She found an area labeled Extraracial territories on the map. She'd come across the word while studying her monitor.

Extraracial was sometimes used to describe the natives of the different moons, an attempt to be more precise in naming the group of races that weren't human, instead of using the term, 'aliens.' But it wasn't a common expression.

Amita understood why. People were lazy and by calling those races alien, it gave the humans ownership of the different moons, as if they were the ones who belonged there and not the Extraracials. Amita had been thinking a lot about the use of language since they arrived here, wondering exactly how the dead body of the Lightening Bug had reprogrammed their minds to understand Nalanda's common tongue.

She followed the passage coming closer and closer to the Extraracial territory. On the map it looked like one of the grand halls from the upper levels, but as she reached the end of the passage, she saw that it was different in a significant way. Not a single window looked out on the stars, but yet there were trees, an entire forest, filling the massive room. They were like pillars running up to the ceiling, filling the air with a living smell. Their massive roots broke the floor, leaving smashed and damaged stones lying about on soft ground that was the result of falling leaves from above. Beyond, on the ceiling, hung powerful lights that could barely penetrate the thick canopy. "Whoa!" Amita said, hearing her voice echo back again. It wasn't as terrifying this time.

Coming down the passage behind her, she heard the padding of feet. She turned to see a few young Ice-Carvers, their large eyes staring at her in surprise. Their tails came up in a defensive position pointing the fleshy tips at their ends in her direction. Amita had read about how the Ice-Carvers could use those tips to spray dangerous chemicals.

Amita held up her hands. "I come in peace. I just got a little lost."

The young Ice-Carvers never stopped moving, looking around, turning their heads, always watchful. "You shouldn't be here. This area is only for the other races," one of them said.

"Like I explained, I got a little lost. I'm new here," Amita said.

"Leave," the Ice-Carver demanded, then the group hurried past, disappearing into the forest. The one that spoke turned his head almost completely around, keeping an eye on her till he was out of sight.

Amita sighed and glanced down at the map. She could see doors past the trees leading into the different homes of the different races. She wanted to explore, to go look further, but she didn't wish to anger the Extraracials so she backed out, leaving their territory behind.

She went higher in the station, taking a set of wide stairs that seemed to climb forever, and came out into a broad hallway where she heard voices. One was a low rumbling and the other was softer and higher pitched. As she followed them, it dawned on her that she was in the first place she'd seen at the station. She came around a corner and found Regin and Fafnir, the giant Drake. They were standing beside the diamond ship. She went to the doorway as quietly as possible, trying to hear what they were saying.

Regin stopped mid-sentence, lifting his head and turning toward her. She hadn't made a sound, but it didn't matter. "Hello, young one," he said in a friendly tone. He didn't seem bothered by her eavesdropping. She couldn't help but notice how different he was from the other Ice-Carvers, sounding confident and wise.

Amita stood out from the wall. "Sorry. I got a little lost."

"The way I hear it, you've a tendency to wander. You're a bit of a curious one, aren't you?" Regin asked playfully.

"Is that a bad thing?" Amita crossed her arms.

"It is here." Fafnir's voice rumbled out while his bright eyes glared behind a beak-like mouth.

Amita turned away from his stare.

"Ignore my friend." Regin came closer. "He is incredibly old and very cranky. Curiosity is not a terrible thing in a child, it is only to be expected." He reached out a furry hand, touching Amita's arm. Amita looked down at his large welcoming eyes. Regin was so different from the other Ice-Carvers. He was friendly and confident, smooth in the way he spoke and the way he acted. His gestures seemed almost human. Amita wondered if he'd adopted the behaviors through contact or if he'd purposefully developed them.

Amita looked down at him. "It's not just curiosity. I need to know what happened to us. How we got here. But knowledge is outlawed. It's beyond frustrating."

"There are worse hardships," Fafnir said, sounding unimpressed.

Amita fought the urge to scream, taking a deep breath. Then she started toward the ship. "What about this? Have you learned anything from it?"

Fafnir blocked her way. Amita was about to go around him when Regin said, "We haven't learnt much. We don't know where it came from or how Tearmai came to be in it. He and Brash were a bit like you, 'curious.'"

"It didn't work out well for them," Fafnir said.

"How is Tearmai?" Amita felt bad she hadn't asked already.

"Not well," Fafnir answered.

Regin added, "He woke for a little while but the madness hasn't ended. We had to restrain him to keep him from injuring himself. Now he's being kept sedated till Eir returns."

"If she returns." Fafnir started forward, putting his cane to the ground and almost on top of Amita. She had to jump aside to keep from being stepped on. "I'm going," he said to Regin, ignoring Amita altogether.

She watched him leave, waiting till he'd turned the corner. While the sound of his staff tapping on the floor slowly receded, she grumbled, "He's a surly one, isn't he?"

"Always has been. He can be very diplomatic when he has to, but as he's gotten older, he's gotten tired of playing nice with you people," Regin said. Amita turned to him, waiting for him to say more, but instead he motioned to the diamond ship. "You may examine it if you wish."

"If I remember correctly, there wasn't much to examine." Amita went to the ship anyway and started up the side.

"I understand your frustration with the monks and their restrictions but try not to blame them. After all, they're only the messengers."

"Of the Æesir?" Amita was standing on top of the hatch, wondering if it was worth climbing in again. She ran her hand along the edges, remembering how Tearmai had been repairing it in the canyon when she met him. She'd almost died trying to get a better look at it. She wondered if the doorway's surface, so different from the rest of the vessel, was a result of his work or if the opening had always looked like a second thought.

"Yes, messengers of the Æesir. Though from what I understand, the Æesir say very little," Regin agreed. One of his hands ran along the reflective side. Amita couldn't tell if he was trying to find something in it, or if he was only staring at his own reflection.

"Can you tell me what the Æesir are? And while you're at it, how does this whole translation thing work? Because I know that word. I know what it meant on Earth, but it seems to mean something else here."

Regin tilted his head, waiting for her to say more. She added, "Back home the Æesir were gods, myths really, from a people who existed centuries ago. Their ancestors don't worship them anymore," she explained.

Regin's ears perked up a little. "Gods, you say? I suppose your mind could be translating our word for these creatures to that. They certainly seem god-like in their power and they are worshiped. They arrived a little over a century ago. The humans were dangerous then, more dangerous than now, if you can believe it. Their different factions had been at war for generations. Sometimes there'd be peace, but it'd only last a short while, then there'd be some new reason to fight. Dynasties rose and fell as they created more elaborate ways of killing each other. The other races were caught in between, just trying to survive. Some didn't."

"The Lightening Bugs?" Amita asked.

"Yes, they were the greatest casualty."

Something was bothering Amita as she tried to analyze Regin's words, her mind working quickly as he spoke. 'Greatest casualty,' so were there more? But that wasn't the question that bothered her most, it was still the translation thing. There was something there, a thread she wanted to pull. "But why Æesir? Why that name?" she asked.

Regin shrugged. He wasn't sure what she meant.

Amita continued, "I mean yes, that's the name for a group of gods, but it's not a common name, especially for me. Why wouldn't it just be gods or deities, or something more general? Æesir is so specific. I was raised Hindu. That's a different set of gods, though they're all sort of related." She looked at Regin and saw that he had no idea what she was talking about. The Æesir were Norse or Scandinavian. That's pretty far from India. The only reason I know about them was because I read a lot. This translation thing, the way Fafnir reorganized our minds, would it do it if we had a word in common?" she asked.

Regin shrugged, "I don't know. Honestly, I've only ever seen Fafnir use the Lightening Bug that way a handful of times. Occasionally, a noble will have such a distinct dialect that he must be retrained a little, or a member of the other races may have had limited exposure to the human language, but always there is a bit of the common tongue to work with. You and your friends are new, so I'm surprised it worked at all. We're lucky it didn't damage your brains."

"Yeah, not that Fafnir would've given a toss," Amita said.

"He probably wouldn't," Regin agreed.
"Still, I wish he'd stuck around so I could ask him."

Regin glanced toward the door. "He'd only chastise you for your curiosity."

"You're right there," Amita agreed.

"Like I said, Brash and Tearmai were much like you. They weren't content to let the monks keep their secrets. I know for a fact that at night they'd go looking about, finding things out about Nalanda, things even the monks didn't know. Andavarri and I had to cover for them more than once."

"Really? Andavarri?" Amita asked.

"Yes," Regin answered slyly. "Of course, that was in exchanged for them sharing what they found. Andavarri is always interested in information and to be honest, I've been accused of curiosity myself."

"Oh," Amita said, sensing that Regin was suggesting something more. She glanced down at the diamond ship, still sitting by its hatch. "I hate to tell you this, but I think Tearmai and Brash were keeping a bit back." She swung her arms wide, motioning to the whole length of the ship.

Regin nodded in agreement. "When they left here, it wasn't together. Brash went first and Tearmai said he was on a mission. He was worried about his friend when he followed him. You must understand, Lightening Bugs and Drakes are from the same world. Before humans, before the purge, they were remarkably close, almost symbiotic. Drakes were lost, directionless without Lightening Bugs, but not Tearmai. He was the last that still had a companion. Brash would never leave him behind unless it was for something incredibly important or for his safety. When Tearmai followed him, I don't know if he was going to try and stop him or help him, or simply because he couldn't stand to be without his friend, but he was desperate."

Amita sensed that Regin knew something more, something he wasn't saying. "Do you have any idea where they went?"

Regin shook his head. "No, but I have a theory."

"I like theories," Amita said.

He motioned to the ship. "This crystal technology, there's only one species I know of that played with anything like it, the Long Wolves, Andavarri's people."

∞

Alex waited outside the Tamerlane domicile. It was on the other side of Nalanda, opposite the dining hall and most of the classrooms. He hadn't been there before and was surprised to see how active it was. It was another grand hall but built closer to the rocky heart of the tiny moon, making it possible to dig into the stone foundation and expand the living quarters. More than a dozen of these doors were carved in the stone, lining the far side of the hall. Each one owned by a different noble family.

Outside these noble enclaves, the massive room, like the dining hall, had windows near the ceiling looking out on Altor. The doors were guarded by human soldiers dressed in the uniform of various royal families. The openings were set back in alcoves while in the center, running the length of the entire room, was an open market. Tables and stalls were run by the servant class, along with members of the other races. They sold food, brightly colored fish, fruits and vegetables, clothing and luxury items too, jewelry, expensive shoes, ornamental weapons and silk bedding. Everything was marketed to the wealthy children of nobles, the ruling class, Alex thought, looking around.

He hung back trying to blend in, leaning against a column and watching the door that was marked with the seal of Maeven's house, a tree with a crossed spear and sword above it. Glancing at one of the stalls, Alex saw a weapon on display that looked just like the one on the crest, like a Chinese broad sword, two-handed with a thick single blade. The two guards who stood outside Maeven's door wore the same weapon on their hips, but they also carried the shock batons used in the combat training. Alex hadn't done much with weapons in his dojo, a little with a bo-staff, but he preferred batons as a more natural extension of his hands. They were better for the style of close quarter fighting he'd practiced.

"Those weapons are outdated, but they still have their uses," Alex heard someone say behind him. He turned to see Edith standing close by. "I've been looking for you," she said.

He glanced down at her boots with their plating, bolts and pistons. Alex couldn't believe he hadn't heard her approach. True, the market was noisy, but in that heavy armor he'd have thought she'd be louder. Edith saw him sizing her up and smiled.

"Is there something you need?" Alex asked. This was the closest he'd been to the combat instructor. She was a little taller than him and the armor made her seem larger, but now, looking at her, he wondered how much of that was the gear. She looked younger up close too, late twenties maybe. Alex realized that it wasn't time that had aged her, but a tough life, years of fighting.

"'Need?'" she repeated. When she smiled, she stretched the scar that ran up the side of her face. Other marks ran back over her ear, under her short, cropped hair. "No, there is nothing I need, but I'm curious about you, Alex. I saw you fight and I was impressed. I was hoping to learn more about your style. One warrior to another."

"Oh," Alex said while looking at the floor and feeling his face become warm. "I'm not a warrior, not really. I've just always practiced martial arts, Jujutsu mainly." He glanced back up at her. The combat instructor was waiting for him to say more.

"'Warrior' isn't a term we used that much where I come from," he explained. "Well, maybe my dad did. I don't know, but I've wrestled since I was a kid and I became interested in where all those moves were from, so I started reading about judo, which is another discipline, then I started going to a dojo near my house. It all kind of works together, the throws and the locks. Then there's striking. I'm not much for kicking, but I can throw a decent punch. I wanted to try boxing, but my mom wouldn't let me. Too many head shots, plus I wouldn't have had time with baseball."

"Boxing?" Edith asked.

"Yeah, it's a sport where I come from. People think it's all about knocking your opponent out, but it's not, it's about landing hits and avoiding them." Alex moved his feet a little bit and his hands went up naturally into a fighting stance. "I like the foot work. You have to keep on your toes," his voice had a little thrill in it.

Edith mirrored him, getting into the same sort of stance. "Like this," she said, putting her left shoulder toward him. "You're making a smaller target. Many of our disciplines start with this form as well," she said.

"Yeah, exactly" Alex said moving a little. He threw a combination that came inside her hands, but that didn't land, coming close to her armor. "See what I mean? It's all about foot work." He smiled.

"So, these different fighting styles are sports on your world, done for fun and competition?" Edith asked. She'd watched his hands move and saw the way his eyes lit up.

"Yeah, but when I graduate high school, when I can go into the service like my dad, I'm hoping some of them will come in handy. That's when I'll be a warrior, or I should say a soldier. That's what I want."

"I see," Edith said. "Here we become warriors much younger. I was fourteen the first time I commanded a picket ship."

"Oh," Alex said, not sure what she meant.

"Can I show you something, something I think you'll find interesting?" Edith said starting to walk away, motioning for him to follow her.

Alex glanced back at the Tamerlane's door, at the guards. He wanted to speak to Maeven, to tell her that he was going to accept her offer. He wanted to wait for her to come out, or at least wait till Ben found Amita and came here, but he was enjoying talking to Edith. 'It probably won't take long,' he thought as he said, "Sure," and fell in step next to her.

Chapter 21

Alex followed Edith through the market, down into a quieter part of the station. He noticed how even in an empty hallway he could hardly hear her footfalls, she moved like a cat. Her matte-black armor seemed to disappear into the walls. He wondered if the lack of sound was some function of the equipment or if it was her. She turned back to him, saying, "I have to confess something to you, Alex. I may look like I know what I'm doing with this teaching thing, but I haven't been at it very long. I'm grateful to Kavaris Dell for taking me on, but I've been forced to learn a lot about dealing with people, especially nobles." She typed a code on a door. "The old monk is a pain sometimes, but he's kind in his way. He gave me a home after the Grannus war and I've tried to do my best by him."

"Kind?" Alex asked. He was thinking of Vyktor.

"In a way. Troopers like me don't always find a place after they lose a war. Luckily Kavaris Dell felt some kinship to me. We're related you see. He's a distant cousin in fact. I sought him out and offered my services. My people have a tradition of teaching, but it's always one on one. A master and student. The relationship is more important to us than family. We're mercenaries, going back generations. Fighting is in our blood. War is the occupation of nearly everyone and we don't give our knowledge to just anyone."

Alex didn't know where they were going, but he felt comfortable with Edith. To others she may have been scary. There was an intensity under her casual confidence that reminded him of his dad. "I kind of assumed that fighting was part of everyone's life, especially the nobles," Alex said, thinking back to the combat field and how young some of the participants had been.

"For the lower houses, maybe. But most nobles don't actually like getting their hands dirty. They fight for honor, but then sit back contently when actual war comes. They let others fight for them, people like me." They'd entered a wide hall with high ceilings and tall roll-up doors lining it. Crates were stacked with wrapped supplies. She turned back to him and added, "Or maybe people like you."

Alex didn't know what to say, but he started to understand why Edith had brought him here. She was a teacher and she saw a student with potential. He was proud, even though it was strange having someone consider his future when he wasn't even sure he had one. He thought about home, about the path he'd mapped out for himself, then, for the first time, he wondered about a life here in this place. He didn't know if he'd ever get back to Earth, or if the Earth still existed to get back to.

"It's not an easy existence, being a mercenary," Edith said, seeming to fill in his thoughts. "But for someone who has enough fight in them and the discipline to make themselves better, it can be rewarding." She came to one of the roll-up doors and took out a metal key, unlocking it and lifting the door out of the way. "I've got my own quarters in the faculty area, but this is where I spend most of my time." She went to the wall and turned the lights on. Alex was shocked by what he saw.

Inside were shelves full of equipment and gear, pieces of technology and hand tools, but that wasn't what drew Alex's attention. Standing against the back wall, over two meters tall was a suit, a weapon really, something obviously meant to kill. Its legs were drawn up beneath it, making him believe it'd be even taller if it were standing. Its center was thickly armored with a broad, robust battle platform, bristling with weapons. Multiple appendages sprouted from it, some of which looked like arms, others were obviously guns or bladed weapons. "Wow," Alex said.

"It's taken me the past year to put it back together. I didn't keep souvenirs before I came here. As a mercenary I moved around too much to hold onto anything, but now, Kavaris Dell has been kind again, giving me some space and allowing me to pursue this hobby."

"What is it?" Alex asked.

"It's a forward operating drop-suit, the ultimate weapon to penetrate enemy territory, to fly in and wreak havoc. I thought it'd be an interesting teaching tool."

"You flew in this thing?" Alex turned toward her.

Edith was taking off her armored gauntlets, placing them on the shelf as she answered, "Flew in it? I nearly died in it, or at least one just like it. I was conscripted to fight in the emperor's fleet when he attempted to invade Grannus. It didn't go well, for him or for me. The Grannusians, human and fish-head alike, were tougher than any of us thought. Luckily for me the Grannusians, the ones with gills, have some strange moral code.

I'd dropped from the sky with the intention of murdering them, but when my suit took too much damage and I sunk into their ocean, they took pity on me. They took me in and nursed me back to life. I'm not sure if I was their prisoner or just their patient, but I spent a year in their underwater city." She removed her shoulder pads and arm pads.

"Wait. You said you were conscripted? I thought you were a mercenary," Alex asked.

She pressed a button on her armor, and with a hiss of escaping air the chest piece popped open. Lifting it over head, Edith took it off and hung it on the wall. There was a tight rubber sleeve beneath that she wiggled out of, leaving her in a simple black tank top. Alex looked at her shoulders. She was muscular, probably as strong as he was, if not stronger and her skin was marked with pale scars.

"Yes, all my people are mercenaries. We won't declare our loyalty to any noble, but as a people we'll serve them for a price. It's been that way for hundreds of years. We're from the southern Islands of Uppsala, the Tamerlane's world, but we're from the harsher side, the hotter side. Territory nobody really wants. Still, they use us in their wars. Young men and women are sent to fight, especially young women."

"Why's that?" Alex asked.

Edith had taken some of the padding off her legs, but she still wore the heavy boots. She sat on a stool and brought out a small toolbox. Picking up a flashlight, she shined it in the access panel on the drop suit that had been left half open as she answered. "To command a picket ship requires a great deal of concentration, an ability to multitask. Thanks to the Æsir, there is only a limited amount of AI that can be used in the drones. They don't like networked AI. So, the drones require a person to guide them. For some reason, women, young girls actually, are the best at it. Something to do with brain chemistry. Lucky us, right?" She touched the side of her head, the marks that ran along her scalp. "The first time I was jacked in and sent to warm, I was still a kid. It's a strange thing commanding a wing of drones. You're out among the stars, so vast, but you feel like you're being pulled apart the moment combat begins, like you're trying to fight with hands you don't have."

Alex pointed to the drop suit, "So how did you end up in this?"

"I survived and I earned it, most pilots can't claim that. Most burn out, get brain damage, but I didn't. They wanted the best for the drop suits and that was me. That's why I wanted to show you this, Alex. It's something you could have. Only the greatest warriors can command a suit. I wanted to show you so you'd know. You see for someone like you with no house, this. . ." She touched the side of the armor. "Might be the best you can hope for."

Alex looked at the armor and at Edith. According to Chooth's instructions, he had to wait another two weeks before he could participate in combat training.

He thought about it and felt a thrill, wishing the time would hurry past. He had no idea if they'd ever get back to Earth, but he knew they'd have to survive here and that meant being strong. He'd never be stronger than in that armor. Then there was his mom. The Lightening Bug had gone through the wormhole with her. They could be anywhere, on any of these moons. As a mercenary maybe he'd have a better chance of finding her.

"Are you offering to teach me?" Alex asked.

Edith turned to him. She stood tall with her back straight, eying him. "There are reasons I'm here on this station, reasons that have kept me a long way from home. That doesn't mean I don't miss my people's traditions, being among warriors. I'm tired of showing spoiled nobles how to fight. I want to teach someone who's already got some fight in them. Is that you?" Edith asked.

A familiar feeling was building inside Alex. Every challenge he'd faced, every wrestling or jujitsu match started this way, with a tickling at his spine that could've been fear. He'd learnt how to use it, to turn it into a live wire that would carry him through anything. He looked at Edith. If she'd been his father, he would've saluted. Instead, he answered. "Hell yes, it is!"

Edith smiled and nodded. "Good. Come on, you want to see what the cockpit looks like?" She asked, getting up, standing on the stool and opening the hatch.

Alex glanced back toward the door for a moment wondering if she'd let him pilot it. If there was even enough room down here to get the machine out. He looked around the metal shelves covered in gear and knew it would never get past them. Then his eyes fell on a large tank, like an aquarium. Inside was a strange fish, a lumpy piece of flesh with no eyes and barely a tail with wires connected to it.

"What's that?" Alex asked.

She hesitated, seeing what he was pointing at. "Another souvenir from Grannus. I've only recently acquired it," Edith answered, "Kind of ugly, isn't it?" She smiled then waved him over, showing him the way up into the armor.

∞

Focus was a struggle for Ben, but he was getting better. There was discipline at the station, and there was fear, which forced Ben to stay ahead of his thoughts, to control himself in a way that he never had before. He still struggled with the classwork, but nobody seemed to care. The teachers were used to nobles. Kids who treated being in class more like an obligation because of their positions while staying indifferent to learning.

Alex, Amita and Ben fell into the routine of life here as the days passed. They received badges to enter the Tamerlane quarters and were given their own rooms, much nicer than the one the monks had assigned. The rooms were painted and had furniture with soft bedding and spare clothing in the closets. They passed through the Tamerlane doors each day and ate at the Tamerlane table. It was weird and it took getting used to, because everyone seemed to give the Tamerlanes a little extra respect. Ben could sense the way everyone watched them.

At first, Kavaris Dell appeared annoyed with the change, but he got over it quickly after Maeven spoke to him. Ben overheard her tell Alex, "The old monk has no interest in politics. Giving you three to the most powerful house in the system is getting rid of a problem for him. He's happy not to be responsible for you and your friends, especially Amita," The princess said.

The monk couldn't really complain about Amita though, not after that first day. Since then, she'd sat through classes quietly and made herself scarce the rest of the time. Even Ben wasn't sure where she went to. The few times he asked her she'd told him in colorful ways, "To mind his own."

Amita hadn't even been eating with them. She chose to sit with the aliens instead. Ben wasn't surprised that she was more interested in the different races. They were aliens after all, but Ben found people more interesting, or at least one person in particular, Tara. Alex and he had been spending a lot of time with Maeven and her attendant. Of course, Alex remained his aloof self, studying the combat manuals contained in the monitor. This only seemed to make Maeven like him more. Everyone else paid so much attention to her, worrying about keeping her happy, that having someone like Alex, who obviously liked her but didn't treat her like royalty, seemed exciting to her. Ben had seen the way the princess's eyes sparkled when she looked at Alex and he'd noticed Alex sneaking back from her room in the middle of the night. Ben's adolescent mind couldn't help wondering how far he'd gotten with the princess. He wanted details, but of course Alex didn't say anything about it. He wasn't that kind of guy. No one mentioned any sort of girlfriend/boyfriend stuff, but it was in their eyes, a closeness grew quickly between the princess and Alex.

During the day Maeven was content to sit next to him while he read. They talked, but his mind always seemed to be somewhere else. The first live combat exercise Alex got to participate in was coming up. He'd be fighting for house Tamerlane and it was the most excited Ben had ever seen him. Alex was getting extra training too. Each evening he'd go off for about an hour with Edith, then show up for dinner, sweaty and sometimes bruised. Maeven would joke about taking care of his wounds later while Tara smiled. Ben got the feeling that Maeven wasn't as discreet about talking to her handmaiden.

Tonight, they all had somewhere else to be. A transmission was waiting for them in the communications room. Grannus had lined up with Nalanda Station, making a direct signal possible. Chris was waiting on the screen as the monks showed the three in.

"Hey guys," Chris said. It was a poor signal with a slight delay and the screen was snowy, making Chris's brown skin appear pale. He was aboard a ship that had set off from Anchor Home the day before.

"So how is Grannus?" Ben asked.

"It's pretty. I met the queen and was nearly executed when I first got here," Chris said.

"What, why?" Alex demanded.

"I kind of attacked the prince." Chris shrugged. "Bad idea, right? I don't know if you guys realized this, but Cormack is an actual, legitimate prince, like with a castle and everything? The whole noble thing is more than just a title."

"Yeah, we figured that out. We've been hanging with royals too," Ben said.

"He was going to have you executed?" Alex broke in.

Chris waved his hands. "No, not him. He defended me actually. It was his mom. As it turns out, going after one of these nobles, when you're not one of them, is a big no-no. So, you guys might want to remember that . . . Luckily Cormack was pretty cool about it." Chris's voice trailed off a little.

"You still hate him, don't you?" Ben smiled.

Chris looked off screen for a moment, then his hand came across the camera, moving it. Katy came into view while Chris said, "Hate's a strong word."

"He's going with us and Chooth to find Eir," Katy added. Her voice was soft and nervous. Even though she couldn't see the screen, she kept her head down. "Apparently Eir was investigating the mass poisoning in their food chain. Chooth wants to find her worse than we do. The people here and the Grannusians got along pretty well until this. So, it's important," Chris said. Then he asked, "Anything on your side, you know about getting us back home or finding Mom?"

"Nothing yet," Amita said, "But I'm working on it."

Alex and Ben both stared at her as if surprised by this answer. "Anyway," Alex said turning back to the screen. "Try to be safe, you two."

"Hopefully, we'll be back soon," Chris said. The signal ended. He turned and looked at Katy. They were both wearing something very much like a wet suit made from a bioengineered material. He tried to ignore the smell. The people on Grannus only wore them when they were going deep, down into the places where the ocean was cold.

Chapter 22

Standing up in the sub was hard for Chris without bumping into something or someone. They'd been traveling below the sea for two days, into territories where only Grannusians were supposed to go, or those with their permission. They had Chooth with them, though he'd been quiet for most of the trip and much of the time he'd spent outside the sub, only occasionally coming in to catch up with Cormack.

Glass domes on the vehicle looked out from all sides, the largest at the front was where Cormack sat, controlling the ship. Everything was damp, and cold. Outside all Chris could see was the dark blue of the ocean along with the occasional fish shooting by. Pale sunlight shone down from the surface reflecting off the white sand below.

Chris had plenty of time to think about his mom and about Earth on the shuttle, wondering what happened to both. The last thing he needed was more time alone with his thoughts. He looked at Katy, wondering if she felt the same way, when Chooth, who had briefly come aboard, sat next to him and explained, "It'll only be a few hours more. The largest of our cities, Twilight is ahead of us, deep in the Shallows."

"'Deep in the Shallows?'" Katy asked. "That seems like an odd way to say it."

"No, trust me it fits. There are depths to our world, places even my people don't go. Our city is only a hundred meters down, but it's far into our sovereign territory, kilometers from the floating islands the humans have claimed and further still from the Abysmal Shelf."

"'Abysmal,' that doesn't sound terrifying at all," Katy pointed out.

"And a hundred meters sounds plenty deep to me," Chris said. He'd done a little diving with his dad, but the furthest down they'd gone was a mere twenty meters to look at a coral reef in Jamaica.

"Believe it or not, I agree with you," Chooth said. "We may live below the ocean, but my people have never tried to claim all of it as our own. This is a large world and we only occupy a small portion of it. Out past the ledge where the ocean's bottom can't be found is unsafe and too far for us to go. We are not wanderers like you humans."

"So, we won't be going anywhere near there, near that ledge?" Chris asked. He was sitting on a bench next to Katy, who had been quieter since they left, listening to the strange sounds of the sub, the echoes of the pulsing engines.

"I certainly hope not," Chooth nodded.

Chris looked back toward the window. Something long and sinuous, twisting in the current, moved through the water, waving in a rhythmic pattern. As it moved closer, coming more and more into focus, Chris could see that it had long fins like fans that splayed out from its back and scales that reflected the sunlight in shades of blue and green.

"What is that?" Chris asked, realizing as it approached just how large the creature was, five or six times longer than the sub. He backed away from the glass when its mouth opened to reveal lengthy, jagged teeth, the stuff of nightmares.

Katy looked up at the sound of his voice, waiting to hear more.

Chooth stood and stared out. "Oh, that's a sea dragon. Kind of a small one too."

Chris looked at Chooth as the thing continued toward them, passing over the top of the sub, rocking it, forcing everyone to hold on. Chris watched Cormack struggle with the controls. He couldn't see his face, but he could tell the young prince's shoulders were tight as the sub bucked in the creature's wake. Chris helped Katy hold on, then turned his attention back to the ocean, searching for the creature, but it was empty. "Small?" he asked.

"Oh yes," Chooth said. "An adult can get up to forty meters long."

"Are they dangerous?"

"Not to me, but you might want to steer clear," Chooth answered. "Don't worry though. You won't be getting out of the sub till we're in the city. Dangerous creatures hardly ever go there."

"Great," Chris said. Up till that moment he hadn't thought about the fact that he'd have to get out. He pulled at the suit he wore. It would keep him warm, but it offered no protection against predators. "Will we have weapons or anything?"

Cormack looked back over his shoulder. "You can bring a knife just in case, but larger weapons are illegal inside the city limits. The sub isn't even allowed defensive hardware. Chooth may have played it off, but we're lucky that sea dragon wasn't more interested in us."

Chooth waved his hand dismissively. "It was only a harmless baby." He pointed to the window. "And we're almost there."

Chris turned and searched where Chooth was pointing. He wasn't sure what he was expecting a Grannusian city to look like, maybe like Atlantis from the movies with tall towers and minarets. This was nothing like those places. It was closer to a bowl of rock candy sunk deep into the ocean floor.

Crevasses, deep cuts that ran along the sandy bottom of the ocean surrounded the city. Their edges were shiny and pink as if the sand had been melted and turned to glass. They glowed softly with openings tunneled into the ocean floor, all running to the center, to the main bowl that was lined with more of the glass. It twisted and turned, creating elaborate structures with few edges. Everything flowed and bloomed with wild and vibrant color, looking more like life forms than buildings. In places, the surface was fuzzy. Chris had to wait till they were closer to see that those were plants, flowers and leaves, waving in the currents.

Chris was in awe, looking out. He tried describing it to Katy, but he was being careful, not wanting to make her feel bad. He didn't tell her every detail of the amazing colors and shapes. When his words failed him, he realized everyone else was quiet. Chooth and Cormack were looking out the front of the sub, giving each other a nervous glance. Something was wrong.

Again, much like the sea dragon, Chris couldn't understand the size of the place until they were closer. He thought of the few times he'd flown into a major city like Boston or New York. The way buildings could go from concepts to toy-like structures, to being so large that they made you feel small and insignificant. By the time he saw those plants, which were massive themselves, he could no longer distinguish the structures. The twisting glass blurred together, clinging to the walls of the bowl as the sub descended toward one of the few open spots, where white sand was still visible.

The sub came down just above the empty spot, and Chris heard something fall out of the bottom. "Anchor's away," Cormack said in a flat, nervous voice.

Chooth was looking out the window. His whole body was tense as he said, "This is so strange."

Chris looked at the structures which were like nothing he'd ever seen, nodding his head and agreeing.

"Yeah, it's amazing!"

Chooth turned and for a moment Chris thought he was going to attack him.

"No Chris. You don't understand. They're all gone, the Grannus aren't here." Cormack pointed out the window. "I've never seen Twilight so empty."

"Oh," Chris said feeling silly.

"This was home to three hundred thousand of Chooth's people. It was their most populated and oldest settlement. It was constantly alive," Cormack continued as he went to a gear locker. He took out a helmet and a vest with tanks attached to the back of it. He handed them to Chris. Then he reached back in and took out a knife in a sheath. Next, he pulled out a pair of fins.

Chooth said sadly, "There's only death here now." His whole body rippled, like he was about to fall apart.

"I'm so sorry Chooth," Katy said as she stood and started toward the Grannusian's voice.

Cormack went to him and laid a hand on the smooth surface of his head while guiding Katy forward. "We'll do everything we can to find them."

Chooth pushed the prince away and nearly knocked Katy over as he said, "It won't be enough." He turned and rushed to the hatch in the back of the sub. The Grannusian hurried, turning the wheel, popping it open. Chris nearly panicked, expecting water to come rushing in. But it stayed where it was, a flat surface inside the airlock. Chooth jumped in, falling into his separate parts as he touched the water.

Hugging the gear he was handed, Chris realized he was holding his breath. Cormack helped steady Katy then glanced at Chris. "He'll be alright. Get your stuff on."

"Okay," Chris said while watching Cormack sit Katy down. "I know he's upset, but Chooth almost seems like a different person since we've been here," Katy said. Cormack went back to the lockers and took out more diving gear.

He said over his shoulder, "I've noticed it too," he shook his head. "It'll be better when we can get some answers, I'm sure." In short order the prince had everything but the fins on. Then he came over and helped Chris struggle with the equipment. After dropping a surprisingly heavy helmet over Chris's head, they started to the back of the sub. Chris looked at the hatch, at the pool of water. "How's it staying out," he asked.

Cormack turned back, touching a button on his helmet. "What?" Chris heard the prince's voice echo in his helmet.

"How's the water stay out?" Chris pointing to the pool.

"Pressure," Cormack answered. "Have you ever held a cup under water, upside down. This is the same idea."

"Yeah, but what if someone tips the cup?" Chris asked glancing back at Katy, who'd be staying behind. He could tell that she was listening to them through the sub's speaker.

"We're anchored and buoyed. It'll be alright." Cormack said sitting down to pull on his fins, then disappearing down into the water.

Chris keyed up his mic. "We'll be right back, Katy," he said as he sat down at the edge of the pool. Katy nodded while Chris struggled to pull on the fins.

"Stupid things . . . um, yeah right back," he repeated, feeling like his foot was still half out as he dropped into the water.

The weight of his vest pulled him down as the ocean closed around him. The cold wasn't nearly as shocking as the feel of sudden pressure enveloping him from all sides. He kicked his feet as he sunk, noticing that he was breathing way too fast and one flipper floated up past his face. Looking down, he saw his naked foot, then cursed as he tried to grab it. He kicked off from the bottom and nearly rammed his head into the sub's belly.

"Chris, relax," Cormack's voice came over the radio. He had retrieved the fin and was swimming down Chris's leg to put it back on. The prince tightened it on his foot. "Are you going to be alright?" Cormack asked.

Chris nodded and smiled at his next thought. 'Now I got something in common with Cinderella.' Then he keyed his mic. "Yeah, I think so."

"Use the fins slowly, long kicks, okay? Try to slow your breathing down too. Just stay calm, okay?"

"Okay," Chris said, giving Cormack a thumbs up. He looked around at the city and asked. "Where's Chooth?"

"He went this way," Cormack said as he kicked slowly, moving at a leisurely pace. Chris followed him, consciously trying to take long, deep breaths.

"We aren't far from Eir's lab," Cormack said, looking to make sure Chris was with him. The boy from Earth was watching the subtle glow dancing on the surface of the glass walls. Everything was bright and clear till Chris followed Cormack into an opening.

It was a soft spot in the glass that was marked by a different shade of green. Cormack pushed on it, then disappeared inside. Chris followed and found himself in a tunnel that was less than a meter across. The sunlight was gone and they were left with only the light from their helmets. Chris felt like he was traveling through a vein. More soft valves were ahead as they turned and traveled down the tight space. Eventually they came out into a larger chamber.

It was impossible to tell how big the room was since it was still in darkness. Chris shined his beam over the curved walls, trying to figure out where they were, then swam closer to one of them as he followed Cormack down into the lab.

Feeling like he was sinking into a hole, he couldn't sense a floor below him, but as he and Cormack descended, he noticed shelves along the way with sample tanks and screens displaying information covered in lines of a foreign language. Slowly, as they passed, the displays came to life. Growing inside the tanks, he saw dark green plants with flowing stalks that twisted up into rainbow-colored seed pods woven together like beads. Those same plants were magnified on some of the displays.

Other monitors came to life as something else moved around the room, something that wasn't Cormack. Chris could sense it in the water, swimming with them but much faster in the darkness.

He tried to see what it was, but only saw quickly moving shadows above and below him. He noticed the currents running through the room change as the water was stirred. Chris reached out for one of the shelves, pulling himself closer to the wall, and turned, putting his back to it.

He looked at Cormack, who was still descending and saw the things come closer. Several dark objects rushed toward the prince while more poured down from above. They went past Chris, joining the larger group, coming together next to Cormack, forming a school.

Worried, Chris stared at the light on Cormack's helmet. He was fumbling to key up his mic and warn the prince, but then he saw what was at the head of the school. It was an eel-like fish, Chooth out in the water.

He'd spread himself out searching the whole space. Chris let go of the shelf and dropped down to the others just as Cormack was holding a device out to Chooth. A microphone. Its display showed a spike in activity, then Chris heard Chooth's voice come over his helmet's speaker. "It's in the food supply, in the kelp we eat. Eir found it. According to her notes she was going out to the farms to investigate." Chooth's voice was different, deeper and slower as the machine translated his words through the water.

"Are there any lights in here?" Chris asked, keying up his mic.

The eel head and Cormack both turned to look at him as Cormack answered. "The Grannus can see in the dark. They don't bother with them," he explained.

"Oh, so what do we do now?"

"If Eir went to the kelp fields, then we should follow her," Cormack said.

"I've got some more to look into here, and I can probably do it faster on my own. Besides—" Chooth swam behind Chris, looking at his bottle. "Chris has sucked down most of his tank. You two should probably get back to the sub."

Cormack nodded. "We'll meet you back there. Come on Chris."

Chris's looked down, reading the gauge on his vest, twenty percent. He thought about how long it'd taken them to get here, wondering if he'd have enough to make it back. He started to hurry toward the ceiling and the entrance, but then he heard Cormack's voice. "Slow it down Chris. You're going to use more air if you panic."

'Okay, okay,' Chris thought, consciously slowing his legs down. Then Cormack came up next to him and pressed a button on the vest, which became instantly lighter as sand dropped out in a stream. He took Chris's arm and guided him back out into the vein-like tunnels. Chris felt like it took forever for them to get outside in the sunlit ocean again. They swam toward that first wall and came in sight of the sub.

Chris wanted to glance back down at his gauge, but his eyes were drawn ahead toward their craft. Something was wrong with it. It was listing to one side, no longer level with the ground. Chris thought about what Cormack had said. That the water stayed out using pressure like a cup. Chris stared at the little sub, knowing that if it had tipped, water would rush in. He just didn't know how much.

Thinking about Katy, he started swimming hard across the open distance. Cormack was with him, both hurrying over the white, sandy field. That's when a shadow passed over them. Something large was swimming above and it was getting closer. He

looked up and saw it. The sea dragon had followed
them.

Chapter 23

Amita nodded to the guards as she exited the Tamerlane chambers. Over the past couple weeks, they'd gotten used to her leaving in the middle of the night. They never asked her where she was going or what she was doing. She assumed they were reporting it back to Maeven, but that didn't matter. As long as the princess stayed quiet, not telling the monks or Alex and Ben.

Amita didn't want the boys giving her a hard time, saying it was too dangerous or trying to stop her. She had agreed with Alex's decision to take Maeven's offer. It'd been smart, moving in with the Tamerlanes. They needed allies, the more powerful the better, but Amita suspected he had ulterior motives. Alex seemed all too content to slide into a life here, playing house with a princess. It annoyed Amita, almost as much as the way he'd taken on this sort of dad vibe, trying to protect her and Ben. Amita already had a dad and he was back on Earth.

Then there was Ben. He pursued whatever interested him in the moment and currently that was Tara. He followed her around like a puppy dog. Not to mention, the ghosts and the execution seemed to have freaked him out. To Amita those things only added to her desire to get home, back to her parents, but also to understand this place.

There were secrets on Nalanda Station, things the monks didn't want to know. They choose ignorance on a daily basis, treating this place like it was electricity, too dangerous to touch. Amita couldn't accept their limitations, not while there were still problems to solve.

During the night cycle, when the monks weren't around, was the best time for exploring. Andavarri's warning about the ghost didn't frighten her. She wandered through the main halls and classrooms, finding observation bays with heavy glass windows and libraries of folded manuscripts written in alien languages. Logs were stored in a data base that only the monks were supposed to know about. It tracked visits by the Æesir throughout the system, naming those who their gods had destroyed. The monks logged the murders of the nobles as if keeping a score card. Occasionally there'd be a note, wondering about why some duke or chieftain had been struck down.

Amita forced her way into locked rooms. Apparently, the monks thought the fear of the Æesir was enough that they could get away with using simple locks. It didn't take much for Amita to pick them, using tools she'd borrowed from maintenance. She managed to wake human and alien machines, pulling up displays that hadn't been touched in years and trying to decode entries that'd become corrupted with age. She read about the early explorers of the void space and those who'd been foolish enough to touch down on Einherjar, the dead world. Things like the ghosts, horrible creatures, some solid and some more ethereal had swarmed over the explorers, dragging every living person away, never to be seen again. Despite this, new expeditions were sent to that dead moon, seeking the weapons of a lost race. The Hunters, like the one that came to Earth, were made from a techno-virus that could turn a victim into a killing machine.

Amita read everything she could on Tairnish, the home of the Long-Wolves. Nothing about the crystals they used to control the Fire Golems was directly mentioned in the general files of the crystals they used to control the Fire Golems, but she did find something on a material dug up from their planet, found in the deepest mines, that sounded a lot like what the diamond vessel was made from.

Tairnish was an interesting place. There were hints of early human colonies being established, long before people were anywhere else in the system. Amita found accounts of people surviving on that harsh world, forced to adapt through genetic manipulation, but little was said about how they got there.

A rescue effort was made by some power, and human refugees were deposited on the moon, like orphaned children. She couldn't find out where they came from though, and the story was nearly a thousand years old. She couldn't tell if anyone had ever tried to learn more. The information was missing, either destroyed or forgotten and corrupted.

Each time she went out, Amita would pass Fire Golems in the hall. They stayed quiet, never waking or trying to stop her. The monk's embargo on knowledge had made information a valuable commodity. Amita shared it with a few conspirators, mainly Regin, but Tara had also taken to asking her questions, keeping the princess informed.

Amita wasn't sure how much filtered out to Andavarri, but she sensed that there wasn't much the Long-Wolf didn't know. She'd give Amita sly glances after class, nodding to her in the morning when she passed some new secret to the others.

Amita didn't like the Long-Wolf, but given a chance, she'd love to pick Andavarri's brain on a few things. She was trying to put together a picture to understand how people came to Tairnish. But every time she'd cornered the Long-Wolf and started asking about her moon, Andavarri sent her away, often rudely.

One time, when she brought up the crystal material, Andavarri had seemed ready to attack her. Long-Wolves had sharp teeth and Andavarri had shown all of them to Amita that day.

Still, in the nearly three weeks she'd been out exploring, Amita found little that compared to what she'd seen in the lighthouse that night with Ben. Those machines appeared more advanced and ancient than anything she'd found anywhere on the station. She'd been thinking about it all this time.

Leaving the Tamerlane chambers in the deepest part of the night cycle with one destination in mind, Amita pulled the cloak she had borrowed from Tara tight over herself, trying to disappear into the walls. Her monitor was glowing softly but she turned it toward herself and only checked it when she wasn't sure which way to go. She was attempting to follow the passages that she and Ben had taken that first night. Coming out into the long hallway where they'd first seen that spreading darkness, where they'd seen the ghost, she waited a moment wondering if she needed to worry. Part of her wanted to see it again, another part thought she was insane.

In all her wandering over the past few weeks, the phenomena hadn't repeated. She thought, maybe she'd heard the ghosts a few times, but she couldn't be sure. That metal like swishing of blades dragging across the floor was vivid in her memory, but there were many sounds in the ancient space station. Telling one from another in rooms left empty and in hallways no one ever travelled was impossible. The rumbling and cracking of walls, the whirl of machines, pipes hissing and air rushing with the low humming of energy fields filled her ears. Often, she thought she felt their presence, watching her from the shadows, but she found nothing when she turned to look.

Even tonight as she came to the stairs, she felt she wasn't alone. Going up was more like climbing than walking because of the height of the steps. She was trying to be as quiet as possible. She assumed the lighthouse was empty at night, but she couldn't be sure.

A few steps more and she stopped and listened, waiting to see if she heard voices or footsteps above. She thought of Andavarri's warning after the execution. It, more than anything else, had kept her from this place.

There was no secret to the rules of Nalanda Station. Kavaris Dell was the ultimate authority and he decreed that no student should enter the lighthouse or tamper with the machinery there. Only teachers and monks could enter and even then, it had to be with expressed permission. The charter that governed Nalanda stated, 'To break the laws of the Kavaris, servant of the Æesir, is to court the strictest penalty.' Amita had read that before the execution, but she hadn't understood how serious it was till after she watched Vyktor die.

Amita didn't hear anything from the lighthouse, only the whirl of machines. She started climbing again, taking the last step, and looked into the room. Her eyes were immediately drawn to the glass dome and to the gas giant beyond it. The planet was a shadowy form. Little of its tangerine surface reflected the light from the system's twin suns. Even here on the dark side of the planet, the surface was alive. Crackles of energy exploded beneath the clouds of massive storms, lancing across the globe and disappearing.

Amita didn't bring her eyes down from the dome till she heard a sound. There was a familiar shuffling, sharp metal being dragged across the stone floor. Her heart stopped as she looked across the room. She wasn't alone.

Standing opposite the raised platform, where most of the equipment was set, she saw an ashen grey phantom. A ghost. There was no telltale pool of darkness around it, in fact the ancient machines of Nalanda seemed more active near the creature. There were lights that blazed sharply, pinpoints of shocking brightness on the displays.

The creature's horrible head turned toward her and the black dots of its eyes focused on her from beneath its thickened forehead ridge. It shimmered in the light from the machines, standing still, but seeming to wave and sway, slightly out of phase with reality.

Amita stood motionless, wondering if she'd be able to back down the stairs or if the thing would chase her. It started to move, but instead of coming toward her, it turned away toward the wall. It reached one bladed arm out, touched the surface and pushed its arm through. It took another step forward. The wall swallowed its shoulders and legs and, in an instant, the whole thing had disappeared.

Letting out a long breath, Amita dropped her hands to her knees and looked at the machines on the platform. They were slowly turning back off. She took a step forward, going further into the room. 'I came here for a reason. I've risked this much,' she thought, knowing it'd be safer to turn and run.

The stairs that led to the platform were around the corner. Amita considered them for a moment, stared at the ancient technology, but for some reason she stayed back. Slowly, her steps carried her to the wall where the ghost had gone. A part of Amita's brain screamed at her, telling her not too, but she went forward anyway. There was something about that wall. The first thing she noticed was that it wasn't solid stone like most of the station. The wall was made from separate pieces of rock, piled high with mortar in between. She'd seen other places like this that'd been changed or sealed off throughout the station. Still, it suggested that there was something behind it.

Amita went and held her hand just above the stone. It was the very spot the ghost had gone through. She hesitated only for a second, picturing the creature's spectral form coming back out and grabbing her. She closed her eyes as she lowered her palm.

The wall was cold and unmoving. Nothing reached out to take her. She ran her fingers over the rocks, poking and trying to wiggle a few. She came on one that was looser than the others, high up over her head. Amita looked around for anything to stand on and found a rickety wooden chair. It looked like the kind of simple, low tech thing that the monks would love. She set it below the spot, climbed up, and started to work the stone loose, pushing and pulling at the mortar, chipping away at it with a pointed tool she'd found near one of the computer monitors.

The rock, which was a foot wide and only a few inches tall, came loose. From there it was easy to chip away another and another, making an opening large enough for her to climb through.

Amita pulled herself up into the tight opening with her monitor in front of her. A few rocks bulged into the short passage, but she pushed her head and arms forward, squeezing, getting close to the other side. She could sense an open space, the smell of stale air. Holding the monitor out with a single hand and using the screen to shine light from side to side, she found a room. No ghost waited for her, but the space was far from empty.

A row of pillars much like the one on the dais, black onyx with gold inlay, stood before a massive window. She shined the light on the far wall and saw a doorway with stairs going down. 'Now how do you get there?' She asked herself.

She pulled back from the opening, getting ready to knock the last few stones out of her way and drop to the floor, but as she did, the pillars in the room ahead of her came to life calling her attention back. Lights sparked on their surfaces, welcoming her. Amita glanced at the floor. It'd be a bit of a drop. She pointed the light down, seeing how dust had collected there over the years. It was thick and mainly undisturbed except for a few spots where she saw something that reminded her of the desert back on Earth.

She remembered the day they'd gone out to Joseph Bizahalone's ranch, when they followed the creature that would turn out to be her friend Tearmai, into the slot canyon. They'd followed the Drake's footprints for miles so it was easy for her to remember what they looked like.

She stared at the footsteps in the dusty floor and recognized them. They were the same, large with three toes and long narrow points where his claws had touched the ground. Tearmai had been in this room.

'There must be answers here,' Amita thought as she pushed further into the hole. The thrill she felt as she pictured Tearmai and Brash together, leaning over these machines made her work all the harder, wiggling and twisting forward.

She took the tool in her hand, picking at the mortar, tapping away the last pieces. The rocks fell, hitting the floor, but as they settled, she heard a noise behind her. She was too far in to turn around and look back, but she was sure it had to be Andavarri. 'She's probably curious about what I found.' Hands suddenly gripped Amita's ankles. Taking her firmly, they pulled back. She tried to stop herself, tried to hold onto the rocks but it was no use.

Jerked out of the opening, without enough time to even scream, she fell hard on the ground. The impact forced the air from her lungs and left her head feeling swimmy. She looked up, trying to understand who did this to her. It wasn't Andavarri, but a red-robed Kavaris monk with three others. They didn't look happy.

Chapter 24

The long, sinuous shadow of the sea dragon moved over the white sand, growing larger above Chris. He could see its scales reflecting the strange light of the city and its eyes blazing as they turned on him. Its mouth opened as it dove deeper, coming at him. Cormack's voice shouted over the microphone in Chris's helmet. "Go! I'll distract it."

He'd felt frozen until that moment, watching the creature move slowly at first then banking and speeding down like an approaching train. Cormack's voice broke through and Chris kicked as hard as he could, reaching and pulling with his arms toward the sub, trying to move through the water as swiftly as possible with hurried and awkward strokes. He looked back and saw Cormack diving for the edge of the city.

The prince stopped for a moment, waving up to the monster as it descended toward the bottom. The sea dragon's mouth was a deep and dark cave and its wings were pulled back tight to its sides as it dove on him. Cormack waited till it was uncomfortably close, then ducked, disappearing into one of the Grannusian doorways. With scales shimmering, the creature turned away just before smashing into the glass walls. It spread its wing-like fins and started to rise away from the curving barriers, but then turned, twisting sharply toward the sub.

Chris was just below the little craft. He looked up at the vehicle's hatch and kicked off from the bottom, rocketing toward the opening, certain he'd be snatched at any moment. Because the sub was no longer parallel to the sandy bottom, the hatch was turned at an angle as well. His hands closed on the metal lip and he started pulling himself in, desperate to get his legs out of the water, expecting to feel teeth pull him away with every labored breath. Getting his chest over he flopped forward to the floor, spilling in, immediately feeling heavier as he slid across the wet surface. A foot of water had seeped in through the hatch and the weight of Chris's helmet sent him clumsily splashing forward into it. He tripped into the deepest part of the uneven cabin landing in a corner where the water had collected.

Trying to pull himself up, he grabbed the wall. His visor was fogging up, but he could tell someone was standing in front of him. He touched the mic button. "Katy, are you alright?" He could hear his voice echoing through the sub's radio system.

"Chris—" Katy started to say, but she was cut off.

Something solid tapped on the front of his helmet as someone ordered, "Take it off." Chris didn't recognize the voice.

He tried to do as he was told, but he struggled with the clasps that held it in place, banging at the little metal fasteners. As the air he was breathing became thinner the last clamp finally popped loose. He shoved the helmet off, letting it fall into the water. Then he sucked in a deep breath and looked around for Katy, but his attention was immediately drawn to the barbed point of a short spear gun directed at his head.

A girl was holding it. She wore a tight-fitting top, like his dive suit, but hers was cut to expose her back and sides. Her dark eyes were glaring at him. They were nearly black and larger than they should've been. Her nose looked too small for her face and her skin was a faded grey.

Despite her strangeness, she would have been attractive if she weren't pointing a weapon at Chris. "Who are you? What clan are you from?" she asked sharply.

Chris glanced past her toward Katy, whose hands were tied. She was wet and shivering.

"Answer me air-breather," the girl demanded.

Chris stared at her. His body was cold and his muscles were tired from swimming. That didn't matter though, not with his adrenalin still pumping. His temper turned hot. Chris didn't like being pushed around. He hurried to stand, intending to rush her, but his oxygen starved body moved too slow. His attempt to attack became a clumsy effort to get to his feet. He stood for a second, swayed, then the girl struck him, smashing him on the head with the butt of her gun.

"I didn't tell you to get up." She shook her head as he fell back, splashing near the hatch while Cormack came up from below. Chris rolled, trying to get out of the way. The prince got to his feet and took his helmet off while Chris leaned against the bulkhead, coughing.

The gun was turned toward the new arrival. Cormack's eyes met the girl's, then she said, "The prince of the Sidhe, well, isn't this a surprise. Come to check on your people's handy work?"

"Naiathne," Cormack acknowledged her before looking at Katy. "Is that really necessary?" He motioned to the bindings on Katy's hands.

"You tell me. In fact, you can tell me why you're here while you tie up your fat friend there." Naiathne handed Cormack green binding cords.

Chris realized she was talking about him. 'Just another reason not to like her,' he thought, while rubbing his head where she'd hit him. Cormack took the bindings. "You want to make some introductions?" Chris asked when he eventually held up his hands to be tied.

"Yeah. This is Naiathne," Cormack said pointing to her. "A year ago, you would've met her at Nalanda Station, she even had a room in the Sidhe chambers, but then she was kicked out."

"I left on my own," Naiathne said in defense. "Our noble family and their friends started making volcanos in the ocean I call home. Your people had to be stopped."

"Yeah, that's why you left. It had nothing to do with your knack for ticking off every person you met. It was all a joke to you," Cormack shot back.

"I'm not one of your people," she growled. Chris was wondering if she was going to pull the trigger, firing that little spear through Cormack's heart.

"How can you say that, when you're my damn sister?" Cormack yelled, standing up.

"Wait, what?" Katy asked. She'd been listening quietly.

"Naiathne is my younger sister," Cormack explained.

"But why does she—" Chris started to ask.

Naiathne interrupted, "Look like this?" She pointed to her face, then to her sides where deep cuts ran along her rib cage. Chris stared at them, noticing how they seemed to move. It took him a moment to realize they were gills.

"Look like what?" Katy asked.

"She's a fish person," Chris explained.

"Screw you fat boy," Naiathne sneered.

Cormack turned back to Chris, helping him sit up on the floor as he explained, "A long time before the Æesir came, resources on this world were tight. There were those who believed humans needed to evolve, needed to change to fit the environment. There's very little land on Grannus, but there's plenty of ocean. So, these people, with the help of the Grannusians, altered their genome. They engineered themselves to survive in the water." He motioned toward Naiathne. "The Æesir no longer allow it, but the people who already existed are still around and the traits sometimes come out randomly in certain bloodlines."

"A happy little surprise," Naiathne said bitterly. "Traditionally, people like me, Naiads we're called, are murdered in our cribs, but my father was soft. He kept me alive. Despite our mother's wishes. He gave me back to the ocean."

Chris wanted to know more, but his attention was called to the large glass porthole at the front of the sub where he saw something rushing toward him. The sea dragon had banked around and was coming back. He felt it pass them with the speed of a subway train, causing their vehicle to buck and shake.

"Are you responsible for that thing too?" Cormack asked.

Naiathne leaned toward the porthole and looked out. "I've been training him, but he can still be a bit unruly." She turned back to Chris, "You're lucky you got away. He was probably going to eat you. Plenty of calories." Then she ordered Cormack while motioning with the gun, "Take the controls."

"Why, where are we going?" Cormack asked.

"To the colony. There are people there that will be interested in hearing why you're here. It's funny, but since the poisoning started, nobles have been scarce below the surface." She leaned down and checked Chris's bindings. Her fingers were icy cold.

"We're here with Chooth, looking for Eir," Cormack's eyes widened as he shook his head. "We want to help."

"I'm sure you do." Naiathne said, obviously not believing him.

"It's true," Katy said. "I tried telling you before, we're looking for—"

"Just shut it!" Naiathne snapped at her. "I've heard enough human lies over my life. You should all take note, down here things are more honest. We'll get to the truth and we'll do it back at the colony."

Cormack got up and went to the controls.

"What about Chooth?" Chris asked from the floor as he heard the anchors pulling up.

"He knows the way," Naiathne answered.

"Yeah but I don't," Cormack said.

"Head due west toward the outer ledge of the Abysmal Shelf," Naiathne ordered.

Cormack looked back at her. "You can't be serious."

"What's the matter, big brother? Your people have wanted to know where the colony is for years; how the Naiads kept it secret. Now you know. We've stayed safe perched at the edge of the deepest part of the ocean, out where the monsters are. Now set us full ahead."

Cormack set the course and worked the controls, righting the sub and touching a button to close the hatch. After he turned on pumps to expel the flood water, the inside was still damp and cold, but it was better than it had been. Naiathne told Chris to sit on a bench. She never took the gun off him as she searched for weapons, finding the dive knife and tucking it in her belt. She searched Katy as well, having her stand and move back to where Chris was. They sat next to each other and Chris could feel Katy shivering. Their wetsuits kept most of their body's warmth in which was good as the heaters in the sub hadn't caught up.

"It'll be alright," Chris said to Katy.

"I doubt it," Katy said back. "I doubt anything will be alright again. I keep waiting to wake-up. Being kidnapped by a fish person, it just seems like one more thing."

"Yeah, I know," Chris said, looking at his hands. He reached over and took Katy's. Then she leaned against him. "It could be worse. I mean I escaped

237

being eaten, so I guess things aren't all bad," Chris said, making Katy laugh.

"I suppose so," she agreed.

The sub continued its course for hours, traveling along the ocean bottom. Chris, of course, had no idea how fast they were going or in what direction, but outside he could see the water getting darker. He assumed it was because the sun was setting. The white sand was giving way to grey shadows and gloom, but it wasn't just the darkening water. Rocky islands were starting to rise from the ocean floor as they approached the ledge. Occasionally, Chris caught a glimpse of the sea dragon swimming next to them, keeping pace with its mistress.

Standing behind Cormack the entire way, Naiathne never sat. Her brother tried making conversation, tried asking how she was doing, but Naiathne's stern expression never broke. She was one of the few people Chris had ever seen that Cormack's charm didn't work on. She'd give him course corrections, telling him to bring the sub over this far or that far. Eventually she ordered, "Drop to quarter speed and come about three degrees to port. We're close." She glanced around at the inside of the sub, listening to the sound of the engines as they slowed. "Still pretty damn noisy," she muttered.

She looked at the controls, then glanced out the porthole. "We're over the edge. Take us down seventy-five meters and cut your propulsion." Her voice was tense.

Chris stood and went to the closest porthole and looked down. The white sand was gone. Below them was only darkness going on forever. Naiathne stared daggers at him but didn't tell him to sit back down. Chris looked toward the other porthole and saw a sheer rock wall passing next to them. Uneven dangerous looking ledges jutted out, so Cormack moved them a little further away, firing the engines up for a moment.

"What are you doing?" Naiathne demanded sharply as she heard the engines kick on. "We need to be quiet." She reached over and killed them. But it was too late. Something had heard.

Chris was the first to see it a distant light down below, out a little from the cliffs, like a fire in the deepest part of the ocean. It cast out in blooms, rolling and unfolding. "What is that?" Chris asked.

Naiathne was busy leaning over the consul, reading the controls. "Dive faster," she said to Cormack.

He stood to look out the forward porthole. "That'll bring us closer to it."

"I know. That's why it's there. It's been hunting near the colony. Just dive, we've got to beat it to the opening. It's too late to run."

Chris watched the thing. Massive, it looked like a web of light spreading out as a many pointed star. It was growing larger and larger as it moved toward the cliff wall. In a moment, he could see that they would be trapped between the rock wall and this creature. Horrible things moved across its surface, long appendages that waved and twisted out toward them hungrily. It was like a fishing net come to life with wormy mouths. The living webbing, the glowing part, was sort of beautiful, but the tentacles with their snapping teeth were terrifying.

One slammed into the sub. Roughly the thickness of an oak tree, it hit just as hard, twisting the sub around. The teeth tried to take a bite out of the sub but it couldn't get purchase. It pulled back while another launched itself at them.

"There, there's the opening!" Naiathne pointed to a cave in the rock face. She didn't have to tell Cormack to head toward it. He fired up the engines and put them into a nosedive, slamming the throttle forward. It felt like a race, like they had a chance, but then they were hit again, which sent the sub into a tailspin. Another hit, then another hit, till they didn't know which way was up. Then the sub slammed into the rock face. The motors whined but it didn't move. They were being pushed into the wall and were surrounded by the glow from the monster.

With their hands still tied behind their backs, Chris and Katy tried to stand. They'd been thrown around, landing on top of each other more than once. Chris saw the porthole at the front of the sub begin to crack. Then he saw the one next to him splinter as well.

"I'm opening the hatch," Cormack yelled, already reaching for the controls. "We've got to swim!"

"What?" Katy screamed, reaching out for anything to hold on to.

Chris felt Naiathne grab his arm. He was looking up at the porthole again, seeing one of those awful mouths attempting to swallow the whole thing. The light from the sub shone down into a mouth full of undulating teeth that went far back into the tunnel-like orifice.

Naiathne handed him a small, floppy, living thing. "Put it in your mouth, it'll help you breathe," she yelled in his ear as the hatch opened and ocean water came pouring in. Very quickly she cut his hands free, then Katy's. He took the thing from her, but rather than putting it in his own mouth he slammed it into Katy's. "This will help you breathe," he said as she tried to spit it out. Chris held it in her mouth, till she stopped fighting.

They were upside down. Cormack had to drop from the front of the sub down into the water, nearly landing on their heads. Katy was making muffled sounds as Cormack and Naiathne shoved her and Chris out the hatch while Chris did his best to take a mouthful of air into his lungs.

Because there was so much light from the creature, he could see far clearer than he wanted to. The opening that Naiathne had been aiming for was just past a forest of the creature's seeking arms. Chris swam anyway, holding Katy's hand, knowing there was little chance of making it through.

The mouths seemed to sense them. The writhing, wiggling forest turned toward them, pulling back to strike. The mouths were open. Chris could feel Cormack swimming down, helping him guide Katy. He could feel Naiathne grabbing his arm. In a moment they'd be torn apart and they all seemed to want one more human touch before they became lunch.

241

Something rocketed past them. The sea dragon lunged into the thickest group of tentacles with its mouth open, driving its long fangs into the fleshy worms. He viciously tore at them, filling the water with blood and gore, opening a passage for the group.

They swam down, heading for the opening, while the sea dragon stayed behind guarding their backs. Before going into the cave Chris looked back. The sea dragon's tail had been caught by the worms. It turned to pull them off, but more came and sunk into the dragon's neck. Very quickly the battle turned one-sided as more of the stalks came forward, closing in on the creature. It struggled and twisted, but the dragon couldn't fight those numbers. Stalks closed in from all sides, devouring the sea dragon.

The group disappeared into the cave entrance with the glow from the monster lighting their way. Chris looked ahead, then at Katy with the fleshy creature jammed over her mouth. His lungs burned. He wasn't sure how much longer he could hold his breath. Already the temptation to open his mouth was overpowering. His whole body was screaming, 'just take a breath, you need to breathe!' But of course he was underwater. He began to flail a little, still trying to stay with the others and swim forward.

The girl Naiathne looked back at him. She shook her head, then came over and placed her mouth on Chris's. He felt air forced into his lungs, one long sustained breath, then another. He started to relax.

Naiathne pulled back, but she continued to swim for both of them kicking with webbed feet, going deeper into the cave.

Chapter 25

Maeven grabbed Alex's arm. "You need to wake up," she said, shaking him.

Alex looked at her, confused. He'd been in her chambers earlier, but he'd left and slept in his own room, as he did each night. There was a 'sense of propriety that had to be maintained,' she insisted, even though the two of them had become close over the past few weeks. The other nobles snickered about it and whispered, but no one was foolish enough to talk openly of their relationship.

He rubbed his eyes and sat up, "What's the matter?" he asked. He was surprised to see her in his room. She'd only come a few times. Usually, she preferred to enjoy Alex's company in her own chambers. Even just waking up, Alex was in awe of her. He felt himself stirred just looking at her, but when he saw the concern on her face, he cleared his head focusing on what she was saying.

"It's your friend, the girl Amita, she's been arrested. The monks have detained her," Maeven said in a hurried voice.

Grabbing his clothes, Alex moved to the edge of the bed. "What, why?"

It took Maeven a moment to answer. She hadn't told Alex what Amita was up to. "I don't know what she's looking for, but she's been going out almost nightly. They found her in a forbidden area." Maeven paused for a moment watching him dress. "It's one of the worst crimes, going to those secret places."

Alex heard the concern in her voice. Maeven didn't show much emotion around others, but in front of him she'd started to let her guard down.

"Will they treat her like Vyktor?" he asked, remembering the way the big kid's eyes had looked as the monks opened the doors to space.

Maeven looked at the floor. "I don't know, maybe. They've given your group more leeway than most, but—" Her eyes came back up. "I can give her sanctuary here. If you can get her, I can keep her safe."

Alex nodded and picked up his monitor. "Show me where they're keeping her." He pointed to the map.

Maeven leaned forward, highlighting an area. It wasn't far from their old quarters, but it was deeper into the monk's territory, down through darkened corridors. Alex turned to go, but Maeven grabbed his arm first and pulled him back. "Be careful," she said, kissing him on the cheek. The kiss moved around to his mouth.

When she pushed him away, it took Alex another moment to clear his head. Alex wasn't someone given to falling. He had girlfriends back on Earth, but he'd always been so busy, focused on sports and trying to get into Annapolis. Even here, he'd tried to remain motivated, thinking about protecting his people, putting them in a position that was sound, but he had to admit it, Maeven had him. She was impossible to resist.

Alex didn't wonder how the princess knew about the arrest. Even at this late hour well into the night cycle, Maeven had her spies. They sought favor with her father through her. If they hadn't come with the news about Amita, she would've been cross. And no one at the school seemed willing to upset her. It was enough to worry him when he thought about the future.

He shook his head trying to clear his thoughts as he passed a few Fire Golems. None of them stirred, even the four that marked the entrance to the monk's area remained still, guarding an otherwise unremarkable passage.

Alex didn't think he'd have to worry about them. Their size and darkened shape may have given him pause, but he knew they weren't under the monk's control. Andavarri was their master. Alex wasn't sure if she controlled all of them, or if the other Long-Wolfs shared a connection too, but he knew Andavarri's loyalty, for what it was worth, was to Maeven. He'd been around the princess enough to see how often Andavarri came to her, serving as one of the Tamerlane's spies.

The Long-Wolf was ill-tempered and flippant to everyone else, but subservient to the princess. She didn't speak back or sneer. Instead, she bowed low, staying polite, knowing she was addressing the daughter of the emperor.

Alex had been studying the Tamerlanes. They'd always been a powerful house, but Maeven's father was the first to be emperor. He'd taken control of the family through murder and seized power through war, moving across the system in a way no one had seen since the arrival of the Æsir. Since they didn't intervene, it was assumed that he was chosen by them. Then Grannus happened. The Tamerlane invasion of the water world failed. The emperor was left ruling three moons but couldn't take the fourth. Still, he was powerful enough to control the Tairnish, the Long-Wolves, Uppsala and the fuel reserves on the ice moon Oighear. 'And I started dating his daughter,' Alex thought. Maybe that was too strong a word, he wondered. It implied that they went out together, open and public, and that there might be a future for them. Alex wasn't sure if that was possible given Maeven's status.

He stopped, hearing something, a crunching sound. Alex looked back at the Fire Golems. They were still standing tall and dark at the entrance but their heads, all four of them, had turned to follow him. Alex watched their eyes glowing in the center of their shapeless faces. They were slowly becoming brighter. He waited to see if they'd move in his direction, if he'd been too confident.

The glow never traveled to their arms or chest. Remaining still, they only watched. Alex let the air out of his lungs, then gave the creatures a nod as he headed on, knowing he was being observed.

Not long after turning a corner, he stepped into a darkened chamber to find a monk sitting on a stool with a monitor in his hand. The glow lit his face. He looked up at Alex, then reached for a switch to bring the lights up. "What are you doing here? You're not supposed to be out during the night cycle."

All that time traveling through the corridors, Alex hadn't come up with a reason they should let

Amita go. He had no plan. "I was told my friend was here," he said.

The monk stood up and put his tablet on the stool. He wasn't very old, maybe early twenties. He looked fit too. Alex sized him up, wondering if the monks had any martial arts training. He'd been sparring with Edith while preparing for his first combat simulation. Edith was an amazing teacher. Everything she showed him was practical with no wasted flourish in the way she fought. He felt good about his abilities but wondered if he was overconfident.

"She violated the laws of Nalanda Station. We don't think it's the first time either. She's been sneaking out, going into places she shouldn't. She'll have a trial in the morning and the Kavaris Dell will decide what to do with her."

Alex looked at the monk's robes, wondering if he could be hiding a weapon under them. "I'd like to see her," he asked.

The monk stared at Alex for a moment, then nodded, pointing to a doorway.

Alex moved cautiously to the opening, having trouble seeing in the dark. "Amita, are you here?" he called.

He sensed movement in the shadows and heard her say, "Alex?" Then he turned the glow from his monitor toward her, seeing a doorway with bars. He looked in at her, noticing, as if for the first time, how small she was.

Amita was the youngest of the group from Earth, a few months younger than Chris, but even at that, she was small for her age. With those big brown eyes, it was easy to feel protective toward her. Even though, Alex had to admit, he didn't know her nearly as well as he knew Ben who'd become his 'wingman' over the past few weeks. At least that's how Ben referred to himself.

"What were you thinking?" Alex asked.

Amita snorted. "Really, that's the first thing you're going to ask me?"

"You're risking everything, being stupid." Alex tightened his hands on the bars.

"I'm trying to understand what happened to us!" Amita shouted. "I'm trying to find a way back," she lowered her voice. "What's the matter? Are you too busy playing house, pretending it's all hunky-dory, to see that this isn't where we belong?"

Alex felt instant anger. He remembered now why he didn't spend much time with her. "I have been busy. I've been trying to keep us safe. I put us with the most powerful people around because we can't learn anything if we're dead. You want to find a way back? Well, they're our best chance."

"How pragmatic," Amita sneered.

"It's the whole reason I moved us in with Maeven."

"Oh bollocks, that's not the only the reason?" Amita folded her arms.

Alex was tempted to leave. "It's the most important reason. Not that it matters to you, you still managed to get yourself in trouble. Do you know what they're going do to you? Can't you remember Vyktor, the big guy they killed?"

"Of course, I remember," Amita said, backing away from the bars, "but it doesn't matter."

"What do you mean?"

She shrugged. "If we're stuck here, Alex, then what could it matter? Any hope we have of getting home is in knowledge and that's outlawed. They might as well flush me out an airlock if they're not going to let me solve this."

"For a smart kid, you can be pretty dumb," Alex said. He was holding the monitor up to the lock. It was a keypad. "Do you have any idea what the code is?"

Amita had tried paying attention when they locked her in. "It's four digits. At least two, the first two, are in the top row and another is in the bottom," she said, watching Alex press buttons in random sequences. He was too busy to hear the monk come in.

"What do you think you're doing?" the monk asked from the doorway.

Alex turned. "You need to let her out," he said balling his fists and moving toward the man, threateningly. This guy knew the code and if Alex was going to get Amita out, he was going to have to get it from him.

The monk didn't back away. He turned his feet a little, coming into a fighting stance, then reached behind his back and took out a large knife. The monk held it like he knew what he was doing too.

'Crap!' Alex thought, wondering if he was about to get stabbed again. Then someone stepped up behind the monk. Alex watched a black armored arm go around his neck. There was a quick jerk of the monk's head and the man collapsed to the floor. Edith stepped over his body. She went past Alex and straight to Amita's cell, where she typed in a quick code.

Alex and Amita watched in shock. In the darkness they were both asking the same question. Did they just witness a murder? Did that really happen? Neither of them was moving as the cell door swung open. "You needed to be back in the Tamerlane domicile five minutes ago," Edith said.

"What, why? Why did you do that?" Alex asked, motioning to the body.

Edith stared at him with eyes that glinted in the shadows. In an icy cold voice, she said, "I have no idea what you're talking about. I was never here. You never saw me. Now get back to Princess Maeven."

Alex grabbed Amita's hand and the two took off running, leaving Edith alone in the dark, her armor blending into the shadows.

Chapter 26

Maybe it was just the euphoria from almost drowning, but as Chris hugged tight to Naiathne he felt happy. She gave him a few more breaths. She was doing some of the work of swimming for him too, staying close and guiding him along. They passed through a dark, tight passage, leaving the light from the monster far behind. Chris tried looking back to see Katy, who had that weird lump in her mouth. He hoped it was actually working. She and Cormack were silhouettes against the rocky passage. He wondered for a moment if they were sharing air as well in the same way, or if the prince had incredible lung capacity. He pictured Cormack leaning into her in the dark the way Naiathne was for him and felt a little of the euphoria fade away.

They swam straight for another minute as the cave tightened and turned darker. Chris couldn't see where the rock wall was, but he could feel it, sense its jagged edges cutting close to him. Naiathne was the only one who could see, which made the going even slower as she moved around the group, guiding them. There was the sense that they were turning a corner. The cave began to brighten and they swam up.

Cormack went ahead, swimming for the faint glow as quickly as possible, leaving Katy behind. He'd been the only one holding his breath this entire time without help. It had been a long way even for an expert free diver. Naiathne had to take Katy's hand to guide her up. Chris didn't let go of the Naiad, clinging to her like a lifeline.

When they surfaced, Chris took a deep breath and felt Naiathne push him away. "Would you get off?" she said. She spat into the water. "Yuck. I hate doing that with you nasty air breathers."

Chris looked at the girl for a moment, then his attention was taken up by their surroundings. They were in a lake of sorts, deep underground in a massive cavern. A city lined the walls and flowed out over the water. Buildings and windows flickered with light as it rose from the shores of the lake. Above, on the cave ceiling, were large patches of a glowing material. It was impossible to tell from the water what they were, but they seemed to throw off warmth as well as a yellowish red light that mimicked a summer sunset, bathing the city below.

Twilight, the city of the Grannus, had been completely different from any underwater fantasy world Chris had seen in movies or TV, but this place felt more familiar.

It'd been constructed by human hands, not all that different from those who built Cormack's city of Anchor Home. The buildings were white stone with columns and arches, though few had roofs. The walls framed common areas and sat over the lake with canals and passages between them.

"Katy, are you alright?" Cormack asked, swimming back over to her. Katy couldn't answer with the thing in her mouth. The lumpy piece of flesh turned out to be some sort of sea slug with a unique ability to create oxygen.

Katy pulled at it but couldn't get it out of her mouth. Naiathne had to come over and help.

The Naiad tugged with both hands till it made a wet, sloppy sound. Naiathne threw it at Chris. The slug smacked him in the head. "I gave you this, because I knew no matter what, the girl was going to need help. I figured I'd have to breathe for her and it wouldn't have been nearly as nasty as breathing for you."

Chris was tired, still treading water. "Well, I didn't know you could do that. I thought I was going to drown. I was trying to be chivalrous."

"You were being stupid," Naiathne shot back. She started to swim off toward the edge of the lake. Cormack and Chris looked at each other with Katy between them, not sure what to do. "Come on," Naiathne ordered. "It's not like you can go back the way we came."

It was a long swim to the outer edges of the city. Chris stopped more than once, treading water and trying to recharge. Each time he started again, he was more sluggish, feeling his muscles tighten. Katy was struggling as well. Even with Cormack's help, she was tiring out.

Naiathne looked back at them annoyed, unwilling to help anymore. Eventually she dove under the water and disappeared. "Well, that's great," Chris said to Cormack, catching his breath.

"That's Naiathne," Cormack answered, exhausted as well.

Chris was about to start swimming again when he felt something bump his leg. The water was extremely clear, enabling him to look down and see a long animal go past. Then there were more, some small and some large. It was a school of fish. He felt them touch him, pushing him up, pulling him toward the city. Chris saw Katy being dragged along as well. Chris was nervous right up until he heard Katy laugh.

"It's okay," Cormack explained. "It's the Grannusians. They're helping us." Chris offered no resistance, knowing he was too tired to make it on his own. When they were close to a long walkway with a sloped ramp, the Grannusians slowed, letting Chris take Katy and guide her the last ten meters to the stone structure.

Naiathne was already there waiting. Chris collapsed onto the walkway. He was drained of strength, trying to catch his breath as he looked back at the water to see a Grannusian's head sticking up, staring at him. "Chooth?" he asked. The creature wagged its head, 'no,' then disappeared back beneath the surface.

Katy sat next to him while Cormack got up. He was staring at the city in awe. "I had no idea the colony was this big," he said.

"What about Chooth?" Chris asked. "If he followed us, he's going to have to get past that thing?"

"He'll be fine," a voice said from the water. "We Grannusians don't have to fear the Cirean-Croin as much as you humans do." The Grannusian who carried him had surfaced again. He pulled his parts together. The small individual pieces of his body all swam into one form as he climbed up the ramp. "I'm Julta. Welcome to the colony." Others were with him, Naiads like Naiathne. While the Grannusian nodded to the group warmly, the Naiads looked less friendly. Chris noticed that all of them were armed with long spears. Some were strapped to their backs, but others held the weapons down, ready to use.

Cormack seemed to ignore this as he asked, "So it is true, you can control that monster?"

"No, nothing controls that thing." Julta said, smiling as if he found the idea funny.

"And very little escapes it." Naiathne added bitterly as she started walking away. "Of course, that wouldn't have been a problem if you hadn't started your engines." she added as her people reached out, touching her back kindly.

Chris watched Naiathne and saw her dark eyes wet with tears. He hadn't thought about the sea dragon that'd rescued them. Naiathne must've loved the thing. He'd still been thinking of it as the monster that nearly ate him, instead of the one that saved him from a second monster— that also nearly ate him.

Julta waved them forward. "Please follow the path, we are going to the council chamber, we have much to discuss." Chris got to his feet, then gave Katy a hand. He glanced over his shoulder and noticed that the Naiads with the spears were right behind them. His eyes met Cormack's, silently asking if they were going to be alright.

Cormack smiled, trying to be reassuring. "So, if you don't control the Cirean-Croin, why is it guarding the entrance to the colony and why is it attacking the mining platforms?" Cormack called to Julta. He sounded every bit the part of a confident noble.

"The creature is attracted to noise, like your island makers," one of the Naiads snapped. "That's why they keep coming up from the depths, coming to the shallows. Now it's waiting where it knows there's food outside our home. It's your people's fault that it's here."

The Grannusian held his hand up to silence the Naiad before adding more gently, "I misspoke as well when I said we didn't have to worry about the monster. You see, it's just that over time my people have learned how to be silent, to move without being noticed and we also have the unique ability to scatter and protect our most essential parts."

"'Essential parts?' Chris asked.

"Yes, there are pieces of us that are more important than others. Small things that make us who we are, our mind and our soul. We can be hundreds of miles apart, but still maintain some sense of self as long as those pieces are unhurt. It's not ideal. We may lose memory or purpose, but there's more than that to life." He gestured again with his hand. "Please. I'm sure you're tired, but the Naiad council is waiting and as we are their guests. . ."

They followed Julta, while the armed Naiads stayed directly behind them.

They headed toward the center of an open area dotted with streams and paths, feeding from every part of the city to a large amphitheater that floated on the surface of the water with a large entrance way. Naiads from across the city were going ahead of them. The word was out about the new arrivals. They passed through the gate and saw that the theater swirled like the inside of a nautilus shell. At the bottom was a group of five elderly Naiads, sitting on a raised platform, just above a dark pool.

They followed the walkway down, passing Naiads who lined the sides. They had to be careful of their step because the path was damp and slippery from ribbons of water that ran down toward the bottom. The entire community seemed to be coming out for this. The lower they went, the more Grannusians they saw. They were coming up from the bottom, from the pool of water.

Eventually they reached a platform just above the pool. The elderly Naiads sat with their dark eyes staring at Cormack. Julta jumped into the water and swam across, holding his form together till he reached the other side, where with a graceful leap he sprung from the water to stand with the council.

He was given a chair. The Grannusian sat and looked back at Cormack and Chris with his large eellike eyes. His was the only friendly face they saw.

Chapter 27

Ben wandered to the dining hall in the morning before class. Usually he waited for Alex, but no one answered when he knocked on the door. He wasn't sure what was going on between Maeven and his friend. He knew they spent a lot of time together, everyone knew that, but it wasn't like they held hands in public or kissed or anything. They were definitely into each other, but neither one mentioned the whole boyfriend/girlfriend thing. Maybe they didn't have that here.

Most guys back on Earth were happy to spill on everything they'd ever done with a girl, but Alex wasn't like that. He didn't brag. He kept his secrets. When Ben got nosey enough to question his 'wingman,' Alex would give him that death stare he was so good at.

Ben looked around as he entered the dining hall and saw Tara sitting at the Tamerlane table. She was alone, which was odd. Usually, she was attached to Maeven in case the princess needed anything. Sometimes when classes were over and the princess wanted time to herself, she'd release her handmaiden for the night.

Ben and Tara had hung out a few times. Ben thought she kind of liked him. She laughed at his stupid jokes. Sometimes she laughed at him just because he was being himself. Ben would take it. Any attention from a pretty girl was better than how things usually went for him. He thought of making a move on her, leaning in real cool and stealing a kiss, but he hadn't done it yet.

He may have been low on impulse control, but he wasn't brave around girls, unable to get through the force field that seemed to surround them, especially this girl. She was something else, like magic, so sharp, smart and pretty, confident in a way he never could be.

He had no idea why she liked hanging out with him. He asked her one time. Tara's answer was confusing and maybe a little insulting. "You're simple," she had said. "You're not trying to hide anything. I've never known anyone who says exactly what they're thinking. All the time. Even when they shouldn't."

"Cool. . . I think," Ben had said.

He dropped down on the bench next to her, leaning back on his elbows and asked, "Flying solo today?"

Tara turned. "My mistress had a late-night visitor.
Your friend Alex."

"Really," Ben asked raising his eyebrow. "How inappropriate."

Tara smiled and shook her head. "It is actually. But I don't think he was there for the reason you're suggesting. He came back after dark and he was upset. He had your other friend with him, Amita. From what I understand he rushed her to her room before seeing the princess."

"That's kind of weird," Ben said. He wasn't surprised to hear Amita was up late. He knew she'd been going out at night, though she'd given up on asking him to join her. Ben had his fill of ghosts on that first night. "She must've gotten in trouble, or maybe she found something."

Now it was Tara's turn to raise an eyebrow, waiting for Ben to say more.

He looked at her, unsure if he could talk about this stuff, but he had to trust someone, and moving into the Tamerlane dorms was as close as you could get to picking a side. He leaned in and whispered, "She's been trying to figure out what happened to us. How we got here."

"You mean she's been looking into the void spaces?" Tara asked. She kept her voice low as well.

Ben nodded. "Yeah, that, and anything else that might lead to answers. Alex doesn't know. He'd be ticked if he found out. Maybe that's what she's up to."

Tara looked around for red robes. "Has she found anything?" Her eyes were on the other side of the hall, watching Kavaris Dell come in with several other monks. They were looking over the room, searching for someone.

"I don't know. Amita's always been a bit, um, snooty. She hasn't talked to me much lately. But the first night we went out, we found a room with this big glass dome and all these machines. She got them to work too, made this display come to life. But there was this ghost thing and then Andavarri showed up. That was it for me, no more going out at night."

Tara nodded. She'd heard the story from Maeven weeks ago. Andavarri had reported it to her. "I don't know what she's been up to since then," Ben added.

"Maybe we should go back and find out," Tara suggested, getting up. "You could ask Alex." She was watching the monks, noticing how they seemed to be moving toward her and Ben.

"But I haven't eaten yet. Come on, I'll be fast." He got up to go toward the serving station. Tara grabbed for his arm, but she was too late. Kavaris Dell caught up to them, standing in Ben's way, blocking their path, while glaring at them. Edith stood over his shoulder while monks closed in from all directions, boxing them in. Kavaris Dell waited till Tara and Ben were surrounded before saying anything.

"If you guys are hungry, the food's over there," Ben said, pointing.

Kavaris Dell ignored him and said to Tara, "Your mistress has given sanctuary to criminals." His eyes fell on Ben and his lip curled in disgust. He turned back to Tara adding, "I wish to speak to her."

A look passed between Ben and Tara, neither sure what to say. Kavaris Dell returned to staring at Ben. "Your companion, the girl, was arrested last night for going into forbidden territories. The monk guarding her is dead now and she has escaped."

Tara looked back at Edith with her dark armor. The mercenary's arms were crossed and her face was unreadable, but Tara sensed something from her. It was near the surface. Edith always had an air of concealment around her thoughts, but it was stronger now. Their eyes met and Tara looked away. "I can't imagine my mistress had anything to do with that."

"We believe it was Alex," Edith said, not sounding nearly as harsh as the monk. "He was sighted by Fire Golems, coming and going in that direction. We need to talk to him." The mercenary stayed passive and controlled on the surface, but Tara could tell that she knew more than she was saying.

Edith always boiled a little with an undercurrent of rage. Given her history, that wasn't surprising. And she was no different than anyone else at Nalanda, hiding schemes. However, any time Tara had been close to the mercenary, she'd never felt anything like this. Her emotions were confused. Edith was conflicted about something. Her eyes moved and tightened.

"I'll carry your message to the princess." Tara bowed to the monk and started to back away, still holding Ben's arm and pulling him with her. Tara was trying to avoid Edith's stare. They were from the same planet and the mercenary had once served the emperor. Tara wondered if Edith knew what she was capable of. If she knew about her abilities.

Ben pulled his arm free and pointed at the monk. "Now wait a minute. You can't seriously be accusing Alex of killing someone. Look, he may be a tough guy and a bit of a head case, but he's no murderer. If you told me he knocked someone out, I'd believe you, but there's no way he'd just kill a guy."

"You think you know Alex that well? That he's not capable of it? Have you trained with him, have you seen the fire in him? You know nothing about killing?" Edith moved forward, getting right in Ben's face. "Anyone is capable of it. It's a simple thing."

Ben stepped back, uncomfortable with her intensity. "I trust Alex, and where we come from, you don't just go around murdering people."

"Sounds nice. But you should be careful here, child, giving your trust away so easily can be dangerous. Things aren't always what they seem. People aren't always who they seem." Edith glanced at Tara and something passed between them. A silent conversation.

Tara took Ben's arm again. "Let's go," she said pulling him away. Ben didn't fight this time. He wasn't sure what was going on with Edith and Tara, but he knew he was missing something.

Chapter 28

Chris, Katy and Cormack stood before the council. The five Naiads with their grey skin and dark eyes were staring down at them, along with Julta, the Grannusian who had guided them here.

Looking around at the crowded amphitheater, Chris noticed that it had filled in behind them, like the entire community had come out. None of them looked happy to see him. 'They're probably going to execute us and everyone loves a show, he thought. He glanced down at the dark water in the center. A few of the Grannusians had come out of it, but Chris had no doubt that there had to be some horrible thing with big teeth waiting for him below. Since arriving at Cormack's home a few days ago, he'd almost been eaten twice and nearly executed once. Really, the only way to go out that would make sense was to get hit with both at the same time.

Katy grabbed his hand. "It'll be alright," she said as if she knew what he was thinking.

"Of course, it will," Chris agreed and perked up a little because Julta was speaking. He was the only Grannusian on the stage. Chris liked him, he reminded him of Chooth, who still hadn't made it to the colony, but he also had an older vibe, like a college professor. He seemed willing to listen.

Julta asked Chris and Katy to tell their story. The two did as requested. They told the council everything, starting with Earth and going right up to this cave deep under the ocean on an alien moon. Katy filled them in on Brash and the Hunter, and

Chris covered his mom and the wormhole. Then he finished with Nalanda and the trip here. He even told them about his audience with the queen.

The Naiads listened, but their dislike for surface dwellers was apparent throughout. They liked the nobles that ruled them even less. Chris could see why since, as Julta explained, the nobles had tried several times to wipe the Naiads out.

Cormack didn't get much of a chance to speak to the council. The one time he opened his mouth to add something he'd been shouted down. A Naiad councilor said, "It is only out of respect to your sister that we don't immediately put you to death." Like many of the Naiads, this councilor was convinced the nobles were responsible for poisoning the Grannusian food chain.

Julta had held up his hand to silence the crowd. He said to Chris and Katy, "As you can see, the Naiads are protective of my people."

He explained that generations ago it'd been the Grannusians who'd engineered the human hybrids, just as they'd engineered much of the life on this world. "We thought we were helping the humans, we didn't think about the divide we were creating," he said sadly. "Each Grannusian is so unique that the idea of one part of a species hating another part for some small genetic variation was inconceivable. The human concept of racism had never existed on our world." He'd turned to the crowd and said, "I'm only a guest here, but I would hope my Naiad friends can see a way of working against their human nature and judging these three as individuals, not as some subgroup that deserves to be exterminated."

This seemed to take a little of the venom out of the crowd. Julta turned back to Chris and Katy. "You see, when the poisoning started, we turned to the Naiads for help. The Grannusians are farmers and over the centuries we've developed a very specific diet. We only grow enough food to maintain our population. Unfortunately, this made the poisoning much more dangerous because we had no reserves to lean on."

"We are happy to help." One of the Naiad councilors said before turning to stare at Chris, Cormack and Katy. "The question is, if we accept what you've told us to be true, then what do we do with these three?"

"The answer to that is simple," Julta said.
"We help them in any way we can." He looked up at the Naiads. Their rage had turned quiet, but it was still present.

"I know you are angry, my friends. Those on the surface are poor neighbors. They consider only what affects them. And it may be that some amongst them are responsible for this poisoning."

Julta pointed to the three. "But these young ones had nothing to do with it. In fact, I believe they honestly wish to help. Prince Cormack has been known to my people, and just like his father he has been a friend, not only to us but also to your people. He was instrumental in bringing Naiathne, his sister to Nalanda Station. That act gave your people a voice. He doesn't want you to be forgotten. A forgotten people can be slaughtered at will. Hate them if you must, but help them despite that, because in doing so you help yourselves."

Chris looked at Cormack, then at Naiathne. Her eyes were on the ground and her gray skin had hints of crimson shame. The council retired from the stage, moving their chairs back to confer. When they returned, they agreed to allow Chris, Katy and Cormack to return to the surface.

Someone interrupted from the crowd, screaming, "But they know where we are!"

Julta returned to the front, looking at the spot where the shout had come from. "I will see to it that they don't remember. I promise you, you will remain safe here."

Chris didn't know how the Grannusian was going to do that, but he remembered the way Chooth had sedated Katy and the way the throat of the solar blossom had sedated everyone. He wondered what else the Grannusians could do. 'Could they alter brain chemistry and erase memories?'

Escorted by armed Naiads, they left the amphitheater for one of the villas. Then they were shown beds and given food by the guards who spoke very little to them. The Naiads took up position at the door. Chris wasn't sure if they were there to keep them in or to protect them from the outside.

"So, you got Naiathne to Nalanda?" Katy asked Cormack.

Cormack nodded. "Yeah, for whatever good it did." Katy and Chris waited for him to say more. Cormack sighed. "I did it for my dad. He died a few years back, during the invasion. Before that he'd been secretly meeting with Naiathne in a cove not far from the palace. He brought me with him sometimes. My father was a kind man and he loved her just as he loved me. After he was gone, Naiathne and I continued to meet, not as often, but sometimes. It was never easy after he died. She was angry and I was sad, still we're family. After the truce I convinced her to go to Nalanda. She may have been cast out by my mother, but she was still of noble birth, and according to the laws of the Æesir, the monks still had to educate her. It didn't matter if she breathed air or water.

"So, I snuck her aboard a transport with Chooth's help. My mother would have no power over her away from Grannus. At Nalanda, among other people and races, I thought Naiathne could seek support for the Naiads, try to campaign with the other clans from Grannus and the species from other worlds, to get them to see the Naiads as something more than subhuman. That was the plan anyway."

"What happened?" Chris asked.

"Naiathne was herself. She has extraordinarily little statecraft and even less tact. She made a lot of people angry and I spent a lot of time apologizing. Still, I wish she'd stayed. She was safer there, away from my mother." Cormack shrugged.

"Would the queen have hurt her own daughter?" Katy asked.

Cormack stood up and started to pace. "My mom can be scary. But you must understand, it was her leadership that protected this world and turned back the Tamerlane invasion. She couldn't have done that without the cooperation of the other clans. She would sacrifice anything to protect her people."

Cormack went to a window and repeated Katy's question, "Would she have hurt Naiathne? I don't know. She couldn't do it the first time. When Naiathne was born, she put my sister in my father's hands knowing he'd save her. But that was at the beginning of the war. Once the invasion started, I think she would've done anything to win.

"The Tamerlanes are still out there and my mother still needs to maintain her alliances. Why do you think she took that piece of slime as her consort?"

"That Duke guy?" Chris asked.

"Yeah, to someone like him the Naiads aren't even human and the Grannusians are only a resource. If the island making project upsets them, he doesn't care. Unfortunately, there are many who think like him. My mother keeps him close because she needs his support to rule, but also because he can't be trusted. He's dangerous."

"So, she doesn't actually agree with him?" Katy asked.

"I don't think so." Cormack didn't sound completely convinced.

They slept that night and, in the morning, Julta came to them with another Grannusian, a healer named Eidenthia. She took Katy into the water. If you wanted to be examined by a Grannusian that was part of the deal. Julta stayed with Chris and Cormack by the shore of the small lagoon, while Eidenthia went to work, breaking apart and spreading over Katy. "She'll do what she can for your friend, but it'd really be better if Eir was here," Julta said.

"She's really that good?" Chris asked.

"Eir is special." Julta nodded. "She's lived in the seas for thousands of years. Since before the fall."

"Your people can live that long?" Chris asked. He wanted to add, 'and what fall' but Julta was already answering his first question.

"In a way, yes. Though not every part of us can remain for all that time. You can think of a Grannusian like a city." He pointed to the colony around them. "Over the years the name remains, and some of the streets, maybe a landmark or two, but the buildings change and the beings living in them are born and die generation after generation. A Grannusian is like that. We live for untold years, but not without those years changing us."

Chris nodded, although he didn't completely understand. He looked out at Katy. Parts of Eidenthia were crawling over her. Many were on her face, but she was incredibly calm, floating just below the surface with her hair waving in the lagoon. Slowly Katy sunk into it. Chris could see Eidenthia's pieces making small ripples. They brought Katy back to the water's edge, where Cormack and Chris helped her up onto the stony ledge.

Eidenthia stayed in the water, bringing herself closer together. "I'm sorry. Her eyes are far too damaged, even the nerves are dead. If we had access to our labs, it'd be possible to clone her a new set, but none of the materials I'd need are here. And the damage didn't stop at the nerve. The region of her brain connected to vision is different now." Eidenthia sounded a little confused.

Katy struggled to sit up, still sleepy from the sedation. "New eyes?" she asked slowly.

"Yes, we'd clone them from the originals so they'd be completely the same," Eidenthia said.

"If you say so," Katy touched her face.

"But if her brain's been affected, would that even work?" Chris asked.

"It would be the first step. Replacement is the best option, but as far as the brain damage goes, we won't know until the new eyes are in."

Katy shook her head, trying to clear it. "Did she just say brain damage?"

Naiathne was coming down the walkway. "She did, and she wasn't even talking about my brother," she said.

Chris and Cormack looked back and saw that she was pushing a cart full of equipment. "You've been given permission to leave." Naiathne explained. "And I'm lucky enough to be your guide."

"Does that mean you're going back to Nalanda?" Cormack asked.

Naiathne looked at the ground. "Yeah, I guess so. First, we've got to get you guys out of here. We'll have to get me back on a ship and past your mother later. In other words, there's a good chance none of us will make it, and an even better chance I'll end up being skewered by some noble turd, looking to put a Naiad on his trophy wall."

271

"They don't actually do that, do they?" Chris asked.

Cormack and Naiathne looked at each other. "It's not unheard of," Cormack said.

"That is truly messed up." Katy shook her head while getting to her feet. Her voice was clearer now. Chris took her arm and tried guiding her from the edge. "It's fine, Chris," she said as she shrugged him off.

He stared at her for a moment before turning toward the cart. "What's all that stuff?"

Naiathne pulled one large box down from the top. "This is how we're going to get back to the surface. As you might remember, the way we came is unadvisable. Luckily for us, there's more than one way out of the colony. Unlucky for us, the new way is through the volcanic tubes that formed this cave system. Don't worry, most of them are dormant now."

"Most?" Chris asked, watching her open the case, revealing a dive suit inside. It looked more advanced than the one they'd worn in the sub, with armor plating and heat shielding.

"Someone had the bright idea of making islands by drilling down and setting charges in the planet's mantle. It's made the whole system unstable. The Grannusians were kind enough to help secure this area, but if we're going to make it to the surface anywhere near where you guys can be picked up, we're going to have to travel further, out toward the volcano machines." She pointed to the suit. "These should help protect us, since we stole them from the guys who work on those machines. It's technology that the Long-Wolves developed for their own world."

"Really?" Chris asked, leaning down and picking up the suit. It was bulky but not nearly as heavy as it looked.

"If you're going to mess with volcanos, there are no better creatures to talk to. The Long-Wolves' planet is practically one giant ball of magma." Cormack said, opening another box.

"We're going to be walking and swimming, potentially in some very warm water." Naiathne lifted a handheld turbine. "So, take about an hour to get familiar with the equipment, then grab something to eat because after that we'll be leaving."

Chris asked, "Why so soon?"

Naiathne laughed. "Are you kidding? Most of these people wanted to kick you out last night, no guide and no equipment. Trust me. The sooner we're on our way, the better for everyone." She looked at Katy and grabbed a case off the pile. "I'll help you get suited up," she said. "You boys, I'm sure, can figure these things out for yourselves." She looked Chris up and down. "That's if they even fit."

Chris watched Naiathne take Katy's arm and lead her away, then glanced at Cormack, who shook his head. "Like I said, 'no tact.'"

"But plenty of attitude," Chris added. Cormack just nodded.

Chapter 29

The night of the monk's murder, Alex had left Edith at the cells with the body. It was early morning and the station was waking up when he hurried Amita to her room. He thought of going to Maeven, wondering if the princess was waiting for him, but he wasn't sure he wanted Amita talking to her, not yet anyway. He needed to be careful and he didn't want Amita volunteering information, saying something like, 'Hey, Edith killed a guy.'

For all Alex knew, Maeven might have sent the mercenary. Edith did work for Maeven's father at one time, but he'd rarely seen the two interact on the station. Maeven didn't even take combat training. Considering what Edith had done and what she'd said, 'I was never here. You never saw me,' in that cold, mechanical voice, Alex thought it best to tread lightly and that wasn't a talent of Amita's. Even with all the time he'd had training with her, he didn't think he could predict what Edith would do. That fact was made even more apparent by what he'd just seen.

The day cycle had begun by the time they returned to the Tamerlane domicile. The guards let them through without question. Following Amita inside her room, Alex flipped on a light, then closed the door behind him, wondering if they were safe.

"I came across something," Amita said. "Just before they found me, I discovered a room that had been blocked off, a side chamber to the lighthouse. I think Tearmai was there, maybe Brash too."

"What?" Alex was distracted, not sure what she was talking about.

Amita laid it out for him quickly, telling him about the night she and Ben found the room with its glass dome. She believed Tearmai and Brash had found something, a clue that led them to the void ship. "There must be more," she said. "For some reason they came to our world. I've been trying to pull together where they went before that, find more clues to what they wanted with us." She didn't explain about her deal with Regin, the way she was passing information to the Ice-Carver.

"We know what they wanted, to shut down the wormhole," Alex said, remembering that night in the desert with Brash, hours before the creature grabbed his mother.

A knock came at the door and one of Maeven's guards stood on the other side. "Come with me," he said to Alex.

Alex stepped out into the hall while holding up his hand telling Amita to stay put. The guard looked past him at her. Alex said, "She's going to rest. It's been a long night."

The guard wasn't sure what to do. He'd probably been told to retrieve them both, but he wasn't willing to push the issue with Alex, who had become the princess's favorite. Alex made up the guard's mind for him by closing the door and pointing for the armored man to lead the way.

In the princess's room food was laid out for him and he was told that Maeven would join him shortly. The guard left the door open. Alex could sense him standing outside in the hall.

"Where is she?" he called.

"The communications room," the guard answered, leaning back in. "She's speaking to the royal house of Uppsala, her father the emperor."

Alex nodded, knowing this could all end badly. He should tell her everything, tell her it was Edith. Then he remembered that Maeven had been covering for Amita. She let her travel out at night, going on these excursions. He knew Maeven had her secrets. 'How couldn't she with the position she held?' But he thought they had an understanding. That she knew his people were his to protect.

In the time they'd been together, she'd confided in him, told him about the pressures of being heir to the throne, and he told her all about the world he came from, the life they'd left behind. Even talking for hours there were many things left unsaid between them. They didn't talk about the future and she didn't mention current politics. In fact, any time someone had come to her with an update, he'd left, not wishing to impose on her. He wondered if he should've been like everyone else here, listening and gathering information. If he should've tried harder, maybe joined Amita in finding a way out of all this.

Edith came to mind, the person he'd spent so much time with over the past few weeks. An hour had passed, but he still couldn't get over the shock of watching her murder that monk. It hadn't moved her at all.

Alex thought about the sparring sessions with her, the things she'd shown him, the life he'd considered as someone like her. 'Was that really what he wanted, to be a cold-blooded killer?' He shook his head. But in the back of his mind, he wondered. 'Maybe that's just who you have to be to survive here.'

Between Edith's training and Maeven's company, he'd started to believe he could have a life in this place. He ran his hand back over his head, mumbling to himself, "So stupid."

"Maybe," Maeven said from the door. "But I'm sure you didn't have a choice." Alex looked up and saw her standing just inside. She'd come in quiet as a cat. He felt the air in his lungs catch, looking at her. Back on Earth, he'd never had trouble meeting pretty girls, but he'd always been careful not to become distracted. Maeven was beyond that. She was perfect, or as close to it as possible. It was almost off-putting the way she seemed beyond human, almost ethereal. Her hair was tied back revealing her long neckline, and she smiled at him, her pouty lips closed and her emerald eyes twinkling.

"You can leave," she said to the guard. Then she shut the door, turning back to Alex. "It's never easy talking with my father," she said as she crossed the room. "There's a delay you see. Uppsala is a bit further out, so there's these pauses. It's only for a few seconds, but it makes for an awkward conversation, not that it's ever been simple talking with him." She touched Alex's shoulder. "I try to be so much like him. Everyone says I play a fine part too, but it's hard. I worry that I'll never be allowed to be kind. That I'll always have to intimidate others to maintain our dynasty."

Alex stared at her, not sure where she was going with this, but loving the touch of her hand.

"I've never intimidated you, have I, Alex?" she asked as she sat down across from him.

"Is that what you're trying to do now?" He felt his skin turn hot.

She touched his face. "There'd be no point. You've proven that, haven't you? You're vicious."

"What do you mean?" he asked, though he knew the answer. Her eyes were on him, and there was a thrill behind them. Alex didn't know how he felt about that.

"I mean that I knew you were protective of your friends, but I didn't know you had this in you." Her hand left his face and went to his arm. "Of course, you must understand that your actions have caused a bit of trouble for me. Kavaris Dell is calling for your arrest. You will only be safe here in the Tamerlane domicile."

"Was that what you were talking to your father about?" Alex asked.

Maeven smiled again, this time broader, showing her flawlessly white teeth. "I've just spoken to the emperor. What could I possibly tell you about that? Nearly everything I say to him is privileged, state secrets and what not." She stared at Alex for a moment, thinking. Then she added. "I suppose it's okay to say some things." She played with her hair while Alex waited.

"The news about what you did hasn't reached the emperor yet. He was too busy being cross with me to even ask about you and your friends. You'd think he'd be more interested in people who came through the void space." She leaned forward, crooking her finger toward him to draw him closer and whispering, "There are things that even an emperor is careful of. The Æsir are always listening. Even in coded transmissions, it's unwise to talk about Amita's investigations." She leaned back, her eyes never leaving his.

"You should've told me what she was doing."

Maeven looked away, and when her eyes returned, they were sorrowful but still with a playful edge. "Will you forgive me?"

Alex couldn't bring himself to be mad at her, though he knew he should've been outraged. "My friends are my responsibility."

"I understand. It won't happen again." Maeven assured him. "Back to my father. You see, much like you, I was rash, and it's caused a bit of trouble for him. It was that whole thing with Vyktor a few weeks back."

Surprised, Alex pulled back as he asked, "You didn't have anything to do with that? Did you?"

He watched Maeven's eyes widen in mock innocence, "Of course not, but still many know that I wasn't happy with him. Not with his failure that day, or his blundering ways the rest of the time. His people think I may have had something to do with his attack on Cormack. Of course, taking up with you right after made them even angrier. You can see how provocative that was, given that you were the one who stopped him."

Alex remembered how he'd thrown himself in Vyktor's way without a second thought. He had no idea it would lead to the thug being tossed out an airlock. He was only trying to protect someone, but the guilt was still there. It was the same thing as last night. Alex placed his head in his hands. "What if I'm not the person you think I am?" he asked Maeven.

Maeven waited for him to say more.

He looked up at her. "It bothers me what happened to Vyktor— and what happened last night."

Her eyes were expectant, waiting for him to say more. What would he lose if he told her it was Edith? What would he gain? He looked away saying, "I didn't go there to kill anyone. I just wanted my friend safe."

Maeven took his hands again. She stood and pulled him up with her. Her arms went around him, holding tight. "It's alright, Alex. This is all new to you. I'm sure you're worried, but you and your people are safe here." She held on for a long time before kissing him. Alex felt his blood pulse and slowly forgot about last night, enjoying Maeven's touch.

The kiss became more impassioned as their hands traveled, and in a moment, it would've gone further, but a knock came at the door, followed by a more incessant banging.

"Go away!" Maeven screamed and the knocking stopped.

As she turned back to Alex, she heard Ben call, "Hey man, we need to talk." The door was nearly soundproof to everyone else, but somehow Ben's voice managed to make it through. "You know . . . when you're finished in there and what not."

Alex looked at Maeven. Neither of them wanted to open the door, but they knew Ben wasn't leaving.

"It is kind of important though," Ben added. Alex shook his head.

∞

Not far from the Tamerlane domicile, only a few doors over in the market hall, were the quarters of the Bogatyr collective, Vyktor's people. Their door was marked in a dull red with a massive hammer on it. It was the most color they'd allow in their barracks. Two large guards stood by it, watching the hall. It would be easy to assume they were common soldiers, but they weren't.

These young men were first cousins to Vyktor. Someday they'd be high in the leadership of the Bogatyr. Still, they stood guard as common as any other. This was the way of their people, those who colonized the harsh world of Tairnish, who lived beside the Long-Wolves. Each man and woman had to do their duty. Even those who led and made decisions were part of the collective and had to do their part. According to their philosophy, no one was special, but to harm one was to harm all.

They'd seen Maeven hurry back from the communications room. She kept no guard with her, confident enough in her father's power to think that no one would be foolish enough to attack her. But her father was far away.

They'd heard the news from last night. The princess's new toy had murdered a monk. He was the first at Nalanda to be so bold, risking the very wrath of the Æesir. It was worth some measure of respect that he'd do such a thing and that he'd taken Vyktor down so handily, but respect wouldn't spare him his punishment. It was only a matter of time before the Æsir came.

That wasn't the Tairnishman's concern though. For decades, the Bogatyr had been allied to the Tamerlanes.

They'd been at the invasion of the water world Grannus and had failed with them. It had strained diplomacy, tested their loyalty to the emperor. The emperor had shown weakness, something the Bogatyr hated, but they'd held onto the alliance these past few years, building their strength in secret, waiting for the right moment to break ties.

The emperor still controlled the most powerful fleet and the wells of raw energy on Oighear, the ice moon. He still needed his allies, the nobles of his own world, and the ingenuity of the Long-Wolves. But Long-Wolves were fickle, going to whoever fed them. They'd been working closely with the nobles of Grannus, building their island, making volcano machines.

The cousins watched Ben and Tara hurry by, looking over their shoulders as they passed the Tamerlane guards. Tara glanced back toward the Tairnishmen. She was lovely, but frail looking, unfit, as were all the nobles of Uppsala. The cousins sneered at her. They knew she was the last one to speak to Vyktor before he lost his senses.

Of course, that wasn't proof that Maeven had anything to do with Vyktor's dishonorable behavior, but at the trial, she hadn't spoken up for him either. That had been Vyktor's one chance, a word from the emperor's daughter might have saved his life.

Instead, she'd held her tongue that day and watched him die.

Now it was time for the Tamerlanes to be humbled. It was time for them to feel a measure of loss.

Chapter 30

"It's not true, right Alex?" Ben asked as soon as he was through the door. "Tell me you didn't do it."

Alex sat down. He started eating, keeping his eyes low. His cold food suddenly became more appealing as a way to ignore Ben's question. "I don't want to talk about it," he mumbled.

Ben waited with his mouth hanging open and his arms crossed. For the first time in a long time, he couldn't find anything to say. 'I don't want to talk about it,' Alex's words repeated in his head. His answer should have been 'No. Obviously I didn't kill anyone.' Ben thought as he looked at Tara, then at Maeven. The princess was sitting on the edge of her bed acting bored, watching Alex and Ben.

"The guy that runs this place is accusing you of murder. They were like two seconds from grabbing me because of you," Ben said, sitting down across from Alex.

"I said I don't want to talk about it." Alex still didn't look up.

"Did you do it?" Ben asked pointedly.

Alex slammed his fist on the table and stood up. "Knock it off Ben!" he yelled.

Ben looked at his balled fists. He was thinking about that day Alex had fought Vyktor, the way he'd slammed that knife into the big guy's leg.

Maybe he could've done it. Ben's stomach churned. Maybe he is a killer. Ben didn't really know Alex that well. It'd only been a few weeks. He looked around the room again. Maeven, Tara, Alex, he was surrounded by strangers. Something broke loose deep inside of Ben. He felt his emotions suddenly well up.

"You know what? I'll just leave you alone," Ben said, hurrying to the door.

"Where are you going?" Alex asked.

"I don't know, class maybe." He felt himself choke a little, but he didn't want to cry in front of these people, so he went to his room instead.

Maeven watched him leave, then turned to Tara, "Go with him, make sure he doesn't get in any trouble." Tara nodded. Her eyes fell on Alex for a moment. She could tell in her way that he was hiding something. She didn't know why, but he was being dishonest. Going toward the door, she didn't say anything. When she looked back at her mistress, her thoughts were on Ben. Even if Maeven hadn't ordered her to go, she would've wanted to make sure he was alright.

Maeven touched Alex's shoulder as the door closed behind Tara. "I know that was hard, but the less your friend knows the better. They'll question him again." Alex didn't look up, but his shoulders relaxed under her touch. After a moment, her hand fell away and she went over to her nightstand, picking up her monitor. "I need to go," she said.

"What? Where?" Alex asked.

"I've still got class, and I'm sure I'll be delayed by the monks. They'll want to talk to me, convince me to give you up." She smiled devilishly, but Alex didn't react.

"Oh, don't worry, you're perfectly safe here. I'll protect you." She ran her hand back through his hair.

285

"But I can't hide out with you. I must be out there where they can see me." She leaned down and kissed him. Then she left. Alex looked around at Maeven's room. It was the nicest place he'd seen at Nalanda, giving the impression that it was part of a palace and not a cave cut into an asteroid. The white wood, the elegant furniture, the lighting that mimicked a sunny day, it was all so nice, but it might as well have been a prison cell.

∞

Tara waited outside Ben's room. She didn't knock at first, giving him a moment to collect himself. Anxious, she wanted to tell Maeven about Alex, and about her reading of Edith. They were both keeping a secret and Tara had a feeling she knew what it was.

Tara and Edith were from the same world but opposite sides. They came from different cultures, but she'd heard of the way Edith's people, the mercenaries, would pass on their knowledge, student to teacher. Each one was a warrior and it was important for them to create more like themselves. That student-teacher relationship was sacred to them.

Tara had noticed the way Edith had taken to Alex. Edith had been training him and giving him more attention than any of her other students. Edith had always been a puzzle box. She didn't have loyalty to anyone, but at one time she would've died for her emperor. She almost did on Grannus. Tara wondered if some of the devotion still existed.

Maeven was the emperor's proxy on the station, but would he really trust all his dealings to his daughter? She was young and sometimes reckless. No, Tara was certain there were other actors here, fulfilling the emperor's will. But how could he keep them from going rogue, especially when they'd taken a liking to someone.

She thought of Alex.' He was surly, but he wasn't a killer, not yet anyway.' Edith was. Tara thought of her mistress going over and touching Alex. 'Maybe it was better to stay quiet,' she thought, 'let Maeven have her illusions.'

Tara tapped at Ben's door. After a moment he opened it. "Are you alright?" she asked.

"Yeah fine. I ah, you know— just kind of got a little overwhelmed in there." He stepped into the hall. "I know it seems like I don't let things bother me, like I just go along for the ride because, I mean, what else are you going to do? But you know, a lot of this stuff just hit me is all. I mean, you think you know a guy, right?"

Tara touched his arm. She could see his face was swollen from crying. Ben had a simple way of looking at the world. She liked it, even if it made no sense. It was sad to see his beliefs breaking, but it was probably for the best.

"I should check on Amita," Ben said.

Tara looked down at her monitor. "We've got class, Ben, and your friend is probably resting. I'm sure last night was an ordeal for her. We'll check on her after, okay?"

Ben looked down the hall to where Amita's room was, feeling Tara's hand still on his arm. He nodded and followed her.

∞

Maeven left her room without Tara. The princess missed having her confidant with her. She needed to talk to someone. The past few weeks they'd spent less and less time together, mainly because she chose Alex's company over Tara's.

Tara still spent many nights in the princess's chambers, just like when they were young, but the handmaiden knew when she was wanted and when to make herself scarce, giving the young couple privacy, but now Maeven was lonely. Of course, she was more than capable of going places by herself and keeping her own council, but she still wanted her oldest friend. There were things she didn't want to tell Alex, and she certainly couldn't discuss her feelings about him. After class, she told herself, she'd see to it that she and Tara had some time alone, away from these new arrivals.

Tara didn't seem to mind spending time with Alex's companion, Ben. Maeven didn't think much of the young man. He was loud and annoying, but she was willing to tolerate him for Alex's sake. 'It was a good lesson,' she told herself as she thought of her father. Many nobles in his court would be put to death if they weren't necessary to maintain his empire.

Some did disappear from time to time, but he kept the secret of those political assassinations to himself. For the most part, even the emperor couldn't just get rid of someone who annoyed him. 'Being the head of state meant you had to tolerate a number of idiots,' she thought, as she stepped outside the doors of the Tamerlane domicile, passing her guards. She looked to the Bogatyr collective's door, and smirked.

Vyktor's cousins are still staring daggers at me, she thought. She was fairly certain that's who they were. She had a hard time telling Tairnishmen apart. They were all giant, thick necked brutes with that purple tint to their skin.

That color was a genetic alteration adapted from the Long-Wolves. It protected people from the radiation in the air of Tairnish. A human would die within a few months of being on their awful world without it. Maeven looked at her hands, certain they were the perfect color, not pale, like Tara, or dark like Alex, but warm, more like that Amita girl. 'Humans came in so many unique colors, but purple wasn't supposed to be one of them,' Maeven thought. 'Maybe I'll do something about that when I'm ruler.'

"Mistress," one of her guards said, catching her attention before she walked off.

She was surprised. Usually, the guards only bowed respectfully. They hardly ever ventured to speak to her. Again, she thought of how much she missed Tara.

The guard cleared his throat while she stared at him. "Master Kavaris Dell was here. He wishes to have an audience with you. I told the lady Tara."

"And what did Tara say?" Maeven asked.

He looked at the other guard for help, before answering. "She nodded, acknowledging it."

"Fine then. It'll be taken care of. Tara will set the whole thing up and if I need to meet with him, I will.

She keeps my appointments." Maeven started walking away, going toward the market.

"Yes, mistress. It's just that he was insistent that you speak to him as soon as possible," the guard added.

Maeven turned and glared at him. She didn't recognize the man and wondered if he'd just started this post. A ship was in dock from Tairnish and some of her soldiers would be traveling back on it to her father's holdings. However, anyone given the task of guarding the princess was supposed to be handpicked by her father's top advisers. They could only come from the royal palace on Uppsala and it'd been over a month since any ship arrived from their world. One was in route, but it'd still be a few days.

Maeven shook her head. "Did he say where he'd be?"

"Yes, he's supervising the cargo transfer for the next few hours in hanger three, after that he said he'd be in his office."

Looking at the clock on her monitor, Maeven saw that she was already late for her first class. The conversation with Kavaris Dell wasn't going to be pleasant, at least not for him. She'd need to make it clear to him that Alex and his friends were under her protection.

Maeven let out a long sigh, bringing the monitor up. Nalanda Station was a big place and she'd never felt an urge to learn all of it. She had no idea where hanger three was, or two, or one, or even how many hangers there were. Usually if she needed to go there, she'd have Tara show her the way. She pulled the location up on the monitor, annoyed by how far it looked, then turned and started off.

The guard, who wasn't new, stepped back to his position. Of course, he couldn't signal Vyktor's cousins, who were still standing at their door. He couldn't let on in any way that they'd approached him, showed him pictures of his father taken a day before.

His father hadn't looked well. They'd beaten him and they promised to do worse if he didn't speak with the princess. Now it was done, he simply prayed that no one else would find out.

∞

Maeven followed the map, annoyed by the whole situation. The hallway she was in was wide and empty, large enough to drive a supply truck through. Weak lighting shone down from above, making dark shadows on the far walls.

Maybe she was to blame for this mess, letting Amita go out at night, allowing her to wander in places where few people went. Hallways like this were lonely enough during the day cycle. There were so many secrets to Nalanda Station and they weren't allowed to explore any of them.

'The artificial gravity alone would be amazing to understand. Imagine if the girl had found the machine that made it possible,' Maeven thought, as she felt the pull through the floor. If they could control momentum in star ships, negate the effects of acceleration, they could travel so much faster between worlds. She could be home on Uppsala in a day- home and away from this place. Her father used to tell her about the machines on the station and his voice would warm with an excitement that was rare for him.

One time, before the Æesir, there'd been people who studied such things, who tried to learn and develop new technology, but not anymore. Everything would stay the way it was forever, just as the Æesir demanded it.

Maeven wondered what Alex would think of her world, if she'd even be able to bring him home. When she was of age, she'd be expected to marry another noble, someone whose position would benefit her father, but that didn't mean she couldn't keep Alex in secret. She could give him ships and warriors, armies to command. She knew he had it in him to be a leader, a great warrior. Someday he might even be able to succeed where her father failed, conquering Grannus, bringing the water world to heel. Then what could anyone say?

It was a thrilling thought, but even Maeven knew it was a fantasy. 'Enjoy what you have now,' she thought, 'before father takes it away.'

A short distance from the hanger bays, she climbed a flight of stairs, coming out on a metal walkway that echoed under her feet as it ran down yet another long corridor. She could hear machines up ahead and smell oil and exhaust. Disgusting, she thought, but it was the shortest route to where Kavaris Dell would be.

Cargo, supplies from the volcanic world, were taken off the Tairnish ship. She was surprised the headmaster deemed it necessary to supervise this himself, but he'd always been a bit hands-on. He was a monk after all, and not of noble birth.

The machinery sounds were getting louder. Looking ahead, she saw the thick shoulders of a Tairnishman standing at the entrance to the hanger bay. For a moment she hesitated. She hadn't spoken to any of these people in the past few weeks. They all seemed to be holding a grudge against her.

She went up to the man and announced, "I'm here looking for the Kavaris Dell."

"Yes, the headmaster wanted to speak to you." The Tairnishman did not look up, his attention on a monitor.

Obviously, he wasn't one of the cousins who'd been standing at the door to the Bogatyr barracks, but he looked just like them, only older. He was wearing the brown uniform of the servant class. They all looked the same anyway, she thought as she asked, "Would you get him for me?"

"One moment. I'm checking our manifest. The transport is leaving soon and we need to make certain that everything, every piece of cargo is loaded." He finally looked up at her and smiled. "Give me a moment and I'll be more than happy to help you." Then his eyes went back down.

Maeven waited, tapping a heel. The tiny monitor looked ridiculous in the large man's hands. Looking at a Tairnishmen it was easy to think they'd be simple, or slow. Their size seemed incompatible with speed and intelligence, but Maeven had seen them fight. She knew they were capable of lightning quickness and decisive thinking.

It was a shame that Vyktor, the one chosen to lead them, had been such a lummox. She wondered who would replace him. Eventually she'd have to smooth things over. That's what her father was trying to do. Why he'd been so upset with her earlier. "Everything is political!" he'd shouted at her, "Every action you make or don't make carries consequences."

The emperor didn't know she had anything to do with Vyktor attacking Cormack, but he, like the leaders of the Bogatyr, thought she should've spoken up for him at the trial, not just let him be executed. Of course, they didn't have to live with him like she did. She wanted to tell her father what she'd done. How clever she'd been. If Alex hadn't intervened, she would've been rid of two annoyances in one move. Instead, she got to see what Alex was capable of. Then last night he proved it again. He was the better prize, handsome and dangerous, kind and protective as well. She thought of him and felt a thrill.

For a moment Maeven's thoughts were back in her room, remembering his every touch, then something brought her out of her reverie. Heavy, stomping footsteps behind her came down the metal walkway. She turned and there they were, the two cousins from the door.

Their faces were carved without mercy as they glared at her. What could they want? She wondered, feeling an uncomfortable taste of fear and buried it beneath outrage.

Maeven turned to the man with the monitor. He smiled broadly and said, "Ah, it looks like we're ready to load our last piece of cargo."

Maeven looked one way then the other. She considered running but there was no place to go. The man with the monitor moved in front of her and the two cousins blocked the way back. She tried to scream, but as she opened her mouth, she felt the man's massive hand go over it. She struggled but there was no point, he was too strong.

Chapter 31

Chris, Cormack, Katy and Naiathne were moving slowly through hot tunnels, constantly going up. There was climbing, lots of climbing. They wore their dry suits so they wouldn't have to carry them.

'Dry suit, yeah right,' Chris thought feeling sweat drip down his spine. They called them 'dry' because they kept water out, unlike wet suits that kept you warm with a moist layer that adhered to the skin. Dry suits were insulated, thick, heavy and uncomfortable, especially these since they were made for working near volcanic shoots.

Of course, as good as they were at keeping heat out, they were just as good at keeping it in, hence the sweating, hence not all that dry. 'It's hard to believe these things are made to swim in,' Chris thought, as he looked down at the controls on his gloves. They had packs with motorized turbines, like small jet drives that would push them through the water. That'd be cool when they were actually in water, but as they hiked, they were only adding weight.

Beams from their flashlights were shining ahead of them in the claustrophobic cave, bouncing around and moving over the dark volcanic rock. The only thing that made Chris the least bit happy was the fact that both Cormack and Naiathne were struggling even harder than him. He may not be an all-star swimmer but walking and carrying heavy things . . . that he could do. Go ahead, make a fat joke now. He watched Naiathne fall behind. Then he realized that she was only trying to stay with Katy.

Katy was using an aluminum poll to help her navigate, swaying it in front of her to look for obstacles.

When they came to places they had to climb over or under, they'd all slow down and work together to get her through. Luckily, the cave was mostly uniform, made from magma, then smoothed over by ocean water which had been drained by the Grannusians when they helped build the colony for the Naiads.

Time passed. There was little talking, even when they took a break. At one point Chris asked Cormack if he thought Chooth was alright.

"He knows where the colony is. He'll find his way there," Naiathne answered in that tone of hers that made it sound like she thought everything he said was stupid.

Chris ignored her attitude. "Speaking of which, Julta said he was going to make us forget where the colony is. He never did."

"That's kind of funny, isn't it?" Naiathne said.

"Hope you're enjoying your water."

Chris looked down at the straw that came up from his suit's neckline. It ran down to a bladder canteen. He'd been slowly sipping it, trying to stay hydrated.

"It doesn't taste funny, does it?" Naiathne asked smiling.

"He spiked it," Katy said, spitting out her own straw.

"Not yours, sweetheart," Naiathne said to her. "For obvious reasons he wasn't worried about you finding your way back. But the boys. . ." she held her hands up. "I'm just saying don't drink too deep, Chris. You might forget your own name."

Chris looked back at her, then at Cormack. "Don't worry," Cormack said. "The Grannusians can tailor their bio-chemicals to be very specific, nearly surgical." "Yeah, you won't even know what you forgot. I had him tailor mine so I don't have to remember sharing air with you," Naiathne teased. Chris shook his head and pushed on. He stomped forward, leading the way. Any more talking would've been tough as the tunnel climbed even sharper, getting closer and closer to vertical.

"Hang-on," Naiathne called to Chris. She came up to him and retrieved two meters of cord from his suit, pulling it down and attaching it to Cormack. She tugged another from the prince and hooked it to Katy, then took a final stretch from Katy's suit and attached it to herself. "Go ahead," she said to Chris. "Lead the way."

Chris looked back, shining his flashlight the way they'd come. It wouldn't have been a sheer drop, like off the edge of a cliff, but if someone slipped, they'd probably start rolling and get banged up enough on the way to make going forward tough. Chris was on his hands and feet pulling them forward as the air got hotter.

He reached a peak and the tunnel turned directions, starting to curve down, a much easier walk. They stayed tagged together because in a half kilometer the tunnel started to fill with water. It was gradual, just a little bit of dampness at first, then a centimeter splashing under their boots. A strong smell of sulfur filled the air and little bubbles popped on the water's surface as it rose to their knees. The floor was still curving down. The steamy air was difficult to breathe.

Chris saw living things moving below the water, pale crabs with long pincers and small barnacle-like creatures with fleshy nubs that pulled-in as they passed. The crabs scurried away from them or occasionally tried and failed to pinch their armored suits. The air was bad, forcing them to put their helmets on, even Naiathne. The suits started dropping their body temps and pumping fresh, breathable air. Immediately Chris felt relieved, wishing they'd put them on sooner.

"Will we have enough air in these things to make it to the surface?" Chris asked.

Cormack looked at a read out on his wrist. "Definitely, this suit has CO_2 scrubbers. It can recirculate the air we're breathing, making a single tank last way longer, and it can use the air in the cave after filtering the chemicals out."

Chris sniffed deep, feeling like he could still smell the Sulphur, wondering if it was making it through the filters or if the smell was still stuck in his nose.

Katy kept pushing forward, reaching out with her pole, jabbing it into the water, even though all she really had to do is follow the tug of Cormack's line. She felt Naiathne next to her, moving in the water and felt the other line pulling in that direction. With the helmet on she could no longer hear. The space around her ears filled with the sound of her own breathing. It was odd having another sense cut off as she plunged through darkness.

Naiathne's voice cut in over the speakers in her helmet. "I'm going to adjust your ballast and make you more buoyant. It'll make it easier to move." She felt Naiathne touch controls on her arm, and her feet slowly start to leave the ground. She could bounce along now, barely touching the bottom with her toes. Soon the water was above her head, reaching the ceiling. Even through the armor and insulation she could feel it pushing in from all sides.

The tunnel went down again, then started rising. "We should be coming up on a pressure valve. It regulates how much water gets into these caves. Something the Grannusians invented," Naiathne explained over the speaker on everyone's helmet.

"Does it look like a giant scary mouth?" Chris asked, shining his flashlight up the tunnel, which had started climbing at a steep angle. He could see long, white, jagged edges pulsing, tightening, contracting and covering the walls ahead of them. He couldn't tell how far it went, but it looked like they squeezed down to nothing.

"That's sort of what it is," Naiathne said. "They grew it here." She leaned past him looking at the opening.

"So, it's alive?" Chris asked.

"Most everything the Grannusians create is," Cormack said.

"Don't worry it only eats small fish. It wouldn't be able to digest you." Naiathne added, extending her line so she could move up to the edge. "But I don't think you're going to want to take your time going through either. It'll contract if it feels too much pressure change. So, point straight, right toward that black spot in the center. That's open ocean." She pointed the way.

Chris aimed his flashlight straight ahead. "Open ocean?" he asked. He caught sight of a fishtail stuck to the wall. It was flapping, trying to escape, impaled on one of the white spikes and slowly being pulled in closer. 'That's not a small fish,' Chris thought.

"Maybe you should go first. Since you've done this before," Chris said to Naiathne.

"I've never done this. Why would I come this way?"

Chris turned to her. "Wait, what?"

"The only reason I'm wearing this stupid suit or taking you guys through this awful tunnel is because I'm trying to get you back to your people. This was the shortest route. I'd never be here on my own. I'm not a big fan of climbing through caves or being boiled alive. Not to mention I can breathe underwater and if I ever needed to travel this far, I would've used my sea dragon."

"Well, that's awesome," Chris said touching the small joystick next to his palm, gently pushing his thruster back as he moved ahead. The controls were similar to the EVA suits astronauts used. He bounced around in the cave a little, getting comfortable with it.

"What are you doing? Just go," Naiathne called.

"Hey, you let us play with these for like five minutes back at the colony. I'm sorry if I don't want to go shooting through a giant mouth at full speed."

"Relax. You'll be fine," Cormack said but he was talking to Naiathne. "I know you don't like tight spaces."

Naiathne snarled. "I'll be fine as soon as we get this over with. Are you done goofing around yet round boy?"

Chris threw his arms up. "Yeah, whatever, I guess I'm good." He touched the controls forward. "Try to keep the line tight and keep Katy in the middle," he said as he felt the cable pull Cormack behind him. With only two meters between them, they moved in a chain, leaving barely enough space to use their jets.

Chris went into the opening, resisting the urge to gun the controls and get this over with faster. Looking ahead at the dark spot, he thought of the open water, both eager and afraid to get out there. He watched the white teeth move past. They were set in a pink gummy substance with small polyps growing on it.

The teeth were softer than they looked from a distance. Their pulsing was more of a sway, moving in the current like seaweed and barbed with tiny hooks. As the opening got tighter, he felt them brush against him and try to grab hold, but they broke off on the suit's armored plating and floated away.

The wall creature didn't seem to appreciate this and the edges began to contract. Chris pushed the controls forward a little more, bringing his feet up to get them out of the way. The dark spot he'd been aiming for was now almost gone. He pressed the controls forward even harder, barreling through the white teeth, which caused more to break off on his side. Occasionally he felt one get purchase on him, but the jets were stronger and he managed to push through. "You guys doing okay?" he asked over the comms. He tried looking back over his shoulder, but it was impossible in the cumbersome suit.

"Just keep going," Naiathne called, her voice tense.

Only a moment later he was out, floating in the dark. Turning, he saw Cormack come out behind him, then Katy. She didn't have her jets on. Instead, she was pulled along by Cormack's tether. As he shut his jets down, Chris watched the two of them get tugged back towards the opening.

The line stayed taunt then suddenly it snapped. A sheared end floated up from the white teeth, severed and the opening was gone, completely closed with no sign of Naiathne.

Chris called out over the comms, "Naiathne, are you okay?"

"My jets are jammed," she yelled in a panic. "Pull my line!"

"It's torn," Chris called back. Reaching down to his side, he grabbed his dive knife. It was bigger than the one Naiathne had taken from him on the sub. He fired his jets full blast and rocketed back into the opening, driving his shoulder and the armor plating into the teeth. They'd turned rigid when they closed. It was like slamming into a wall. Still, some of it broke off. Chris pushed off with his legs and fired the jets again, smashing it a second time.

"It's trying to get in my suit." He heard Naiathne call.

Chris took the knife and started to dig his way in, chopping like a lumber jack. Cormack came down and helped. In desperation they hacked the edges of the plant. As the teeth floated up and away, Chris saw Naiathne's hand. Her gloved fingers were reaching out in front of her, trying to wiggle free, but the mouth was pulsing, pulling her back.

Chris grabbed for her hand, then reached further down, punching through the closed off teeth, managing to get a grip on her shoulder.

"Hang on," he called, feeling her fingers closing on his.

He moved his thumb over his jet controls and pushed off with his legs, struggling to control the pack while keeping his grip on her at the same time. Slowly he felt her shift, coming toward him.

Grabbing her under her arms, he strained feeling the teeth pull at his feet. Getting her in a bear hug and with one great effort, he pushed off. With a pop, they broke free. The jets blasted them up and away, tugging everyone else behind them.

Chris didn't let go of Naiathne until they were a good distance from the opening. Cormack and Katy were dragged along. When he stopped, the three bounced into each other, twisting around Naiathne, swinging her and tying her in tight in front of Chris.

"Are you alright?" Chris asked. The domes of their helmets were pressed against each other. It would've been uncomfortably close without the barrier of the suits between them.

"I'm okay," Naiathne said. "But next time I'll go first." She looked away, struggling to get free from the line. When her eyes came back up to Chris's again, she said more quietly, "But thanks for getting me out."

Chris nodded, going to work to untangle them. Naiathne was able to swim up and out from the middle while Chris and Cormack pulled themselves apart. They floated for a moment to get their bearings.

The opening they'd come through was at the bottom of an underwater mountain range. Jagged peaks and ledges wandered out in front of them along the sea bottom. They used the jetpacks to ascend the cliff face, going toward the surface. As the water became lighter, they could see more of the mountain range. It wasn't as silent as it first appeared.

In the distance the water was cloudy and colored white, as plumes of gas rose in the ocean. In valleys and on the edge of ledges were flashes of light, popping like explosions, then going dark as material poured out onto the ocean floor. Long pipes ran down from the surface, pulsing with energy, sinking deep into the ocean floor, drilling into the rocky surface. Everywhere they touched, rock was bubbling to the surface and there were more explosions.

Katy could feel them bursting through the water. Even at a distance the pressure waves were hitting her as the cold ocean water touched the hot lava, making tremors and detonations. Chris saw Naiathne's mouth moving. "What's that?" he asked keying up his mic.

"I said they're so noisy," Naiathne answered, shaking her head as she watched the eruptions. The magma poured out, flowing over the mountains, slowly growing higher and higher. Someday these volcanos would be islands. The natural process would've taken millions of years, but with the machine accelerating their development, they'd be born in under a decade.

Cormack pointed up. "The drilling platform is up there. I'm going to raise them on comms and let them know we're coming. They'll probably be shocked."

"That's one word for it," Naiathne said as they started ascending to the surface.

Chapter 32

Maeven didn't show up for any of her classes. History, math, planetary mechanics, or as Ben thought of it, the toughest calendar making project ever. Ben sat in the class that taught how the days and seasons worked on each world, feeling like he'd never be able to do the equations.

He took notes and did the calculations, but he still couldn't figure how long a day was on Uppsala. He had the excuse of not growing up on one of these moons, but even for the other students, understanding a structure with multiple worlds spinning around a massive gas giant with a binary star system in the center, was no easy task.

Ben looked at an empty seat and thought of Amita. Each time she'd finished one of these practice problems, calculating orbits, mass and other variables, she'd come up with the right answer, then say something like, "it doesn't seem possible."

"What's the matter?" he'd ask. "You've got it right there. The nights are thirty hours long on Oighear. No wonder it's the ice world." Then he'd try to copy her. Too bad she had to stay in her room today, avoiding monks and potential execution.

Amita would always shake her head in class and say, "It's just too perfect. All these worlds, they fit together too well." She'd stare at the right answer like it was a puzzle that she couldn't solve, even though she had literally just solved it.

Ben didn't see the problem then, just as he didn't see it now. He guessed that was why Amita had kept going out each night, risking everything. Sure, she wanted to go home, but also, she couldn't stand it when things didn't make sense.

He glanced at Tara. Since Maeven skipped class, lunch, and breakfast before that, he'd gotten a whole day alone with her. It was awesome. 'Speaking of things that didn't make sense,' he thought, while watching her move a strand of pale, blond hair away from her face. Her eyes met his and she smiled at him. He didn't get it, but all signs pointed to yes, yes indeed, a girl from another planet was into him.

The teacher, Regin, the Ice-Carver, called for their assignment to be turned in. Ben looked down at his orbital calculations that were plugged into a planetary model that went crashing as it accelerated. He shook his head, not sure if it was worth submitting, but he got up anyway and went to front desk. To pass his work to Regin he had to plug his monitor into a dock. Wi-Fi wasn't a thing on Nalanda, there was too much interference and most kinds of computer networking were on the list of outlawed technology.

Regin looked up at Ben as he pushed the button to send. The Ice-Carver seemed like he wanted to ask him something, but Ben was too fast. He hurried out into the hall and waited for Tara, not wanting to explain to the teacher why he'd sent his ice moon flying off into space.

Ben called to Tara as she came through the crowd. "So, I think Amita's probably gotten enough rest by now. I'm going to check on her."

"And I should check on my mistress," Tara agreed.

It was evening and everyone else was heading for the dining hall. "Or we could just go get some dinner," Ben suggested.

Tara gave him that look, the one that said you should know better.

"Fine, lead the way," he bowed a little holding his hand out. The number of people in the corridor thinned as they headed toward the Tamerlane domicile. Ben felt Tara's cool hand reach down and take his.

He remembered that Tara and Maeven sometimes walked this way. Maybe she was missing the princess. He looked down at his hand. Don't over think it, he told himself. She'd let go by the time they reached the Tamerlane door.

They went straight to Maeven's room. Tara knocked and opened it at the sound of Alex's voice. He was sitting almost exactly where they left him that morning, with his shoulders rolled forward looking bored. Ben didn't go in, choosing to stay in the corridor and go check on Amita, but he dragged his feet, listening to Tara and Alex talking. "Princess Maeven isn't here?" she asked.

"She was going to class last time I saw her. At least that's what she said," Alex explained.

"I never saw her. She attended none of her classes. When did she leave?" Tara's voice was tight with tension.

"This morning, right after you guys. She said it was important she be seen." Alex got to his feet. "You don't think the monks would've arrested her, do you?" He headed toward the door.

Tara stopped him, placing her hand on his chest. "No, they wouldn't dare. Besides, I would've heard about it. Everyone would've heard."

Ben expected Alex to come storming into the hall. 'Going to break more necks?' Ben thought as he heard Alex say, "We should go look for her."

Tara pushed him back. "You'd be arrested the moment you stepped outside. You need to wait here. I'll contact Andavarri. If anyone knows where Maeven is, it's her. I'm sure everything is fine, but please don't leave. It'll only make things worse." Her voice became incredibly calm, but when she walked out into the hall, Ben saw the look on her face.

He went to her and touched her shoulder. "Are you alright?"

"I'm fine. I'm sure it's nothing. Come on," she said as she walked down the hall to her own door. Her chambers weren't nearly as large as Maeven's, but they were in the same area, around a bend in the corridor and sharing a wall with the princess's. When Maeven had her suite built, Tara's room was added with a private entrance to hers, a back door in case she needed something.

Tara came around the corner and her eyes widened seeing her door slightly open. She stopped, staring at it.

"What's the matter?" Ben asked.

Tara held still, looking in at the shadows. She glanced back at Ben for a moment. "Come on," she said going forward. She moved cautiously as if expecting something to happen, expecting someone to come walking out. Ben followed. He could see how worried she was.

Tara had been at Nalanda for five years and had been Maeven's handmaiden even longer. Never once had she been worried that someone would invade her private quarters, but she'd always been careful, always made certain to secure the door. 'What could anyone want from me?' She thought. 'The only reason anyone would break into my room is to get to Maeven's, and Alex had been in there the whole day.'

She swung the door open and reached for a light, certain she'd find someone inside. Those extra senses of hers told her the room wasn't empty but looking around let her know she was wrong. No one was inside.

Her room was simple. A bed, a desk, and a cabinet. Her eyes went over it quickly, looking at the back door, the one that led to where Maeven slept. She missed the fact that her cabinet had been left half-open.

Ben walked in behind her. He touched the cabinet door, letting it swing open further. Outfits hung inside, and below them was something strange. He heard it bubbling.

"What's this?" he asked, pointing to a glass tank.

Something moved inside.

Tara turned back to him. Coming closer, she looked just as confused when she felt something coming from the tank.

"Is that a fish?" Ben asked, staring at the sluggish thing. If it was a fish, it was just about the ugliest he'd ever seen. It had no eyes, barely any fins and a mouth like a worm.

"Ben, close those doors," Tara said.

He looked back at her. "I said close them!" she demanded, pushing past him and flinging the cabinet doors together herself. "You need to go. You need to go right now." She pointed to the exit.

"Okay, alright, chill," Ben said, raising his hands. He backed out of the room, worried he'd done something to upset her.

Tara slammed the door shut, while Ben stood in the hall, staring at it, completely confused. He turned and started shuffling away, feeling like he'd just been slapped. He figured he'd go check on Amita, but he was having trouble focusing. He tried not to get angry, tried to remember the feel of Tara's hand.

It was the tank that upset her, not me, he told himself. He had no idea what the thing inside it was, but something about it reminded him of Chooth.

Chapter 33

Chris and Katy sat back enjoying the sun. "What are you two, plants?" Naiathne asked, standing over them. They were far above the ocean surface.

Chris glanced up, then patted a spot. "Sit down and join us. It's good for you." The morning sun was rising, heating the deck of the drilling platform. By noon it would probably be too hot to be out, but for now Chris was treating it like a welcome vacation, sipping a cold drink. He'd slept like a rock last night in the medical bay, then they'd eaten a little in the cafeteria before coming out. It was hard to tell through the atmosphere that they were enjoying the heat from two stars.

Naiathne dropped down on the other side, next to Katy. They were at the very edge of the platform. Netting ran just below the surface in case someone slipped, but it was still concerning the way Katy's feet dangled over the side. "Did you get anything to eat?" she asked Naiathne.

"No, they didn't have fish heads or sea slugs, so I skipped out," she said smartly.

"That's got to be tough for you," Katy said.

Naiathne looked away. "I'm kidding. I didn't feel like going in there with all those people."

"I can grab you something." Chris stretched back, getting ready to get up. He didn't know how long they'd been underwater. Between the trip in the sub, being kidnapped by Naiathne, and their night in the colony, not to mention their hike through the caves, he figured they'd been down below for just under a week.

When they surfaced last night in the dark at the platform's dock, they were peeled out of their suits like a bunch of shrimp. The doctors from the drilling platform, at least he assumed they were doctors, poked and prodded them in their medical bay. They checked them for decompression sickness and any other problems.

Parasites were a big concern after hearing how much time they'd spent with the Naiads. Apparently, that was one of those racially insensitive things surface dwellers believed about altered humans. At least that's what Naiathne accused them of as they started their tests.

Chris could see it in the way they looked at her, that to them she was less than human. They'd have been more than happy to toss her over the side or worse if she hadn't been under Cormack's protection. From the moment she'd taken off her helmet on the loading dock, the prince had made it abundantly clear that she was not to be harmed. That hadn't stopped the platform workers from staring at her and whispering though.

"Honestly, Chris, I'm not hungry, but thanks for the offer," Naiathne said, leaning back on her elbows.

Chris had trouble getting used to her being nice to him. Saving her life in the caves had subdued her a little, but he didn't expect it to last. He peered over the side, feeling the drill's power through the entire facility. The platform sat thirty meters above the water's surface, safe from storms and hopefully from the other dangers of the deep. They were in a choppy part of the ocean, far away from Anchor Home. The water had a dark color, almost green. It went on forever in every direction.

He pictured the explosions they were causing deep below. He'd seen the pop of magma surfacing and touching cold water down in those mountains, and he thought about Naiathne's warning that they were too noisy. Chris could see scarring on the legs of the platform as they splayed out and dove beneath the surface. He pointed down at the scars, "Are those from the same thing that tried to eat us at the entrance to the colony?"

Naiathne leaned forward. "The Cirean-Croin? Probably," she said. "The damn things are surprisingly good climbers. There aren't many other predators that could've gotten that high up," she said it so dryly that Chris thought she was joking.

When her dark eyes looked at him, they were grim. "No, seriously. They've been a real threat in these waters lately. And all this noise—" she pointed back to the buildings on the platform. "That's why this place has been built up like a fortress. Look at those barricades. That's because they've already been attacked. I'd say it's happened a couple of times. Once something like that comes up from the deep, it doesn't leave, not if it's got food. Running an operation like this is like ringing a dinner bell."

She pointed down to the ocean. "Look down there. You see the movement in the water, the dark spots going against the tide? Those are schools of fish. They're attracted here and big things eat little things. It goes on and on, till you get to something that'll take a run at a drilling platform. The Cirean-

Croin was spread out like a net when it attacked us, but it can curl up tight and make itself more like a column." She pointed down again to the scars on platforms legs. "It'll wrap itself around something like that and worm its way up. It's tried getting into the colony that way before, but it was too big. The tunnel was too tight."

She shrugged and sat back, looking out at the water. "But at least you guys have a nice view if it does attack."

"Sure do," Katy said cheerily. Naiathne and Chris weren't sure how to react as Katy smiled.

Cormack came out and walked up to them. "Well, I couldn't put it off any longer."

"What's that?" Chris asked.

"Calling my mother. She wasn't happy."

"You must've told her about me then?" Naiathne said.

"No, I definitely didn't do that, but I'm sure someone else will." He glanced back over his shoulder at one of the buildings on the platform. It had a few antennas on top of it. "I had to tell her about the sub though. She's sending a skimmer to pick us up. It should be here in a few hours. She said our mission is over."

"Wait, so we're not going to keep trying to find Eir?" Katy asked.

"Not without a transport and I don't think my mother is going to give us another."

Chris thought about going on, going back down under the water again. He glanced at Katy's pale eyes, then back out at the ocean. He felt selfish, but there was a sense of relief that he didn't have to go down again, didn't have to face any more sea monsters. The sooner they were on dry land, the happier he'd be. "I bet you Chooth is still looking for her," Chris said. "Maybe when he finds her, he'll bring her back to the palace."

"Yeah maybe," Katy's voice was soft. "Or maybe I should just get used to this." She got up and started walking back toward the buildings. It was impressive how she managed to navigate without sight. When she got close to the door, she slowed down, feeling along the wall.

Chris was about to follow her, but Naiathne put her hand on his shoulder. "I'll keep an eye on her. It's not you. She's angry at the world. I kind of get that." She paused in front of Cormack, "How do you think this is going to go? Me going back to Anchor Home?"

"You're my sister. You know I'll protect you no matter what." Surprisingly Naiathne leaned in and gave him a hug. Then she went off and followed Katy.

Chris watched the exchange. Despite himself he was starting to like Cormack. The prince nodded to him. "You good?" Chris asked.

"Yeah," Cormack said. "It's just one of those things, you know. . . I mean there are so many of those things here. Nothing is ever simple. I love coming home, but sometimes it's simply better to be gone. Family, you know?"

Chris thought about Alex, wondered how he was doing. "Yeah, I know," he said.

∞

It was getting near lunch and there was still no sign of the skimmer. Chris was hungry and a little bored. He wasn't sure where the others had gone, but he'd been sitting outside by himself for a while. Wandering inside the facility, he looked for the cafeteria or the others. It was a big place, but much of it was taken up by machinery, massive pumps and cooling systems that hummed and smelt like fuel.

'No harm in checking it out,' Chris thought as he wandered. A flight of stairs took him down from the main deck to a lower level to a long hall with offices on either side. One he noticed had a door with a seal on it. He went toward it and saw a glass observation window. Seeing movement, Chris peered through at a man in a white coat, wearing a respirator and goggles. He took a tray full of samples and placed it on the table. Chris ran his eyes quickly over the room and saw tanks holding plants. They had long green stalks twisting up into rainbow-colored beads.

Chris tried to look closer at what the man was carrying. The tray was covered by little cups that had the seeds in them. That's what was in Eir's lab, that's the plant they eat, Chris realized. 'What were they doing with it?' He watched the man dropping something onto the samples, some chemical compound. 'Was that the poison? Could this be where it was made?' He hated that the idea had entered his head.

He backed away from the window wanting to find the others. That's when a sudden noise from outside echoed through the entire platform, a smashing sound as the structure shook and an alarm went off.

The man in the window looked up, saw Chris and pointed to him. He was saying something, but Chris couldn't understand with the glass in the way. He started toward the door as Chris turned and ran.

∞

Naiathne was behind Katy, who was wandering down the hall. Katy didn't know where she was going, only that she wanted to avoid people. So, whenever she heard voices, she would pointedly turn away. This led her to a set of metal stairs that ran up one of the antennas. Her hand found the rail and she started to climb.

Naiathne stayed quiet as she followed her. Katy ignored her till she reached a door she couldn't open. Naiathne didn't help. She just watched as the blind girl pressed at it. When Katy finally gave up struggling with the handle, she said, "I know you're there."

Naiathne stayed quiet.

"Are you going to help me or what?" Katy waved to the door.

"Why should I? You don't even know where it goes."

Katy threw her hands up in frustration, starting back down. "You're right. And it doesn't matter anyway." Her shoulder banged into Naiathne. She was almost at the bottom when she heard the wind above her. Naiathne had gone past her to open the door.

Katy started back up the stairs, pushing past the Naiad again. "I knew it was you. I knew you were following me."

"Yeah, my footsteps aren't as loud as Chris's," Naiathne pointed out.

"And you smell like low tide," Katy shot back.

"Ouch. A fish joke from the blind girl, didn't see that coming."

Katy snickered a little despite herself. "I'm just looking for a place to be alone."

"Yeah, I get that. Mind if I join you?" Naiathne went out the door ahead of her.

Katy didn't know what to say, but she followed Naiathne out into the wind.

"I know, I'm annoying, right?" Naiathne asked as they started to climb higher and higher, reaching a landing well above the deck of the platform. To go any further, they'd have to climb a ladder. Naiathne saw it but she didn't point it out to Katy, who was content to lean over the rail. Naiathne leaned over too, staying quiet.

"Sorry about the low tide crack," Katy said after a bit.

"It's cool, I get it," Naiathne answered.

Katy waited for her to say more. Naiathne stared out at the ocean before finally explaining what she meant. "Your friend Chris is a really nice guy and I think base-line you're probably pretty nice too. It's hard to be really mean to someone like him. Even I couldn't keep it going for long and niceness is not something I've ever been accused of. But that's what you want to do right now. Things are starting to settle down while you're still worried and you just want to tear into someone. You probably haven't gotten to do that since you lost your sight? Am I right?"

"I don't know. I feel like I've gotten to be a pretty big witch." Katy was thinking about the transport, the way it'd taken days and a lot of help from Chooth for her and Chris not to break out in an argument every time they talked.

Naiathne shook her head. "Oh, sweetheart, you haven't been half as pissy as you could be. At least not from what I've seen."

"I did run off to an alien world."

"Yeah so, who was going to stop you? Chris? It's not like he lost his sight."

"It's more complicated than that. My brother's back on Nalanda and the others from Earth. And it's not like getting angry ever helps," Katy said. "I should just suck it up, right?"

"Sure, maybe."

"You think I'll ever get there?" Katy asked.

"How the hell should I know, I've never gone blind before. Now keep your eyes open for the skimmer. They're going to be bringing me to see the mother that tried to have me killed at birth."

"Wow," Katy said. "I mean, just wow."

"Yeah, I know I get that reaction from a lot of people."

They stayed up there waiting, hiding from the world, till Naiathne said, "Here they come." She could see the skimmer flying over the waves, moving quickly and casting spray behind it. "They're really in a hurry to pick us up," she said, watching their fast approach.

"I'll take your word for it," Katy said. That's when they felt the entire platform shake and sway.

The girls clutched the rail, feeling another impact radiating up through the structure. "What is that?" Katy yelled.

"I don't know," Naiathne said, taking her hand. Naiathne pictured the scars she'd seen on the platform, imagining what an attack by the Cirean-Croin would be like. It'd roll itself up, coiling and twisting into the platform while its long wormy mouths went everywhere.

Out in the open wasn't good. They'd be easy prey. She moved toward the stairs when she heard a crunching sound. Massive metal struts were screaming, pinched under the weight of something heavy. She had to get Katy inside, but Naiathne's curiosity got the better of her. She leaned over the rail to see what was attacking them.

She expected to see a coiled horror, the thing that'd killed her sea dragon. Instead, she saw a white shell and long clawed arms, over two dozen of them, splayed out like the feet of a pill bug, grasping one of the platform's legs, gripping and releasing in waves as it climbed.

Naiathne knew this creature, and it was no monster. She grabbed Katy's hand. "Come on," she said, starting down the stairs, hoping to see an old friend.

Chapter 34

Following Naiathne, Katy nearly slipped. The Naiad held her hand as they raced down the stairs.

"Where are we going?" Katy asked.

"We've got to get out there before anyone starts shooting." The steps echoed loudly under her feet. Naiathne pulled her along as the alarm sounded.

They charged down the hall and pushed through the door to the outside. Naiathne helped Katy through, then let her hand go, moving further ahead. "What is it?" Katy called, wandering behind her.

Squinting in the glare from the sun, Naiathne watched the creature's head come up over the edge of the platform. It was massive, with armor plating and a mouth like a strainer, filled with baleen fibers similar to a whale's. It had twelve eyes held on stalks that dangled in clusters from either side of its head. They spun around strangely, taking everything in. Its front claws were the largest of its multiple sets of appendages. They clamped down and held to the edge of the platform, while the rest of its body hung below, clinging to the leg.

Naiathne moved toward the creature as a shot slammed into the deck, right near its broad head. She turned, looking for the shooter. A worker from the platform had gone up on the roof of a building. He was taking aim with a rifle. "Don't shoot," she yelled, waving her arms.

He ignored her and another shot blasted through the air. It hit the creature squarely in the side of its head and ricocheted off, only leaving a little dent.

Something fell out from beneath it. A hundred or more smaller animals poured from below its mouth, flopping onto the deck in a pool of water.

Wormy, little fish and clawed-crustaceans, swam in the puddle. Quickly they started to pull together. The large creature's eyes focused on them for a moment. It made a sound, then let go, dropping back off the platform. Naiathne ran to the side and watched its entire mass flop into the water with a giant splash. She could see it swimming down under the surface.

When she turned back to the animals that it released on the deck, the puddle was gone and so were the creatures. Standing in their place was Chooth in his humanoid form. Naiathne went forward and hugged him. "I had a feeling it was you," she said.

"Hello," he said simply.

Still by the door, Katy felt it fling open behind her. Chris came running out and grabbed her. "What are you doing out here?" he asked, ready to pull her back in.

Cormack wasn't far behind, along with several workers from the platform. They streamed out into the open. "It's okay," Cormack said. "It's just Chooth making an entrance."

"Yeah. . ." Chris said looking at Cormack, wondering if he knew about the lab. If the people here had told him that they were experimenting on the crops. He looked around at the workers, who weren't happy to see Chooth. His presence made them nervous. Was that because these were the very people responsible for poisoning his species? Were they afraid he'd call up that creature that'd delivered him here or some other terror from the deep?

Cormack's people blamed the Grannusians for the attacks by the Cirien-Croin. Chris had heard the queen's consort accuse them. Maybe the poisoning was revenge.

Naiathne and Chooth were speaking, but Chris couldn't hear what they were saying. He took Katy's hand, approaching them and asking, "What was that thing?"

"It's a part of me. Sort of," Chooth said.

"It's called a Caleth-gul. The Grannusians use them for heavy labor," Naiathne offered.

"We don't 'use them.'" Chooth shot back.

"Sorry," Naiathne said.

"We are not always together, but they're still part of us. There's always a connection to them . . . It can be disconcerting being that spread out." Chooth said looking at the water. The creature was still below, swimming around the platform's legs, but it seemed like something else was bothering him.

Cormack came over. "Glad you could make it, buddy," the prince said, touching Chooth on the shoulder.

Frowning, Chooth twisted away from him. "Are you?" he asked. Then he turned to the others. "I think I know where Eir is. She is unsafe." He was about to say more when he was interrupted by the royal skimmer's arrival. Its engines screamed, pushing it into a vertical climb up from the ocean's surface, drowning out any conversation.

It rose above the deck, then touched down softly. The gangplank fell forward, releasing armored soldiers who stomped out in rows with their rifles on their shoulders and flags waving.

One of the soldiers wearing the markings of an officer stepped ahead of the others. "Prince Cormack, we've come to retrieve you by the queen's orders."

"I understand, captain. Just hang on one moment." He turned back to Chooth. "Where is she?"

"Down below," Chooth said. "I went to the farms on the outer rim, where the poisoning started, searching for her. Do you know what I found? The fuel trail of a royal submarine. Strange, right? Why would they go there, so far from their precious volcanism project? Did you think you could hide your stink crossing the ocean from someone like me?" He motioned to the deck around him, pausing, waiting for Cormack to say something, but before the prince could open his mouth, Chooth began again. "I found a lab that Eir had in the farmer's quarters." Chooth looked at the deck and shook his head as if deciding what to say. "It was half destroyed." His voice was shaking and fumbling, struggling to find the words. "More questions," he spat out. "And no one to ask. Everyone is gone. The farmers weren't there, neither was Eir. Where are they?" he demanded.

Naiathne broke in. "The farmers came to the colony. They were the first to become ill. They were looking for help."

"But what happened to Eir then?" Katy asked.

"Or why was there a lab set up here," Chris added. All eyes turned to him. "I found it just before the alarms went off."

"I'm sure there's an explanation," Cormack said, looking back at the workers.

Chooth laughed, his voice sounding distinctly human and bitter, almost sad. "I've heard enough. I'm going to find that sub and get Eir. I'm going to bring this news to the others. Your people have been so afraid of a war with mine. It'll be over before it even begins." In the short time Chris had known Chooth, he'd seemed so calm and reasonable. That was gone. He sounded nearly insane, seething as he struggled to keep his body together, to hold his humanoid form. His alien eyes were pinpoints, staring like a predator at Cormack.

He turned to walk away, but Cormack reached out for him again, "Wait," he said grabbing his shoulder.

Chooth swung, his body twisting as his arm swiped Cormack across the chest, leaving a long, ragged wound that started to bleed.

Immediately the soldiers dropped their weapons into firing position, taking aim at Chooth. "No!" Cormack shouted putting himself in front of them. Naiathne joined him, throwing her arms up.

For a moment something broke and a look passed over Chooth's face. He stared at Cormack's wound, then at his hand. Tiny, raised spines were tipped in Cormack's blood. He came to the prince's side. "I'm sorry," he said. "I didn't mean to do that."

Cormack looked up at him. "Stay here, then. Help me figure this out."

"I can't." Chooth seemed to be fighting a battle against himself. "I've no control." He turned back toward the sea, ready to walk over the side, but Katy stood in his way.

"You promised you'd help. You said we'd find her together," she said it softly holding her hands out.

"Fine," Chooth said, that frightening edge came back to his voice. He grabbed her arm and in a single motion, holding Katy tight, he leapt from the edge. She screamed in surprise as she fell toward the water's surface.

"No!" Chris yelled, running forward with his arms outstretched. He looked down and watched them disappear beneath the waves. Chooth's body had come apart and he had encircled Katy in an attempt to protect her as they fell. It was impossible to tell if it worked.

Chris looked down at the water. In a moment, without thinking, he jumped. Behind him he heard Naiathne call, "Chris, don't!" But he was already in the air and falling. It was far enough down for him to realize his mistake. He tried to point his feet toward the water's surface, tried to make himself as straight as possible.

It didn't matter. When he hit, pain shot through his legs, sharp and intense, lancing through him. He felt bones breaking as the force of his body brought him further and further down, deep and away from the sun. Consciousness slipped away as he focused on not obeying his body's need to inhale. 'Don't breathe, hold your breath,' he thought as his head became fuzzy.

Before him, he saw something spark to life and glow as it approached him. It was beautiful, like an angel. Chris was too hurt to worry. His last thought as he passed out was, 'I hope that thing, whatever it is, doesn't eat me.

Chapter 35

Ben banged on Amita's door after she'd been in her room for almost twelve hours. She opened the door with red rimmed eyes and fought the urge to rip his beating heart from his chest, or more likely his voice box from his throat.

Amita wasn't much of a sleeper, averaging only four hours a night. Back home, when she was supposed to be deep asleep, she was usually reading. Her parents always said she wasn't a morning person. When waking her, it was an unwritten rule that you didn't talk to her. The rest of the day she was respectful of her parents, but that first half hour, as she ate her breakfast and slowly came back to consciousness, they knew that discussing anything would be risking the loss of a limb.

Ben was talking faster than usual, which is saying something for him. It was about Tara and Maeven and about Alex and a fish tank and the monks. He came back to the monks a few times and this brought something to Amita's mind, something she'd been trying to forget. She didn't like the monks, but that didn't mean she was okay with what happened to the one guarding her.

An image of him being lifted from his feet as a black arm went around his neck and another went around his head came to mind. She heard the snap again and shivered, remembering the way the man in his red robes had slumped to the floor.

She held her hand up to Ben. "Stop, stop, please stop? Give me a minute."

"Right, sorry," Ben said. "I was coming to check on you. Make sure you were doing okay."

"Yeah, I got that part, but just give me a minute?" She rubbed her eyes, then went to the tiny sink in her room to splash water on her face. She stared at her pale reflection in the mirror. Her light brown skin looked ashen and dark circles had formed under her eyes. Her hair was wild and disheveled. She reached for her scarf and tried to pull it back out of the way. It was a poor attempt. She came back to the door and grabbed Ben's arm. "Come on," she said.

Ben went with her. He opened his mouth to say something, but Amita reached up and put her hand over it. "Not yet," she said. "Just walk." They were heading to the common room of the Tamerlane Domicile.

The dining hall was where most students took their meals, where they were expected to eat, but the Tamerlanes had a space set aside for those who didn't wish to mix with the other noble families or who couldn't. It was mainly self-serve. Though in many cases such as with Maeven and Tara, a noble from a greater house was served by one of the lesser.

Amita searched through the pantry and the cooler, till she had a small meal in front of her. The machine that made tea and other hot concoctions worked relatively fast, but not quick enough for her.

Standing in front of the machine waiting for her cup to fill, Amita hoped Ben would wait till she had some breakfast before he started talking to her again. Of course, he didn't. He pulled out a chair and flopped down at a small table, making as much noise as possible. The chair legs had barely stopped screeching across the floor when he started telling her all about his visit to Tara's room, the tank he'd found and the way she'd kicked him out. He was coming to the end of his tale when suddenly he went quiet.

Amita looked over her shoulder and saw Alex. "Where's Tara? Has she found Maeven yet?" He was talking to Ben, but Ben refused to acknowledge his presence. He crossed his arms and stared forward, not saying a word.

'Thank god, he's gone quiet,' Amita thought, knowing it wouldn't last.

"Ben?" Alex stepped behind him. "Come on, this is important."

"Yeah, so is what happened last night." Ben looked at Amita. He saw the change on her face, the way her eyes flared and her shoulders tightened. "Wait, you were there too. I should've asked you."

Finally, her tea started to pour, filling the cup. 'Thank goodness,' Amita thought, picking it up from the machine and watching the steam rise as she pushed last night away.

"Amita!" Ben insisted, sitting forward.

"Leave her alone Ben," Alex said, looking at Amita pointedly. "We're not supposed to talk about it."

Amita's eyes were still on the steam. She wasn't sure if the drink was too hot, so she held it under her nose enjoying the smell. "Are you even paying attention?" Ben asked her.

Amita took a deep breath. "I pay attention to everything. It's kind of my thing." She used her drink to point at him. "You're bothered because your sort-of girlfriend kicked you out of her room when you found a fish tank there." Then she pointed to Alex, "And you're worried about your definite girlfriend, the princess from a powerful empire, who has flitted off somewhere. But neither of you are nearly concerned enough about getting us back to Earth. You're all quite content to let me deal with that." She took a sip. "Oh, and you don't want me talking to him." She pointed back to Ben. "About last night, when you and I witnessed a murder."

"So, you didn't do it?" Ben was happy, turning back to Alex. "I knew you didn't have it in you."

"Shut up Ben." Alex's eyes were across the room, where Andavarri had just come in. Her dark purple skin blended in with the shadowy stone walls and her tail waved contently behind her. Amita cursed silently, feeling a thrill of fear as she thought of everything she'd just blurted out.

Andavarri cocked her head a little but didn't do anything else to give away how much she heard. "Where's Tara?" she asked, slithering forward, coming into the light.

"That's what I was just trying to find out," Alex said.

"Did you check her room? That's where I saw her last," Ben asked, trying to sound more civil, uncomfortable with how Andavarri was staring at him.

"She had some sort of tank? Such as a water tank? Is that what you said? Was there anything in it?" Andavarri asked, coming uncomfortably close to Ben, slinking down just in front of him.

Ben eyed the others, looking for help. Apparently Andavarri had heard quite a bit. "Um. . . Tell you what I'll go get her, okay?" He started backing away from the table.

Andavarri pointed her long fingers toward the hall, but her gaze was on Alex. "We'll all go. I need to report something to her that will be interesting to your whole group."

Amita looked at her tea and at her breakfast sitting on the counter. She put it down on the table glumly before following the others.

They went to Tara's room and Ben knocked on the door. "Tara," he called.

"It's not a good time, Ben. I told you that," she said. Then she opened the door a crack. "Look, I'm sorry I made you leave like that but—" She stopped, looking past Ben to see Alex and Andavarri. "Oh, you have company." Tara stepped out into the hall, closing the door behind her.

She looked at Andavarri, "I was just going to contact you. I haven't seen the princess all day. I was hoping—"

Andavarri held up her hand, silencing her. Her voice, which had been aloof a few minutes before, now took on a solemn tone. "That's why I'm here. The princess has been kidnapped. It's the Tairnishmen, the Bogatyr, they have her aboard their transport.

They've barricaded the loading dock and are due to depart in the next hour."

"What! Why did you wait to tell us?" Alex demanded. Andavarri stared at him as if he were beneath her notice.

Alex shook his head, took a long breath and turned to Tara. "How many armed men do you have?"

Tara was still trying to comprehend what Andavarri was telling her. Alex's question forced her to focus. "We have eight guards in the domicile, but I can get more bodies from the other royal houses that are still loyal to us." She looked down at the monitor. "Many of them are still in the dining hall."

"This isn't common knowledge yet," Andavarri said. "The monks are trying to keep it quiet so there won't be a conflict here in the station."

Alex started toward the exit, waving for Tara to follow him. "I'll take the guards with me. All of them. You go to the dining hall and round up as many loyal people as you can. Do you have access to weapons?"

Tara nodded, taking his arm and steering him toward the armory and the small barracks for the guards. Two would be on duty at the door, while the others would be in the room where the weapons were stored. "We've mainly got stun batons," she said, then glanced over her shoulders and whispered. "But there are some nastier things in here that we're not supposed to have."

"We may need them," Alex said. He had his monitor in his hand and he was pulling up the map of the loading docks as they walked.

Andavarri looked at Ben and Amita. "Aren't you going with them?" she asked.

Amita gave her a withering look, letting her know she thought it was a stupid idea but Ben nodded, surprised it hadn't occurred to him before. "Right, right. Yeah, I should go." He started to follow Alex and Tara, but then he glanced back at Amita. "But you should stay here where it's safe."

"I was going to and you should as well," she said dryly.

Ben was hurrying away, following Tara. Before he disappeared around the corner, he called, "I'll be fine. Alex is going to handle this." Amita still didn't feel awake, nor did she want to be arrested again.

She looked back at Andavarri. "I'm going to go eat my breakfast."

The alien nodded. "Very pragmatic."

"Always," Amita said holding up her tea.

The Long-Wolf seemed to be waiting for her to leave. Amita shrugged and walked away. She was trying to shake off the sense that something bad was about to happen and she wondered what she could do to stop it.

Chapter 36

Chris heard Chooth's voice. The words came from so close that it felt like the Grannusian was inside his ear canal. "I've given you something for the pain, but you're still going to feel discomfort."

He felt a strange pressure against his eyes, making it hard to open them. He felt it against his whole face, but that wasn't the worst part. Something was in his throat tight against his teeth, slippery and slimy, going down into his lungs. He reached up to his mouth, his hands moving through a viscous fluid that was thicker than water. He touched his jaw running his hand over his lips and teeth. A fleshy tube blocked his airway. His eyes opened in shock and found everything was fuzzy. It was like looking through Vaseline.

Chris started to panic, but then he heard Chooth's voice say, "Relax."

He followed the command whether he wanted to or not as a warm happiness crept into his system. 'He's drugging me,' Chris thought, not able to work up the rage he knew he should feel.

"You broke both your legs following us and you suffered a concussion," Chooth said. "I'm attempting to heal you, but it's going to be a while. You're lucky you didn't damage your spinal cord."

Chris reached up, touching his ear, feeling something twisting and moving, buried deep in it. He would've torn it out if he weren't medicated. Instead, his finger tips played over it, dancing on his earlobe. Through the haze he was having trouble telling where he began and where the creature ended, which he thought was odd. 'Ears were such strange things anyway.'

He could see a little. Chooth's parts were swimming all around him, and Katy wasn't far away. Her form was outlined and floating in the same fluid. She had a breathing tube in her throat as well. There was no chance of speaking. Not that they would've been able to hear through whatever this stuff was. Still, it was nice to know he wasn't alone. Pulsing lights moved all around them, bathing Katy, then darkening. She appeared as a spectral form.

"You're doing very well, Chris. Both you and your brother are fast healers. Your legs will be cast by the time we get to the sub. That's where we are going, by the way, to the royal sub. I would not have chosen to take you with me. Katy, yes. I promised to take her to Eir, but you . . . you would've been safer with Cormack. Now sleep for a time. My friend will care for you while I handle some things." Chris felt more of the warmth from the drugs coursing through him. He wouldn't be awake long, but before he passed out, he touched Katy. She startled a little, pulling back. Then she felt Chris's fingers running down her arm seeking her hand. Grabbing it, she held tight. Chooth was in her ear as well. He told her about Chris's injuries and where they were going, to find Eir. "Just as I promised," Chooth said in a strange voice, almost regretful.

Katy never saw the creature they were inside, but Chooth told her about it. It was similar to a jellyfish, only much larger. It sailed beneath the ocean, pulsing and pushing water out through its body in small jets. Most of Chooth was outside the creature, but as they came closer to the sub, he left Chris and Katy alone. He swam down toward the Caleth-gul, which had been following them since the drilling platform. The large, armored creature stayed low, where it blended in with the ocean's sandy bottom. A Caleth-gul wasn't usually an aggressive creature, but with its powerful claws and its sheer size, it could be dangerous if a Grannusian chose to use it as a weapon.

∞

The next time Chris woke he was on a metal deck plate that curved and pointed down at a weird angle. For a moment he thought he was back on the drilling platform. He cleared the viscous jelly from his nose, smelling an oily machine odor tinged with smoke. The subtle glow of emergency lights lit the room. Katy was leaning down next to him. "Where are we?" Chris asked, wiping the stuff from his eyes. His whole body was soaked in jelly, as was Katy's. They both looked like they'd just been vomited up, which wasn't far from the truth.

The large, industrial chamber featured chain falls hanging from the ceiling and cargo containers thrown everywhere. Ramps and walkways led to a massive set of doors in the center of a half-flooded floor. They were sitting on one of the walkways above the main level.

"Chooth said we were on a royal sub and he put these on your legs," Katy said, running her hand over the cast.

Chris reached down and felt it. A bone like material covered him from knee to heel on one leg and a second cast was formed around his ankle on the other.

"He said I broke bones in both my legs," Chris explained. "First time I've ever broken anything." He looked around the room. Everything was wet. A deep pool of water covered the sloping floor where it met the far wall. He couldn't tell if the massive set of doors in the floor were compromised. They looked solidly closed, but the room was so flooded that he had to assume they were cracked. Three smaller subs like the ones they'd taken to the city of Twilight were piled in the wreckage of machinery and cargo smashed in the far side of the room. His eyes went up the wall, attracted by a pulse of light coming from a crack just above him. It was a ragged cut in the outer skin of the sub and it wasn't small.

Outside, the jelly-like substance clung to the hull, keeping the ocean back. Chris got the sense the room had just been drained. He thought back to what Chooth said on the drilling platform. He'd never mentioned the sub being damaged. 'When did that happen? What caused it?' Chris wondered.

Something shuddered in the ship. They felt it through the floor and rail. Chris thought he heard the distant sound of an explosion. It popped and went quiet so fast that he couldn't be sure.

"Where's Chooth?" he asked, reaching for a rail and struggling to get to his feet. His legs didn't hurt, but they didn't move very well either, especially on the uneven ground.

"Don't know," Katy answered as she struggled up the walkway, moving on her hands and feet toward the top of the room. Chris reached out to help and nearly fell over. 'A fine pair we make,' he thought.

"What do you think happened here?" Chris asked.

"I heard something in the water, explosions, I think. Chooth came back for a moment and said the sub was attacked, maybe it was that thing from the colony. But Chris, he's acting really weird," Katy said.

"Yeah, I picked up on that when he tossed you off the side of the drilling platform. I'm assuming by your scream you weren't expecting that?"

"No. And I didn't expect you to follow me either," Katy said.

Chris looked over the room. "Seems to be a theme with us."

"It felt like we were falling forever," she said.

"It was pretty high. You should've seen it- Oh . . . sorry," Chris apologized as he leaned heavily on the rail, moving stiff-legged toward Katy, though he wasn't exactly sure where she was going.

"It's alright. It was probably one of the few times I was lucky to be blind," she said. Chris thought about being inside the jellyfish, about the sea monster at the colony with its hungry mouths tearing apart the dragon and even about that fish struggling in the mouth of the caves. He was glad he wasn't blind, but he could've gone without seeing any of those things.

"Where are we going?" he asked.

"I don't know. Up, I guess. I figured if we're underwater, we should probably seek the highest point, just in case."

"Sounds logical." Chris said struggling after her.

"I wasn't just talking about the jump from the platform by the way," Katy added. "Chooth seems agitated. He took off the moment we got here, like he was looking for someone or something."

Chris shrugged, though Katy couldn't see it. He was about to say that he didn't know, but then something caught his attention. The pool of water that half flooded the room had been still until then, like a dark mirror that swallowed everything including the walkway they were on. Chris looked and saw a ripple. Something was moving beneath the surface. He watched as it broke through.

Something stared at him. It was grey and its intelligent eyes were alien, "He's looking for me," the thing said, watching them sharply. It was one of Chooth's people. It spoke and its voice sounded female, ancient and raspy. "But who are you people? You're not part of the crew?"

Katy stopped moving as Chris stiffly turned around. "Um, we are—" He started to answer, then stopped, looking back at Katy, hoping for help. Of course, she had no idea who he was talking to. The eel-like head waited patiently. She was a different color from Chooth, pale white. She looked tired, possibly sick. "It's a long story, but we're friends of Cormack, Naiathne and Chooth. Who are you?" Chris asked.

Her voice came weakly. "I'm Eir, first healer of the Grannusians and I'm afraid we all may be in terrible danger." As she said this, as if to punctuate her statement, the sub rattled again. There was that same pop, but this time it was louder and closer. The vibrations came through the metal deck as the sub shifted. The whole room turned and the vessel plunged deeper into the ocean with its nose pointing down.

Katy, who was above Chris, slipped. She lost her hold on the deck and fell toward him. Chris reached out to pull her in, but he lost his own footing in the effort. He let out a grunt of pain as he tumbled, slamming onto the shifting walkway, barely managing to hold onto the rail as it turned vertical. He pulled Katy back to the side of the walkway, where she could grab hold again. Chris's legs started to throb from his hips to his toes, feeling the impact and the strain.

"What's happening?" Katy asked, catching her breath.

"The sub is going deeper. Most of it is flooded already. This room is one of the few with any air left. The rest are being torn open systematically," Eir said, motioning with her head toward the crack. "The creature will only be able to hold the water back for a little while. As we sink deeper, the pressure will increase. You should not have come here."

"We were looking for you," Katy said. She was feeling her way along the rail, climbing down and getting closer to Eir. "I came really far to see you."

Chris watched her go, watched her blindly reach out for each cross bar, moving toward the water. His shoulder hurt from grabbing her and the discomfort in his legs was getting worse. He wished Katy would just hold still. He tried to breathe through the pain, but then another rattle moved through the walls shaking them, followed by a distant explosion.

The sub shifted further, going almost vertical. The walkway became a slide as Chris lost his grip and fell toward Eir. He slammed into Katy on the way down, knocking her off the rail. It was the cast that hit her, smashing her with a solid blow. They both splashed into the water. Chris felt Katy next to him, felt the walkway as well. He tried to swim, but with his legs frozen in the cast, he sank deeper in the water while his fingers reached out trying to grab the rail. It was impossible to fight panic as he slipped deeper.

Then he felt something under him. Eir had swam down and using her head she slowed him enough so he could catch the rail. He tried to control his fear as he started to climb. He knew he'd hit Katy and was worried he may have really hurt her, but as he got closer to the surface, with his lungs burning, he felt someone grab him from the top. He surfaced and saw that it was Katy reaching down. She had a handful of his shirt and she did all she could to pull him up.

Blood was in the water, streaming down from Katy's head, down her face and her arm. "I'm alright." Chris managed to get out as he clung to the rail, struggling to breathe and coughing up sea water. He looked at her, at the gash on her skull. "I'm sorry." He reached up to touch her head.

"It's okay," she said feeling the spot. They were both in freezing ocean water up to their waist, clinging tight to each other, holding the same rail. The jelly had washed away from their skin, leaving them shivering and the room was almost completely vertical.

'We're probably going to drown,' Chris thought as he tried holding his hand over Katy's wound. "It's a lot of blood," Chris said. He turned back to Eir. "Can you help her?"

"I can try," Eir said swimming next to him. Her pointed nose was so close that he could smell her fishy breath "But in the state I'm in. . . I've been exposed to the poison. The toxin inhibits my ability to stay in contact with the rest of me. I'm losing myself, soon I'll be too diminished to even speak. It's happening faster than I thought."

Chris looked around in the water. There were parts of Eir swimming nearby, but they didn't seem organized. Some were bumping into him and Katy and some were struggling to get around the walkway.

"Who did this to you?" Katy asked as a few small wormy creatures climbed from Eir onto Katy's shoulder. They squirmed through the blood toward her forehead where it was streaming out.

"I did it to myself," Eir said weakly. "Only a little while ago, in the lab on the sub."

"Why?" Chris asked.

"To test the cure. I had to let the poison run its course to see if it'd work. I was waiting till the final stage, but then we were attacked. I was in a tank being transported back to my lab when it happened."

"Wait! You made a cure, here, on the royal sub?" Chris asked. He was thinking about the lab on the drill platform, wondering if he'd jumped to the wrong conclusion.

"Yes, the human scientists were assisting me," Eir said. She looked away sadly for a moment. "When the ship flooded, they were killed, murdered. We were so close. I didn't see it till it was too late, but he hasn't been himself for quite some time."

"Who?" Chris asked.

She looked at them both. "Your friend Chooth. He's been compromised," Eir said.

Chapter 37

Andavarri took her hand down from the spot behind her ear, the place where the stones sat. She'd been in the head of her Fire Golems. She'd seen Kavaris Dell through their eyes, calling for them to follow him. He was going to the loading dock to confront the Tairnishmen. For a moment Andavarri considered holding the Golems back, not letting the monk use them as his personal security, but then she remembered that their presence here was dependent on cooperation. Fire Golems, as powerful as they were, were no match for the Æesir and the monks were the chosen of the Æesir. If she didn't give them over now, everything would change. She wasn't sure if the Æesir would come, but she didn't want to risk their wrath either. She knew what they were capable of. They'd scoured Tairnish a hundred years ago, destroying labs and factories belonging to human nobles.

Not to mention that if the emperor heard that Andavarri hadn't tried to help save the princess, she'd find herself skinned and placed on his wall, along with so many of his victims. Most people thought that the emperor's trophy room was only a rumor, but Andavarri had been there. She'd seen what he was capable of.

Giving the command freeing the Golems to act on their own, she told them to follow Kavaris Dell's orders. She knew it wouldn't matter. The old man wouldn't be vicious enough. He'd hesitate and try to negotiate. The Tairnishmen would slip away, breaking their vow to serve the emperor, and their actions would lead to another war.

'And that really didn't matter either,' Andavarri thought, while bending down in front of Tara's door. Humans were always fighting over something, even something as silly as that spoiled brat Maeven. Better that she be kept as a bargaining chip in their games, rather than be given the chance to rule.

Andavarri ran her hand over the lock. It would've been hard to open, with its advanced electronics and heavy bolt. Luckily for her someone had already disabled it, breaking its codes and leaving it in a compromised state. She touched the entry command and pushed.

Tara had been distracted when she left, otherwise she would have noticed that her door couldn't be secured. Something beside the capture of her mistress was bothering her. It had to be something interesting.

Andavarri stepped into Tara's neatly ordered room and heard gurgling water, coming from a cabinet. Opening the doors, she discovered the tank inside, bubbling away. Andavarri had an idea what she was looking at. It was something the Grannusians didn't want known, their most vulnerable part. She hadn't expected this from Tara. To do something so sinister, but if her mistress commanded it, Tara would follow orders, loyal to the end.

Loyalty was a strange concept to Long Wolves. Andavarri could understand it from a distance, but she'd never felt it herself. Her ancestors were solitary scavengers surviving on a barren wasteland of a world. They trusted no one. It didn't mean that Long Wolves had no society or understanding of the interrelations necessary for a species to survive and advance. They were simply incredibly good at weighing all their options before choosing a side, and they never choose that side out of some misplaced sense of duty.

It was a tough concept for humans to grasp, with their nobles and their houses. None of what they had would've been possible without loyalty. Though often the ones who ruled them, who sat at the top of their pyramid of duty, were the least trustworthy of all.

Andavarri tapped the side of the tank and watched the thick, eyeless fish inside, thinking about the other races. They had their own ideas about loyalty, more honest than what the humans professed.

The slow thinking Drakes had lived in a symbiotic relationship with the Lightening Bugs for millennia. Drakes were easily made into slaves because of their sense of loyalty, desiring nothing more than to be guided. The male Ice-Carvers were constantly hunted by their mates. They survived only by working together.

Then there were the Grannusians, their bond was beyond loyalty. Their entire being was determined by cooperation, from their smallest parts to the whole of their society. It was in their very cells.

And look what they'd done with it. They controlled nearly every aspect of their world, but it all started in their center, in those specialized organisms that made up who they were. When they hatched, each looked alike, the crustaceans, the worms, the fish, even the parts they weren't always connected to, like the massive Caleth-gul. They all came out looking like ugly slugs, popping from egg sacs, impossible to tell apart. Then as they grew, they'd take on the form of the piece they were to play. They would develop eyes, or claws, or tails. They'd go and join a host, one of the Grannusians already in the world.

Only one part stayed unchanged as it grew, always looking like an ugly slug. This rare part never went on to join a preexisting being. It would form its own collective. Some thought it contained the 'self' of the Grannusians, but they denied this.

Their 'self' was defined by all their parts, even those they could sacrifice. No, this part, which they called the hub, was more like a communications center, a telepathic broadcasting point that sent signals through some unknown medium, reaching thousands of miles to all the other parts of a Grannusian. Others like it ran through a Grannusian's body, like a nervous system, but this little fish that clung under the eel-like head, which was their mouthpiece, was the part, more than any other, that controlled the whole.

Andavarri stood back, considering the tank. She was fairly certain that the ugly thing inside of it was a hub and she didn't know who it belonged to. Only a few Grannusians were on Nalanda. Their survival out of water was a complicated thing, so they didn't often travel.

'What is the point of keeping this one? An experiment maybe, to see if a Grannusian could be controlled by its hub?' Andavarri wondered. An interesting thought. The hub wasn't something many knew about. The Grannusians didn't advertise their biology openly, but over the years the always curious humans had learned a great deal. Of course, that kind of research was usually conducted in a secret lab somewhere dark and horrible, not in the middle of a school by a princess's royal hand maiden. This was no experiment. Andavarri realized there was a purpose behind it.

Sensors were in the water, metal rods tied into a display. Tiny wires ran to the creature, hooked into its skin. Andavarri let her long fingers run over the display, bringing it to life. The display wasn't overly elaborate, looking like it'd been thrown together from parts and pieces. There was a log-in to get into its command codes, but conveniently they were unlocked. Andavarri pulled up the last few commands, a list of orders that'd been typed into the display, then repeated over and over again filling the screen.

Find the cure, destroy it, destroy Eir.
Find the cure, destroy it, destroy Eir.
Find the cure, destroy it, destroy Eir.

The words formed as a block of text running down the entire screen with time stamps on the side, each only minutes apart. Andavarri looked at the clock and saw that it was coming up on that time again. She watched as another line of commands came across automatically. Find the cure, destroy it, destroy Eir. As the words stopped moving, the metal wires in the tank began to pulse with light, causing the creature to twist and quiver in pain.

'Eir was home on Grannus,' Andavarri thought, as she realized what she'd just witnessed. She knew the hub could be far from its host, but she had no idea it could be on another world.

Her mind started working quickly now, wondering what to do with this information. Tara, or more than likely Maeven, was controlling a Grannusian, maybe even one on their home world. 'Could they be responsible for the poisoning?' She wondered at the deviousness of it. But now what to do with this information?

If she kept her mouth shut, it would spare Maeven and Tara any repercussions. But Maeven had been kidnapped. If that transport left with her, she'd never return to Nalanda again. She'd be kept as leverage against her father. And Tara, who was she? Just a servant, even if she was of noble blood.

She meant nothing to Andavarri and would mean even less to the emperor when he heard his daughter was taken. No, the value in this secret was not in keeping it, but in choosing who to tell. If she told Kavaris Dell, he'd probably try to keep it quiet too, but Regin and Fafnir would be outraged and the Grannusians— Andavarri could only imagine their anger.

Loyalty was not something that Andavarri understood, but she saw that it was something others valued. She decided she'd be loyal to the extraracial stewards and see what that gained her.

∞

It didn't take long for Alex to gather the royal guards. They were unlocking closets, opening cases and arming themselves. Ben held a stun baton, pressing the button and watching the electricity spark at its tip. This wasn't the first time he'd held one. He had to take combat classes just like everyone else. He had the bruises to remind him of the two hours of hell he put up with every other day.

At first, the week after they arrived, Edith hadn't made him participate. She let him sit on the sideline with Alex, but as the time went on, and as Alex started taking a more active role, Ben was expected to join in. He followed along with the drills, going through forms and practicing moves. Eventually, she had him go into a few sparring matches. As he pressed the button on the baton, he shivered remembering the feel of one of these things jammed into his ribs. He'd been on the ground with some kid on top of him, who hadn't looked that tough a moment before. The guy put enough juice through Ben to make him flop like a fish on the floor.

That was awful enough, but it wasn't the worst part of the encounter. The baton that zapped him had been his own. The guy he was fighting had come in the center without a weapon, trying to make it a fair fight. He'd taken Ben's own baton from him. Now he was going into battle with those big Tairnishmen. 'This should go really well,' he thought.

Ben pressed the button again and looked at the royal guards, who were wearing armor and assembling rifles that fired vicious looking flechlettes.

The ammo came in little solid blocks that fractured into shrapnel with barbed tips. One guard opened a case with bracelets, handed them out, then pointed his fellow guards to a container holding small dark orbs like ping pong balls. They floated up and attached to bandoliers across their chests.

Alex looked at him with a raised eyebrow. "Grenades," the guard said. "They've got simple navigation, so you can get them right up next to an enemy. They're low yield though, made to throw up a graphite screen. Still, if you pop one in someone's face, they can cause quite a bit of damage." The guards were all trained soldiers, young men and women who'd probably seen combat. Despite that, they seemed to be listening to Alex. At least they were willing to let him tag along and contribute.

Alex nodded. "Alright, let's hurry. We're fighting time here." Alex didn't bother with any of the other toys, only picking up two batons. He wasn't trained with the rifles or the other weapons so they'd only be a liability.

Unfamiliar with the terrain, Alex pulled up schematics on the monitor, holding it in front of him as the guards made their way out of the Tamerlane Domicile. He didn't see Ben put on a bracelet and sneak grenades into his pocket before running to catch up. Ben pointed to the screen in Alex's hand toward the loading bay's main entrance. "That way is going to have a ton of guards. Last time we tried something like this, you know when Chris went to get Katy, it only took a couple of monks to grab me."

"They're tougher than you think," Alex said.

"My point is that it's a tight spot, put two Tairnishmen in the walkway and you've got a wall."

"Then we go through them," Alex said.

"Or," Ben's hand reached over to the screen, moving the image out further, showing a number of entry points. "We can try a different way." He nodded to the guards and lowered his voice. "Let these guys hit them through the front, while we use a backway."

Alex thought about it, then agreed. "But which one?"

They were walking past the little kitchen area again where Amita was sitting with her breakfast. She looked up, listening to the guards and her friends. She felt more awake, alert enough to know how stupid their mission was. Amita stood, getting in Alex and Ben's way. She took the monitor from his hand, knowing what Ben was suggesting. "Hold on a tick," she said waving him over.

She touched the monitor screen while Alex watched the soldiers get further away, headed toward the exit. He was anxious to follow them, but Amita grabbed his shirt before he could sneak around her. "Just wait!" She demanded while her eyes stayed on the monitor.

Amita's hand went over the controls, moving a wire frame map. She pointed. "Here, these doors are for bulk supplies, but there's a set of service stairs that'll take you to that level. If the Tairnishmen have half a brain, they'll have them secured."

She bit her lip while problem solving. After a second, she added, "But these doors are on the top level. They move supplies through them using a sky hook on the ceiling." Her hand moved over the screen to show the top of the room. "In this hall is a door for getting into the hook's control room. You could go down the chain, drop right on top of the airlock. It's completely mad, but most likely your best chance."

"Awesome," Ben said taking the monitor back while Alex nodded.

"Awesome and stupid," Amita pointed out while still holding Alex's shirt. "This is foolish and you know it. You shouldn't be out there."

"I have to," Alex declared, then added more softly, "It'll be alright." He moved Amita's hand away, then headed out. Ben fell in step behind him. He looked back to wave.

Amita shook her head. She didn't want to admit it, but she was scared for them.

Chapter 38

Standing before one of Vyktor's cousins, Kavaris Dell wasn't happy. The situation was simply unacceptable. The young man was unmoving, as were the other two other Tairnishmen behind him. With their heads nearly touching the corridor ceiling, they were probably the largest members of their collective, but they weren't part of the ruling line so Kavaris Dell had never bothered to learn their names.

The Tairnishmen may claim they're a brotherhood, a collective, as they said, where everyone was equal, and that may have been true at one time, but over the centuries even they had developed their hierarchies. These massive men held simple weapons, clubs and knives. As imposing as they were, Kavaris Dell was surprised to see so few. They must've known the Fire Golems would make short work of them, he supposed, but then they told him what they were willing to do.   Kavaris Dell looked back over his shoulder at the Golems. The four stood still. The heat from their core burned hot, lighting the way, bathing everyone present in a red, hellish glow. A few monks stood with them.   Letting the words of Vyktor's cousin sink in, Kavaris Dell knew Tairnishmen didn't bluff. They said that if anyone tried to force their way onto the transport, they'd blow the securing clamps and depart early. "Charges were already set," he'd added.

Unscheduled departures were extremely dangerous. Not only did it mean their course would be wrong, risking shooting off into deep space rather than making it to one of the moons, but Nalanda was inside the gas giants rings, a storm of rocks and dust that would tear the ship apart.

The systems at the station that brought vessels in were automatic, technology left behind by whoever built Nalanda. They controlled gravity fields and were the only way such large transports could get enough speed to dock but nothing helped leaving the station.

Ships simply dropped away, falling as quickly as possible through the debris field of the ring. It was always risky but doing it without perfect timing was suicidal. That was the threat. They'd set off and risk destroying the transport rather than give up their prize, the damnable princess.

Running his hand through his thin hair, Kavaris Dell considered his options, annoyed that he really had none. He looked at the Golems and wondered if they could get the princess off the transport before it crashed into a rock. Special commandos were trained to do such things but none of them were here.

The Fire Golems were a possibility. They were so agile they could probably find her, but how would they bring her back? Certainly, they had managed to drag that drake, Tearmai, through space, but he wasn't a princess or the daughter of the most powerful man on three worlds.

"Do you know the wrath you'll face? What the emperor will do to you?" Kavaris Dell asked the Tairnishmen.

Vyktor's cousin nodded. "Don't concern yourself with our politics, old man. The Bogatyr Collective is one. We survive together and we die together."

Kavaris Dell turned, hearing footsteps. The guards from the House Tamerlane were armed as they charged down the corridor. "For certain you'll die together!" their leader shouted as he shouldered a rifle and fired at the Tairnishmen. A blast of needles came flying out, cutting through the large man's body. It was an impressive shot, fired from fifteen meters away and past the Fire Golems and monks who crowded the hall.

With amazing precision, the guard avoided hitting anyone else, even though the needles widened as they dispersed. The other Tairnishmen moved back to find cover just outside the corridor, while Kavaris Dell turned and held his arms up. "Hold your fire!" he screamed.

The Tairnishman hit the ground hard, blood streaming from him. His shoulder joint was blown apart, rendering his left arm useless, but his other hand was searching his belt. He grabbed a transmitter and was struggling to pull it to his mouth. Kavaris Dell fell on him, trying to tear the device from the big man's hand, which was still incredibly strong.

"No, no! You don't want to do that," Kavaris Dell snarled, hearing the Tamerlanes approaching to finish their butcher's work. He turned to the Golems, "Stop them!"

The rocky creatures went into action. The lead guard was moving past the first Golem with his rifle ready to fire, when in a sudden motion the creature's stone fingers took hold of his armor, lifting him from the ground. It slammed the man against the ceiling, taking the rifle from his arms and throwing it to the floor. Its stone foot smashed the weapon while the guard fell and slumped unconscious.

The other Golems descended on the remaining eight guards like a landslide. The metal plating in the corridor shook as the Golems stormed forward. The guards opened fire, blasting with needles across the rocky bodies. The needles pinged off, taking some rock with them, but mainly falling away or ricocheting. The men in their body armor were tossed left and right. The sound of stone fists falling on flesh was like a butcher's hammer. Four men fell quickly, crumpled to the ground, while the others backed away, still firing. Eventually they turned to run, but they didn't make it far. Kavaris Dell watched over his shoulder, still bent down by the cousin on the floor. His hands never released the transmitter. "Don't do it," the old man begged. "I've stopped them for you."

The Tairnishman's hand relaxed and Kavaris Dell fell back with the little device. "Good," he said, then he looked up past the loading docks entrance out into the vast industrial space. It was nearly empty with shipping containers and machinery sitting idle. Two more Tairnishmen stood at the airlock guarding the way, looking toward the corridor, waiting to see what would happen. They were distracted and weren't about to look up after hearing the weapons fire.

Kavaris Dell's eyes went to the airlock. Then sensing movement, they traveled up toward the vast open space above the loading dock at the catwalks and platforms. He gaped at what he saw coming down through the shadows. It took him a moment to understand what it was as he closed his mouth and tried to keep the surprise from showing on his face. Smuggling the transmitter away in his pocket, he considered what to do.

∞

"This is a terrible idea," Ben said, staring out the glass dome of the sky hook that ran on a track high above the loading dock. The dome pointed down toward the floor with a control consul at the front of the cabin. The operators chair was pointed at an angle and had a four-point harness. It was one of five machines going along the ceiling. They had picked the one closest to the airlock.

Far below, they could see the entrance corridor, where Vyktor's cousin stood with his two cronies, facing off with Kavaris Dell. Two more Tairnishmen posted in front of the airlock were directly below them.

"It was your idea," Alex said, looking through a box of safety gear near the back of the control booth.

"No, actually, it was Amita's," Ben said. He was holding the operator's seat as he glanced out. The hook was all the way up. They'd both agreed it'd be too noisy to use the chain to descend, afraid the sound would alert the guards. Not to mention that climbing down a chain for what amounted to a five-story building wasn't appealing. "All I said was we shouldn't go through the main entrance," Ben pointed out. He was looking down through the window again, feeling his stomach twist, as he stared at the floor. "She was the one who came up with this goofy idea. Dropping from the sky like a, like a— I don't know, special ops guy or something." The windows all curved down, like the gun turrets on a World War 2 bomber, so the operator of the sky hook could look below at what he was doing. The operator would work the joystick controls while strapped in for safety.

Alex pulled two harnesses and a long coil of rope from a storage container in the back of the cabin and held one harness out to Ben, who stared at it. "This is stupid and we're both going to die." Ben grabbed it from Alex's hand, then watched him climb into his, pulling the thigh straps tight and the shoulders over. In the center of the belt was a metal ring with a device hooked into a carabiner.

"We're out of options," Alex said. They'd already checked the stairs that ran down to the floor and found monks guarding them.

Of course, Alex and Ben didn't know about the ultimatum that the Tairnishmen had given Kavaris Dell, but they knew they were better off avoiding the monks, since Alex currently sat on top of their most wanted list.

Alex went to a hatch on the glass dome, banged the emergency latches and swung the window out. This wasn't the way you were supposed to get out of the skyhook, it was only for emergencies. Ben watched Alex tie off his line to a rail. They were close to the loading dock's outside wall, the side where the Tairnish transport was parked. Ben came forward as Alex climbed back in. From a distance he thought they'd be able to walk down the wall, but then he saw they were still a good three meters from it.

"Come here," Alex said, leaning down and looking at the device on Ben's belt.

The auto descender was a little different from anything Alex had seen before. It had a squeeze lever to let the rope through and mechanical brakes for the pulleys. Alex didn't like that. He liked simple things with less to go wrong. Still, it was probably better for Ben, he couldn't really mess it up and they could descend on the same rope, not needing a brake line.

Alex only found one rope that he hoped was long enough to get them to the floor. The descender already had a short piece of safety line. Probably just enough to get out of the skyhook in an emergency. He looked at the coil he'd left on the floor, considering. It was probably strong enough, why else would they have it up here?

He took the short rope out of Ben's descender and started lacing in the new one. He had to open the little device to side-load it, running the line through the pulleys. "Are you sure that's how it goes?" Ben asked.

"Yeah," Alex said impatiently, knowing the clock was ticking. His hand brushed across Ben's pocket where he felt something solid. "What's this?" he asked.

Ben took the grenade out and held it up. As his fingers widened, the little orb floated up a few centimeters above his palm.

"Ben, hold absolutely still," Alex said, while his eyes widened.

"What?" Ben said. Not sure why Alex was so scared.

"You don't have any idea how to use those, that's what. Now slowly close your hand, just like you opened it."

Ben did as he was told. The little orb floated down as he folded his fingers. "I thought they might be helpful," Ben said.

Alex shook his head, taking the bracelet off him. There weren't many instructions on it, just a little note that said, 'tap twice to arm.'

"Do you have any more?" he asked.

Ben pulled out four more.

Alex shook his head. "You kept them in your pocket? Do you know what could have happened if they went off?"

Ben shrugged.

"The Virtanen family name would've ended with you," Alex said, looking for something to store the grenades in. When he couldn't find anything, he reluctantly dropped them into his own pocket.

"Hey, what about the Johnson family name?" Ben asked.

"I've got a brother just in case," Alex said, working the rope through his own descender.

He went to the hatch and picked up the coil, threw the rope out into the air, holding a few coils back, and waited to see where it ended before letting off a few more lengths. Ben had to stand by him, right near the edge, so Alex could estimate the slack. When Ben climbed up to the opening, touching the sill around the hatch, he immediately regretted every decision that had brought him to this moment.

"Ben, it's going to be alright," Alex said looking at his pale face. "Look, man, if you need to stay here—"

"No," Ben said cutting him off. "I'm cool. I'm here to help."

Alex nodded, then turned away.

Ben grabbed his shoulder. "Hey, if this goes badly, I just want you to know I'm glad we had all this time together. That we've become, you know, wingmen."

Alex laughed a little, amazed by how Ben had started to grow on him. He was even willing to bump Ben's fist, which waited in the air.

"Yeah, wingmen," Alex said, tapping knuckles, then he turned and leaned out the window, carefully watching where the rope ended.

Alex's hand was on the frame when he heard yelling come from the corridor. It was followed by the compressed sound of a flechette gun firing below. The Tairnishmen came out to take cover, while Vyktor's cousin fell back, blood spurting from his shoulder. The red of Kavaris Dell's robes covered him as the old man dropped on top of him.

"We've got to go now," Alex said, feeling his heart jump as he stepped out the window. Hanging in the air, he pulled out a baton and squeezed the descender to release the brake.

Ben didn't have a second to think as the line went taught, dragging him out behind Alex. He bit his lip to keep from screaming, struggling to get his hands on the line and trying to keep himself upright. His legs found the rope first. He clung to it, looking down at Alex hurrying toward the ground. Trying not to hyperventilate, Ben closed his eyes while his hand searched for the descender. Just a squeeze and he'd be on an express train to the floor. His baton was on his back, ready to use.

Ben glanced down again seeing the Tairnishmen. 'They don't see Alex coming, and they're not going to see me either,' he thought. He squeezed the descender. It buzzed as he plummeted.

∞

"No," Kavaris Dell said silently to himself never taking his eyes off the rope and the two troublemakers. He turned, looking back at the Golems. They were returning from dismantling the Tamerlane guards. Kavaris Dell pointed up at Ben and Alex. "Stop them," he demanded.

The first Golem turned its single flaming eye toward them, staring for only a moment before its stony form went silent and the flame shot from it, aimed toward Ben and Alex.

Seeing it come for him, Alex squeezed the descender even harder, forcing it to release and let him fall faster. The guards in front of the airlock still hadn't looked up. Alex pointed his feet. The line ran out a meter above one of their heads. It was only then that the two large Tairnishmen glanced up to see where the Fire Golem was going.

Alex plowed into the guard's head like a steam engine, smashing the man, who was older and larger than Vyktor, into the ground. The guard crumpled into a heap. Alex ignored the pain from the impact and rolled away with one baton out while reaching for the second. The remaining Tairnishman was unprepared for how fast Alex was as he stormed ahead and drove the shock batons into the guard's stomach. He held the charges on, causing the large man to convulse and fall over.

Alex spared a single glance up at Ben, who was holding his hands up defensively toward the flame. It stopped directly in front of him, still for a moment. "Hey there," Ben said to the living flame. "We're not doing anything, I swear." He was four meters up.

The flame danced in front of Ben, then whipped across the rope. The hot plasma cut the line and Ben started to fall, this time without any hope of stopping himself. He hit the ground hard and collapsed. Ben let out a moan and a heavy breath as his eyes closed. He wasn't moving.

Alex watched his friend fall and heard him hit the ground with a sickening thud. He paused looking toward Kavaris Dell, feeling rage course through him. Then he refocused on the problem in front of him, knowing he only had a moment before the Fire Golems would have him too. He ran up the steps to the airlock, toward the inside door and found it closed.

'What now,' he wondered going to the controls, looking for a release. There were all sorts of buttons. He pressed them all, but nothing happened. The door refused to budge because it was sealed from the inside.

Alex tried to think, knowing he only had a moment before the Fire Golems would be on him. He came out of the airlock and took the grenades from his pocket. 'Tap twice,' he thought as he tossed the little devices into the doorway. The red indicators lights blinked as they landed. He covered his eyes and his face waiting for them to pop.

When the explosions went off, they were unimpressive, no more powerful than the salutes he and Chris lit on the fourth of July. The puffs of smoke billowed out, filling the room. He looked at the two unconscious guards on the ground, realizing too late that they would've been his best chance of getting the doors open. The outer door started to close. For a moment he thought of running through them but when the shuttle left, if he couldn't get the inner door open, he'd find himself in a vacuum.

He looked at Ben's slumped form and realized for the first time how stupid this whole plan had been, how helpless he was. How he failed in the one thing he thought of as his responsibility. 'What was I thinking? They are going to take Maeven no matter what I do.'

He wasn't getting on the transport, not without help. He went over to Ben, bending down to check on him. Thankfully, he was breathing. In the distance stony footsteps approached. He looked toward the corridor where Kavaris Dell stood and saw the Golems move past him. It was too late to run.

Chapter 39

Trapped in a doomed vessel, sinking deeper into an alien ocean, Chris realized that they'd finally found Eir, the healer. 'Mission complete,' he thought, trying not to laugh. He glanced at the recked machines below him, having trouble believing that Chooth had done all this. Taking a final glance at the destruction, he tried to put it from his head, looking back at Katy instead who was still clinging to the rail.

Chris took a deep breath and held tight to Eir's eel-head as she dove down under the water that filled the cargo bay. Chris was beyond cold, shaking uncontrollably.

They hadn't talked about how they were going to stop Chooth or how to get the cure to Eir or even how their friend could possibly be responsible for all this. Their only goal was surviving and the mini subs that had tumbled down toward the bottom of the room were their best chance. Unfortunately, the machines were under two meters of water, falling further as the sub shifted. A few more distant explosions rattled through the hull. That was the sound of Chooth searching, trying to find Eir.

Chris was stiff legged, incapable of swimming with anything but his arms. Luckily Eir was willing to be his propulsion. A red light from the emergency signs glowed in the distance, and a few spotlights stayed lit above with their own power, but it was still dark below the surface.

There wasn't much hope of activating the subs. They were smashed and flooded, but Eir had explained that they had dive equipment on them and that the hatches shouldn't be locked. Since Chris remembered where the suits and tanks were stored on Cormack's sub, he figured it'd be easy enough to get to them, but his opinion changed as Eir brought him to the sub's side and he went to work.

Chris reached out to touch a dormant mechanical arm, pulling himself along till he found the top of the sub. It was laying on its side on a pile of other equipment. He pulled the hatch open, feeling small air bubbles move past him. Chris's lungs were already burning. What had it been, thirty seconds? Cormack would've been fine, he told himself.

Chris wasn't raised on this world and he wasn't an expert free diver. He thought about playing that game with his brother when they were kids, where they'd hold their breath under water in the pool. It was one of the few things Chris could beat his brother at. He'd almost gotten two minutes one time, but he'd nearly blacked out doing it. It's all about trying to relax and ignore the pain, he reminded himself as he went through the hatch.

Naturally, his body floated to the top. He didn't fight it, telling himself again and again to calm down, but the fact that he was underwater and had a roof over his head brought on the mother of all anxiety attacks as his whole body screamed for him to surface and breathe.

No, no, Chris told himself, nearly blind in the dark of the mini-sub. He couldn't see anyway he was going to get this done. His hands searched frantically for the hatch, trying to find his way out. Instead, he felt an air pocket above him. Gripping the ceiling, which was the side of the sub, he turned himself over. He wanted to pull his whole head up in it, but there was only room for his face, which he stuck out of the water, pushing his nose into the wall to take a deep breath. A little bit of seawater got into his mouth causing him to cough. He ignored the tickle it left behind.

'Okay,' he thought, calming himself, 'now what?' He pictured where he was, what he needed. The lockers couldn't be far. Taking a deep breath, he kicked off the ceiling with the one leg that wasn't completely encased in a cast, launching himself to the back of the sub.

He banged into the lockers, then reached out till he found the tanks. pulling them loose from their holders, he started for the hatch, glad they were so buoyant. He shoved them out, seeing Eir waiting. She nosed the bottles, pushing them toward the surface. She struggled, not used to only being able to use a single part of herself. It was like suddenly having all your limbs amputated.

Chris returned to the air pocket, took another breath, then went back for the bags of gear, which were much heavier. He dragged them across the sub, walking along the bottom wall. He would plant the leg with the long cast, then push off with the one that had the short cast. It was slow and painful work. He had to stop at the air pocket twice before he got them to the door.

With a final effort he lifted them and pushed them out the hatch. His heart sank as he watched them fall. Chris didn't know how far down this pool of water was, but he knew he didn't want to go any deeper to recover the gear so he tried grabbing the straps. He was half hanging out the hatch when they pulled him out and down with them.

He held the straps, sinking, as Eir swam deeper, a black shadow against the distant lights. She returned pushing a large tightly packed bundle toward him. Chris couldn't tell what it was. With her mouth Eir pushed a cord into his hand. He gave it a hard tug and the thing started to expand.

The raft inflated rapidly and rushed toward the surface with Chris hanging on. He shot out above the water holding its side with the gear still in his other hand, glad his shoulder hadn't been dislocated on the way up.

Eir surfaced near him. "Are you alright?" she asked.

"Sure, I do this kind of stuff all the time. Can you push me over to Katy?"

Eir nodded, then dove under, driving the raft, Chris and the gear toward the walkway, where Katy was clinging onto the rail. "We got a ride," Chris said.

Katy climbed in, then helped hoist the gear over the side. She tried to assist Chris as well, but he was too heavy. He had to go over to the inverted handrail and climb it like a ladder, before dropping into the raft. Laying in it, staring at the ceiling, only the fact that Katy was in a hurry to get into her suit got him moving again. He sat up and helped her pull the bags apart. Each one had a wet suit, a regulator, a face mask, a dive knife, fins and a weight belt. 'No wonder they almost drowned me,' Chris thought.

The suits weren't warm on their own, but they'd help insulate against the cold, help keep their own body heat in. Chris tried not to look while Katy got into hers, taking her wet clothes off first. He almost asked her to turn around as he pulled his own on, feeling strange having her stare right at him with those pale eyes. Taking out a knife he had to customize his suit so it'd fit over his casts, cutting of a good part off the legs.

There wouldn't be much chance of him getting the flippers on. Chris attached Katy's tanks and gave her the regulator. It locked into her face mask, which had a radio connected to it. They'd be able to talk while they were submerged. 'So now we won't die right away if this place floods,' Chris supposed as he stared at the water where Eir was waiting patiently.

"Maybe now you can tell me why you two are down here with Chooth? Neither of you look like you're from Grannus," she pointed out.

"We aren't. We're from somewhere much further away, but we've come to find you. We wanted to see if you could fix my friend's eyes."

"I have so many questions . . ." Eir's voice drifted off as she stared at Katy.

Chris waited for her to say more. "Um, can we do something?" he asked.

"To fix your friend?" she asked in that same far-off tone.

He shook his head. "Well, yes, but I meant to get us out of here first."

"Getting out should be easy for you. We need to make an exit then you two can just swim up." Eir said.

Chris shook his head. "But you said there was a cure, that Chooth did all this—"

Katy cut in. "There's got to be something wrong with him. I mean we've only known Chooth for a little while, but I can't imagine he'd do this, hurt all these people and why would he poison the Grannusians?"

"He's not doing it. Not really," Eir said. "Allow me to show you something." She swam up onto the edge of the raft, driving her head and most of the eel's body over the gunwale. A small flap opened just below her head. It looked like a second toothless mouth.

It took Chris a moment to realize it was a separate creature clinging to a spot just below her neck. "It's the last piece of me still holding on. Soon the poison will force me to let it go, but for now. . ." she paused with her rasping voice overcome by emotion. "We call it the hub, it's our communications center, the only way we can exist as we are, as a collection of beings all working together. Some believe it's the place where a Grannusian's soul resides. . . That's what I believe and I feel it slipping away. . ." She had to gather her thoughts to continue. "From a scientific perspective, if there was one part of us that's most important to the rest, it's this. It looks like nothing, but without it we are nothing and I believe Chooth's is missing."

"So, when you say it wasn't him, you mean it's because he doesn't have this part?" Katy asked.

"No, it's not enough that it's gone. Our hubs can speak to us from thousands of miles away. In fact, in the early days of space travel our people would leave their hubs behind in a safe place, so some part of them would survive if things went bad. What I believe has happened is that someone found a way of using this part to control him. It's a terrifying thought. I can only imagine how they must be torturing him."

Chris was having a hard time wrapping his head around the idea that while most of Chooth could be on this sub looking for Eir, part of him was somewhere else. He stared at the little slug-fish. How would you even torture something like that? It had no eyes and no mouth that he could see.

"So, we need to get you to the cure? That's got to be our first move?" Chris asked.

"Where is it?" Katy added.

Eir looked between the two of them before answering. "Much of it was in my lab, but that's already been destroyed. It was the first place Chooth hit. The captain had another sample though. He stored it in his quarters before the attack."

The rattling came again followed by an explosion that was close enough to make ripples in the pool filling the cargo bay. "How do we get there?" Chris asked.

"The main passageways are flooded," Eir answered. "Chooth is out hunting. He's tearing the ship apart one door at a time looking for me. The entire ship will be destroyed soon."

"Would the captain's quarters be flooded as well?" Chris asked.

375

"I have no idea," Eir said. "I've been working my way there," She nodded toward a hatch at the top of the room. "I've been using the flooded service tunnels and pipe chases."

"So, we'll keep going that way," Katy said.

Chris looked up at the entrance to the service tunnel, which was ten meters above their heads on the ceiling that had once been the side wall, before the vessel started sinking, and pointing its nose down. With the chamber drained it was impossible to get to it.

"You see why I stopped here?" Eir asked.

"Yeah, I don't think that's going to be an option," Chris agreed and looked at the tear in the wall, where the jellyfish creature was. It was a little over two meters away, still sealing the ragged wound in the sub's hull. "Can you talk to that thing or is Chooth the only one with control over it?" he asked.

Eir looked annoyed, as if she were ready to give him a lecture about how they didn't control creatures like that, that they worked with them, but she held her tongue and simply asked, "Why?"

Chris bit his lip, and stared down at his face mask, ready to pull it on as he said. "Because I want you to tell it to let go. To let the water in."

Chapter 40

Tara tried to put the tank from her mind as she headed to the dining hall, just as Alex had asked. She was glad he'd taken the lead and given her orders. She needed something to do and without Maeven she was afraid she wouldn't know what.

She worried about Ben going to the hanger bay to fight the Tairnishmen. Then she considered Alex. 'Even if they were successful, he was opening himself up to arrest. He must truly care for her,' she thought, then wondered if the princess felt the same. That could make things difficult down the line with Maeven's father.

When Tara came into the dining hall, her eyes fell on the empty Bogatyr table. It made sense that they'd be gone. Any of them who hadn't helped in the abduction would stay in their barracks where they'd be safe from reprisal.

The Tamerlane nobles were altogether at their table. They looked up at her as she called, "They've taken the princess. Maeven's been kidnapped."

Food and forks were dropped as the shock of what she said settled in. Questions were shouted at her, but Tara waved her hands to quiet them. "The Bogatyr took her. Their transport is about to leave. I need your help to stop them." She beckoned for them to follow as she started to turn.

The nobles jumped up, incensed at the actions of the Tairnishmen. It didn't matter if they liked Maeven or not. She was their princess and to attack her was to attack them. A small mob of Tamerlanes of all different ages gathered ready to fight and follow Tara. She wasn't sure what they'd do when they got to the loading dock. Maybe the monks had a plan or maybe the guards, or Alex. Tara wouldn't find out.

A noise echoed from the corridor as a massive dark form stormed in. Fafnir was like a boulder falling from a mountain. He roared as he flung himself at the Tamerlanes' table, bringing up his staff and crashing it down, sending the nobles flying across the room. They fell back in shock and confusion as the smashed and splintered pieces of the table rained down on them. The massive Drake stood, breathing heavily. Tara looked up from the ground. She had ducked to the floor to avoid being crushed.

Three young men who'd gotten out of Fafnir's path tried rushing him. They grabbed knives and dashed forward, attacking, darting below Fafnir's staff. He swept it over their heads, forcing them to dive lower, while stomping with his foot, smashing into the floor and breaking a large piece of stone loose. It rose like a rocky cliff in front of the young men. They tripped over it as Fafnir brought his other hand forward, flinging them away, sprawled across the room with the rest of the Tamerlanes.

Fafnir stood in the entrance, blocking it with his hulking shoulders that were covered in twisted barbs. He watched the nobles, holding his staff like a club, ready to strike again. Younger Drakes came to his side as Regin, the Ice-Carver, and Andavarri, the Long Wolf, stepped out from behind him.

Tara looked up at Andavarri and knew why they'd come, what the Long-Wolf had found in her room.

Silently Tara cursed Maeven, wondering if she'd been the one who had put the tank in her closet. The aliens from three different worlds stared at her. She knew what they came to accuse her of, torturing and attempting to control a Grannusian.

Breathing loud and rapid, Fafnir's chest heaved while he stared at Tara. Despite coming off as cranky to most, he was usually a creature of extreme calm. He was long lived with more years behind him than any other Drake. In all that time his thoughts had become quicker, but rage had grown as well. Andavarri had found him in the medical bay with Regin, outside the door where Tearmai was held, carrying on a private conversation. They'd gone quiet when Andavarri entered, but that didn't last.

She told them what she'd seen, describing the tank and the electrodes. "I think they mean to enslave the Grannusians. Force them to serve against their will," she'd said.

On parts of Tairnish, Long-Wolves and humans still used Drakes in their mines, forcing them to go deep beneath the surface, extracting valuable metals. Fafnir himself had served in the mines till the Æsir came. He hated slavery and made it his life goal to see it ended. He'd negotiated and bargained and fought most of the past hundred years with that goal in mind. He'd always sought a peaceful path. But peace was the furthest thing from his mind when he heard the humans on this very station were seeking to enslave another race.

Regin tried to calm him, tried to hold him back, advising that they go to Kavaris Dell. Ignoring him,

Fafnir went off to find the girl responsible. He'd see her arrested, even if he had to do it himself. He pointed a clawed hand at Tara.

"You," he said, "where is your mistress?"

Tara got to her feet. "She's not here. The Tairnishmen kidnapped her. They've taken her to their ship as a prisoner."

Fafnir glanced at Andavarri, who held up her hands. She looked between Fafnir and Regin. "I would've told you, but you left so quickly. That's where Kavaris Dell is now. He wanted to keep it quiet, to keep from making a scene."

Edith came sauntering into the room from the other side of the hall, looking around at the mess. "Making a scene? It seems you've taken care of that." She wore her armor and carried a weapon, an assault rifle that she held pointed at the ground.

Fafnir turned back to Tara, "You'll answer for this if your mistress can't. I want this girl arrested."

Edith snorted a little and smiled. "Yes, sir," she sneered. "Though the way I see it, the only one doing anything wrong here is you." Her hand was firmly attached to the rifle.

Fafnir glanced at Andavarri. "Tell her what you found."

Briefly Andavarri explained about the tank and what she thought it was for, then Andavarri asked, "Shouldn't you be at the loading dock trying to rescue Princess Maeven?"

"Kavaris Dell sent me away," Edith said. "The monk wanted me to come here to make sure her people didn't try to escalate things." She motioned toward the Tamerlanes. "Looks like you've already taken care of that. The head monk doesn't want any more ill-conceived rescue attempts getting people hurt. He's letting them go. He doesn't want to risk the Bogatyr leaving early and damaging their transport."

"He can't just let them escape," Tara pleaded. She was considering Edith's words, wondering if Alex and Ben were okay.

"He can and he will," Edith said. She slid her weapon to her back and offered a hand to Tara. "Now why don't you show me this tank?"

Tara stared at the mercenary. Edith's face was friendly and kind, but Tara could sense the lie behind it. She always knew when someone was lying.

Chapter 41

'This is trust,' Chris thought, while climbing the handrail like a ladder. The walkway and the entire room were vertical. He looked up at the ragged opening in the hull of the royal submarine and reminded himself, this is your plan. Water was pouring in past the giant jellyfish. The seal it made against the ocean was imperfect and it was about to get even more so. Everything was slippery and wet, including the creature tucked down in his wetsuit. Eir's hub squirmed next to him, sticking out under his neck, where the zipper was undone. She'd just told him how important these things were. Now he was going off with it.

The hub fish was odd next to his skin, not just the fact that it was slimly, but also because it had a slight current, a weak electrical charge that made his skin tingle. Chris could feel it trying to connect with him. 'That's what it does after all,' he realized, as he felt it tickle his brain. The creature's presence in his head wasn't as clear as words or thoughts, more like a faint sense.

Chris wondered if a person could become part of a Grannusian collective. He pictured himself covered in fish and worms and shivered a little in disgust. He certainly would not be the first to volunteer for it.

He was climbing with his hands and his less damaged right leg. He had to constantly drag the left one behind, posting it on the rail, then pushing up. It was a slow process, but he was getting closer. Feeling the spray from above cascading down like a shower, Chris looked at the eel-part of Eir in the water and at

Katy floating in the raft. Eir had told him that she could communicate with the jellyfish if she could touch it.

With no way to get the eel-part up, it was too big and he was already climbing in full scuba gear with casts on both of his legs, he was left carrying the hub.

As he reached the opening and the glowing body of the jellyfish, he turned his attention to the problem in front of him. When the creature let go, the water would come pouring in, and on him. Near the opening, just before it, he saw a place where he could hold on, a place above the flood. He looked down at Katy and Eir. "Paddle to the other side of the room," he called, not wanting them to be directly under him. Eir pushed the raft with her snout as Chris climbed higher.

He locked one arm around a rail and took the slug out of his suit, trying not to drop it, but also trying not to squeeze it too tight. Leaning down, he looked at the glowing bioluminescent seal. He had a hard time believing that he'd been inside this creature and had traveled across the ocean in it. The slug touched the jellyfish. "Go ahead and tell it to let go," Chris said, feeling silly talking to the slug-fish.

Unspoken communication passed between the two creatures; Chris felt it rattle in his skull. Then slowly the jellyfish started to peel away. Chris hurried, bringing the slug back in as the jellyfish removed its flesh. It was like a pipe bursting. In less than two seconds the flow of water went from a small rupture to a full water main, to a waterfall. It was blasting into the room.

Holding the slug tight to himself, Chris tried to keep his feet from slipping with the force. He was out of the flow, but it didn't matter because the breeze it was making was pushing him and the raft to the far wall.

Katy was smart enough to have her mask on already. Chris struggled to get his on, watching the boiling, bubbling surface come closer and closer. Eir's eel body was nowhere to be seen, forced under by the pressure of the incoming current.

Chris had his mask up above his face. All he had to do was pull it down, but he had Eir's hub in one hand and the rail in the other, holding on for dear life. He pushed his head and the mask against the bar, trying to shove it down.

The water was now just below him. The waterfall had been covered by the dark rising surface, but the current coming through the opening was still churning away with deadly force.

Chris couldn't see with the mask half over his eyes, but he could feel that the water was at his waist and rapidly moving toward his chest. He pushed his head harder against the rail feeling his feet slip out from under him. The mask wasn't in the right place, but it was sitting close enough to where the valve on the regulator popped open. Air churned inside the face mask as he was blasted deep into the water by the current. Metal rails slammed into his tank as he was pushed off the walkway. Somewhere along the way he lost his grip on the hub but he was too busy struggling to survive to worry.

Using just his arms, he swam up toward the ceiling, bumping into the bottom of the raft. The force of the current had pushed them both into the same corner of the room. He swam out from under it and saw the ceiling get closer while the water poured in. Chris held the side of the raft, finally getting his mask in position. "Katy, can you hear me?" he asked, using the com unit.

"Yeah, I'm here. Are you okay?"

"A little banged up, but I'll be alright. I lost the hub," Chris said right before he felt something touch his leg. He looked down to see the creature swimming next to him and touching the side of his suit. He'd been so worried about the thing as he climbed that he'd forgotten water was its natural element. "Never mind, I found it. Hey, little guy," he said.

He was just about to reach out and touch it when Eir's eel head appeared. The hub flicked its tail as it turned and found its spot below Eir's neck, clinging to it again. "That was frightening," Eir confessed, "With the poison I could barely connect."

The water started to slow as air was forced to the top of the room. A small pocket would stay for a time, eventually escaping as the water forced it out. Katy dropped out of the raft, and Chris turned on his head lamps. He found a tether on his belt, a half meter of line that he hooked to Katy. Below the surface he could see the opening in the sub and the dark ocean behind it.

'This is my plan,' he reminded himself as he swam down. Rather than trying to make their way through the sub where Chooth would be hunting for Eir, they would go outside, try to get into the captain's quarters that way. Chris didn't know if it'd work, but he knew that if Chooth's intention was to kill Eir, then staying in one spot was a bad idea. Using his arms, he swam with Katy toward the opening. He was picturing the creature from the drilling platform with all its legs and claws waiting just past the jagged, ripped sides, ready to tear them apart.

They swam on, going through the tear and out into the open water. Nothing waited for them outside but the endless dark of the ocean. In the distance he could see the jellyfish creature swimming away with the last touch of light. The way it shone and pulsed was beautiful with its tentacles waving and spiraling below it. Katy didn't get to see that. At the thought, he suddenly felt a little selfish. He looked down at the long hull of the sub, the broad surface seemed to go on forever. It was the size of a building, tilting down into the darkness. He started to swim across its curved surface, going in the direction Eir had described. She was right next to him, helping guide him.

They wouldn't be able to talk with her while they were submerged, but she'd given him a pretty good idea of where they needed to go. The sub was shaped like a long flat blade with large engine pods on either side. On top near the stern, like the dorsal fin of a shark, was a conning tower. With its heavy crystal windows, the bridge sat at the bottom of it.

Chris and Eir both assumed that if Chooth's mission had been to destroy or disable the sub, he would start there, tearing into the bridge and taking out the command crew first. A pressurized hatch on top of the tower was still in one piece and they could use it to enter. The captain's quarters, where the sample cure was secured, was behind the bridge.

They had to swim around from the sub's bottom, going across the vessel and up to its topside. As they circled, they could see emergency lights shining out from the bridge. Chris kept pulling with his arms, disheartened by the distance and feeling exhaustion creep into his muscles. Katy was swimming as well, using her whole body and moving much better through the water. He had to ask her a couple of times to slow down. Eventually Katy said, "Just point me in the right direction and I'll do the work," a lifetime of surfing had made Katy an amazing swimmer. She was able to use the long dive fins much more effectively.

Chris still used his arms, but it was much easier now that he let Katy tug him along by the guide rope. "I keep thinking it'll be good when this is over and we can go home. I kind of forget that's not an option anymore," he said.

"How long has it been anyway?" Katy asked.

Chris thought about it. Doing the math to understand how long they'd been gone. Most of it had been on the transport from Nalanda. He thought back to before that. In his mind it all started the day he and Alex arrived in the desert with their mom.

Everything strange had followed. "A few weeks, less than a month I'm pretty sure," Chris answered.

"I hope the others are okay," Katy said.

"Me too. We're almost there."

They came around the corner of the vessel's upper deck. The conning tower rose like a gravestone against the dark surface of the endless ocean. They were close enough to the bridge, which yawned like an open mouth. Then the details inside came into view. Chairs, controls consuls and bodies drifted about aimlessly.

"They're all dead," Chris said. The crew hadn't had time to get out when the water came flooding in. The crystal windows, made to stand up to the heaviest pressures in the ocean, had been cracked open. The crew died at their posts, slammed by an unescapable surge of ocean. They hadn't expected an attack.

Chris approached slowly, looking ahead. Eir had told him before they left where the captain's quarters were. She'd described the captain as well, since he had the key to the cabinet in his room. Chris would have to search the bodies to find it. He wasn't looking forward to that.

Eir swam beside him. He waved his hand to get her attention and pointed to the conning tower, trying to tell her to go there. He wanted her to stay out of the way where it was safe.

Eir seemed to understand and swam up. "You should go with Eir," Chris told Katy.

"No, I'm coming with you. For moral support if nothing else," she answered.

"Katy," Chris started, ready to talk her out of it, but he changed his mind knowing he didn't want to be in there by himself. "Fine, just stay nearby."

Katy pulled at the tether. "Where am I going to go?"

"Alright then." Chris examined the air gauge on his harness. He'd already gone through half his bottle, then he shined his light on Katy's. Hers was much fuller. He shook his head, swearing he was going to get in better shape as he swam up through the window. He didn't know how deep they were, or how long it'd take them to surface and wondered, not for the first time, if they'd be better off cutting their losses and running away, getting to the surface and hoping for rescue. But he'd made a promise to Eir.

Inside, the room was smaller than Chris would've imagined for such a large ship. It wasn't like the bridge of starships in the movies. Everything was tight and not made for comfort. Chairs were bolted to the floor behind darkened control boards. The room was inverted like the rest of the ship, everything pointing down toward the ocean floor. Pipes ran across the ceiling and along the walls. "Watch your head," Chris said, turning around to guide Katy.

"Thanks," she said when she felt his hand.

Chris would've been happy to stay close to her, to look only at Katy, but that wasn't why they were here. He turned to the bodies, which were thrown around the room, tossed in every direction. In the low glow of emergency lighting, he saw seven of them floating listlessly. Two were wearing armor like the soldiers on the surface. He didn't bother going to them, but he'd have to check the others.

He swam up to the center of the room to a chair surrounded by monitors. It was the captain's, but the captain was no longer in it. At the back of the room was a small hallway with a ladder. Three bodies were squeezed in it, pressed together.

Chris swam over, reached out and grabbed the first body, pulling it down by its belt and out of his way. Eir had told him what the captain looked like. 'I don't want to do this, I don't want to do this,' he thought as he watched the woman's long hair waving in the water. He knew this wasn't the captain, but he still had to move her to search the others. The face came around. She was young. The glow from his head lamps focused on her eyes as she seemed to stare back.

Chris felt awful. He knew whatever happened after this, he'd never be able to unsee what was in front of him.

"Are you alright?" Katy asked again. She'd asked him a few times, but this was the first time he couldn't answer right away.

"Um, yeah. I'll be fine," he said after a moment, pushing the body out of the way. He tried to keep Katy to the side as he swam a little further up the hall to grab the next body and pull it back. This man had a greying beard.

"I found him," Chris said, turning the captain so he could reach the zipper in the man's jacket. Not wanting to have another terrible memory rattling around in his head, he was careful not to look the dead man in the eyes. The zipper came down easily, and the key came floating up on its chain. Chris reached for it and pulled, tugging the chain over the captain's head. Chris glanced up the ladder as it came loose and saw why they'd all crammed into the hall.

The open hatch of an airlock was ahead of him. That's where they were trying to get to, the only safe spot. If they could've gotten in and managed to shut the hatch, they would've been able to drain the water. They could have survived, but the attack happened too fast. Inside the airlock Chris saw spare air tanks and dive equipment. He was glad, knowing they needed to come back here before they left.

"Alright, I got it," he said to Katy, pulling himself back down the hall. He was just about to start searching the captain's room when he saw movement out of the corner of his eye, where the captain's body was floating.

"Awesome," Katy said. "Let's go find the cure."

"Yeah, let's," Chris said slowly, turning back around.

Katy was close enough to feel him move. "What's the matter, Chris?"

He looked at the captain, drifting in the water. "Nothing, I just thought I saw him move. It looked like he turned his head."

"Who?"

"The captain."

"But he's dead."

"I'm pretty sure," Chris agreed as he approached the body. It'd been the dead man's mouth. It looked like the jaw had opened on its own. Was that a muscle contraction, was that a thing that dead bodies could do? The captain's beard covered most of his jaw and lips in thick fuzz, and his greying hair swayed a little. Chris stared at the jaw and saw something in the dead man's mouth.

"What the—" Chris started, falling back in shock.

A set of eyes gazed out from behind the dead man's teeth. A small creature poked its head out, climbing onto the captain's chin. It watched Chris questioningly.

Chris recognized it immediately. It was part of Chooth and it was looking right at him.

"We need to move." Chris turned around, swimming fast.

"Why, what's the matter?"

"We've been made. Chooth knows where we are," he answered.

Chapter 42

Chris's voice was full of panic. Katy could hear it. He was tired and tense and whatever he saw on the sub's bridge bothered him more than he was saying. He was feigning calmness, but she could tell that the bodies were getting to him. She didn't know how many were floating around them but in her imagination the entire room was full. She stayed surprisingly relaxed.

Katy had been going through life feeling removed since she lost her sight. Everything was at a dream like distance that made it hard for her to focus, even when they were in danger. Chris's words, 'Chooth knows we're here,' didn't bother her nearly as much as it should have.

Being under water made that distance feel so much worse. The pressure tightened over her from all sides, cutting her off. Occasionally she could sense the vibrations through the ship, but she had no sense of reference where they were coming from. Without her eyes or her ears, the only connection she had was Chris's touch and his voice. She clung to it as her only lifeline to the real world.

More vibrations came from the distant echoes of decompression as parts of the sub were pulled apart. Chris took her hands, pulling her forward till she felt a bar just ahead of them. "Take this," Chris ordered. "It's the bottom of a ladder. I need you to climb it." The ladder was angled like everything in the bridge, pointing at better than forty-five degrees. Things bumped into her, soft things. 'Bodies,' she thought.

"You'll go through a hatch. When I tell you, close it behind you. There'll be another hatch in front of you that's already closed. As soon as the bottom's locked, go to the top. It opens the same way. Get out and start swimming. Go up, toward the surface." Chris paused, listening. Something was coming. He whispered even though they were in a closed com system. "Drop your weight belt and go. Hopefully Eir will be with you. Do you understand?"

"I think so," She felt him unclipping the tether. "What are you doing?" she asked as she felt him swim away.

"Getting the cure. Chooth is on his way. Go! I'll still be on coms. I'll try and join you, but if Chooth gets in the way I want you guys to have an escape plan."

"Wait. That was a plan?" Katy asked as she started to climb.

"Yeah, if I don't get back, go up and get the hell out of here. Hopefully Eir will follow you."

"That's an awful plan," Katy said, feeling Chris push her along. She didn't resist.

The ladder went further up than she expected. She passed through the hatch, reached out and touched it, trying to understand how it closed. It wasn't complicated. Then she went further and checked the top. More vibrations rocked the sub. They were closer than before. Things were being destroyed just below her. Banging and the sound of machines being smashed carried through the water. She couldn't be certain, but it sounded like something large and angry was in the bridge.

∞

The bridge was shaking in the light of Chris's head lamps. He was grateful Katy hadn't argued with him.

There wasn't time. Hoping Chooth's little spy didn't wander out any further to watch him, he turned the captain's body away. He had the key wrapped around his hand. He wasn't swimming anymore, not really. Using the pipes and control panels he pulled himself along, moving much faster back to the bridge. Only two other hatches came off that main room. One was behind the ladder, going back further into a hall. In a vain attempt someone had closed it when the bridge flooded.

The other hatch hung open. It was smaller and tucked behind abandoned workstations. Chris pulled himself toward it and ducked in as something moved outside the bridge's broken windows. A moment later an incredible force came smashing down through the sub's top deck. It burst in, destroying bulkheads like a train off the tracks. Walls and supports were shredded as the Caleth-gul swam out and turned back again.

Under normal conditions it wouldn't be a frightening creature. Only its considerable size made it scary. Chris caught a glimpse of its glowing eyes floating on stalks on its boulder-like head. Its pincer-claws still had twisted metal sheets hanging from them as it turned and started swimming toward him.

Chris closed the hatch to the captain's quarters, hoping to buy himself a few seconds. The captain's room wasn't large, containing only a bunk, a desk and a chair that was bolted to the floor. In the light of his head lamps Chris spotted a safe under the desk. He pulled himself across the room and swam down quickly, putting the key in. It was a perfect fit. Outside the room he could feel things being destroyed, slammed about as Chooth searched.

Chris lay with his belly on the deck. He didn't have long. He struggled to pull the safe open against the pressure of the water. The ocean flooded in soaking papers and making them dance. Chris reached past the pages, expecting to find a vial or some sort of chemical container. He felt something else, a pistol.

He lifted the weapon out and looked at it. It was different from any gun he'd ever seen on earth with round cylinders near the back and multiple barrels lined in a row down its flat front. Several cartridges lay in a stack next to it. Carefully, but quickly Chris put one into a slot near the front of the weapon and felt it lock in place. Chris pointed it away from himself at the captain's bed and pulled the trigger. Compressed air fired a projectile that tore a large hole through the side of the bunk. He put the gun down on the deck and searched further into the safe. His hand touched a number of syringes. The needles were capped and closed.

He gripped them and heard rending metal travel through the water and felt a pressure change in the room. Over his shoulder he saw where the hatch had been a moment before. The walls shook as the whole side of the cabin tore away like paper.

Unzipping his suit, Chris shoved the syringes in and pulled the zipper up. As he tried reaching for the gun where it had fallen when the room shook, a large claw came barreling toward him and grabbed his leg, dragging him from the cabin. In a panic Chris reached out for anything to hold on to. He found the pistol again, but he was being pulled through the water so quickly that he didn't have a chance to take it by the handle. Hugging it like a passed football, he tried to cover his head as he was bounced through the bridge.

In the light of his helmet, he saw the Caleth-gul but only the front of it. Its head and part of its body were inside, filling the bridge, but the rest hung from the window, twisting its tail around the conning tower. Chris was pulled to the hall with the ladder. The creature went from dragging him to shoving him. He was pushed past the bodies, then up toward the airlock where Katy waited.

The claw released him just before the hatch. He glanced up and saw Katy above him. Suddenly something else came at him, a school of smaller fish charged, led by Chooth's eel head. Its teeth grabbed onto his suit, dragging him through the hatch. He watched them swim back, twisting their bodies around the handle like fingers, closing and sealing the opening. Chris reached out for Katy, who was turning around, confused, reaching and feeling the different parts of Chooth as they swarmed and bumped into her.

"I'm here," Chris said, taking her hand. He held the weapon down low on the other side, while watching several fish swim to a control panel. A red light went green under their touch. Then the water in the airlock started to bubble and churn, quickly draining away.

Chris tried to watch Chooth come together, but the water was too agitated to witness his reconstitution. He wanted to see his friend's face. He wanted everything Eir told him to be wrong, but as he looked over, meeting Chooth's eyes, seeing the pain, the suffering and conflict, he knew.

When the water was below their necks, Chooth said, "You can take that mask off now."

Chris hesitated for a moment, then lifted it up and away. The water dropped further to his waist. Chris looked at Katy, who was taking her mask off as well. It was hard to find good footing on the curved walls of the airlock as it was tilted at an angle with the rest of the sub. He reached out to Katy for help standing while trying to keep the gun out of sight.

'Chooth doesn't know where Eir is, otherwise he wouldn't be bothering with us,' Chris thought. 'But does he know that she'd helped them? He came here so quickly that he must have had his suspicions.'

"Why did you attack these people?" he asked, hoping to set Chooth on the defensive.

Chooth stared at him with his dark inhuman eyes. Back on the transport it'd taken a while for Chris to get used to them. He wasn't certain he'd ever learned how to read them. "I didn't want to." Chooth said. "I haven't been myself for quite some time."

"We can help you," Katy offered, going toward the sound of Chooth's voice and reaching out her hand to touch him.

He recoiled. "No. I must do this. Then the pain will stop. That's how it's always worked before. I follow the commands and then they release me." He was struggling to keep himself together, to maintain his form. "You should've stayed where I left you. I was coming back. I never wanted to hurt you two. You're my friends."

"That's right, and we're in this together," Katy said, moving forward again hoping to comfort Chooth. She hadn't seen him pull away from her, nor had she seen all the lives he ended today. She had no idea the horrors of which he was capable. Chris tried holding her back.

"Together?" Chooth spat the word out, suddenly reaching for her. His arm, comprised of smaller animals, stretched across the room going to her throat. They grabbed Katy, twisting and worming around her neck, tightening. "Are we together?" Chooth asked. "I don't think so. I think you two are playing games."

"Chooth, stop!" Chris begged, trying to pull the creatures off Katy.

Chooth ignored his plea and demanded, "Where is she Chris? Where is Eir?"

"Let her go," Chris shot back. He gritted his teeth as he dug his fingers into the arm. The creatures squeezed tighter like a wet knot.

"You wouldn't have been able to get here on your own, not without her help," Chooth pointed out coldly. He was going to kill Katy. He'd kill all of them if he weren't stopped.

"You'd be amazed by what I'm capable of," Chris said, outraged, as he brought the gun up. He didn't hesitate to pull the trigger. Compressed air blasted through the barrel and fired an explosive projectile. Chris finally saw something in Chooth's eyes that he was sure he recognized. It was surprise.

Looking away, not wanting to see what he'd done, the horror that would be left where his friend had been, Chris turned to Katy, hoping the shot had been enough to break her free. Some of the creatures still clung to her throat though. He took his dive knife and in a panic, started cutting them away, tearing them loose, trying not to hurt her in the process. He could hear the sounds coming from behind him. A wet slopping noise came from Chooth's body as he tried to maintain its form.

Chris cut enough of the arm to let Katy breathe, then looked back over his shoulder just in time to see the rest of Chooth come flying at him. Like a thick tree trunk, Chooth's mass smashed into Chris, tossing him up and across the room. He banged into air tanks and pipes, rolling over the wet surface toward the top hatch where he found another switch for the airlock.

"Katy, get your mask on!" Chris called as his hand came banging down on the lever. Valves opened in the wall and water came flooding back into the room. Chooth came apart in the spray. As a school of fish, he swam around Chris, who was reaching for the hatch, trying to force it open, but it held. He wouldn't be able to get it to budge till the room was full and the pressure equalized.

Chris still held his dive knife and was slashing out at the little creatures attacking him while he tried to get his mask in place. Most of Chooth's parts didn't have teeth or large mouths but they could twist together and wrap themselves around him. Their tiny pincers stung his flesh and tore at his suit as they dragged him from the hatch.

Cutting and tearing, Chris fought for his life. "Katy, swim! Get out!" he screamed while struggling to keep the mask on. Chooth was pulling at it trying to drown him.

Katy found the hatch and broke it open. Chris saw her go. He'd been pulled all the way to the bottom of the airlock, still fighting. He stopped and took a moment, kicking off as hard as he could.

Parts of Chooth still swam around him in chaos. Chris reached out for the hatch and missed, touching Katy's hand instead. She was above grabbing hold of his arm and pulling hard, dragging him out, then she slammed the hatch shut, trapping most of Chooth inside.

Chris pulled the few parts of the Grannusian still clinging to him away. Then he looked around and asked. "Where's Eir?"

"I don't know," Katy said.

Chris shook his head, having trouble believing he'd asked such a stupid question. His eyes searched across the dark water, but he saw no sign of Eir's pale form. Below him he could feel the conning tower shaking. He knew the Caleth-gul was on its way.

Chooth's mouthpiece, the eel head, may have been gone, but that didn't mean he ceased to exist. He wasn't one creature but hundreds, thinking and acting together, and the Caleth-gul was part of that.

"Drop your weight belt," Chris said to Katy. "We've got to swim away from here. We've got to try and make it to the surface."

"How far is it?" Katy asked.

"I have no idea," he said as the shaking below them became more violent. Their belts fell away, hitting the deck of the sub and they started to swim. Chris looked back seeing the pale surface of the sub get smaller as their own buoyancy carried them away. He searched the dark water, looking for Eir. Something moved in the distance. It was large and coming toward them. His eyes searched further and he saw that it wasn't alone. Lights moved beneath it, falling away, then turning toward them.

'What now?' Chris thought, quite certain he didn't have the strength to survive anything else, but then the things came into view. He saw that they were submarines. Small, fast moving ones. The larger thing in the distance was a royal sub, a massive vessel like the one they had just left. It was coming to their rescue. Between the sub and them was a small pale creature followed by a school of fish. It was Eir, and she was making her way toward the fleet of royal vessels.

She was almost to it when the conning tower beneath them ripped in two. The Caleth-gul burst up through the airlock, splitting the top of the sub wide open. Chris watched metal fall away into the dark as the last couple of air bubbles escaped. The creature's orb-like eyes glared at him as the rest of Chooth came swimming out around it.

Eir was struggling to get to the sub, to escape but she was moving much slower than the Caleth-gul, which was now pursuing her. In only a moment it would have her.

Explosions of air came from the mini-subs. Long lances fired out, blasting through the water. Leaving a trail of bubbles. They shot past Eir rocketing through the water.

The Caleth-gul didn't have time to turn. Its long tail was skewered by two torpedoes and a third hit its head, right in its baleen filled mouth, going through the thick fibers. The creature flailed, desperately twisting in its death throws as the slight glow in its eyes darkened. It went rigid and began to sink.

"What's happening?" Katy asked.

Chris watched Eir reach the subs, then looked at the massive broken vessel below them. The Caleth-gul was sinking down beside it.

He searched the dark ocean for the rest of Chooth. All those parts of him had scattered when the subs fired. There was no sign of their friend. Like dust Chooth had scattered across the ocean.

Chris touched his tattered wet suit and felt the syringes. "I think it might be over." He said, watching one of the mini subs approach. He reached over and took Katy's hand, carefully guiding her down towards its hatch.

Chapter 43

On Nalanda station two monks carried a tank into the auditorium and placed it on a table in the center of the room in front of the lectern. Kavaris Dell's eyes followed it as his body fell further, hunched with exhaustion. He'd already examined the Grannusian part and followed the instructions that their home world had sent for removing the wires and probes. He glanced over at the few Grannusians still at the station. They were staring at the tank in horror.

The little creature was such an ugly fish. It swam very little, staying flaccid barely floating around in its tank. Kavaris Dell had heard the report from Grannus. Chooth had poisoned his own people. He'd done it on his last trip home, the one where he supposedly discovered the poison. He wasn't completely responsible, of course. Someone here had been torturing and controlling him.

Kavaris Dell wondered why they had bothered having him return to Nalanda. Why they'd give Eir the chance to go back to Grannus and investigate. Maybe they wanted to keep Chooth as an agent, to use him here again, next time against Cormack and his family.

It was such an evil plan but fitting for the emperor. Kavaris Dell remembered the young Cyrus Tamerlane when he was only a boy, just another student of Nalanda. The monk had liked him. Tamerlane had been a good student and a hard worker, unlike his daughter Maeven. Kavaris Dell didn't know what the Tairnishmen were going to do with the princess, but he thought as his eyes fell on Tara, at least I have one of her cronies to punish.

The student body crowded together waiting to hear his verdict. The room was so full that it'd be hard to find anyone in the halls of the station. Even the staff and the servants were loitering out in the corridor, waiting to hear the results of the tribunal. 'They'd be the same as always,' Kavaris Dell thought, 'justice would be served.'

Tara stood chained in the middle of the room. She'd said little in her defense but claimed she had no idea how the tank got in her cabinet. It'd been Andavarri's testimony that had damned her, and her own refusal to name anyone else.

Maeven was gone and there was no harm in blaming her, but Tara wouldn't speak against her mistress. She stubbornly refused to confess or name anyone else, so the punishment would be hers alone.

Kavaris Dell had already been in contact with the emperor. The man had been in a cold rage on the comm channel. He was angry with the monks for their failure to protect his daughter. The emperor had heard the report from his guards, the way they'd been attacked and held back from helping. When Kavaris Dell explained why he detained them, the emperor had nodded. He understood the monk's reasoning, but that didn't mean he was happy about it. Still, he held his tongue, not daring to threaten the monk.

After all, to harm one of the monks was to invite the Æsir's wrath. Kavaris Dell had worn that threat like armor for years. He turned his attention to the other prisoner. Alexander Johnson, the oldest of the five who had come through the void space.

Kavaris Dell wasn't sure if what he was doing would please the Æesir, but the boy had murdered a monk. Andavarri's testimony had been damning to him as well. She'd seen him go into the detention area, through the eyes of the Fire Golems. And she'd seen him come out with Amita, leaving a monk's murdered body behind.

Alex refused to confess as well. He refused to even suggest anyone else was responsible only saying, "It wasn't me."

"Who else could've killed him then?" Kavaris Dell had shouted. "Not your friend?"

"No," Alex said. "Amita hasn't done anything wrong."

"She's done plenty wrong and if I had my way, she'd be standing beside you, paying for her crimes." Amita was still in the Tamerlane domicile. He didn't know how long the emperor would allow her to stay under his protection or if the emperor even knew she was there. The girl was a small matter.

She was a troublemaker, but that was all and she was too small to break a man's neck. Kavaris Dell looked at Alex, who was maybe seventeen and not overly large, but with a strong body that he'd already shown to be highly capable.

The boy was a killer, Kavaris Dell was certain, and he would be punished as such. The trial was done. Both had been given their chance to speak. The alien stewards stood witness, angry at more human plots to subjugate them. They wouldn't do anything to stop this.

Kavaris Dell asked the final question of all those gathered. "Does anyone wish to speak on the accused behalf?" No one would witness for Alex, the monk was certain. Most of the nobles hadn't been happy with the way Maeven had taken to him. His friend Amita was in hiding and the other one, Ben, was in the medical bay. He hadn't woken since his fall during their ill-fated rescue attempt.

Kavaris Dell's eyes ran quickly over the room. He didn't notice the look on Edith's face. The mercenary had stood back through the entire trial, pointedly looking away from Alex and Tara.

The monk's eyes fell on the emperor's supporters who sat silently watching Tara. Some of them may have been willing to speak up for her, but word had come down. She'd fallen out of favor with the emperor. It wasn't her fault Maeven had been taken, but she'd still be held responsible. Her friends and family members watched coldly while Kavaris Dell said to the hushed room, "Very well then. We shall commence with justice."

He nodded to the monk by the heavy doors with their observation windows. He hit the switch and the doors opened on an empty airlock. A light went on inside, shining down on the place where Vyktor died.

Tara and Alex looked at each other but neither moved.

Kavaris Dell cleared his throat, looking for Edith. She was gone though. She'd silently left the room.

Kavaris Dell wasn't happy about that. As head of security this was her job.

He motioned for two of the monks to escort the prisoners instead. They stepped behind Alex and Tara, pushing them toward the double doors. The prisoners offered little resistance, though Kavaris Dell could see the anger in Alex's eyes. He was thinking of fighting, but there was little he could do while restrained. The shackles were around his feet and hands with a chain running to his neck, making it impossible to take anything but small steps. Tara was chained also, though she was far less of a concern. As a lifelong servant she was accepting of her fate. She'd watched so many others go this way, but Alex- he thought he was special.

'They'd all see,' Kavaris Dell thought, while looking at his students. 'No matter where they came from, what family, none of them were special in the eyes of the Æsir.'

∞

Alex tried planting his feet at the door, but the monks pushed harder, striking him in the back, driving a fist into his kidney, then shoving him forward. Alex struggled to stay on his feet. Tara's eyes were on the far wall. She didn't turn around, even when the airlock closed behind them. She wouldn't give them the satisfaction of seeing her face.

She kept her hands closed in front of her and her eyes on the floor. Alex was looking up, staring at the doors, waiting for them to open. No sound came from the auditorium. He looked at Tara. "I'm sorry," he said.

"For what?" Tara asked, finally turning toward him.

Alex wasn't sure, and by the time he tried to answer, the airlock was starting to open. He didn't see the doors move, but he heard the wind whistle by as it sped toward the opening. There was a space that widened as the breeze turned to a gust. All the air came out of the room and it was instantly cold. By the time Alex thought to hold his breath, his last gasp was out of his lungs. In the distance he could see the surface of the gas giant with its tangerine-colored clouds. Despite the pain tearing at his whole body, the sight made him long for more from the world. He stayed on his feet while Tara fell over, slumping in a pile.

'Is this where I die?' Alex wondered, having trouble believing it could be true. That's when he saw something moving across the bright sky of the gas giant Altor. A dark shadow, like a cloud raced across the surface of the world and came rocketing toward him. The airlock filled with darkness and a crackling purple glow that clung to a horrific figure that stepped from its chariot and onto the floor of the station. The Chariot wasn't much more than a platform that glowed softly as it hung in open space. The dark creature turned and pulled the airlock doors closed. Its clawed fingers were burning hot and the metal melded together with its touch.

Alex still couldn't breathe as he stared at the spikes and nightmarish armor. It looked ancient, nothing like the gear that the soldiers or Edith wore. Towering over him, it stepped heavily, rippling like waves as if it weren't quite real. It punched its fist into the glass observation window, making a hole for air to flow in from the tribunal room. Then as if that weren't enough to satisfy it, the creature grabbed hold of the door and pulled it completely free from its tracks, throwing the massive door across the room.

Shadowy clouds rolled across the floor while the students in the bleacher seats backed away in fear. As panic spread, they started climbing over each other to get away from this thing, knowing that it was the god that the monks warned them of. This was the creature that gave them their laws, the Æesir. Few had ever seen them and survived. Now, one was standing in front of them, like the very embodiment of death.

Dropping to the floor, Alex breathed in deeply, filling his lungs. He crawled over to Tara, struggling to put his hand on her carotid artery, checking for a pulse, he a weak but regular thump.

The Æesir's voice filled the room, echoing and reverberating off the walls. "You were told to educate them, not to judge them. Those that came through the void space are ours," the Æesir shouted, sounding like it came from a place beyond.

Kavaris Dell opened his mouth to speak, but before he could get the words out, the Æesir took a black dagger from a shoulder harness and flung it at the old man as if dismissing a servant. It shot across the room with the force of a javelin, lifting the monk off his feet and throwing him back against the wall, pinning him to it. The monk looked down in surprise to see the long, black spike sticking out from the center of his chest.

"Clear the room," the Æesir demanded as he turned, going back toward the airlock.

The crowd panicked, rushing for the exits. The Æesir stopped next to Alex, who was kneeling on the floor. "You should go too Alex," it said to him, pointing with a clawed finger toward the exit. Then it brought the hand toward him. The pointed tips of the claws glowed red again. It reached out and touched the chains on Alex, cutting them like soft butter.

Alex stared up at the Æesir. This god knew his name. How was that possible? It had no eyes to look into, only blackholes in the center of a dented, gunmetal grey helmet.

"Go," it said again.

Alex nodded, then bent down and picked Tara up. He held her in his arms as he ran off leaving the tribunal room before collapsing in the hall. The door closed behind him with a heavy thud.

Through it he heard the outer airlock explode and air rush out as the Æesir left. Tara's breath moved across Alex's arm. His nostrils flared as he filled his lungs and when he let it out, a short forceful laugh came with it. His whole body began to shake, and he closed his fists in front of his face as his emotions surged. Opening his fingers he covered his face. They cooled his face like icicles.

Epilogue

Amita left the Tamerlane domicile in the fallout from the trial. The pain-laced moans of Maeven's guards recovering from the fight with Fire Golems could barely be heard above the sound of machines beeping in the strange honeycomb of rooms that made up the medical ward.

She sat at Ben's bedside, watching his chest rise and fall. He had a tube down his throat and his skin was pale. A machine counted out his slow pulse while scanners said there was swelling inside his head. He needed help soon.

The Fire Golems had moved through the guards with indifferent purpose, unconcerned about causing lasting harm. Ben was no exception. Amita wanted to blame Andavarri, but from what she was told, it'd been Kavaris Dell who gave the command.

The Golems were autonomous. They followed orders without compromise, so it was Kavaris Dell who was to blame, and he'd already been held accountable.

Tara and Alex were healing too, but they weren't in the medical ward. They'd gone back to the Tamerlane domicile to rest. Amita wasn't sure how it worked, but Tara still had some authority as Maeven's chief aid. Tara wasn't in any shape to give orders at the moment though. She was recovering from her exposure to hard vacuum. Having her there was enough to make certain that Alex and Amita didn't get booted by any of the other Tamerlanes.

Not that it mattered. Apparently, they had someone else looking out for them. Alex was in rough shape, but he still took the time to tell Amita what happened. Amita had asked. "Why did it protect you?"

"I don't know, but it knew my name," Alex said. Amita considered this, then got up and went to the exit. She had left the Tamerlane domicile, going straight to Ben.

Uncomfortable with the stares she got, Amita passed through the halls. Everyone at Nalanda was talking about the visitation. Most had never seen an Æesir. They were like bogey men. To have one show up and leave witnesses was strange enough, but to have one actually save a person, that was unheard of. Amita didn't understand it any better, but she knew one thing, the monks no longer had any power over her. Their gods had come down and picked a side. Everyone who came through the void space were a protected class, especially Alex. Amita didn't know how far she could push that, but she doubted anyone would arrest her for going to see her friend in the medical ward.

"I'm sorry," Amita said, reaching out to touch Ben. "I wish you hadn't listened to me." She choked back a sob, knowing that it had been her plan that caused this. Ben wouldn't have fallen if she'd never told him to climb. He would've ended up in here, beaten up like these guards, but he wouldn't have been this bad. With no way past the Tairnishmen Amita had come up with a solution. 'Sometimes it was better to just leave things alone,' she thought.

She turned at a sound, hoping to find the Grannusian healer behind her.

The room was still empty though. She heard it again. A scratching noise. She got up to see where it came from, expecting to find one of the six guards in the ward sitting up. She looked at each bed. None had moved. The sound wasn't coming from that side of the ward anyway.

She followed it to a locked door, knowing who was behind it. She could hear him awake and moving around inside. It was Tearmai, the Drake that'd brought them here. Usually, he was chained down or so sedated that he couldn't move, but slowly they'd been giving him more freedom in between his fits.

There was a small window on the door made of heavy glass with a flap covering it. Amita moved it out of the way, so she could look inside.

There he was, standing at the wall, digging his clawed fingers into the stone. At first Amita thought he was trying to dig his way out because there was a pile of rock and dust gathered around his feet. Then Amita saw the marks weren't random. Tearmai was drawing something and she recognized it. Turning to look back at Ben, she knew he'd be excited to see this too. Or he would've been before his fall. The form Tearmai was carving was simple and it easily could have been confused for a person if not for the single eye in the center of its face and the flames over its shoulders.

Amita could only see a little of the image, but she could tell more was carved on the wall. She leaned far to the side to see more through the window, but the opening was small and Tearmai was so broad that it was hard to peer around him. She thought she saw the point of the diamond ship and something else in the distance. It wasn't a mountain, but something like it.

Amita's hand dropped to the door handle. She tried pulling, but of course it was locked. She tried looking at the keypad and even entered a few combinations, pushing the handle after each try.

"Bugger," Amita cursed as she went back to the window, hoping to take another look, not noticing that the scratching had stopped. When she looked in, a pair of strange blue eyes covered by a heavy brow were staring back at her.

"Open it," Tearmai demanded.

It took a moment for her to answer. "I can't. I don't know the combination."

It didn't seem like he recognized her. His eyes still had that crazy rage behind them. "Open it!" he shouted.

Amita backed away. She could hear him screaming, "OPEN IT!"

The door shook as he smashed it while still yelling. Amita took one last look at Ben, then hurried down the ramp, nearly falling as she ran off, going to look for help. She needed to find the healer for Ben and she needed someone to calm Tearmai down before he broke out. It was a while before she realized what Tearmai had carved into the wall, what the Fire Golem had been standing in front of. It was a mountain, but one without a top because it had been destroyed, blown off in a volcanic explosion. Tearmai had been drawing one of the moons around Altor, the home of the Long Wolves, Tairnish.

Katy, Chris and Ben

Alex, Amita and Tearmai

Kavaris Dell and Regin

Fire Golem and
Andavarri

Fafnir

Chooth, Cormack and Naiathne

Pete A O'Donnell is the creator of

 Illadvisedstories.com, a children's story podcast where kids can listen to free and funny tales. He's a firefighter and EMT in his day job. He holds a degree in journalism and creative writing from Queens University. His first book, The Curse of Purgatory Cove won the Royal Dragonfly award for best new author.

The Stars Above the Ocean is his fourth book and the second in a seven book series that began with The Stars Beyond the Mesa. You can download a free character guide at his website PeteAODonnell.com He is a life-long lover of Science Fiction and can't wait to dive further into alien worlds in the series.